Praise for the Hope Meadows series

'An adorable read [with] a real sense of village community'
Bookworms and Shutterbugs

'A stunning, emotional, beautiful tale of friendship, love, and
the importance of being who you need to be . . . I laughed,
I cried, and I cannot recommend [the novel] highly enough
– it really has got it all!' *Books of All Kinds*

'[A] lovely romp through the glorious Yorkshire countryside
. . . a really lovely summer read and the start of a promising
new series' *Jaffa Reads Too*

'Just the right amount of nostalgia . . . wonderful and very
poignant' *The World is a Book Blog*

'An incredibly lovely story' *Rachel's Random Reads*

'The author creates a perfect balance between the human
and animal stories in this book . . . this is an absolute *must
read* for animal lovers' *The Book Bag*

About the Author

Lucy Daniels is the collective name for the writing team that created the bestselling children's book series Animal Ark. Hope Meadows is a brand-new Lucy Daniels series for adult readers, featuring the characters and locations that were so beloved in the original stories.

Sarah McGurk, the author of *Summer Days at Sunrise Farm*, has the twin advantages of being passionate about Animal Ark, and a fully qualified vet. Sarah writes fiction related to her work in general practice and in emergency and critical care. Her special interests include anaesthesia and pain relief, and low-stress techniques in small animal handling.

Sarah currently lives in Norway. She has worked for two years in a local veterinary practice and speaks Norwegian fluently.

The Hope Meadows Series

Summer Days at Sunrise Farm

LUCY DANIELS

HODDER

First published in Great Britain in 2019 by Hodder & Stoughton
An Hachette UK company

1

Copyright © Working Partners Limited 2019

The right of Working Partners Limited to be identified as the Author of the
Work has been asserted by them in accordance with the Copyright, Designs
and Patents Act 1988.

A CIP catalogue record for this title is available from the British Library

Paperback ISBN 9781473682436
eBook ISBN 9781473682443

Typeset in Plantin Light 11.75/15 pt by
Palimpsest Book Production Limited, Falkirk, Stirlingshire

Printed and bound in Great Britain by Clays Ltd, Elcograf S.p.A.

Hodder & Stoughton policy is to use papers that are natural, renewable
and recyclable products and made from wood grown in sustainable forests.
The logging and manufacturing processes are expected to conform
to the environmental regulations of the country of origin.

Hodder & Stoughton Ltd
Carmelite House
50 Victoria Embankment
London EC4Y 0DZ

www.hodder.co.uk

Special thanks to Sarah McGurk,
BVM&S, MRCVS

To the real Helen Steer,
a very dear friend

Chapter One

'That's the last patient gone,' Helen Steer announced as she opened the door to the reception area of Hope Meadows Rescue Centre. It was the end of a busy afternoon at Animal Ark Veterinary Clinic where Helen worked as a nurse. It was always a joy at the end of a long shift to take her flat-coat retriever, Lucy, over to Hope Meadows to play with the rescue dogs.

The centre had been open almost two years now, but it still felt new. It smelled of warm wood from the beams that held up the arching roof and somehow it always seemed filled with peace. To Helen's left, the huge glass window looked out onto the steep fellside where puffy white sheep grazed among the heather.

'Mrs Ballantyne came for Dylan at last?' Blond-haired Mandy Hope, one of Animal Ark's veterinary surgeons and the owner of Hope Meadows, glanced up and smiled. She was crouching beside a small brown terrier with a black muzzle and bright button eyes. Mandy had left the clinic to begin her evening chores, leaving Helen to discharge the last of the post-surgery animals.

'She did,' Helen replied. Helen had watched the

rambunctious Golden Retriever go with some relief. He had spent the afternoon barking in his kennel and the enormous buster collar that Helen had fitted had ricocheted off every single chair in the waiting room before he managed to make it through the door. She didn't envy Mrs Ballantyne the task of trying to settle him for the night.

Mandy got to her feet and looked down at the terrier, who was gazing up at her. 'Good boy, Bobby,' she said. She gave him a treat and the stubby brown tail wagged back and forth on the ground.

'Are you taking him out?' Helen asked.

Mandy nodded. 'Him and Flit,' she replied. 'Can you hang on to Bobby while I get her?' she asked.

Helen took the lead and grinned up at Mandy. Though she was five foot eight, Helen always felt small when standing beside Mandy, who was almost six foot tall. Helen's thick brown hair and hazel eyes were in contrast to Mandy's Scandinavian colouring, but they shared a love of animals and a passion for their work. 'See you outside,' she said.

Flit had recently arrived at Hope Meadows. She was an attractive Welsh Collie with intelligent eyes and one ear that flopped to the side, but she had a tendency to get overexcited. Helen knew that Mandy would take her time getting the fidgety collie to calm down before taking her out of the kennel.

'Can you take Sky, too?' Mandy called as she opened the kennel door. 'Go on, Sky.' There was a clicking of claws on the flagstone floor as Sky, Mandy's gorgeous collie, rose from her bed in the corner. She scampered across the floor to join Lucy, who was waiting patiently at the door.

It was a beautiful summer day. Helen and the three dogs wandered outside and into the paddock. By the time they had reached the gate, Mandy had appeared with Flit. The collie's ears pricked up and she began to bark when she saw the three other dogs.

Mandy stopped. 'Sit,' she told the wriggling collie. She leaned down and fed Flit a treat, placing it on the ground and making her wait for permission to eat it. Once Flit had calmed down, Mandy gave her plenty of lead while she met the other dogs. They walked through the gate together. 'You can let Bobby off the lead,' Mandy said.

Helen unclipped the leash. Bobby wagged his tail and licked her hand, then galloped off to join Lucy and Sky, who were running across the grass beneath the apple trees.

Even though the sun was starting to set, it was very warm. In the distance, the rocky outcrop of Axwith Tor looked peaceful under the arching blue sky. Beside them, Flit panted as they came to a halt near the wall that marked the end of the field. They climbed over the stone stile and continued up the sloping fell until they reached a crooked hawthorn bush growing out of a rock.

Helen perched on the rock and looked down at the village of Welford. Beyond Animal Ark and the cottage where Mandy had grown up, the church spire rose tall above the slate-tumbled roofs. Her eyes followed the road that led up to the Beacon on the far side of the village. Farms dotted the hillside and the familiar names came into her head: Upper Welford Hall, Old Dyke, Black Tor and Bleak Fell.

They set off back down the hill. Flit was walking well now, though she was still rather jumpy. As they came nearer to the paddock, she began pulling on her leash. A Jersey cow with a dished face and long eyelashes blinked at them over the wall with quiet curiosity. Mandy stopped and crouched down beside the restless collie. 'It's only Fluffybonce,' she told her.

The Jersey was another of Mandy's rescues. She'd come to them from a petting zoo in Sheffield which had closed down when its owners became too old. Many of the animals had gone to another centre on the outskirts of Leeds, but Fluffybonce had come to Hope Meadows accompanied by an outsized Flemish Giant rabbit called Lettuce.

'Haven't you thought of another name yet?' Helen protested. The cow's name had become a running joke. 'What about Honey? Or Bramble? Or . . .'

'Fluffybonce suits her,' Mandy insisted.

Helen rolled her eyes, but it was hard to argue. Above her placid face, Fluffybonce had the most ridiculous tufty forelock. 'Poor Fluffy,' she said.

A dark green van drove up the lane and turned into the drive that led to Animal Ark. 'Seb's here,' Helen told Mandy, who was still on her haunches beside Flit.

Seb and Helen had been going out for two years. She watched as he climbed out of the van and waved at them before vanishing out of sight behind the rescue centre. A moment later, he appeared at the gate to the orchard and began walking towards them.

'Are you coming to Gemma's leaving party?' Helen asked Mandy.

'Of course.' Mandy stood up. 'I'm going to miss her at the post office. Gemma always knows everything that's going on.'

Helen laughed. 'Always knows everything that's going on' was a polite way to say Gemma had the juiciest gossip in the village.

Gemma Moss was Helen's best friend. She had worked in Welford post office for the past five years, but now she was heading off on an extended summer break. 'Sounds like an amazing adventure,' Mandy added. 'Riding across France with her cousin. And you're incredibly generous to lend her Moondance.'

Moondance was Helen's horse, a sixteen-hand grey warmblood mare. Helen and Moondance had ridden out many times with Gemma, but now Gemma was taking her to France and Helen would not see her for nearly three months. 'Moondance will love it,' she said, though she felt a pang as she spoke. She was going to miss her beloved horse at least as much as she would miss Gemma. 'And it's been fun getting her fit to go.'

They had been on lots of long rides over the moors. Lucy had come too, running beside them.

'Maybe you should go trekking across Europe next year,' Mandy suggested.

'There's too much going on here,' Helen said, shaking her head.

'Well, that's true,' Mandy admitted. 'Animal Ark and Hope Meadows would grind to a halt without you.' She waved at Seb, who was crossing the paddock towards them. 'I must put the dogs back and change my trousers,' she said, looking down at her hair-covered jeans. 'See you in a minute. We can walk to the pub together.'

'Come, Lucy!' Helen called. Lucy raced up to her and sat down. Helen stroked her dog's smooth domed head. It had been magical riding Moondance across the moors with Lucy at their heels. She reached out her hands and smoothed Lucy's silky ears. In this weather, being on horseback all day would be heavenly. Gemma was very lucky, she thought.

'Penny for them?' Seb's voice broke through her reverie. Lucy's tail began to wag.

'Sorry, what?' Helen squinted up. Seb was standing in front of her in a halo of sunlight. His spiky ash-blond hair stood up above his sweet-natured face. He was smiling, his deep-set brown eyes crinkling.

'You were miles away,' Seb said. 'Penny for your thoughts.' He reached out a hand and pulled her upright.

Helen smiled. 'I was just thinking what a great summer Gemma is going to have.'

Seb turned to stand beside her, looking down the valley, then put his arm around her waist. 'She is indeed,' he said. He pulled her in closer and kissed her hair. 'Shall we head down?' he suggested. 'We don't want to miss the party. Come on, Lucy,' he called as they set off down the grassy slope.

Ten minutes later, they were outside the Fox and Goose. It was an ancient inn that stood at the crossroads in the heart of Welford. Terracotta flowerpots filled with begonias stood along the window ledges and a pair of jaunty hanging baskets swung on either side of the black-painted front door. Through the open windows they could hear the low hum of voices, but as they rounded the corner and approached the entrance to the beer garden, they could hear music playing. Peals of laughter rang out above the chatter of a party in full swing.

'Helen! Mandy! Seb!' Gemma sashayed towards them as soon as they opened the gate. She was wearing the biggest sunhat Helen had ever seen. It was made of straw, about the size of a wagon wheel, and had miniature stirrups and horseshoes dangling from the brim. She reached out her arms, green eyes a-glitter, and wrapped them round Helen's neck. 'Thanks for coming,' she cried. 'Seb!' She hugged him in turn. 'Mandy!' She opened her arms a third time. 'Is Jimmy coming?' she asked as she stepped back.

'He'll be along soon,' Mandy told her. 'He's just

7

finishing up. There was a hen party in this afternoon.'
Jimmy Marsh was Mandy's boyfriend. He ran an
Outward Bound centre on the outskirts of Welford.

'It's so lovely to have you all,' Gemma said. She turned
to look for her husband, then held out a hand to him.
'Look who's arrived, Luke!'

Luke sauntered over. He had a pint glass in his hand
and a huge grin on his sunburnt face. His shiny brown
hair was clipped very short. 'Afternoon, all.' He waved
his glass at them. 'Can I get you guys a drink?'

'I'll get them,' said Seb. 'What'll you have, Mandy?'

Mandy glanced towards the open door that led into
the bar. 'How about a glass of Pimm's?'

Helen suddenly realised how thirsty she was. 'Brilliant
idea,' she agreed. She linked her arm through Gemma's.
'Would you like one too, Gem?'

'Don't mind if I do!' Gemma beamed.

'I'll get a jug.' Seb regarded her with a smile. He really
was very sweet, Helen thought. He almost brought to
mind a puppy, with his adoring eyes and willingness to
please. He trotted off towards the door.

Helen squeezed Gemma's arm. 'So,' she said, 'are you
ready for the off?'

Gemma giggled. 'I'm ready for *anything*,' she said.

Luke was watching Gemma with a benevolent gaze.
'What about you, Luke?' Helen asked. 'Won't you miss
her like mad?'

'Of course I will,' Luke replied. 'But it'll be worth it
in the long run.'

Mandy looked puzzled. 'In what way?'

Luke's grin widened. 'Well, next time I want to go on a fishing trip, she'll have to let me,' he said. 'I'll have three months of trips in hand. A lifetime's worth, don'cha think?'

Gemma frowned up at him. 'I've never once made a fuss about your fishing obsession,' she declared.

Luke laughed. 'You were pretty mad at me last month,' he reminded her, winking at Helen and Mandy.

Gemma looked outraged. 'That wasn't about the fishing,' she protested. 'You blocked the kitchen sink with your stinky fish-scales. You'd have been mad too, wouldn't you, Helen?'

Helen held up her hands in mock surrender. 'Don't involve me in your fishy arguments,' she said.

'Hi, Mandy. Hi, Helen!' A booming voice sounded behind them and Helen turned. It was Douglas MacLeod, larger than life with his huge red beard and his hair all standing on end. Beside him, Mandy's good friend Susan Collins looked positively petite with her smooth cap of dark brown hair. Both of them looked wonderfully happy, Helen thought. They'd only been together since Christmas, but you could tell at once they belonged together.

'Where's Jack tonight?' Mandy asked Susan. Jack was Susan's five-year-old son from a previous relationship.

'He's at Mum's,' Susan said. 'We thought we'd make a night of it,' she added. She was clutching a long-stemmed champagne glass. 'Douglas and I have been together six months today.'

9

Douglas put his arm around her, pulling her to his side. 'Best six months of my life,' he declared. His blue eyes twinkled.

Out of the corner of her eye, Helen spotted a movement. The side gate had opened again and Toby Gordon appeared. Toby was the latest addition to Animal Ark's veterinary staff. This evening his usually immaculate hair was ruffled and his face looked slightly pink. Despite that, nothing could hide the impressive bone structure that lay beneath his smooth tanned skin. He had high cheekbones, an aquiline nose and an understated self-confidence that made him look distinguished even when everything was chaotic around him. Beside him, Douglas MacLeod looked more dishevelled than ever.

'All okay?' Mandy asked Toby. 'Did you get your foot-trimming done?' He had left for Tom Hapwell's in Twyford at lunchtime, Helen remembered. Had the call really taken him all this time?

'More or less,' he said, 'but I could do with a cold beer.' His tone was so intense that Helen wanted to laugh.

'You sound very much in need,' she teased him. 'Did the nasty cow wear you out?'

Toby raised his eyebrows and regarded her. 'I'll have you know,' he said, 'that the cow in question was number 272.'

Gemma frowned. Luke, Susan and Douglas looked equally mystified. But Mandy's eyes widened and Helen found herself looking at Toby with new-found respect. Cow 272 was well known in the local farming community. She had been known to kick out at head height with a speed that made Usain Bolt look positively glacial. She had hospitalised her owner one year at calving time and Mandy and her father Adam, also a vet, always treated her with the utmost respect. If Toby had managed to trim her hooves without breaking one of his own limbs, it was practically a miracle.

'What's so special about 272?' Susan asked.

Mandy laughed. 'She's the fastest kicker in Yorkshire,' she said. 'Infamous. Tom Hapwell is lucky to still have his wedding tackle, or so the story goes. He spent a week in the infirmary the first time he tried to calve her.'

'Really?' Gemma turned to look at Toby and raised her glass in a toast. 'How on earth did you manage?'

'Nice hat, Gem,' Toby commented with a grin. 'I managed to sedate her, but even that was touch and go. She almost had me a couple of times, but I finally got the needle in. I used my own special mix of sedatives.'

He had studied anaesthesia before he'd come here, Helen remembered. He'd had a high-flying career at Glasgow University and it had been something of a mystery why he'd chosen to come to Welford, but he had settled in so well over the six months since he'd arrived that she'd almost forgotten.

'Why on earth does Tom Hapwell keep her if she's such a menace?' Susan asked.

Mandy shrugged. 'She's a great milker,' she said. 'The

best Mr Hapwell's ever had, but I reckon the real reason she's still alive is sheer bravado. The great and the good in Welford's farming community were taking bets on how long it would be before she was made into burgers, once Tom Hapwell was out of hospital. I think he decided not to let anyone win!'

Douglas let out a huge guffaw, making Helen jump. 'Lucky old 272,' he said. 'She'll probably live out her days in splendid notoriety. The cow they couldn't kill!'

'Not so lucky for the vets who have to treat her,' Helen put in. There was a clinking sound behind her and she turned to see Seb approaching carefully over the grass. He was carrying a tray laden with a large jug of fruit-filled Pimm's and several glasses. 'Seb?' He set the tray down on the table beside her. 'Could you go and get Toby a pint, please? He's been out at Twyford, wrestling with number 272's feet!'

Seb blinked. 'I haven't the faintest idea what you're talking about,' he said, 'but I'll gladly get Toby a drink.' He turned and walked back into the bar.

He returned five minutes later with Jimmy Marsh, who put his arm round Mandy's shoulders. He was looking very tanned, as he always did at this time of year. 'Afternoon,' he said. He raised a brimming pint glass to his lips and took a long draught, then breathed out. 'Oh, that's good,' he said, gazing at his drink for a moment. He looked up, his green eyes twinkling. 'I thought I was going to miss all the fun, but I see you're just getting going.'

'How was this afternoon?' Mandy asked.

'About an hour and a half too long,' Jimmy replied. He took another mouthful of beer, then lifted his other hand, stuck a finger in his ear and wiggled it. 'Pretty sure I'm deaf on this side now. The bride-to-be shrieked so loudly when she hit the netting after the rope swing I thought she'd broken something. If I'm ever tempted to book in another hen party, just remind me I don't want premature hearing loss, will you?'

Helen laughed. The Pimm's was very refreshing and slipped down with alarming ease. They drank the first jug and ordered another. Helen sat on the wooden bench, leaning against Seb and watching her friends and neighbours mill around her. It was great to see so many people turn up to wish Gemma well. Jimmy had just returned with yet another round of drinks when Gemma, whose hat was now at such a jaunty angle it was a wonder it hadn't fallen off, clambered onto a picnic table. She stood there, swaying slightly. Luke picked up a teaspoon and chinked it on the side of a glass until silence fell.

'Thank you, everyone, for coming,' Gemma began. 'I've had a lovely time. I'm really going to miss you all . . .' She threw out her arms, then winked at Susan's boyfriend. 'Yes, Douglas, even you!'

Douglas roared with laughter. Helen couldn't help joining in. It was such an infectious sound.

Gemma waited until they were all quiet again. 'First of all, I want to say thank you to a very special person.' She raised her glass and grinned down at Helen. 'Helen

Steer has been mad enough to trust me with her wonderful mare Moondance.' Helen could feel her cheeks reddening as everyone looked at her. 'And I want to promise you, Helen, that I'll look after her and bring her back in one piece.' Gemma took a generous drink and waved at Helen with her free hand.

Helen raised her own glass. 'You'd better,' she said, then pursed her lips into a mock pout. 'Otherwise you'll have Seb to reckon with. He is our local animal welfare officer, after all!'

A ripple of laughter ran through the crowd.

Gemma held her hands up, scattering amber droplets of Pimm's on the people standing nearest. 'Most of all,' Gemma raised her voice again, 'I want to thank the most wonderful man in the world: my handsome husband Luke. He's given me his blessing to go away for three months. I'm pretty sure it's not just to get me out of the house so he can put his stinky fish in the freezer.' She smiled down at Luke. 'I really am very, very lucky,' she said. 'He's the very best person in the world. Look at him, everyone. Isn't he gorgeous?' She reached out a hand as if to pull Luke up beside her, caught the heel of her shoe on the edge of the bench and, for a moment, wobbled on the brink of disaster, but Luke reached out and caught her easily.

'Don't go hurting yourself now.' He looked down into her giggling face and shook his head. 'Can't ride a horse with a broken leg.'

Gemma wrapped her arms around his neck and kissed

him hard. Douglas whooped. Cheers and catcalls sounded from all around.

To Helen's left, Jimmy cleared his throat. 'I'd like to raise a toast,' he said, 'to Gemma. I hope you have a wonderful time on your travels.' He paused for a moment, looking round at the cheery faces. 'And a toast to Luke as well, for letting her go.' He lifted his glass. 'To Gemma and Luke,' he cried, and the crowd raised their glasses in return.

'Gemma and Luke!' they chorused.

Mandy beamed up at Jimmy with a loving look of pride. Jimmy reached out and wrapped his arms around her, holding her tight. Helen had rarely seen Mandy looking more contented. She and Jimmy seemed so perfectly suited.

Susan had made her way to Gemma's side with Douglas in tow. 'We're going now,' she said. 'We have a table booked in Walton.'

Gemma opened her arms and hugged first Susan, then Douglas. 'Thank you for coming,' she said.

An overly loud burst of giggling made Helen turn and look over her shoulder. Toby was standing behind her, surrounded by a throng of young women who were tossing their glossy hair like a herd of well-groomed ponies. Most of the young women were unfamiliar but Helen recognised Imogen Parker-Smythe pressed against Toby's left arm. She was home from university and had brought her dog into Animal Ark a week ago. From the way she was gazing into Toby's eyes now, it looked to

Helen as if she had more than her dog's health in mind.

Toby was telling them about his visit to Twyford and embellishing the story with some lurid details about the injuries 272 had inflicted over the years. The high-kicking cow might have hospitalised Tom Hapwell, but Helen was pretty sure she'd never escaped and run amok in Welford churchyard chasing the vicar. She made a mental note to tease him tomorrow morning about his tall tales, but Imogen and her rivals were lapping it up. Toby reached out and touched one of the girls' forearms. Her face went red with pleasure.

Mandy came up beside Helen and nudged her. 'Quite the heartbreaker, our Toby,' she whispered.

Helen felt laughter rising in her throat. 'Should we tell Mrs Ponsonby he's cheating on her?' she murmured. It was a running joke in the practice how often Mrs Ponsonby, Welford's stalwart of the Women's Institute, had brought her Pekinese Fancy in to see Toby. The little dog knew his way straight into the correct consulting room.

Seb joined them, followed by Gemma, battling her way through the crowd. When she arrived, she reached out and put a hand on Helen's arm. 'I wanted to thank you again,' she gushed, 'for lending me Moondance.' Helen noticed Gemma had tears in her eyes. 'You really are the most incredible friend. I wish you were coming with us. I know how much you'll miss your gorgeous horse.' The tears were now overflowing, and Helen had to swallow a lump in her throat before she managed to smile.

'It really is fine,' she insisted. 'I know you'll look after her. And the two of you'll have a great time, I know you will.'

She felt Seb lay his hand gently on the small of her back. It was a typically restrained gesture. He knew better than anyone how hard it would be for Helen to say goodbye to her horse for the summer. But Helen wished suddenly that he would wrap his arms around her and hold her tight, as Jimmy had with Mandy earlier. It was going to be a long summer without her wonderful mare.

Luke was holding on to Gemma and Seb had taken his hand away. Helen found herself wishing with a fierce intensity that she was the one leaving for France tomorrow. How wonderful it would be to head off with Moondance and Lucy for company and a horizon full of adventure ahead of them.

Chapter Two

Helen rubbed her eyes, then pressed her fingers to her temples. It did nothing to relieve the pounding in her head or the gritty feeling whenever she blinked. Five a.m. was early even for a normal morning; the day after a party it was madness. But Moondance was being loaded up for her extended holiday and nothing would have induced Helen to miss saying goodbye. Beside her in the yard at Six Oaks Stables, Gemma looked deathly white with a greenish tinge around her mouth. Despite the huge sunglasses she was sporting, she still seemed wary of the early morning sunlight.

Moondance, in contrast, was looking fabulous, Helen thought. Her eyes were calm and her mane and tail were perfectly groomed. Helen watched as Molly Future, the owner of the stable yard, walked the long-legged grey mare up the ramp and into the lorry.

Molly's red pixie cut was immaculate, as were her jodhpurs and shiny boots, despite the early hour. She reappeared, having tied Moondance up, and with quiet efficiency raised the ramp and bolted the door into place. She turned and regarded Gemma and Helen as if they

18

were a couple of feeble geldings that needed pepping up. 'I'm starting to think it was a wise move to miss the party last night,' she said.

Gemma groaned. 'I'm going to sleep all the way to Southampton,' she muttered.

'I do hope it's a not a rough crossing,' Molly said, with something approaching a smirk.

Helen laughed as Gemma grimaced and wrapped her arms around herself. 'It'd better not be,' she said with another whimper.

'Did you remember to pick up the saddlebags?' Molly asked. 'They were in the tack room.'

Gemma yelped, then winced as if the noise had bitten her. 'Thank you for reminding me,' she whispered, and tottered off across the cobbles.

Helen walked over to the lorry, opened the jockey door in the side and clambered up the steep steps. Moondance was pulling at the hay net that Molly had filled for her. She was looking very smart in her green travelling rug and matching leg wraps. Helen reached up and wrapped her arms round Moondance's neck. A lump rose in her throat as the mare rested her head on her shoulder for a moment, then blew in her ear.

'I'm going to miss you so much,' Helen whispered. 'Be good for Gemma, won't you? Don't you go falling for any of those fancy French stallions.'

Moondance twitched an ear backwards and tossed her head as if the idea was ridiculous. Helen smiled, though there were tears in her eyes. It was so strange to think of all the amazing adventures that were coming Moondance's way: adventures she wouldn't be sharing.

There was a sound from the doorway and Gemma appeared carrying the saddlebags. Helen ran her hand down the velvety hair on Moondance's neck, then turned and hugged Gemma. 'Have an amazing time, both of you,' she said. She patted Gemma's shoulder, glanced at Moondance one last time, then climbed back down and stood beside Molly. A moment later, the engine roared into life and the vehicle lumbered down the driveway. Helen watched until it rounded the corner.

'You know you're welcome to come over any time,' Molly said. 'You can ride any of the horses while Moondance is away.'

'Thanks,' Helen said. She smiled at Molly. It was going to be very odd, not having Moondance around. Lucy would miss her too, though she would probably appreciate all the extra attention.

Helen set off for the walk down into Welford. The morning air was fresh and she began to feel better. She was going to be incredibly early for work but it would give her a chance to catch up with some of the chores she hadn't had time for in the last few days. It was comforting to enter the waiting room at Animal Ark and switch on the coffee machine before she set about the familiar tasks, checking the consulting rooms were fully stocked and that each room had a stethoscope and thermometer. Next she went to the store cupboard to update the inventory; she was pretty sure Emily Hope, the practice manager and Mandy's mum, wanted to place an order today.

A car pulled up outside the window just as she was finishing. Helen walked into the waiting room to see whether it was an early client. Mandy was outside, rooting through the boot of her RAV4. Two minutes later, she rushed through the door clutching several empty injection bottles and a container filled with discarded plastic gloves and used syringes. She looked at Helen, eyebrows raised as if surprised, then she seemed to remember why Helen might be at work early. 'Did Moondance get off okay?' she asked, her eyes sympathetic.

'Fine, thanks,' Helen replied. 'Although Molly was the only one fit enough to load her. Not sure Gemma would have got off without her.'

Mandy smiled. 'Good job she was there,' she said. She looked down at the rubbish she was carrying. 'I just need to put this in the bin,' she said, 'then maybe you could give me a hand with the rescues? I know you don't usually in the morning, but I really need to get on. I've got to be at Upper Welford Hall in an hour.'

Helen nodded, suspecting that Mandy was deliberately trying to keep her busy to stop her dwelling on saying goodbye to Moondance. 'I'll go and make a start,' she said.

★ ★ ★

It didn't take her long to feed the cats and clean out their litter trays. Her favourite at the moment was a large white chinchilla breed with piercing green eyes. His name was Emerald, and he had come to the centre when his owner had died. When Helen picked him up to put him back in his cage, he purred so loudly that she couldn't resist cuddling him. He was still purring like an engine five minutes later when Mandy put her head round the door. 'I've finished cleaning the dogs,' she said, 'but I need to take Flit out for a few minutes. Could you see to Lettuce, please?'

With a last snuggle, Helen put Emerald back in his cage. Mandy had brought Lettuce to show her when he first arrived, but this was the first time Helen had fed him. He was far too big to fit into one of the standard rabbit kennels, so Mandy had put him in the isolation ward in one of the cat cages. When Helen opened the door of his kennel he hopped out, lolloped twice around her legs, then stopped right in front of her with his front paws on her feet. His whiskers twitched as he gazed up at her. Helen crouched down and tickled him under his floppy ear and he leaned into her hand with a satisfied groaning noise. His fur was so soft. 'Let's get you fed,' she said, unable to resist smiling at him. He really was enormous, easily as big as Emerald and definitely heavier.

She stood up and checked the chart that was clipped to the front of his cage. Each of Hope Meadows' furry tenants had one of these charts, which detailed everything from health information to food preferences. 'It says here you like carrot tops,' she said, looking down at the oversized rabbit. 'And that you need six cups of chopped vegetables.' Lettuce twitched his whiskers.

To Helen's delight, he lolloped after her as she walked through to the fridge. He was incredibly tame and in very good condition. He had been well looked after at the petting farm, Helen realised.

Mandy arrived back as Helen was putting a handful of timothy hay in the corner of Lettuce's cage. 'Thanks for sorting him out,' Mandy said. 'It takes ages to chop all his veg.'

'He seems to be enjoying my efforts,' Helen observed. Lettuce's broad head bobbed a little as he chewed.

Mandy nodded. 'He certainly loves his food.' She pulled her mobile out and checked the time. 'Must get off to Welford Hall,' she said, thrusting the phone back into her pocket. She smiled at Helen. 'Mrs Bell will be arriving with Croissant in a minute. Could you see to him, please?'

Helen had been in the clinic with Mandy yesterday when Mandy had diagnosed Croissant Bell's diabetes. He had gone home for the night but was coming back this morning to start on insulin. He would be hospitalised for a few days until they had him stabilised.

'I've written the plan,' Mandy said. 'Bloods first, then insulin, and we'll take it from there.'

'No problem.' Helen gave a brisk nod. Starting an animal on a treatment plan that was going to make a big difference to their health was the kind of task she enjoyed best.

Croissant meowed loudly as Mrs Bell carried his basket inside. Anthea Bell was a retired teacher with short grey hair that fitted her head like a cap. She was normally known for her common sense and she had an apologetic look on her face as she held out a well-filled plastic bag to Helen. 'I know it's silly,' she said, 'but I've brought along a few of his things. Michael wanted me to bring them. We're both worried about him.' Michael was Mrs Bell's husband. Like Mrs Bell, he was very attached to crotchety Croissant.

Helen took the bag and looked inside. She wanted to laugh when she saw the contents. Mrs Bell must have brought all Croissant's toys as well as his favourite blanket and a full set of grooming brushes. As well as a ball with a bell in it, there was a toy fishing rod with a goldfish attached, and a large fluffy toy mouse with a well-chewed ear. She swallowed her amusement and smiled with sympathy at Mrs Bell. 'I know it's a worrying time,' she said, 'but I'll take good care of him for you.'

They walked into the cattery and Helen set up the cage where Croissant would spend the next few days. She folded his blanket up and placed it on top of the absorbent pad and set the ball and mouse beside it. 'I'll pop Mr Fishy in here,' she said, propping the toy fishing rod in the plastic tub attached to the cage bars, where normally they stored any medications. Croissant's insulin would be kept in the fridge. 'I'm afraid we don't have space for his grooming kit, though.' She closed the bag and handed it back to Mrs Bell. 'We've grooming equipment here if we need it, but if you'd like to come in and spend some time with him each day to do your own brushing, you'd be very welcome.'

Mrs Bell managed a smile. 'You're very kind,' she said.

Helen opened the box and gently lifted Croissant out. He was a large, handsome cat with a chocolate brown coat and huge golden eyes. He stared at Helen as she cuddled him for a moment before putting him down on his blanket. He turned round twice, then walked over to press his nose to the bars. 'He'll soon settle in,' Helen said.

Mrs Bell nodded. 'He's already calmer than I thought he'd be,' she said. 'I know he's in good hands.'

'I just need to get some paperwork sorted out before you go,' Helen told her. She had already printed out the consent information and the treatment plan Mandy had put together.

Toby arrived as Mrs Bell was signing the form. He peered over Helen's shoulder at the computer screen, then disappeared into the cat kennel. He must be checking Croissant out, Helen thought.

By the time he came back out, Mrs Bell had gone. He sauntered over to the reception desk, where Helen was entering the details onto the computer. 'I see you've made Croissant comfortable,' he said. 'I love the fishy on the string. Is that part of his treatment? Two fishy sessions, ten minutes each, twice a day?'

He was standing close behind her. So close that Helen had to twist round and look up to see his face. He grinned down at her, his eyes twinkling.

'Some people know how to look after their pets properly.' She narrowed her eyes at him, pretending to scowl, and he laughed.

'Speaking of people who love their pets,' Toby went on, 'I heard you slipped a little something into Moondance's saddlebag. Strict instructions to give her a piece every evening before bed! Now that is dedication.'

Helen sat up very straight. Who could possibly have told him? Was it Gemma? Helen wasn't going to give him the upper hand by asking. 'Moondance can't survive without her Kendal Mint Cake,' she said. 'And Gemma had better look after Moondance even better than I'm looking after Croissant.'

'I'm sure she will,' Toby said. His voice had lost its teasing tone. He patted her on the shoulder as if he'd realised this might be a touchy subject. 'You're very caring,' he said. 'Seb's a lucky guy.'

If Helen hadn't known better, she could have sworn he sounded almost wistful. She risked a glance up at him and he was smiling again. He really was a heart-breaker, she thought. Thank goodness she and Mandy were both immune.

'He is,' she replied with a brisk smile, 'but you won't be so lucky if you aren't ready when your first client arrives.' She nodded at the window. A car had just pulled up.

'I'm on it,' he said. He patted her shoulder again, then strolled towards the door of his consulting room, whistling.

He was incorrigible, Helen thought as he disappeared inside. It was amazing he was still single. Every other week, he seemed to have a new date, though until now none of them had lasted past the first few outings.

The client came in with a large pet carrier. Helen registered them and Toby called them through. Alone again, Helen stood up and began to sort through the leaflet rack that stood by the door. It was odd, she thought as she shuffled the pamphlets into place. Toby had been here for half a year, but she knew next to nothing about him. He hailed from some remote part of Scotland and he'd had a glittering career at Glasgow Vet School as an anaesthetist before he'd come to Welford. That was all she knew. Asking him questions didn't help. Any time she tried to get him talking about himself, he turned the conversation around. It sometimes felt as if he was deliberately trying to be mysterious.

Adam Hope opened the door that connected the cottage and the veterinary practice just as another car arrived. His greying hair was neatly brushed and he was already wearing his white coat. Mandy had grown up in the cottage with her adoptive parents since she was a tiny baby. Both Adam and Emily were vets and they had worked together for years until Emily had been diagnosed with MS a couple of years ago. Now Emily had stepped down into the role of practice manager, but Adam seemed as sprightly as he had six years ago, when Helen had first come to work at Animal Ark.

'Everything ready?' he asked.

'Theatre's all set up,' she replied. Adam's first patient this morning was a plump Labrador retriever called Tampa. He had a lipoma – a fatty lump – behind his shoulder. Helen had put the surgical kit out and set up the anaesthetic machine first thing. 'Here's the consent form.' She held out the papers and Adam took them. 'What would we do without you?' he said, then whisked off to open the door to the theatre before she had a chance to reply.

The surgery went well. Helen enjoyed watching Adam operate. He worked with a minimum of fuss, often with Radio 4 playing quietly in the background. He put in the last stitch and pulled away the sterile drape so Helen could clean up Tampa's flank. 'You can turn him off now,' he said, as he always did.

'Already done,' Helen replied. She liked to turn off the anaesthetic gas when he was putting in the final suture. That way the patient woke up as soon as possible after the procedure. Staying too long under anaesthetic could lead to all kinds of problems, above and beyond the initial need for surgery.

'Give me a shout when you need to lift him onto the trolley,' Adam said, pulling off his gloves. 'I'll get the notes done and we can go next door for a coffee if you like.'

Helen nodded. 'Thanks,' she said as Adam pushed his way through the double swing doors.

Emily was looking well, Helen thought as she walked into the cottage kitchen. The dark rings that had shadowed her large green eyes had gone. Her hair was still golden red, though it was starting to be streaked with white strands. An open laptop lay on the table in front of her, but she stood up when Helen came in and walked over to put the kettle on. 'I hear Moondance got off safely,' she said, turning back to Helen.

Lucy, who had been in the kitchen since Helen's early start that morning, came pottering over and pushed her damp nose into Helen's hand.

'She was totally calm about loading up,' Helen replied. 'Gemma not so much,' she added. 'I'd say of the two Moondance was in a better state.'

Emily laughed. 'I did hear it was quite the party last night,' she said.

Helen crouched beside Lucy to give her a hug and Lucy leaned her weight into Helen's body, her tail brushing the ground. Emily watched as Helen gave Lucy a kiss. 'She's been as good as gold,' she said. 'Sit down and I'll get you a cup of coffee.'

'Thanks,' Helen said, straightening up. She pulled out a chair at the scrubbed pine table.

The door opened and Adam came in. He walked over and kissed Emily on the side of her head. 'You sit down,' he told her. 'I'll get the coffee.'

'Thanks,' Emily replied. 'I've been working on the website. Mandy asked me to update the rescues that are ready for rehoming.' She looked at Helen. 'I'm just adding Lettuce,' she said. 'I've written down that he's a Giant Flemish and that he's sandy coloured. What else?'

Helen laughed. 'He's absolutely enormous?' she suggested.

'That does seem to be his most distinguishing feature.' Adam grinned.

'Also that he can eat his own weight in vegetables,' Helen added.

The kettle boiled. Helen watched as Adam poured out three mugs of coffee and put them on the table.

Emily lifted her mug and took a sip, then looked at Helen, her expression humorous. 'Do you have space in your life for an oversized rabbit?' she teased. 'I'm sure Lettuce would be quite large enough to keep up with Lucy.'

Helen wrinkled her nose. 'I'm sure he could,' she said. 'But I'm not sure what Lucy would make of a bunny sibling. Don't you think he'd look good hopping round the kitchen here?' She waved a hand round the comfortable room with its cheerful flowered curtains and wood stove.

Adam looked scandalised. 'Tango would never agree to that,' he said.

Tango was an ancient ginger cat that had come into Hope Meadows a year and a half ago. Adam and he had become great friends. A month later, he had officially moved into the cottage, though he spent as much time in the clinic, supervising the dogs as they went in and out.

'Where *is* Tango?' Helen asked, looking around.

Adam shrugged one shoulder. 'Nobody knows,' he said, his voice mysterious. He grinned as he lifted his mug. 'He comes and goes as he likes. You know he hates being shut in anywhere,' he added in a more normal tone.

Oh, to be so free! Helen found herself wondering where Moondance was. Hopefully not stuck in a traffic jam on the M1. Beneath the table, Lucy's warm head slid onto her lap. Helen reached down and stroked her silky ear. *Just you and me, girl, for the summer. We'll have to find our own adventures!*

Chapter Three

Helen drove home in bright afternoon sunshine. Midsummer was almost here, and the sun was still high over the fells that rose beyond the little village of Kimbleton, just before the turn-off to Helen's home. She topped the summit of Kimbleton Bank and dropped down the steep road that led to Sunrise Farm. Helen had rented the converted granary from Anneka and Steve Mellor for the past three years.

Anneka and Steve had bought Sunrise Farm ten years ago, abandoning city life in Rochdale to begin a new life growing fruit. The little valley had already been filled with densely planted fruit trees in a wonderful orchard of apples and pears. Behind the trees, the Mellors had erected a series of polytunnels to stock with strawberries, raspberries and gooseberries on long raised planters. Two additional fields were given over to ground-growing strawberries, warmed in rows of yellow straw. The evening air was often scented with the sweet aroma of ripening fruit or of the wonderful jam Steve cooked on the farmhouse kitchen stove.

Helen climbed out of the car and stretched. She smiled

at Lucy, who was waiting patiently in the back seat. She opened the door and unclipped Lucy's harness from the seat belt.

'Lucy!' A happy shout and the sound of running feet across the yard heralded the arrival of Anneka and Steve's three children. Nine-year-old Barney led the way, followed by seven-year-old Connie, then Harry, who was only four. A rather roly-poly basset hound brought up the rear.

'Hello, Birdie.' Helen bent to rub the basset's ear, and he sat on his haunches and groaned with pleasure as he leaned into her hand.

'Daddy's making jam,' Connie told Helen. Her wide blue eyes almost filled her small round face.

'We helped,' Barney piped up. He was a sweet-natured boy with a halo of brown curls.

'I can see that,' Helen replied, trying not to laugh. All three children were covered in scarlet juice.

'Rice pudding and jam for tea,' Harry said, then put his red-stained thumb in his mouth.

'Dad said we could bring you a jar, once it's finished,' Connie told her. 'Can we bring it round later, please?'

'Of course.' Helen smiled at the earnest little faces. 'That would be lovely, thank you. Anyway, I'd better get Lucy inside. Come on, Lucy.'

The black retriever was sniffing around the gravelled yard with Birdie, but came as soon as Helen called. Lucy would have stayed outside quite happily, but Helen wanted nothing more after her long day than to escape into the peaceful granary and put her feet up for half an hour.

It was blissfully quiet in her tiny stone-flagged kitchen. Helen felt herself starting to relax as she opened the fridge and poured herself a glass of wine. She tossed spinach, tomatoes and red onions in a bowl, then sat down on one of the two leather chairs that stood on either side of the unlit stove in the living area. It was cosy in winter time, but in summer it was blissfully cool. Helen sipped her wine and Lucy lay down at her feet with a sigh. Helen's mind was drifting on the subject of Lettuce when she heard the click of the front door latch. Lucy's tail began to wag and she jumped up and rushed out into the hall.

'Hello.' Seb sounded as if he was smiling. A moment later, he appeared in the kitchen doorway. 'And hello you,' he said to Helen. He walked over and gave her a kiss, then held out a closed fist. 'Guess what I got for you today.'

It had become something of a joke between them that he always brought her a tiny gift from his day. It had started with small romantic things: a flower from the verge or a square of her favourite chocolate. Gradually the offerings had become more and more corny. Helen raised her eyebrows. 'I have no idea,' she said with a grin.

He opened his hand to reveal a small sachet of tomato ketchup. His eyes were laughing.

'Just what I always wanted!' Helen reached out and

took it. 'Perhaps you'd like it on your salad,' she suggested.

'I couldn't possibly eat it!' he exclaimed. 'I brought it for you.'

He walked over to the fridge and poured himself a glass of wine. Helen pulled herself up from her chair and assembled the rest of the evening meal as he leaned on the counter and watched her. They took their plates outside and sat at the tiny table that stood in the little patch of grass outside Helen's back door. Lucy lay beside them, enjoying the slanting rays of sunlight that dappled the valley floor.

'I had a chat with Lisa today,' Seb said as he finished the last of his rocket leaves and sat back in his chair.

Lisa was his supervisor at the Animal Welfare Unit for Walton Council. 'We were talking about career development. I've been on the same grade for three years now.'

'Did she have anything to suggest?' Helen asked. As a veterinary nurse, her own career path was limited unless she was willing to leave Welford, but she had always been so contented at Animal Ark that moving had never crossed her mind.

'She thought I should think about night school for professional development courses. Maybe consider moving to a different area if a promotion comes up.'

'Sounds like a good idea,' Helen replied. She smiled as she gazed at him across the table. There were several offices not too far from Walton he could try. It wouldn't be impossible to commute to York, and Richmond would be easy. Even if Seb was in Leeds, he wouldn't have to spend too long on the road each day.

She looked out across the valley. The trees in the orchard were casting long shadows. There was almost no breeze and it was very still. A bumblebee buzzed across the lawn and Lucy followed it with her eyes, though she was too sleepy to chase it. It would have been a lovely evening for a ride, Helen thought. 'Have you had any thoughts about a holiday?' she asked, turning back to look at Seb. 'It'd be lovely to do some travelling like Gemma. Not that we could go away for as long as that, but a couple of weeks maybe. We could go somewhere exciting. India, maybe.' They were both young and free. Now was the time for adventure, surely?

Seb frowned. 'A holiday would be nice,' he said, 'but wouldn't it be better to do something that would cost a bit less? I'd actually been thinking . . .' He paused for a moment and reached over to stroke Lucy's head. 'How would you feel about starting to save up for a deposit?' he asked.

Helen felt her shoulders go tense. Of course she sometimes thought about the long-term future, whether she and Seb would marry and settle down. She had tried to picture him dropping on one knee and proposing, but she had to admit that this scenario didn't fit with his personality. But she'd hoped he might manage a little romance when it came to looking ahead. Now here he was, casually talking about a deposit for a house.

'You mean buy a house together?' she checked. They weren't even engaged. Buying a house felt like a huge commitment. Though she tried to temper her voice, the words sounded a little sharp. 'That's quite a big decision, isn't it?'

Seb blinked, as if he had assumed she would jump at the idea. 'Well, if you don't want to buy,' he said, 'could we rent somewhere together? It seems stupid paying out on two separate places when we spend almost every night together.'

Helen felt as if she'd had a bucket of icy water poured over her. Here she was craving adventure and Seb seemed to want to chain her to a kitchen sink. Career pathways and house deposits? Moving in together to cut costs? She shuffled round so her arm was leaning on the sturdy stone wall of the granary. It felt warm in the evening sunshine. Seb was watching her, but she couldn't raise a smile. She was perfectly happy living here with Lucy, she thought. 'I don't think I want to move,' she said, knowing she sounded petulant. 'Specially not just to save money.'

Seb was looking pained. 'That wasn't what I meant,' he said, shaking his head. 'It really wasn't about the cost. I'd like to see more of you. We both work long hours. If we lived together . . .' He trailed off. His neck had become rather red.

Helen could feel heat rising in her own face. They could see one another more if they went on holiday together. A new experience for them both. Special memories to share. Frustration rose in her chest. She spent her whole life in the clinic being practical. What was wrong with wanting to do something exciting? Something different, before they thought about settling down?

To her dismay, she realised her hands were shaking. She and Seb never disagreed about anything. She had pictured an evening spent planning their Indian adventure. Instead he was asking her to forget that so they could save money. She risked a glance at his face. There was a puzzled, rather hurt look in his eyes she hadn't seen before and she felt a stab of guilt. 'I know you weren't just trying to economise,' she said. She swallowed. 'It's just such a big step,' she went on, hoping he would understand. 'I'll think about it, I promise.' But she couldn't imagine that she was going to feel magically different any time soon.

Seb seemed mollified. 'Take your time,' he said, his blue eyes earnest.

Helen nodded. The headache she'd had this morning had returned, and she didn't think she could blame last night's Pimm's. Seb smiled at her, though his eyes were still a little sad. 'Shall we go for a quick walk with Lucy?' he asked. '*The Supervet*'s on later.'

They often watched *The Supervet* together. They were as enthralled by the man's expertise as they were troubled at the amount of money spent on individual animals when so many others were being mistreated. The programme covered both of their careers and they'd had some great debates about the morality of certain treatments. Tonight Helen thought she wouldn't care if they built an entire cat out of robot parts.

She forced herself to smile. 'That'd be nice,' she said. She stood up and lifted her plate, piling his on top, and he picked up the glasses and salad bowl and followed her inside.

Helen paused at the door to the cat ward, gathering herself for the battle ahead. After a few days in the clinic, Croissant had become wise to all her ruses to distract him when he needed to provide a blood sample. For most of the day, he was a fluffy charmer who purred at anyone willing to rub his ear. But at 10 a.m., when his daily tests were due, he became a terrifying ball of claws and teeth and yowls of protest.

'Preparation complete?' Toby asked. His voice sounded tired. He had been looking rather wan all morning and Helen had wondered whether he would agree to help her with Croissant, but when she'd asked, he had agreed immediately.

Helen nodded, waving the huge blanket that was her latest salvo in the ongoing Croissant wars. 'Ready.'

She had never expected Croissant's treatment to be a walk in the park. Cats rarely appreciated having their blood taken. Ever since Mandy had converted Helen to taking blood from the large jugular vein in the neck (it went against the grain to use the blood vessel nearest the teeth

– yet it was so much quicker than using a leg), she had grown in confidence that there was no cat they couldn't sample, but Croissant was testing this to the limit.

She pushed open the door and peered round it. There was no hope of catching Croissant unawares. He was sitting bolt upright, glaring at her. He opened his mouth and let out an ear-splitting meow. As Helen walked forward, he slunk into the corner of the cage, then turned to face her again. His eyes were bigger than ever and his hair stood on end like that of a cartoon cat in shock. Helen was careful not to look directly at him. Most cats responded well when she approached crabwise, blinking her eyes, but Croissant put his ears back, growling, bracing himself for a fight.

'Can you open the cage door, please?' Helen didn't take her attention off Croissant for a moment.

Toby undid the latch. 'Take care,' he murmured.

The cage door swung open. Grasping the blanket, Helen pounced on the angry cat, thrust the blanket underneath him and gathered him into her arms before he had a chance to move.

'Open the door,' she cried to Toby. A wail came from the inside the cat parcel, but Helen held on tightly as she rushed into the prep room, where she had laid out syringes, needles, a swab and a tourniquet. With a quieter patient, she would have transferred him to a cage, but she didn't dare let go of the blanket. They had one shot at this.

In theory, with the blanket wrapped tightly round him,

Croissant should have begun to relax, but nothing could have been farther from his mind. Helen took a steadying breath. The next stage was even trickier. 'His head's at this end,' she told Toby through gritted teeth, nodding at the end of the blanket from which the enraged growling was emanating. 'I can't loosen my hold,' she said. 'Once he gets his claws into the blanket and gets some traction, we're done for. I need you to reach inside and try to extract his hind leg.'

Toby seemed to grasp that time was limited. Helen couldn't help but feel relieved that he was on the ball. Rachel Gill, who worked on reception at Animal Ark some evenings and weekends, had told her that Toby had been seen last night in the Fox and Goose with Imogen Parker-Smythe. 'Faces glued together,' had been the phrase Rachel had used, and Helen had laughed. They'd left together apparently. In Welford that was often enough to cause marriage speculation.

Toby reached inside the blanket and a moment later he had extracted Croissant's hind leg. The area over the vein was already shaven.

'You'll need to use the tourniquet,' Helen told him. 'I have no spare hands to raise the vein.'

Toby reached for the band and put it around Croissant's leg. 'You're very efficient with that blanket,' he observed. He glanced up at her. The twinkle seemed to have returned to his eyes. 'Croissant has no idea how lucky he is to have your arms wrapped around him.' Helen rolled her eyes at him and he laughed as he reached for the syringe. 'You're just lucky I'm a gentleman,' he said. 'Imagine what might happen other- wise, with your arms all taken up like that.'

'A gentleman? Are you sure about that?' Helen teased.

'I am more certain of that than of anything else,' he said with a grin. 'And to prove it, I'll make you a coffee when we're done in here.'

'You have to get some blood out of that leg first,' Helen reminded him.

'I shall do that immediately.' He smiled at her again, then bent to his task. A moment later, he held up the syringeful of blood like a trophy. 'There you go!' he said. He picked up the test tube and transferred the blood. 'I'll take this through to the lab,' he said. 'Will you be okay getting him back into his cage?'

'I think I can manage,' Helen said. She adjusted her grip on the blanket. Croissant already seemed more relaxed. 'Are you sure you know how to make coffee?' she asked, and Toby glared at her playfully, then tossed his head and flounced out of the room.

He was as good as his word about the coffee. It was the first he had made her, Helen realised. Not that she often made the coffee, either. In the practice where she'd started out, cleaning and coffee-making were considered to be 'things nurses did'. Here at Animal Ark, more often than not, Adam or Emily made coffee for everyone in their kitchen, but today they were both out. Now Helen and Toby were sitting in the little rest area of the clinic they used when nobody was in the cottage.

'This is lovely, thanks.' She lifted her mug in a toast and Toby smiled and raised his in return.

'Did Croissant go back into his cage okay?' he asked, taking a biscuit from a tin that lay on the bench beside him.

'He did,' Helen replied. She shook her head, making a face. 'He's an angel until you want to get blood out of him. Poor Croissant. He'll be glad to go home. His blood levels have stabilised so hopefully it won't be long.'

The phone in her pocket buzzed. 'Mind if I get this?' she asked. Toby shook his head and reached into his pocket for his own mobile.

'Hi, Dad,' Helen said. She stood up and carried her coffee into the empty waiting room. She could guess what he was calling about. Her father had recently started online dating, and he'd taken to it as if he hadn't lived most of his life before the internet even existed. Helen had helped him with his profile, choosing a flattering but honest photo and discussing what to write.

'Hello, love.' His voice was warm. He and Helen had always been very close, even though her parents had divorced when they were younger than Helen was now.

'How did it go last night?' she asked.

He had been out on another first date, his third in a month. The other two had ended amicably but there had been no spark, or so he'd told her. This time he sounded enthusiastic. 'It went really well,' he said. 'She likes steam trains so we're going to have dinner on the Pickering Pullman next week. She's called Sue, she has two grown-up sons, and she's got a wonderful sense of humour.'

'Sounds marvellous,' Helen said. It lifted her spirits to hear him sound so happy.

'I was just wondering,' he went on. 'She has an account on Twitter. I was wondering if I should get an account too.'

Helen couldn't help but smile. Her dad was so keen to keep up with new technology. Gemma's parents weren't even on the internet and refused to have mobile phones. 'I can help you if you like,' she said, 'but it sounds like things are going well enough already.'

'Okay, love. I'll have a think and let you know. And I'll take some photos of the engine when we get to Grosmont!'

'Some photos of Sue would be nice too!' Helen said. She hoped Sue was as enthusiastic about steam trains as her dad seemed to think. Still, dinner on the Pullman would be a treat. 'Have a great time, and I'll see you soon.'

'Thanks, love. Love you.'

He hung up and Helen put her mobile back into her pocket. Toby was still drinking his coffee. He put away his phone when she walked back in. 'That was my dad,' she explained. 'He's wondering whether he should join Twitter.'

Toby's eyebrows lifted at least an inch. 'Wow!' he said.

'Why "Wow"?' Helen asked. 'Aren't your parents tech-savvy?'

One side of Toby's mouth lifted, as if the idea amused him. 'They're very . . . traditional,' he said. Helen thought she caught a flash of intense emotion in his gaze. Was it embarrassment? But then he smiled and she wondered whether she'd imagined it. 'I'd better get on,' he said. 'I have to get to Twyford before lunch.'

It was Helen's turn to look startled. 'Not 272 again?' she said. One visit in a month to the Devil Cow was more than enough.

'Happily not,' Toby assured her. 'Off to see a calf with diarrhoea. Really quite safe.' He stood up, sketched a wave and was gone.

Chapter Four

Helen put up a hand to shield her eyes from the sun. Was Flit looking in her direction? She had all the collie's favourite treats including some cream cheese, which Flit liked to lick direct from the tube, but she needed to be sure the dog was paying attention before she called her. If she shouted when Flit was distracted, there was no way she would obey, and Helen would have taught her that it wasn't important to listen to commands.

Unlike most dogs, Flit wasn't very food oriented. She preferred to carry *things*, and she didn't like to give them up. Anything from a tug toy to a twig or leaf would do. Helen was trying to stop her picking up stones. She'd assisted with more than enough foreign body operations.

'Come, Flit!' she called, clapping her hands on her thighs as the collie's eyes latched on to her. Tail high, Flit bounded towards Helen. She was carrying a rope bone in her mouth. As soon as she arrived and sat, Helen grabbed one end and started to pull. 'Good girl, oh, good girl,' she panted as they danced around one another.

It was important Flit knew that when she responded to recall, it would always be fun. Helen suspected that her previous owners had made the mistake of punishing her for coming too slowly in the past.

Mandy appeared just as their game finished. 'Thanks,' she said. 'I'm not sure who's working harder!'

Both Helen and Flit were panting. 'I've done some work with Bobby too,' Helen said once she'd caught her breath. 'He's a quick learner, isn't he?'

'He is,' Mandy agreed. 'I don't think he'll be with us much longer.' She reached down and stroked Flit's ear and the collie leaned into her hand. 'I think I've found a home for this lovely girl, too,' she said. 'Once we've done a bit more work.' Helen knew Mandy wouldn't let Flit go until her recall was reliable. 'Shall we go in?' Mandy asked. 'We've got a new arrival.'

'Oh yes?' Helen bent to clip on Flit's leash. The collie was much calmer now she'd had a good run. They followed Mandy into the rescue centre, where a large cardboard box stood on the floor beside the reception counter. A small, shaggy-furred shape cowered inside the box. Helen quickly returned Flit to her cage and joined Mandy to study the new dog.

'Poor little poppet,' Mandy said, crouching down and laying one finger gently on the dog's head.

Helen looked down at the pitiful little dog. She might have had some Bedlington Terrier in her, judging by her distinctive Roman nose, but other than that, it was impossible to tell her breeding. She had rather short

legs, a long curly tail and fluffy ears that were currently
about as far back as they could go. 'What happened to
her eye?' Helen asked. The dog's left eye had a large
white patch on the cornea, right over the place where
her pupil should have been.

'Not sure,' Mandy said. 'She came in from Raleigh's
practice in Walton after someone found her on the fell.
There's no microchip and she doesn't look like she's
had a decent meal in a while, so I think she was dumped.
She bumped into the table, so they checked her other
eye and she seems to be blind. She's still young, poor
little thing. I've named her Isla.'

For a moment, when Helen spoke, Isla's ears had
twitched forward, but now she was huddled down inside
the box again. Helen wanted to pull the skinny grey dog
into her arms and hug her tightly. Instead she approached
her slowly, speaking all the time so Isla knew she was
there. The little dog still jumped when Helen reached
out and touched her ear. Helen ran her hands over the
tense body. 'You'll be okay now you're here,' she said.
The tension in Isla's muscles began to relax as Helen
stroked her.

'I'll make up a cage,' Mandy said. 'She seems to like
you,' she added with a smile. 'I couldn't get her to calm
down at all.'

Helen carried Isla through to the kennel a few minutes
later and slipped the little dog into the cage. Mandy had
put in loads of blankets, a bowl of water and a small

amount of food in a bowl. Isla sniffed round the kennel and in a moment she had found the food. She ate ravenously, ears pinned back as if she was afraid someone would come and take the food off her. Once she had finished it, she backed away until she felt the wall of the kennel behind her. She sat down again, shoulders hunched, looking thoroughly sorry for herself. Helen felt another pang of pity. How difficult this must be for her: a new place, an unknown kennel, and Isla couldn't even see where she was.

Lucy had followed Helen into the room. She walked over and sniffed the newcomer through the bars. Helen was about to call her away when she noticed that the tip of Isla's curly tail was twitching. The little dog's ears were no longer flattened against her skull. Lucy stood very still as Isla shuffled to the front of the cage. The two dogs touched noses and, for the second time, Isla's ears moved forward.

'Good girl, Lucy,' Helen murmured.

Mandy appeared in the doorway. She smiled when she saw the two dogs together. 'That's the first time she's looked happy since she arrived. You're a good nurse, Lucy, just like your owner.' She walked over, making enough noise to let Isla know she was there, and attached some paperwork to the front of the cage. 'She's a sweet little thing,' she said to Helen as she stepped back, 'but it'll be difficult to find her a home.'

Helen patted her on the shoulder. 'If anyone can, it's

you,' she said. She glanced over at the cage. 'Come on, Lucy,' she called, and with one more sniff, Lucy followed Mandy and Helen into the reception area.

'Lettuce next,' Mandy said, opening the door to the room where the enormous rabbit was kept. 'No idea how I'll find him a home either. How many people have space for a rabbit the size of an elephant?'

Helen laughed. 'Whoever they are,' she said, 'they'd better like chopping cabbage.' She was pulling open the fridge when a blast of high-pitched, frantic electronic music blared out behind her. She jumped, then looked round.

Mandy was pulling her phone from her pocket. 'Hi, Jimmy,' she said.

Helen turned back to the fridge. Lettuce needed three different kinds of vegetables. She pulled out a box of carrots, a chunk of cucumber and two round lettuces and set them all on the table.

'Of course I'll pick them up,' she heard Mandy say. 'See you later.'

'That was Jimmy,' Mandy told her unnecessarily as she stuffed the phone away again. 'He's got to stay late. I'll have to pick up Abi and Max from school.'

She sounded pleased, as she often did now when talking about Jimmy's ten-year-old twins. Helen couldn't help feeling relieved. When Mandy and Jimmy had first started seeing each other, taking on stepmotherly duties hadn't come naturally to Helen's animal-loving friend, and she had wondered whether Jimmy and Mandy's relationship would weather the storm. A few challenging moments farther on, both Mandy and the twins had found an *entente cordiale* that was warming into a very real and affectionate connection.

Helen grabbed a knife and began slicing the first lettuce. 'What on earth was that ringtone?' she couldn't resist asking.

Mandy looked embarrassed, then laughed. 'I let Abi change it,' she said. 'It's the latest K-pop sensation.'

Helen turned to look at Mandy, one eyebrow raised.

'K-pop!' Mandy was still grinning. 'Korean Pop to you and me.' She grabbed a knife and one of the carrots.

Helen frowned. 'I didn't even know that was a thing,' she said, taking another lettuce.

'It's all the rage,' Mandy informed her, starting to chop at high speed. 'At least Abi says so. Some of them are actually not unbearable!'

Helen grinned. 'You know,' she said, 'anyone would think you'd forgotten all about being a wicked step-mother. You seem almost maternal.'

Unexpectedly, Mandy flushed. 'They're really not so bad,' she said. 'Abi's developing the attitude of a seventeen-year-old and Max worries about almost everything, but they're my family now.'

Helen's knife paused again as she looked at Mandy in amazement. 'I think I need to hear more about this miracle,' she said. 'Hold the front page: Mandy Hope likes children!'

'I was never that bad!' Mandy protested. 'Let's feed Lettuce before he passes out from hunger. We're due a break after that, I think.'

They fed the giant rabbit then walked into the reception area. Beyond the floor-to-ceiling windows, the sky was still a blazing blue. Helen sat down opposite Mandy. 'I don't mean to tease,' she said. 'I'm really pleased you're getting on so well with Jimmy's kids.'

'It's strange,' Mandy said, rubbing at a patch of dust on the knee of her jeans. 'I never really saw myself settling down, but everything's different since I came back to Welford. This place,' she waved a hand to indicate the rescue centre, 'Mum getting ill, meeting Jimmy . . .' She trailed off, then shook her head as if her own reactions were as much of a surprise to her as they were to Helen. 'I've changed,' she said. 'I feel like I finally know what I want.'

'Which is?' Helen prompted.

Mandy's whole face glowed. 'Jimmy,' she said. 'A family, and not just Abi and Max. I want to have a baby of my own.' She paused and Helen waited, trying not to show how shocked she was. Somewhere inside, she'd always known that she wanted children, but she had never had even a hint from Mandy that she felt the same.

'You know I'm adopted?' Mandy said.

Helen nodded.

'It's never mattered to me,' Mandy went on. 'Mum and Dad couldn't have been any more fantastic, and

I couldn't love them more than I do. My real parents died in a car crash when I was a baby so I don't even remember them. Mum and Dad have given me everything I dreamed of, and more.' She glanced round the reception. As well as sharing Animal Ark with Mandy, Helen knew Adam and Emily had invested heavily in Hope Meadows to get Mandy's project off the ground.

Mandy looked back at Helen, her eyes steady. 'Seeing Jimmy with Abi and Max . . .' she blinked, her eyes shining, '. . . well, it's made me think about how it would feel to have a blood relative. Someone who looks like me, shares the things I love. Now I've met Jimmy, now I've seen what a wonderful dad he is, I know he's the one I want to share my baby with.'

Helen could feel tears welling up in her eyes. She reached over, grabbed Mandy's hand and gave it a squeeze. 'Thanks for telling me,' she said. 'I think you'd make incredible parents.' She corrected herself. 'You already are, to Abi and Max. But a new baby would be amazing!' She was still gripping Mandy's hand when a cold nose bumped her fingers. Helen glanced down to see Lucy glaring up at her. She gave a sudden bark and Helen laughed.

'Oh, I'm sorry,' she told Lucy, letting go of Mandy's hand with a grin. 'You're still my favourite.' She scratched Lucy behind her ear.

'Thanks for listening,' Mandy said. 'I've been dying to tell someone.'

Helen sat back in her chair. 'So Jimmy doesn't know about this?'

Mandy shook her head. For the first time, she frowned. 'I haven't had the chance to talk to him yet,' she said. 'I know it's old fashioned, but I'd really like to be married before I have a child.'

Helen pursed her lips. 'In that case,' she said, 'hadn't you better get on and propose?' She was teasing, but to her surprise Mandy nodded.

'I might just do that,' she said. 'What about you and Seb?' she prompted. 'You two are so lovely together. Seb hasn't popped the question, has he? I've always thought it was just a matter of time.'

Helen's mind went back to the row she'd had with Seb about getting a place together. Should she tell Mandy that she and Seb had argued? It would spoil Mandy's announcement. 'He hasn't said anything like that,' she said, keeping her voice light. 'That's a long way off.'

Mandy stood up. 'I'm going to take Sky out for a quick run,' she said. 'Want to come?'

Helen shook her head. 'I think I'll see how Isla is settling in,' she said. 'Lucy and I might join you in a few minutes.'

Mandy called Sky. A moment later, Helen watched them stride up the field together. Mandy's conviction about her future with Jimmy had thrown her row with Seb into sharp contrast. She was going to have to talk to Seb, she thought. She needed to find out exactly where he thought they were heading.

She felt a nudge against her arm and looked round to see Lucy staring hopefully at her. 'You want a biscuit, don't you?' She rubbed Lucy's silky head. 'It's easy to tell what you're thinking,' she said.

If only she could read Seb so easily. Life would be much less complicated.

Chapter Five

Six o'clock was early for a Saturday morning, Helen thought, suppressing a groan, but when she looked across the dale at the early morning haze it was almost worth it. It was going to be another scorching day. She walked through the orchard and emerged into the fields and polytunnels on the far side. Lucy trotted behind her and Birdie brought up the rear, panting, though the sun had not yet burned through the dawn mist that lingered on the valley floor.

The Mellors had gone for a rare weekend away and Helen had agreed to fruit-sit. The mayhem of summer harvest had not yet set in, and for now all Helen had to do was make sure the irrigation system was switched on in the morning and evening. Everything seemed to be functioning perfectly as she walked through each of the tunnels. Now and then, she reached out and plucked a ripe strawberry. They tasted wonderfully sweet, and smelled of summer.

Next she inspected the Pick Your Own section, which was uncovered. There was one field of strawberry plants and one of raspberry canes. In a few weeks they would be heaving with customers, but for now the ripening fruit grew quietly. A wood pigeon called from somewhere in the orchard, and a trilling blackbird seemed to reply.

Her tasks complete, Helen headed back to the granary. In return for the fruit duties, Steve and Anneka had said she could use their garden and patio for the weekend. They had a beautiful walled rose garden with a grill at one end and a small pond with a miniature waterfall at the other. Helen had decided to host a lunchtime barbecue. She opened her fridge and pulled out tomatoes and red onions. She would chop and dress those first, she thought, then prepare the cucumber, radishes and Romano lettuce. There was a tub of pre-cooked rice too. She would dice some peppers and fry some halloumi cheese to mix through. She hummed to herself as she worked. Seb was away at a meeting for the day, but Mandy's old school friend James was coming over from York with his partner Raj. Mandy and Jimmy were bringing the twins, and Susan and Douglas would come with Susan's son Jack. Toby was coming too. It would be great to host everyone here for a change, although she might be less generous with the Pimm's than Seb had been at Gemma's leaving do!

Helen stowed the last of the bowls in the fridge and glanced at the clock on the wall. It was still only 10.30. Her guests wouldn't arrive until one. She still had plenty of time and there was no more food to prepare. She grabbed the two bags of charcoal she had bought, deciding to set up the grill and put out the chairs. Twenty minutes later, she glanced around the patio with satisfaction. The long wooden table was set with plates, cutlery and napkins on a red-checked tablecloth. It was too early to light the barbecue, she thought. If she lit it at midday, it would be ready to go when her friends arrived. Helen suddenly felt tired. She'd been up for five hours already, she realised.

A pair of sun loungers stood on the edge of the grass. Perhaps she could have a quick rest in the sun before lighting the barbecue. Helen lay down and Lucy flopped beside her with a loud sigh. A sparrow swooped above them, wings whirring, and began to splash in the little bird bath on the edge of the pond. Helen closed her eyes, enjoying the warmth of the sun on her eyelids. It was very peaceful lying there, listening to the sound of the little waterfall.

She woke with a start as a shadow flickered across her. Toby was looking down at her. There was a gleam of amusement in his eyes. 'Hello, Sleeping Beauty,' he said.

Helen struggled into a sitting position and swung her feet round onto the ground. Her watch read 12.40. She'd slept for nearly two hours.

'I did think of waking you with a kiss,' Toby said, 'but having seen you wrestle with Croissant, I thought if you responded with a right hook, I probably wouldn't be able to get out of the way in time.'

Helen tried to laugh but it came out as a strangled snort, which left her feeling even more flustered. Her face burned as if it was bright red from the sun and her hair must be everywhere. She pushed herself upright, adjusting the straps on her top. How did Toby always look so polished? she wondered. He was wearing a pale blue shirt that complemented the dazzling blue of his eyes. His dark blue linen shorts revealed a muscular pair of tanned legs, lightly covered in bronze hairs. Helen felt her face grow hotter than ever.

To her relief, Toby changed the subject, holding out the two laden bags he was holding. 'What should I do with these?'

Helen led him into the kitchen and put the bread and rolls on the table. The other bag was filled with clinking bottles. She pulled one out. 'Wow!' she said. It was a bottle of Bollinger. She peered into the bag. Another two bottles remained.

'Pre-chilled,' Toby said with a nod, as if bringing Bollinger to a lunchtime grill was the most normal thing in the world.

'Thanks very much.' Helen didn't know what else to say.

'We could have some now,' Toby suggested. He had a way of opening his eyes very wide when he made a suggestion. *Entirely up to you,* said his expression.

For a moment, Helen felt a surge of pleasure. How tempting it sounded, but she really should get everything sorted out before she started drinking. 'I need to get the barbecue started,' she said, 'and the table finished up. Then . . .' She sent him a wicked grin and his face lit up. It was going to be a great party!

It only took a few minutes to get the grill lit. Helen passed an eye over the table. She needed a few more glasses and then all that was left was to bring the salad out. 'You could open that bottle now,' she told Toby. He began to peel off the foil as Helen pulled wine glasses and tumblers from her cupboard.

Toby eased the cork from the bottle with what looked like a very practised hand. '*Voila*!' he said a moment later, holding the cork to his nose. 'Smells fantastic,' he added.

Helen put two wine glasses on the table. Pity she didn't have any proper champagne flutes, but Toby seemed unfazed. He poured two generous glasses, lifted both and held one out to Helen. 'To a wonderful afternoon,' he said. Their glasses touched.

The champagne smelled fruity like baked apples with a hint of spicy sweetness. Helen realised Toby was watching her. 'Okay?' he asked.

'Very okay,' she replied. She took another sip. I could get used to this, she thought, but when she glanced up again, Toby was frowning.

'This is a fruit farm, isn't it?' he asked.

Helen nodded.

'And they grow raspberries?' He sounded so serious that Helen wondered for a moment whether something was wrong, but how could that require raspberries?

'Yes,' she said. 'There's a pick-your-own field at the end of the lane, just beyond the orchard.'

Toby let out a satisfied sigh. 'Well, in that case,' he said, 'I shall pick some at once. You deserve the best and the best thing, in my opinion, would be to have a few freshly picked raspberries with this fizz.'

Before she could stop him, he whisked out of the door and strode off down the track. Helen took another sip of the champagne and then another. It was delicious, even without the fruit.

It took several trips to take all the different salads outside and line them up in the middle of the table. There was a bowl of coleslaw as well as the rice salad, green salad, tomato salad and avocado. There were some unchopped tomatoes left over and Helen stacked them on a plate. They were deliciously ripe and would only need a little salt to dress them.

'Here we go!' There was a yell from the end of the patio and Toby emerged into the garden brandishing a full punnet of raspberries. His hair was standing on end as if he'd charged through a hedge, yet somehow he still looked dashing.

He put down the container, plucked out three of the largest berries and dropped them into Helen's glass. 'Try that,' he said.

Helen felt very decadent as she took a sip and then another. 'Delicious,' she pronounced, tasting the sharpness of the fruit. She was starting to feel light-headed but she was enjoying herself too much to stop.

Toby hefted the punnet in one hand. 'I must pay for these,' he said. Reaching into his pocket, he pulled out a tenner and handed it to Helen. 'I can't have you thinking I go round scrumping raspberries for my Bollinger!'

'You're really pushing the boat out today,' Helen said. 'Bollinger *and* raspberries. Are the Hopes paying you too much or have you been moonlighting for the cash?'

Toby's grin vanished. 'Not many outgoings,' he said briefly. He suddenly seemed miles away. Helen felt a flicker of panic. Had she offended him? Asking about money could be a minefield, but she'd only been joking. What should she say? Should she apologise?

But Toby was smiling again. 'Anyway,' he said, 'what are friends for if you can't spoil them now and then?' He winked and the tension was gone. 'You've been busy,' he commented, looking appreciatively at the table. 'Yum,' he said, 'tomatoes!' His eyes lit up, filled with mischief. He lifted up the three largest and began to juggle with them. Helen found herself chuckling as his movements became more and more extravagant. He threw them higher and higher, catching them with impressive accuracy. His hand flashed to his mouth and he took a large bite, threw the tomato up again and took a bite from the next.

A movement near the ground caught Helen's eye. Birdie and Lucy were looking on with amazement and

Birdie was sidling forward, his head on one side. He barked with a sharpness that made Helen jump and one of the tomatoes splatted to the ground, then a second. Toby caught the third and looked at Helen with a look of consternation that made Helen laugh out loud. 'I'm so sorry,' he gasped. He put the remaining tomato back on the plate and looked helplessly at the mess.

'It really doesn't matter.' Helen picked up the worst of the mush. Birdie rushed over, sniffed at the seeds, and slunk away.

Toby laughed. 'I don't think I've ever seen a dog look more disappointed,' he said.

A car pulled up on the far side of the wall. Helen looked round. It was Mandy and Jimmy. Sky erupted into the garden and, close behind her, Simba, Zoe and Emma, Jimmy's dogs. Abi and Max followed. To Helen's surprise, Max was carefully holding Isla on a short lead.

'Watch her with the wall,' Abi warned.

'This way, Isla,' Max said. 'You don't want to bang your head.'

Mandy stopped beside Helen, but continued to watch as Abi and Max took Isla on a tour of the garden. They seemed determined to describe every plant and feature. 'They're so good with her,' Mandy said. There was so much pride in her voice that Helen half wanted to laugh. 'I'm trying to get Isla out and about,' Mandy explained. 'It's important to get her used to different places if she's going to settle in a new home.'

'Sounds like a great idea,' Helen said. Isla's ears pricked up when she heard Helen's voice. 'Come here, Isla,' Helen called, and to her delight the little dog started in her direction. 'Come on, girl,' she said again, and Max followed as Isla made a rather wobbly beeline towards her. Helen crouched down to scratch the curly little head. Lucy, who had been cantering round the garden with Sky, Simba, Zoe and Emma, came to a standstill, then trotted over. She sniffed Isla gently.

'You could try letting her off the lead,' Mandy suggested to Max.

Max unclipped the lead and patted Isla, giving her a little nudge to let her know that she was free to move. Helen watched as Lucy walked away with Isla beside her. They found a shady patch under an apple tree and lay down.

'Fantastic,' Mandy breathed.

'Lucy's so good with her,' Jimmy commented. He wrapped his arm around Mandy's waist. Helen found herself wondering whether Mandy had popped the question yet. They'd make an announcement if they'd got engaged, surely?

'Ahoy there!' A grinning face with wire-framed glasses and straight brown hair peered over the wall.

Mandy disentangled herself from Jimmy, rushed to the gate and threw her arms around the newcomer. 'James!' she cried. James Hunter was Mandy's oldest friend and they had grown up together in Welford. He and Mandy shared a love of animals and Helen knew the pair had been rescuing them long before Mandy had set up Hope Meadows.

There was a yelp of delight as Lily and Seamus, James's dogs, arrived in the garden and for a moment the lawn was a sea of racing hounds with wildly wagging tails. Helen was pleased to see that Isla was running too, hemmed in the middle of the pack.

'Hello, Raj.' Helen greeted James's partner, Raj Singh Bhuppal. He was looking very handsome in a red turban and a short-sleeved green shirt. He and James had got together last summer. James had been devastated a year earlier when his first husband Paul had died of bone cancer, but Raj had slipped into James's life in a way that seemed natural to everyone. James ran a café in York and Raj imported food from around the world.

He held out two large carrier bags. 'I brought desserts as you asked,' he said. 'And in the other bag is some new wine I want you to try. I'm just back from a buying trip, actually. James picked me up from the airport on the way.'

'Gosh, it's good of you to come! I hope you aren't too jet-lagged.'

Raj inclined his head. 'I treated myself to business class so I feel fine,' he said. 'And I'm not going to miss lunch with James's dearest friends!'

'Well, your presence is greatly appreciated, as always,' Helen said with a smile. She peered into the bag with the desserts, paper-wrapped cakes which smelled deliciously of syrup and spices. 'I'll pop these in the kitchen,' she said.

It was cool inside the granary. Helen pulled a packet of olives from the fridge and put them in a bowl, then filled another with crisps. She heard a sound from the doorway.

'Can I help you with anything?' It was Toby.

'You could take these out,' Helen suggested, holding out the olives. He took the bowl and carried it outside. Helen followed with the crisps. She expected Toby to put the olives on the table and resume drinking, but he offered them round carefully. Mandy was drinking champagne with raspberries, Helen noticed, as were James and Raj. Helen felt a wave a gratitude. Without Seb here, there might have been a lot to do, but Toby seemed to be stepping up and hosting alongside her.

Susan and Douglas were last to arrive. Douglas was wearing a ghillie shirt and kilt with walking boots and Susan was looking enchantingly young in a summery floral skirt and blouse.

'Hi, all!' Douglas's voice boomed out and the dogs began another circuit of the lawn.

Susan and Douglas had brought brown paper packages filled with burgers, sausages and steaks. Helen carried them over to the grill and for several minutes she was busy basting and flipping. Mandy's vegetarian food was being cooked on a portable grill, watched by Jimmy.

When the food was ready, everyone dragged a chair

over to the table and sat down. The burgers were particularly delicious, flavoured with apple and incredibly juicy. Douglas finished his third and sat back in his seat, licking his fingers. 'That was excellent,' he pronounced. 'Can't beat a good barbecue. The last time I had food cooked on a grill like that was when I was walking the Camino Way.'

Raj looked at Douglas, his head on one side. 'That's the pilgrims' trail, right? That ends at Santiago de Compostela in Spain?'

'That's the one.' Douglas nodded. 'Though I decided to go all the way to Finisterre, which is where the pilgrims used to finish hundreds of years ago. They thought it was the actual end of the world. *Finis terre*. That's how it got its name.'

'Fascinating!' James said. 'Were you on any kind of pilgrimage, or was it just a walk?'

Douglas laughed. 'It was a pilgrimage to blistered toes,' he said. 'I was full-on worshipping the god of Elastoplast by the time I got to the end.'

Laughter rippled round the table. Everything was going well, Helen thought. Toby poured out more champagne.

'When are we going home?' Abi put her elbows on the table, her eyes on Mandy. 'I'm bored.'

'We're going to be a little while yet,' Mandy replied, 'but could you do something for me?'

Helen expected Abi to look sulky, but the girl nodded eagerly.

Helen could remember a few times when Abi and Max had come to the clinic early in Mandy and Jimmy's relationship. Abi hadn't been outright rude, but it had been obvious that she resented her father's new girlfriend. Judging from the way she was responding now, Mandy had turned things around big time.

'You see all those dogs over there?' Mandy said, pointing to where the herd of canines were flopped in the shade. 'I think they might be a bit thirsty. If you go over to that little waterfall, you'll see the water disappears into the ground. But if you walk straight down the garden,' she pointed again, 'towards that gate over there, you'll find it comes up again in a stream. Do you think you and Max could take the dogs down?' She smiled, as if coming to the best part. 'I seem to remember Helen told me it was a lovely stream for paddling,' she said, 'only Isla won't be able to paddle on her own. Do you think you could make sure she doesn't fall over anything?'

Max was sitting up very straight. 'Can I go too?' he asked Mandy. 'Please?'

Mandy looked at Abi. 'Can Max help?' she said, raising her eyebrows.

'I suppose so,' Abi said, 'but I want to hold Isla this time.'

'That sounds fair.' Mandy nodded. 'Thank you very much, both of you,' she said. 'I appreciate it and the dogs will too.'

James was bubbling over with laughter, but he held

it in until Abi and Max were out of earshot. 'Who are you, and what have you done with Mandy Hope?' he demanded. 'I thought you were allergic to kids.' He grinned as he looked over at Jimmy. 'You're very lucky,' he said. 'I always wanted to have children. I never thought Mandy would beat me to it.'

Mandy looked thoughtful and for a moment Helen wondered whether she was going to say something then and there, but Toby leaned over and picked up one of the bottles of wine Raj had brought. 'Anyone for a top-up?' he drawled.

Mandy held out her glass, but Jimmy put a hand on top of his. 'Driving,' he explained.

'Me too,' Susan said as he proffered the bottle.

'Would anyone like coffee?' Helen asked. She could do with one herself after all the champagne. There was a chorus of yesses from around the table and she pushed back her chair and walked inside.

'We're starting off in Mumbai.' Raj was speaking when Helen returned to the table. She put down the tray with the coffee jug and cups and sat down to listen.

'I'm looking forward to seeing the place where Raj grew up,' James put in.

He and Raj made a striking couple, in Helen's opinion. Raj was very different to Paul, James's late husband, but James seemed very happy. 'After Mumbai, we're going to Agra,' he went on. 'One of Raj's uncles runs an elephant sanctuary there. I'm going to meet some of Raj's extended family.'

Raj reached out and took James's hand. 'I'm happy to be sharing them with you,' he said.

Helen caught a flash of movement at the bottom of the garden. Max ran up to Mandy. 'Abi wants to know if she can take her trousers off,' he panted, then, as if he was being very daring, 'and can I take mine off too?'

Mandy thought for a moment. 'Not just now,' she said. 'We'll be going quite soon.'

Max looked at her, his eyes wide. 'I think Abi's trousers might be a bit wet already,' he admitted.

Mandy smiled. 'Don't worry about it, Max,' she said. 'I expect they'll dry. Just tell Abi not to get any wetter before we have to get back in the car.'

Max looked relieved. 'Okay,' he said. 'Thanks, Mandy.' He scuttled off again.

'You really are good with them,' James remarked. He lifted up his wine glass and took a sip, then looked across at Raj. 'Like I said before,' he said, setting his glass down, 'I've always wanted children. What about it, Raj? I know we have Seamus and Lily, but how do you feel about two-legged babies?' He grinned lazily. Helen had rarely seen him more relaxed, and she wondered whether Toby had been a little heavy-handed with the champagne.

Raj had gone very still. He took hold of James's hand and Helen realised that he was shaking. She glanced at Mandy in alarm but Mandy was staring at the two men.

'I have always wanted a child,' Raj said. His eyes

dropped for a moment, then he looked at James again. 'There's something I have to tell you,' he said. 'There's a very special reason for going to Accra.' His gaze was so intense Helen almost winced. 'I haven't had a chance to tell you, but this feels like the right time. The elephant sanctuary isn't the only adventure I've been planning.'

James looked confused and Helen felt a shiver run down her spine. Was Raj going to propose? He had an air of seriousness that didn't quite fit with the jokey atmosphere a few moments ago. Helen shot a glance at James, hoping he wasn't going to feel embarrassed about being put on the spot. James was a very private person.

Raj carried on. 'Just before I met you,' he said, 'one of my cousins died in childbirth. I grew up with Chandra, loved her like a sister, and I knew I had to do something to help. The child's father wasn't in a position to raise him alone, so I stepped in. I truly believe it's what Chandra would have wanted.'

There was a hush around the table and a sense that everything had gone into slow motion. Helen felt a sickening sinking feeling in the pit of her stomach. Somehow she knew that a bomb was about to land on her peaceful, laid-back lunch.

Raj tightened his grip on James's hand. 'It was very complicated because I'm based in the UK now, and I have no plans to move back to India. But last week, while I was away, I got some wonderful news. My application for adoption has gone through,' he said. 'Since yesterday, I've had a son. His name is Taresh.' He sounded so proud that Helen felt a lump in her throat. 'I'm sorry I didn't tell you before,' Raj went on. 'I was almost certain it would come to nothing, but now everything has moved very fast.' He smiled, still gazing into James's eyes. 'I know it's a lot to ask,' he said, 'but I want you to share this with me. You just said you wanted become a father. Did you really mean it?'

Chapter Six

Helen realised she was holding her breath. James had gone very red and his eyes blinked rapidly behind his glasses. She and James weren't super-close, but she knew he tended to steer clear of the limelight. He often ran fundraisers for Hope Meadows at his café-bookshop in York, for example, but always stayed in the background. Right now, the poor man looked as if he couldn't be more uncomfortable. How would she feel if Seb made such a massive announcement in public? Helen wondered. She didn't mind other people's attention, but she hated being railroaded.

James opened his mouth as if he was trying to say something. Helen felt a stab of pity as a strangled squawk came out. James stopped, swallowed, then tried again. 'I don't understand,' he said. 'Why haven't you said anything before?' There was genuine dismay in his eyes. 'Even if you weren't sure, you could have . . .'

His words were interrupted by a loud shriek from the bottom of the garden. There was a splash, then the sound of thudding feet. Max dashed up, followed by an excited pack of very wet dogs. 'Abi's fallen in!'

Mandy and Jimmy leaped to their feet and hared across the grass. Everyone else pushed their chairs back and stood up to watch. There was a collective sigh of relief when Jimmy pulled a dripping Abi out of the water and lifted her onto the bank of the stream.

One by one, people sat back down. James sat down last, his shoulders heavy as he slumped in his chair.

Raj was looking at James with fear in his eyes. Helen felt a jolt of pity for him. 'I'm so sorry,' he said with a gulp. 'I should have waited and told you at a better time, but I didn't have a chance on the way here and . . . oh . . . just what you said about children. I wanted to share it with you. I thought . . .' He tailed off. There were tears in his eyes. 'My timing's awful,' he said.

James blinked as if he was fighting back tears of his own, but he reached out and touched Raj on the arm. 'It's okay,' he said, though his voice sounded breathless. 'It's a lot to take in. I'm glad you told me.' He pushed his glasses up his nose and added, 'Congratulations, I guess.'

On the far side of the table, a chair scraped and Susan stood up. She took Douglas's plate, stacked it on top of hers and lifted them up. 'We should be heading off,' she said in a calm voice. 'Where would you like me to put these?'

Beside her, Douglas tossed back the last of his spring water. He heaved himself to his feet and looked at Helen with a sympathetic smile, eyebrows raised.

'Please just leave everything on the table. I'll sort it out in a minute,' Helen said.

'Are you sure?' Susan checked.

Helen nodded. 'Toby'll help,' she said, 'won't you?'

Toby looked a little surprised as his eyes met hers, but he nodded.

Raj had pushed his chair back. He was looking at Susan with a worried expression. 'Please don't leave because of my big mouth,' he said.

Susan shook her head. 'We're really not,' she assured him. 'My son Jack's with my mum. If we don't get there soon she'll have fed him so much chocolate I won't be able to scrape him off the ceiling.'

Raj managed a laugh

'And for what it's worth,' Susan continued, 'I think it's wonderful you're adopting your cousin's baby . . .' She tilted her head. '. . . Taresh, is that right? You must bring him over to see Jack when you get back. And Frostflake our kitten. Taresh will love him.'

Raj was smiling properly now. 'That's very kind,' he said. 'I can see that my son's going to have a busier social calendar than me.'

James had turned very pale, Helen noticed. 'Can I get you anything?' she asked him quietly. 'Cup of tea or another coffee maybe?' She shifted her gaze. 'Raj?'

'Do you have any peppermint tea?' James asked.

'I'll have a coffee please,' Raj said.

Helen stood up just as Mandy reappeared with Abi beside her. Abi's clothes were dripping. 'Birdie fell in the stream and I rescued him,' she declared proudly.

Mandy pursed her lips, but Helen could see she was

trying not to smile. 'More like Birdie went in for a swim and you decided to follow him,' she said.

Helen suppressed a chuckle. The stream was barely deep enough for Birdie to swim. Abi must have gone full length to get as wet as she was.

'There are towels in the cupboard outside my bedroom in the granary,' Helen told Mandy. 'Do go in. I'll just clear a few of these things, then I'll come and get the coffee . . . and your peppermint tea.' She smiled at James.

'I'll get the tea and coffee,' Toby offered.

'Thank you,' Helen said.

Toby headed towards the granary. As Helen collected the plates, she noticed Raj had moved closer to James. 'Sorry,' she heard him murmur. 'I didn't mean to put you on the spot.'

James let out an audible sigh. 'I know you didn't,' he replied. 'And it is good news. It's just a lot to take in, that's all.'

Helen busied herself with the cutlery. That had to be the understatement of the year, she thought. She was glad when Jimmy and Max returned noisily to the table, followed by all the dogs. Seamus and Lily rushed round the table to James, wagging their tails as if they hadn't seen him for days. James leaned forward and lifted them both onto his knee.

'See you in a minute,' Helen said. Clutching a pile of plates, she headed for the kitchen.

To her surprise, Toby had rolled up his sleeves and was washing up. 'I thought I'd make a start while I was waiting for the kettle to boil,' he said, looking over his shoulder with a grin.

'Brilliant.' Helen found herself grinning back. His easy smile was hard to resist. She picked up a tea towel.

'How's James doing?' Toby asked as she joined him at the sink. 'He looked like a train was heading towards him, poor bloke, and he didn't know which way to jump.'

Helen picked up a plate and started to wipe it dry. 'I'm sure they'll sort it out,' she said. 'I think Raj should have taken James somewhere and told him before they arrived, though. It's difficult to keep something like that in.' She glanced at Toby again. He was staring studiously at the washing-up water and she wanted to laugh. Toby was Mr Mystery. He probably never blurted anything out by accident.

There was a scratching of claws and Lucy trotted in, closely followed by Isla. Lucy walked over and sat in front of Helen, and Isla, Lucy's little shadow, did the same. Helen reached into her pocket and gave them each a treat. She was rubbing Isla's curly ear when Mandy appeared down the stairs with a slightly less damp Abi. 'You go on outside,' Mandy told Abi. 'Tell your dad I'll be out in a minute.'

Abi left, squelching with each step. Mandy was looking at Lucy and Isla, who were still sitting side by side. 'I can hardly believe how well Isla's done today,' she said. 'I wasn't sure how it would go with all the dogs around, and in a strange environment. Lucy's brilliant with her.'

Helen felt a wave of pride. The big black retriever

was the first dog Helen had taken on, rescuing her from a family who'd had no time for her. She'd been wholly untrained when Helen stepped in, putting Lucy right in the centre of her life. She looked down again at the two dogs. Lucy's eyes were on hers. Isla was looking up too, almost as if she could see.

'Why don't you leave her here?' Helen said impulsively. She'd helped Lucy. Maybe now Lucy was going to help Isla.

Mandy raised her eyebrows. 'You want to foster her?' she asked. 'Are you sure? It'll be a lot of work.'

Isla was still sitting shoulder to shoulder with Lucy. 'Why not?' Helen said, feeling a surge of optimism. 'Lucy seems to like having her here and Isla seems to trust her. And I've got lots of time with Moondance away.'

Toby stopped washing up and turned to inspect the two dogs. 'They do go well together,' he agreed. 'Lucy seems to be a natural guide dog. One of our Jack Russells at home went blind and the same thing happened. She'd always been great friends with our corgi Linnet and when Persia lost her sight, she became Linnet's shadow.'

Helen couldn't help but feel a touch of fascination. Toby, the man who never mentioned his home life, was actually admitting to something from his childhood! 'Do you think that's true?' she asked him. 'Are some dogs natural guide dogs?'

Toby shrugged. 'Seems like it,' he said. 'Guide Dogs

for the Blind are very selective about which dogs they use. Some must be more suited to it than others.'

Helen looked at Mandy again. 'I'd like to give it a try,' she decided. 'I'm sure Lucy and I can help Isla.'

'That's fine by me,' said Mandy. 'I'm sure Isla will be much happier here than in kennels.'

Footsteps sounded outside the door and Jimmy's head appeared in the doorway. 'We should get off soon,' he told Mandy. 'Abi needs to change.'

'The twins are due back at their mum's tonight,' Mandy explained, then turned to Jimmy. 'Isla's going to stay here. Give Abi and Max a shout. They'll want to say goodbye.'

Both Abi and Max seemed delighted that Isla was staying with Helen and Lucy. They crouched beside the little dog and explained in serious voices that Isla would be fine and that she would be well looked after.

James carried a brace of empty wine bottles into the kitchen. He still looked as if he wasn't sure whether he was coming or going, but he thanked Helen politely. 'We're going to head off as well,' he said.

Helen followed them all outside. 'Bye, Helen, and thanks for everything,' Mandy said. She opened the rear door of her RAV4 and the twins scrambled in, followed by Sky. Zoe, Simba and Emma jumped into the boot.

'Thanks, Helen.' James opened his arms and hugged her.

'Sorry for dropping such a bombshell,' Raj told her.

He gave her a contrite smile. 'Hope I didn't spoil it too much.'

Helen threw out her arms and hugged him too. 'You didn't spoil anything,' she promised. She gripped his hand for a moment. 'Best of luck with everything.' She patted James on the shoulder. 'You too, James,' she said. He just nodded.

Helen watched as James strapped Seamus and Lily into the car. A moment later, they followed Mandy up the track.

Toby appeared in the gateway. 'I should be off too,' he said. He was standing very close, and Helen caught the scent of his aftershave. She could kiss him from here, she thought suddenly. What would he do?

For a moment, she found herself strangely tempted, but then she reached out and pulled him into a hug. 'It's been great having you here,' she said. She stopped, swallowed and took a step back. He was just a charmer, she reminded herself. And it turned out that even she wasn't immune. She felt a stab of unease and stepped back again, putting what felt like a proper distance between them.

Toby was grinning as if he could read what had just flashed through her mind. 'It's been fun,' he said, his voice filled with energy. 'We should do it again,' he added. He looked at her, his eyes twinkling. Helen stood very still as he strode across the gravel, climbed into his car and rolled the window down. 'See you around!' he called, waving as he pulled away.

Helen walked back in through the gate and round to the patio. Most of the tidying up was already done. She picked up a wine glass that had been left on the wall behind the grill and straightened a couple of chairs. Where were the dogs? 'Lucy, Isla, Birdie,' she called, and the three dogs trotted towards her across the lawn. She popped Birdie back into the Mellors' kitchen. She would let him back out later, but for now the old chap could have some peace. She closed the door and strolled back round to the granary. Isla and Lucy ran ahead of her, shoulder to shoulder: her own little team. It had been a great party, she thought as she headed back inside. Good food, good company, and Toby to co-host. It was just a shame Seb couldn't make it.

Chapter Seven

It seemed very quiet when Helen entered her little house. A couple of salad bowls stood on the table, still half full. She would sort them out later, she decided. There were a few sausages left too. She put them in the fridge and turned to look at the dogs. Isla was sniffling her way round the kitchen, moving very slowly. Helen felt a surge of love for the little dog. She really was a sweetheart.

With a start, she realised that she didn't have any extra food or bedding for Isla, and she'd had too much champagne to drive to Hope Meadows. Lucy flopped down on the cool stone floor. Isla pottered to her side, then lay down with a sigh. Pulling the kitchen door to – Isla would need supervision to explore more of the house – Helen walked upstairs and opened the door of the airing cupboard. She pulled out a pile of towels. She could make Isla a reasonable bed from them, and she could share Lucy's food. She went into her bedroom and laid out a makeshift bed next to Lucy's.

By the time Helen returned to the kitchen, Isla and Lucy were sleeping. The afternoon sun was shining in through the window, glossing the dogs' coats. There was still an hour or so until it was time to start the evening irrigation so Helen decided to make herself a cup of tea.

The kettle was coming to the boil when she heard a car draw up outside. She pulled the edge of the curtain aside and peered out. It was Seb. Helen felt a tiny flicker of frustration. She'd been looking forward to a quiet evening settling Isla in.

The door to the kitchen opened and Seb walked in. 'Hello,' he said. 'Is the kettle on?'

At the sound of the door, Lucy scrambled up from the floor, making Isla jump.

'Hello, you.' Seb bent down and scratched behind Lucy's ears. Isla staggered to her feet, her claws slipping on the stone floor, and tilted her head as if she was listening. 'Who's this?' Seb took a step towards Isla. Hearing his footsteps, Isla's ears flattened and her hackles rose. She let out a growl and Seb stopped.

Helen held out her hand to keep Seb still. 'She's called Isla,' she told him. 'She's very friendly, but you just woke her up. She's also blind.'

Despite her tiredness, she was pleased when Seb took a step back, then dropped down and sat on the floor. Lucy studied him with her head on one side, slowly wagging her tail.

'Are you here for the night?' Seb murmured. 'You look like a sweet little thing. Isla, is that your name?' He kept talking quietly until Isla approached him. He reached out a hand, letting her sniff his fingers before he gently stroked the curly fur on the side of her neck. She endured it for a moment, then edged away and walked over to find Helen. Seb stood up very slowly. 'What happened to her eye?' he asked.

'Mandy didn't know. But she can't see from the other one either. Mandy thinks she's only been blind for a while.'

'Poor little thing.' As Seb began to move towards Helen, Isla shifted until she was right on Helen's foot. Seb stopped again. Helen could feel the weight of the little dog, pressing against her. Her body was trembling. 'Why's she here?' Seb asked.

Helen reached down and rested her hand on Isla's head. 'I've said she can stay. Lucy's been great with her.' She stopped, waiting for Seb to reassure her that she was doing the right thing. 'They've been together all day,' she continued. 'Lucy's a natural guide dog!'

But Seb was frowning. 'You do mean just fostering, don't you?'

There was a look in his eyes Helen couldn't read and she felt a stab of irritation that he wasn't being more enthusiastic. Of course she was fostering Isla *for now*. That was what she and Mandy had agreed. But even if she'd agreed to permanently rehome Isla, it was her decision, not Seb's. 'Lucy and I are fostering her,' she said, 'for now.'

'That's good,' Seb said, sounding relieved. 'Fostering's a great idea. She'll be much easier to rehome from a normal environment.'

Helen buried her fingers deeper in Isla's fur. It wasn't a foregone conclusion that Isla would need to be rehomed at all. 'If it goes well I might decide to keep her,' she said. She knew she was sounding defensive. 'She doesn't deserve to be handed round like a parcel after what she's been through.'

Seb raised his eyebrows. 'Nobody's suggesting handing her round,' he objected. 'Fostering's normal for dogs who don't do well in kennels. They still get rehomed afterwards.'

Helen crouched down beside Isla. The little dog's ears were flat against her head and there was tension in her face. Helen felt her anger rising. 'She was doing fine in the kennels,' she said through gritted teeth. 'She came round here and she and Lucy just clicked. Toby agrees. He said sometimes it can just happen that way.'

'Did he?' Seb shook his head. 'The dogs might have played well together this afternoon, but didn't you think it might be more important ask me what I thought first? I love Lucy, you know I do, but taking on another dog's a big deal. Especially one that's going to need lots of extra attention.'

Helen could feel the warmth rising in her face. 'I don't see why,' she said. 'Lucy's my dog. If I want another, it's my decision.' Her voice came out louder than she had meant it to. Out of the corner of her eye, she saw Isla flinch. Lucy padded up to Helen's other side and licked her hand.

Seb stared at Helen. 'Of course it's your decision,' he said. There was a strangled tone to his voice. 'But . . .'

85

'But what?' Helen demanded.

'It'll be much harder to find a rental together if we have two dogs,' Seb said.

Helen realised that her hands were shaking. This was it, she thought. They'd come to the real point about Isla. 'I told you I wasn't ready to move in together.'

'You told me you'd think about it,' Seb argued. Helen could see that his hands were clenched, the knuckles white. 'We've been together for two years.' His voice was strained. 'I don't understand why moving in together would be so awful. Isn't that what people do?'

Helen stared at him, watching a vein throb on his forehead. 'This isn't about other people and what they do. It's about us. You and me.'

'Do you see us together in the future at all?'

'Of course I do.' Helen stopped. The anger which had been burning so brightly vanished and she felt chilled to the bone. Was that true? she wondered.

Seb let out a long breath. 'I'm sorry,' he said. He ran a hand through his hair, leaving it sticking up in tufts. 'What the hell are we doing?'

Helen dropped to her knees. She put an arm around each dog and looked up at Seb. 'I trained Lucy,' she said. 'I can do it with Isla. It's really important to me.'

Seb didn't say anything. Isla edged her haunches onto Helen's knee. The little dog was trembling and a wave of shame washed through Helen. 'I think you should go,' she said to Seb.

He looked down at her with pain in his eyes. 'I just

want some space for tonight,' she told him. 'To give Isla a chance to settle in.'

Seb managed a smile. 'It's always the animals, isn't it?' He swallowed hard. 'We need to talk,' he said, 'but I can see it'll have to wait.' He bent down and held his hand out to Lucy and the retriever wagged her tail on the floor, though she didn't go to him. Seb looked crushed. 'Can I call you in the morning?' he asked.

Helen felt tears prickling behind her eyes. 'Of course you can,' she said. Isla was squirming on her lap, digging her claws in as if she was trying to burrow into Helen. Helen reached down and took Isla into her arms, holding her tightly. When she looked up again, Seb was about to pull the door closed.

'Bye,' she called out.

He turned his head and sent her a fleeting smile. For a moment, Helen wanted to call him back, but Isla was scrabbling at her again and Lucy was whining. She picked Isla up and walked over to her chair and sat down. Lucy followed. She glanced up at Helen, as if hoping she too would be invited onto the chair. Helen reached out a hand and smoothed the silky head. 'You're too big,' she told her. Lucy sat beside her for a while, then, with a sigh, lay down on the floor. Isla lay in Helen's arms, shaking like a leaf. Helen held her tightly. It took a long time for the trembling to subside.

★ ★ ★

It was nearly midnight by the time Helen was ready for bed. Isla had dozed in her arms for almost an hour, but she had woken up when Helen took her outside for a wee. Helen usually cleaned Lucy's teeth before going up, but she was so exhausted she forgot. She was halfway through brushing her own teeth before she remembered. It would be fine to leave it for one night, she thought. There was enough to do getting both dogs settled for the night.

Lucy trotted into the bedroom. She walked towards her bed, then stopped to sniff at the towels that Helen had put on the floor for Isla. Helen couldn't help feeling proud of Lucy. She had recovered from the awful row much more quickly than either Helen or Isla. Helen had had to carry Isla up the stairs. The little dog whined any time Helen put her on the floor for more than a minute.

'Into your bed, Lucy,' she said. Lucy stepped into her basket, curled up and lay down.

'Now Isla, this is your bed for the night.' Helen knelt down and gently set Isla on the pile of fluffy towels. She had built up the sides so it felt more like a proper bed. Isla let out a tiny whimper. Helen reached out and stroked her. She wanted to give Isla some treats, but it was difficult without disturbing Lucy.

She waited until Isla's eyes were beginning to close, then edged upright and crawled into bed. She was so tired her legs felt as if they were made of lead. She glanced at the dogs one last time. How sweet they looked, lying side by side. She put out a hand and turned off the bedside light.

A loud yelping sound woke her in the darkness. She sat up in bed, her heart hammering. She fumbled for the light on the bedside table and switched it on. Lucy was sitting bolt upright, her ears flattened. Isla was cowering in the corner near the door. Helen shoved back the bedclothes and climbed out of bed.

Helen stroked the side of Lucy's neck. 'Come on,' she said. 'Lie down.' To her relief Lucy slumped down. Helen coaxed Isla over. With the little dog in her arms, she moved the towels away from Lucy's bed and closer to her own. Maybe Lucy had woken Isla and given her a fright. She settled Isla back down, got back into bed and watched for a few minutes. Though Isla was not completely relaxed, Lucy was already asleep. With a sigh, Helen switched off the light, but a moment later, she heard a scrabbling noise. She turned the light back on. Lucy was bolt upright again. Isla had crept into Lucy's bed and had curled up into a tiny ball as if making herself as small as possible. Lucy's eyes were fixed on Helen. They seemed to be pleading with her.

Helen crawled out of bed. She reached into Lucy's bed and lifted Isla out. 'Come on now,' she said. Isla lifted her head and licked Helen's face, but she whimpered when Helen tried to put her back down on the pile of towels. 'Do you need to go outside?' Helen wondered out loud. She lifted up the little body and Isla snuggled into her arms as she carried her downstairs.

Outside, the night air was cool and sharp like water. Isla seemed reluctant to move and lingered at Helen's feet for several minutes before she slunk a few steps away and relieved herself.

'Come on, then,' Helen said as Isla crept back towards her. She carried her back up the narrow staircase. She had brought some chews upstairs and she slipped one into Isla's mouth before she set her back down on the makeshift bed. On the far side of the room, Lucy let out a loud sigh.

Helen looked at the clock. It was almost three. She let out a sigh as she saw that Isla had dropped the chew and was shivering again. Helen glanced over at Lucy, whose eyes were still open, though she was blinking as if she was just as tired as Helen. The end of Isla's tail wagged very slightly, and she shuffled closer to Helen and started to edge her way back up into Helen's arms.

It was starting to look as though she wasn't going to settle unless Helen cuddled her. Helen took another look at Lucy. While she had always let the retriever sleep in her bedroom, she had had very strict rules about no dogs in the bed. Helen put Isla back down on the floor. She would lie down beside her for a few minutes. Maybe that would help. Isla settled quickly when Helen was beside her, but as soon as she tried to move into her own bed, Isla began to cry again.

By the time Helen's digital clock read 0400, she was sitting in bed, propped up on her pillows. Isla was lying in her arms. She could almost hear Seb's voice: *Taking on another dog's a big deal. Especially one that's going to need lots of extra attention.* Maybe Seb had been right and Isla was too much for her.

But none of this was Isla's fault, Helen thought as she gazed down at the sweet little ugly-cute face. Isla didn't deserve to be blind and abandoned. Helen was going to have to let the poor dog sleep in bed with her. She manoeuvred the curly body down beside her and tucked a pillow in between Isla and the edge of the bed. Lucy was snoring away in her basket. Isla looked so defence-less, lying like a little person with her head just above the duvet. Helen dropped a kiss on the top of her head, then reached out and switched off the light.

Chapter Eight

It was astonishingly hot. After her broken night, Helen spent the afternoon in the garden on a sun lounger. At first she tried to read the latest copy of *The Veterinary Nursing Journal*, but the sun was so bright that the words danced on the page. Lucy headed into the coolness of the granary kitchen after only a few minutes. Isla tucked herself underneath the lounger in the sliver of shade it provided. It was as much as Helen could do to keep her glass topped up with lemonade and ice.

Seb was playing cricket in Pateley Bridge. He had texted Helen to invite her but she had turned him down. She couldn't imagine much that was more tedious, though she admired Seb's dedication to his team.

The Mellors arrived back in time to do the evening fruit round. She heard their car pull up, and the children shouting as they ran into the house. Rousing herself, Helen glanced at her mobile. It was already six o'clock. She swung her legs over the side of the lounger and pushed herself up. Seb had said that he would drop by after the match. Helen hoped he wasn't going to start talking about moving in together for the sake of saving money again.

By the time Seb's car drew up outside, Helen had set the little table that stood against the wall at the front of the house. Most of the food was leftovers from yesterday: cold sausages, hard-boiled eggs stuffed with anchovies and a bowl of home-made mayonnaise. Helen was still feeling guilty about her part in their quarrel last night. She wanted to show Seb that she wasn't going to carry on being prickly, that everything could go back to the way it was.

'That looks good!' Seb commented when he saw the table of food.

'Come and sit down,' Helen told him. 'What would you like to drink?'

'A beer would be amazing, please.'

Helen fetched a bottle from the fridge and brought it to the table. Then she sat down and started helping herself to salad. When she looked up, Seb was watching her. 'Aren't you going to ask me how the match went?'

'How'd it go?'

'It was great,' he announced, beaming. 'I scored thirty not out and we won by a mile.'

'Where is the cricket ground in Pateley Bridge?' said Helen, wielding the salad tongs to deposit lettuce on his plate. She and Seb had been to the town a few times together. Helen had been charmed by the narrow stone bridge and the steeply sloping high street with its olde-worlde shops.

'It's opposite that park where we had fish and chips,' Seb replied. He lifted his glass and took another sip of his beer. 'I can take you next time we're playing there, if you like.'

Helen's conscience pricked again. Pateley Bridge was lovely, but did she really want to spend the afternoon watching cricket? 'Maybe,' she said.

Seb munched a piece of lettuce. 'Do you remember the ice cream place?'

'I do,' said Helen, spearing a potato. They had driven up into Nidderdale and stopped at a farm which made its own ice cream from a herd of Jersey cows.

Seb spooned some mayonnaise onto his plate and they ate in silence for a while, watched by the dogs. At least, Isla seemed to watch, her ears pricked and her face turned up expectantly. Helen's heart melted when she looked at the brave little dog. She really was settling in, wasn't she?

'Mum and Dad have invited us over next weekend.' Seb broke into her thoughts. 'Can you do Sunday?' He finished his last forkful of sausage and put his cutlery together.

Helen reached out and lifted his plate, stacking it on top of her own. 'Yes, I think so,' she said. She had always been very fond of Frank and Shirley Conway. Compared with her own parents, who had separated almost before Helen could remember, they seemed effortlessly comfortable together, like a cosy pair of slippers. They had welcomed Helen like another daughter from her very first visit, and she often called in to see them even if she wasn't with Seb.

She picked up the plates and carried them into the kitchen. Seb followed with the salad bowls. 'Thanks,' she said, taking them from him and putting them in the sink. She opened the dishwasher and put the plates inside, then piled the knives and forks into the basket.

'Mum and Dad sent their love to you,' Seb said. Helen glanced up at him. He was leaning on the bench under the window, his hair lit up by the sunlight like a halo. 'They're forever asking when we're going to settle down like Bridget.'

Helen straightened up to look at Seb properly. The sun was still streaming in at the window. Seb's eyes were in shadow and Helen couldn't read his expression. Seb's sister Bridget was lovely, but she was eight years older than Seb. It was perfectly reasonable for her to be happily married with two children.

'You'd better tell them they're going to have a long wait.' The words were out of Helen's mouth before she'd stopped to consider them.

'Is that really what you want me to tell them?' Seb's tone was still light, but Helen could tell her comment had hit home. 'I only meant they like you a lot.'

He's lying, Helen thought. Why was settling down so important all of a sudden? Why wouldn't he let it drop? 'I don't know what you should tell them,' she snapped. 'Only you know what they meant by it. Maybe you should tell them to mind their own business.' She folded her arms around herself. 'What is your obsession with nailing down the future? Is it because Mandy and Jimmy are settling down? Do you want me to start breeding like a sheep? Well, I'm not a sheep and I won't follow the crowd.'

Seb reached behind him, one hand on either side, to grasp the benchtop. She could see his fingers gripping the wood. 'I am not a sheep either.' His voice was cold. 'And I'm certainly not forcing you to breed. But I am trying to make some important decisions about my future and I want to know where I stand. I think you owe me that much. Where do you see our relationship heading?'

Helen's heart began to race. She had been so determined not to argue again, but here they were. She had the sudden feeling of being inside a whirlpool: of being sucked under the surface, unable to breathe, whirling out of control.

'Where do I see our relationship heading?' She couldn't keep the scorn out of her voice. 'Are you trying to sound like some kind of marriage counsellor?' She caught a movement out of the corner of her eye. Lucy and Isla were standing in the doorway watching them. Both dogs had their ears flattened anxiously, but for a moment Helen felt a wave of hope. Lucy was comforting Isla! A second later, the awful elation was swamped with shame. Lucy and Isla should not be cowering in their own home. Her anger cooling, Helen turned back to Seb. If she apologised now, perhaps they could discuss this calmly. But she felt the mobile phone in her pocket buzzing. She pulled it out to turn it off, but when she glanced at the screen, the words Animal Ark flashed up at her. 'I'm sorry. I have to take this.'

For a moment, she thought that Seb was going to walk out. He pushed himself off the bench and took two steps towards the door, but then stopped. Helen lifted the phone to her ear. Nobody called her on that line at a weekend unless it was a dire emergency. 'What's up?' she said, trying to keep her voice calm.

'It's Tango.' Emily Hope's voice was high and cracking. 'He's been hit by a car. Toby's going to have a look at him, but he's in an awful mess. I know it's a lot to ask, but can you come?'

Helen felt sick. She knew how much Adam and Emily loved the ginger cat. 'I have to go,' she told Seb, shoving the phone back into her pocket. 'Tango's hurt.' It was as if she had clicked her fingers and erased the anger. All she could think about was getting to the clinic to help Toby.

'Of course,' Seb said. He walked over and patted her on the shoulder. 'Don't worry about anything. I'll sort the dogs out,' he said. 'Is it okay if I stay over?'

Helen blinked. Usually there would be no question of Seb even having to ask. But today, after the things that had been said? 'Of course.' She stood there for a moment, looking at him. There was no time to do anything else. She needed him to look after the dogs.

She grabbed her car keys and set off. Poor Adam, she thought. He loved Tango so much. And Tango was not a young cat. Would they get him through an operation? Would Adam even want to try?

Chapter Nine

Helen drove over the hill and down into Welford in record time, thankful that it was a quiet Sunday on the narrow roads. She parked her car and raced into the clinic, which was already unlocked. The waiting room was in darkness, but the lights were on in the prep room. Toby was standing at the sink, scrubbing up. He turned his head when he heard the door opening and shot Helen a relieved smile. 'Thanks for coming,' he said. 'Poor Tango's face is in an awful mess. Mandy and I have got him anaesthestised and Emily's been wonderful helping, but you know how it is when it's your own . . .'

Helen did know. She had always been careful to let other people take charge when any of her animals were ill. She shrugged into her scrubs and dashed into the operating room. 'I can take over now, if you like,' she said to Mandy, who was standing at Tango's head. Both Adam and Emily were watching too. All three of the Hopes looked glazed, as if they couldn't quite believe what was happening.

'That would be great,' Mandy said. Her voice was strained. 'He's got some awful cuts on his face. He's lost some blood, but Toby's put on an abdominal bandage and it seems to have stopped.'

Tango looked so small, lying on the table. Helen winced when she studied his facial injuries. His cheek seemed to have been torn apart. The skin over his upper lip had been pulled back and his teeth were exposed. Helen couldn't imagine how Toby was going to bring the cat's face back together.

She glanced at the monitor. Tango's oxygen saturation was low as was his blood pressure, but not dangerously so. His heart rate was adequate. She felt for his pulse. It was faint but steady, though the colour of his gums said he'd lost quite a lot of blood. She looked up to see Adam's eyes on her and she sent him her most reassuring smile. 'He seems stable,' she said.

The door swung open and Toby backed in, holding his scrubbed and gloved hands in front of him. He glanced at the Hopes, then at Helen. 'Everything okay?'

Helen was amazed at how calm he seemed. It was challenging enough dealing with an emergency when the animal's owners were strangers. The Animal Ark rule was that no owners should be allowed in the operating theatre, but she couldn't imagine asking the Hopes to leave. Toby was standing in front of the instrument trolley, sorting out surgical kit and the swabs.

'We should go,' Adam said, glancing at his wife and daughter. 'I think Tango's in good hands.' Emily had tears in her eyes. Mandy was very pale, but they both nodded.

'I'll make some tea,' Mandy said, and the three of them shuffled out, leaving Helen alone with Toby and Tango.

Toby cut a hole in the dark green plastic drape and placed it over Tango's head. He looked at the broken face for a moment, assessing the damage, then looked up with a smile. 'Ready to go?' he asked. She nodded and adjusted her position so she could watch Toby as well as keep an eye on the monitors.

It took ages for him to bring the skin together. He pieced it together like the most complicated jigsaw puzzle, putting in stitch after stitch until the little cat's face was a web of knots and suture material. Toby's fingers were miraculously steady. He glanced up now and then at Helen to check the anaesthetic was stable.

'Can you top up his methadone, please?' His eyes looked a little tired now, she thought. A stray lock of blond hair was peeping out from under his surgical cap and Helen had the sudden urge to tuck it back behind his ear. She shook herself. '0.2 mils?' she checked, pulling herself together.

'Perfect,' Toby said. The weary eyes were smiling, though his mouth was hidden behind the surgical mask. He bent over Tango again. 'Not too much longer,' he said, turning round to grab another pack of suture material.

Slowly, slowly, Tango started to resemble a cat again, albeit one that had been sewn out of scraps of cloth with tiny neat stitches. Finally, Toby stood up, pulled his mask off and stretched. There were deep lines around his mouth and eyes, but he looked relieved. He moved back and inspected his work. 'Poor old Tango,' he said. He opened and closed Tango's mouth. 'It's going to be sore for him to eat for a while,' he said. 'I think we should put a feeding tube in and he can stay on fluids until it starts to heal.'

Between them, they inserted the tube down Tango's throat. Helen adjusted the fluids to maintenance rate.

'You can bring him round now,' Toby told her. 'I'll give Adam a shout. Are you okay for a couple of minutes?'

'Of course.'

Toby pulled off the surgical gown and pushed it into the laundry bin. He looked very dashing in scrubs, Helen thought. They were almost the same blue as his eyes. Toby looked up and grinned at her, and for a moment Helen had the disquieting thought that he could read her mind. She felt heat rising in her face and she leaned over the table, busying herself with cleaning up Tango's face.

Mandy and Adam looked very sombre when they trooped in. Helen had disconnected Tango from the anaesthetic gas and moved him into a carrier in the prep room, but he was still heavily sedated. 'Mum had to go to bed,' Mandy told Helen, 'and Toby's having a shower.' She stood looking down at the little shorn face with its tapestry of sutures. 'He's done a wonderful job,' Mandy observed. 'When I started to clean it up, I couldn't see how it would come together at all.'

'He was very meticulous,' Helen said.

'His anaesthetic went smoothly?' Adam checked.

Helen nodded. 'His oxygen sats have risen,' she said. 'They're pretty much back to normal.'

Adam let out a sigh and gently caressed the top of Tango's head. Helen glanced at the clock on the wall and realised with a shock that it was past eleven o'clock. 'You should go to bed, both of you,' she told them. 'I can finish up here. It'll be a while till he wakes up.'

Mandy sent her a crooked smile. 'Thank you,' she said. 'Come on, Dad.'

A moment later, Helen was alone with Tango. 'Just you and me, little puddy tatt,' she whispered, stroking the soft fur on the side of his neck. She looked up as she heard footsteps.

It was Toby. His blond hair was slicked back from the shower and he was wearing chinos and a rather crumpled open-necked shirt. 'How's he doing?'

Helen leaned into the carrier. Tango still had the breathing tube in his trachea, but he reacted now when she touched the corner of his eye. 'Starting to come round,' she said.

'That's good,' Toby replied. He put his hands in his pockets and looked at Helen. 'Would you mind staying a few minutes more?' he asked. 'I want to watch Tango for a while, but I need some strong coffee.'

'I could stay with him,' Helen suggested. 'You've already done so much.'

'Would you really?' Toby sounded so grateful that Helen felt warmth rising within her.

'You should get some sleep,' she told him.

He smiled. 'I promise I will,' he said, 'but first I'm going to make you that coffee I was going to have myself.'

Leaving Tango to wake in his own time, Helen lifted the surgical kit into the sink and left it to soak, then rechecked the operating room. The anaesthetic machine was switched off and the table was clean. She turned off the light, then went back to Tango. The recovery period was almost as risky as the operation itself. She moved the breathing tube a little. Still no reaction. She needed him to swallow or cough before she took it out.

Toby reappeared, carrying two mugs. He handed one to Helen and peered into the carrier. 'Tube not out yet?'

Helen shook her head. 'His temperature was a bit low,' she said. She had put Tango on a heated mat and had tucked some bubble wrap round him, then a blanket over the top.

'That would explain why he's a bit on the slow side to wake up.' Toby smiled. 'I see you've got it all under control, though.' Helen felt her tired face creasing in a smile.

Toby sat down and crossed his legs, his ankle on his knee. He looked remarkably relaxed, sipping coffee in the dead of night after performing major reconstructive surgery. 'What were you doing earlier,' he asked, 'before your evening was so rudely interrupted?'

'Nothing much.' Helen bent over Tango's cage, making a tiny adjustment to one of his tubes. 'What about you?'

Toby pulled a face. 'Not a lot. Chatting in the Anaesthesia Nerds Forum on Facebook is about as exciting as it gets for me on a Sunday night.'

Helen remembered that he had been at the Glasgow Veterinary School before he'd come to Animal Ark. 'What was your position in Glasgow?' she asked, touching Tango's fur through the wire.

Toby put his mug down on the desk and leaned forward. 'My official job title was Clinician in Veterinary Anaesthesia,' he said. 'Basically I was doing some teaching and some research.'

It sounded very different from what he was doing now, Helen thought. She had assumed he'd been doing an internship at the prestigious school, but he'd obviously been a good bit higher in the pecking order. 'Did you enjoy it?'

'Very much,' he replied. 'The research side was really interesting. We were looking at different combinations to control pain.'

Helen nodded. Mandy Hope had always been keen on pain management, and Toby had brought new ideas and some groundbreaking new drugs. Helen knew Mandy was delighted, but it didn't explain why Toby had thrown in his university career. Welford must seem like a backwater compared to Glasgow's bright lights. Surely if he'd already made clinician, he could have gone all the way to the top.

'What made you give it all up and come to Welford?'
Toby shrugged. 'I just fancied a change of scene,' he
said. He sent her a bland smile and leaned over to study
Tango. 'I think he can manage on his own now.' He
reached down and removed the tube. Tango responded
with a feeble cough. He lifted his head and blinked, then
lay back down.

'He's making great progress,' Toby commented. 'You'll
stay with him a little while, won't you?' He stood up
before Helen had a chance to reply. 'I'd better get home,'
he said. 'I'll see you in the morning. Thanks again.' He
sounded brisk and professional, and Helen knew she'd
pushed him too far. Why was he so protective about his
past? Toby tossed back the last of his coffee and left.

Helen rubbed the back of her neck, which was stiff
from bending over Tango. Despite the coffee, a wave of
tiredness washed over her and for a moment she longed
for her bed. Straightening up, she fetched an old
armchair from the rest area and dragged it into the
residential unit next to Tango's cage. It felt blissfully
comfortable after the hard wooden stool she'd been
perching on. She wrapped one of the blankets they used
for the patients round her legs, checked Tango once
more, and closed her eyes.

She was woken at seven by Mandy coming into the unit.
'Are you still here?' Mandy said, gently touching Helen's
shoulder. 'Is Tango okay?'

Helen glanced into the cage. Tango was staggering to his feet, his eyes half open and his fur on end. He turned round once, then lay back down. 'It looks like we both had a good sleep,' Helen commented. 'I'll see if he wants some breakfast.'

Adam's head appeared around the door. 'How is he?' he asked. 'Oh, look, he's awake. Champion.' He looked sympathetically at Helen. 'Why don't you head home for a few hours? We can look after the old chap now.'

Mandy reached into the cage and stroked the big cat's head. Despite his awful injuries, Tango leaned the unhurt side of his face into her fingers and let out a loud purr. 'Oh, bless him,' Mandy murmured. 'You gave us a scare, you silly old thing.'

Helen stood up and folded the blanket. Her legs were trembling with fatigue and her head felt as if it was stuffed with cotton wool. Country practice often meant working after broken sleep, but she was glad of the chance to get home for an hour or two. Seb would have gone to work by now. Helen flinched. It was awful to be glad not to see him, but she couldn't face any more arguments right now.

Chapter Ten

Lucy was in the kitchen when Helen arrived. It looked as if Seb had moved Lucy's bed downstairs. The sleek black retriever got up, stretched, then trotted over to meet Helen, tail wagging. Helen bent down to fuss over her, relieved that she seemed to have forgotten about last night's row. Dogs were so forgiving, she thought wryly. She looked round for Isla, but she was not in the kitchen. Helen walked upstairs and opened the bedroom door. Isla was waiting just inside. She jumped up at Helen, her curly tail beating frantically.

Helen took her downstairs, then clipped on her lead to take her into the garden. Lucy shot past them as soon as Helen opened the door and went to relieve herself in the middle of the lawn. Helen let Isla potter around for a while, then led her back inside. Seb had left a note on the table.

'Good morning,' it said. 'I had to separate the dogs. Isla's in the bedroom. She slept on the floor once Lucy was downstairs, though she woke a couple of times. Hope Tango pulled through. Give you a ring later.'

Helen read the note through twice. He'd signed it 'Sx'

as usual, but she couldn't help feeling a wrench of sadness. The message felt short and clinical, not at all like Seb's usual rambling texts. As she stared at the piece of paper, the words started to blur and she realised her eyes were filled with tears. What on earth was happening to her and Seb? Why did it feel as if they were suddenly pulling in different directions? Helen rubbed her eyes, wiping away the unshed tears. She was too tired to think straight. She should get some sleep.

She went over to the freezer and brought out Lucy's Kong toy. She'd filled it with Lucy's favourite food and frozen it so that it would keep Lucy occupied while it gradually thawed. 'There you go, sweetheart,' she murmured as she put Lucy back into her bed. For a moment, she wondered if she could leave Isla downstairs as well, but Lucy looked up as Isla came near and let out a tiny growl.

'Come on, then, Isla,' Helen said, feeling too tired to argue. She tried to ignore Lucy's sad gaze as she pulled the door closed. Everything had become so bloody complicated. She climbed into bed, then moved over to Seb's side, burying her face in his pillow. She could smell the clean scent of his aftershave and another wave of sadness washed through her. Were they really splitting up? It was beginning to feel like it. Their relationship seemed to be spiralling downwards, and Helen couldn't figure out how to get it back.

* * *

Helen glanced at the clock on the waiting-room wall. Only another hour and she could escape. It had been incredibly busy for a Tuesday at the start of the school holidays. She was feeling the effects of having so little sleep over the past forty-eight hours. She was glad it was Rachel's day for covering evening surgery.

Seb had called her yesterday, as he'd said he would, but not until late in the evening. Their conversation had been stilted. He had asked about Tango and Lucy, but not about Isla or Helen herself. She hadn't slept well after his call. She had tried to move Lucy's bed back upstairs, but Lucy had made such a fuss whenever Isla came near her that Helen had been forced to move her down again to keep the peace.

Helen's heart sank. Seb had suggested coming round tonight and she had agreed, but she wasn't exactly looking forward to it.

Toby's car pulled up outside the waiting-room window. 'Everything okay?' he asked as he came in.

'Yep, fine.'

'That's good.' Toby was hovering just inside the door.

'Is something wrong?' Helen stood up and went towards him but stopped halfway across the room with a yelp. 'What's that awful smell?'

Toby grimaced. 'Sorry,' he said. 'I had to lance an abscess on a bull. Turned out it was under high pressure. There was stinking pus everywhere and I couldn't move out of the way.'

'Urgh!' Helen had a strong stomach, but she was almost gagging.

'Can you get me a plastic bag for my clothes?' Toby begged.

Helen resisted the urge to hold her nose like a child. 'Only if you go back outside first,' she ordered. 'Either you strip off before you come in, or I'll come out in the yard and hose you down.'

Toby raised his eyebrows. 'Right you are, Miss Bossy,' he said. 'Good to see you've found your teeth. I like a strong woman.'

'I'd never have guessed.' Helen studied him. His eyes were twinkling and he was obviously enjoying himself. 'But if you think you're going to pull with that aftershave, you've another think coming. Get outside with you or I'll be forced to chase you with the broom.'

'I can see I've met my match,' Toby sighed, grinning. He opened the door and stepped outside, then winked at Helen through the glass. Helen shook her head and glared at him before heading into the staff area.

She grabbed a plastic bag from under the sink. He'd need a shower too, she thought. From the way his hair had been standing up, he had been covered from head to foot. She took the plastic bag to the door and handed it to him. 'Clothes in there,' she ordered, 'then straight into the shower. I'll get you a towel.' She turned away quickly. She could hardly stand there and watch him strip. She walked into the little changing room and pulled out a towel from the shelf and grabbed some scrubs.

He'd need something clean to drive home in. She placed them on the wooden bench outside the shower cubicle, then went back to the door.

Toby was standing on the drive in his boxers. 'Can I come in now? *Please,*' he added. 'We don't want any clients to find me starkers in the car park!'

Helen tried to keep her eyes fixed on his face. Toby had obviously been in good shape when he was fully clothed, but she hadn't been prepared for the muscular definition of his upper body, nor the perfectly tanned, smooth skin on his chest. His thighs were broad but firm, and there was a scar running across his left knee that Helen suddenly longed to trace with her fingertips. She stepped backwards as he came inside and tried not to watch while he strode to the shower room.

He had left the plastic bag containing his clothes outside the door. Helen picked it up gingerly and carried it at arm's length to the washroom.

By the time Helen had tidied and swept the waiting room, Toby had emerged from the shower. He looked exotically handsome with his blond hair slicked back and darkened by the water. 'I put your clothes in the machine,' she told him. 'They'll be about half an hour. You can collect them in the morning if you like.'

'I'm in no hurry,' Toby said. 'I'll make myself a cup of tea. Would you like one?'

Helen shook her head. Though the waiting room was air-conditioned, she was still very warm after her speedy cleaning session. 'Too hot for tea,' she said.

Toby disappeared for a moment, then reappeared brandishing a bottle of Coke. 'I had this in the fridge,' he said. 'We can share it, if you like.' He fetched two glasses from the cupboard and poured out the Coke. He handed one to Helen, then took a seat on one of the waiting-room chairs. He patted the seat beside him. 'You'll make me feel guilty if you keep doing chores,' he said.

Helen sank gratefully onto the chair. An image of Seb crossed her mind, but she pushed it away. She could chat to Toby if she wanted! They were colleagues and friends.

Toby leaned back and rested his head against the wall. 'How long have you been in Welford?' he asked.

Helen looked at him. How odd that he'd been here months, but they barely knew anything about one another. 'About seven and a half years at Animal Ark,' she said. 'I spent a lot of my childhood in Walton so I haven't exactly come far.' She took a sip of her Coke, then met his eyes again. 'How about you? Whereabouts in Scotland did you grow up?'

'Caithness,' Toby replied. 'Just outside Scrabster, the little port near Thurso where the boat comes in from Orkney.' For a moment, Helen thought she caught a glimpse of melancholy in his blue eyes. Did he miss his home? she wondered. He didn't seem to go there very often.

'Scrabster?' she said. 'And Thurso? I don't even know where they are.'

Toby gave a rueful smile. 'Nobody does. They're right up at the top of Scotland on the coast. Near John o'Groats,' he added.

'Now that I have heard of,' Helen said. 'What's it like up there? Are there lots of mountains?'

Toby lifted his ankle onto his knee. 'Actually, no,' he said. 'It's quite flat, and there are not many trees. It's not what most people picture when they think of Scotland. And nothing like the Yorkshire Dales, that's for sure.' He looked down at his Coke, then back up at Helen. 'This must have been a nice place to grow up. Are your parents still in Walton?'

'Only my dad. My mum lives in Richmond. They split up when I was only a baby. I spent most of the time with Mum, but I stayed with Dad for weekends and in the summer holidays.'

Toby looked surprised. 'Can you remember your parents being together at all?'

Helen shook her head. 'Nope. They were very young when they got married and not much older when they separated. I don't think Mum ever really got over it.' She rubbed the condensation on the side of her glass. 'Dad's going mad for online dating, though.'

'Really?' Toby said. 'Is it going well?'

'On and off. His latest date seemed to go quite well. They're going on a train trip this week. That's Dad all over. If she likes steam engines, she's on to a winner, but there've been some disasters. One time he managed to meet his own dentist in the Fox and Goose. She hadn't recognised him on the website, and her photo didn't look anything like her, or so he said. I think he made some joke to her about opening wide and she stood up and stormed out.'

Toby laughed. 'That's a bit like asking me about cows' arses and arm-length gloves on a date,' he said. 'It gets old after the three hundredth time.'

Helen blinked. Three *hundred* dates? Toby had to be exaggerating, but even so . . . 'Another time one of Dad's dates turned up with her ex-husband in tow. Apparently it was important to her that they all got along. I think he was the one that ran that time.' She took another drink, realising this was the most relaxed conversation she'd had in days. Toby hadn't dodged any of her questions so far. Feeling bold, she asked, 'What do your parents do, up there in Caithness?'

She saw a flash of wariness in his eyes. 'They're mostly retired,' he said. 'Very traditional. Still married.'

'Happily?' Helen prompted.

Toby shrugged. 'I wouldn't know. Emotions aren't something we talk about in our family.'

'Have they been to visit you here in Welford?'

Toby shook his head. 'My father wanted me to go into the family business, but I've never wanted to do anything other than to be a vet. He was . . . disappointed, shall we say.'

Helen felt indignant on Toby's behalf. Was that why he never talked about it? Toby was a brilliant vet. 'That's ridiculous,' she said. 'They should be proud of you. The way you put Tango back together was amazing. Nobody else could have done it.'

Toby smiled at her. 'Good to have a fan,' he commented.

Helen's face felt hot. She'd been gushing like a fool, hadn't she? Embarrassment made her go on the defensive. 'I'm sure you've had lots of fans,' she said. 'Is that why you had to leave Glasgow? Were you running away from all your exes?'

Toby threw back his head and gave a short laugh. 'Hardly,' he said. 'I had a few dates. Met a few nice girls. I'm just not ready to settle down yet.' He shrugged. 'It'll happen one day,' he said, 'but we're still young. We should be having fun!' He looked at Helen and his grin faded a little. 'How's Seb?'

Helen didn't want to answer. She couldn't tell Toby about Seb's desire to settle down, or the way she felt about it. That would be disloyal to Seb. 'It's going okay,' she stammered. 'Seb thinks I'm mad taking on Isla, but I'm going to prove him wrong.'

Toby frowned. 'Mad?' he echoed. 'She's a sweet little dog. I know she's blind, but isn't Lucy helping with that?'

Helen sighed. 'Lucy seems to have gone off the idea. She won't have Isla near her when she's in bed and Isla won't sleep on her own.'

'Oh.' Toby looked thoughtful. 'Well, I'm no expert on dog training. That's Mandy's speciality. But do you think they'd sleep better if they were properly tired?'

Helen shrugged. 'I do try,' she said, 'but it's not easy

to walk them together. Lucy can run free, but Isla has to stay on the lead.'

Toby leaned forward in his chair and put his glass on the reception desk. 'I've got something I've been wanting to try out for a while,' he said. 'And it might help you. One of my friends is setting up a company making harnesses for dogs to run in front of mountain bikes and he's sent me one. Do you think Lucy would like to have a go? I can show you the brochure.' He stood up and went to the pigeonhole where his letters were kept.

Helen studied the photographs of various dogs wearing colourful harnesses and sprinting with their bike-riding, Lycra-clad owners. 'It looks like something Lucy would love,' she said. 'But what about Isla?'

Toby took the brochure from her and stuffed it back into his pigeonhole. 'If Lucy was out in front of the bike on the harness, do you think Isla would run behind? If we had her on a lead?'

He was so earnest, Helen wasn't sure how to reply. Isla walked everywhere quite slowly, on a short lead with constant contact. Suddenly Helen remembered that Seb was coming for dinner. He'd said he'd text to let her know what time he'd arrive. She pulled her phone out of her pocket and looked up at Toby. 'Actually, I'm seeing Seb tonight,' she said.

'Oh. Okay.' Toby sounded disappointed. 'Maybe another day?'

Helen scrolled through her messages. There were quite a few, including one from Seb. 'Very sorry,' it said. 'Have to work late again. Hope you weren't planning anything special. Sx.'

It was Helen's turn to feel deflated. Not that she was dying to see Seb, but there was something about the text that jarred. It was so curt and there was so little explanation. Sometimes he did have to stay late at work. That was just how it was when you worked with animals. But normally he'd have told her what he was doing.

'Everything okay?' Toby asked.

Helen looked up from the phone. 'Seb can't come after all.'

Toby reached out a hand and patted her shoulder rather awkwardly. Helen felt a wave of shame run through her. He thinks I'm upset about Seb, she thought. Apart from the tone of Seb's note, what she mostly felt was relief. Shoving her phone back in her pocket, she forced herself to smile. 'Since I'm free, shall we give the harness a try? I have a feeling Isla might not be up to it, but we can give it a go.'

Toby's face lit up, and Helen had a sudden image of what he must have looked like as a little boy. 'I'd love to,' he said. 'And if Isla won't run behind, I could put her in my rucksack. She'd probably sit in it, don't you think?'

Helen couldn't help smiling, though she wasn't convinced that Isla would sit quietly on his back. 'Mandy'll lend me her bike,' she said. 'Is yours here or do we need to collect it?'

'It's here,' Toby told her. 'I keep it in the garage. There's nowhere to store it at mine.'

'Just give me a minute,' Helen said. 'The washing machine's finished. I'll hang your clothes up and get changed. I'm sure you could borrow some shorts from Adam and there's a spare T-shirt here you can put on.' She carried the glasses to the washroom, suddenly feeling excited. Her tiredness had vanished, and a sunlit evening on the fells beckoned.

Chapter Eleven

With a hiss of frustration, Helen stopped her bike barely two hundred metres up the track behind Animal Ark. The experiment wasn't going well. She had been very proud of Lucy when Toby had put the harness on. The retriever had allowed him to fiddle with all the buckles, adjusting the straps until it fitted properly. Now Lucy was racing ahead of Toby's bike as if she already understood what she had to do, but Isla had begun to whimper before they even set off.

Toby had been encouraging. 'Give her a minute or two,' he'd said. He had taken Lucy, leaving Helen to coax Isla along.

Helen watched Toby and Lucy disappear around a bend in the track, then sighed as she looked down at Isla. The little dog wasn't in a harness, just on a long lead, in the hope that she'd run alongside Helen's bike. 'Come on, sweetheart,' she begged. 'Please give it a try.'

She put her foot on the pedal and set off slowly. The track was smooth and grassy, with nothing that Isla could trip over. But even in the lowest gear, Isla refused to keep up. Her ears were flat against her head, and when

Helen came to a stop again, she sat down on the grass and whined.

'Oh, Isla,' Helen murmured. 'I'm sorry. We'll wait here.' Hopefully Toby would come back when she and Isla didn't arrive at the top of the slope.

'Not going for it?' There was a cheery shout and Helen looked up to see Toby and Lucy thundering back down the path. Toby was grinning and his hair was on end. His legs were stuck out to the sides like a six-year-old's. 'Stop, Lucy!' he yelled. The brakes on the bike squealed. To Helen's relief, he managed to slow Lucy down before she collided with Mandy's bike. Toby was breathless as he hopped off. He looked down at Isla.

'She's refusing to budge,' Helen said apologetically.

But Toby laughed. 'Come on, poppet,' he said. He handed his bike to Helen, and before she knew what was happening, he had scooped Isla up and popped her in his rucksack. Helen had never seen Isla look so surprised, but to Helen's amazement, she didn't seem distressed. Maybe Toby's confident handling had made her decide that this arrangement was okay.

Toby lifted up the backpack gently. 'Can you help me on with it?' he asked. 'I don't want to scare her.'

Helen lifted up the rucksack and held it while Toby pushed his arms into the straps. Isla sniffed the back of his hair, then nuzzled into his neck. 'So far, so good.' Toby sounded as if he did this sort of thing every day. 'Now all we need to do is unclip Lucy from my bike and attach her to yours.'

Helen removed the metal clip from the frame of Toby's bike and fixed it onto hers. She reached down and stroked Lucy's sleek head. The dog's tongue was lolling out as she panted, and her eyes were bright.

'Now, let's try again,' Toby said. 'Lucy will pull the lead tight when she runs, but make sure you keep pedalling. She's not a husky! And once we get to the top, we can chain up the bikes and go for a normal walk. That way Isla will get some exercise too.'

Cycling up the hill with Lucy racing ahead of her, Helen felt like a child again. She hadn't ridden a bike for a while but her legs were strong from walking and horse-riding so she was able to keep up with Lucy. Toby pedalled behind her, avoiding the ruts so that Isla wouldn't be jolted out of the rucksack. Helen was concentrating too hard on steering to look round and see how they were getting on, but she knew Isla was in the safest pair of hands.

When they reached the smooth, rounded fell-top, Helen called to Lucy and they slowed down together. The big black dog looked jubilant, as if she knew she'd done well. Helen made a fuss of her as Toby pulled up beside them.

'This little one seemed fine,' he said, looking over his shoulder at Isla, who was licking his ear. Helen helped Toby lift Isla down, then she unclipped Lucy from the harness.

'I'll chain up the bikes,' Toby said, propping them against a stunted hawthorn tree.

There was a buzz in Helen's pocket. She pulled out

her mobile phone and a picture of Moondance popped up on the screen. A message from Gemma followed. 'OMG so much fun!' it said. 'Rode through Lyons Forest this morning, stopped at Lyons-la-Forêt for lunch. Don't think I ever want to come home.'

Toby came up behind her. 'Anything important?'

'It's from Gemma.' Helen held out the phone to show him. Moondance looked beautiful, her coat spotless and her ears pricked. Gemma stood beside her, beaming. Helen couldn't help feeling a pang of envy.

'Don't you wish it was you?' Toby asked.

Helen sighed. 'Definitely,' she answered, then, feeling his eyes on her, she added, 'though it's nice to be here with you as well.'

Toby laughed. 'Don't worry,' he said. 'I've been bitten by the travelling bug too in my time. Yorkshire is stunning but it pales beside somewhere like Thailand or India.'

'You've been to India?' Why should that be a surprise? Helen wondered. Lots of people had travelled more than she had. The most exotic place she'd been was the south of France.

'I've been to every continent except Antarctica.'

'Wow,' said Helen. Beside her, Isla started to scratch her ear. Helen clipped on her lead and patted her. She clicked to Lucy and watched the big black dog bound away across the moor. Isla lifted her nose to sniff the breeze, then trotted beside Helen, letting the tug of the lead guide her if she veered away.

Helen took a deep breath, filling her lungs. The gorse was flowering, bright golden yellow, its coconut scent lending a sweetness to the air.

'Tell me about India,' Helen prompted.

Toby glanced at her. 'India? It was amazing,' he said. 'The number of people in the cities has to be seen to be believed, and the poverty can be really horrific. But it was beautiful too, especially in the countryside. So many colours, and these amazing cattle with huge horns wandering everywhere. I was there for three months and I feel as if I hardly scratched the surface, to be honest.'

'It sounds incredible,' Helen said. She looked round, checking for Lucy. She was drinking from one of the little streams that criss-crossed the moor.

'It really is,' Toby said. 'You should go, if you get the chance.'

'I'd love to,' she said. She bent down and rearranged Isla's ear, which had flipped inside out.

'Why don't you? What's holding you back?'

For a moment, Helen thought of Seb, and his determination to settle down. His urge to put down roots suddenly felt like chains around her ankles. 'Maybe I will,' she said lightly.

Toby was looking at her as if he sensed she wasn't telling him everything. He shrugged. 'Not everyone wants to travel,' he said, 'but if you want to go to India, you should definitely look into it.'

Isla trotted forward, tugging at the lead in Helen's hand. Helen couldn't help smiling. The little dog looked relaxed and confident for the first time in ages. She couldn't see where she was, of course, but she seemed to love being up here. Toby's idea of bringing the dogs out had been a brilliant one. Helen pushed aside her nagging feelings about Seb. She couldn't sort out their differences while she was here, and she wasn't going to let them spoil this blissful evening.

By the time they returned to Animal Ark, Helen was so tired her legs felt wobbly. They had tramped over the moorland for an hour, then ridden the bikes back down the hill. Helen held Isla's lead while Toby stowed the bikes back in the garage.

'Thank you so much,' she said as he emerged into the sunshine. 'That was a stroke of genius, using the harness.'

'Lucy looks properly tired,' Toby said. The retriever was lying in the shade of the garage, her head resting on her paws with her eyes half closed.

'Isla's tired too,' Helen commented. Isla was sitting on her foot, leaning on her leg. The little dog seemed much calmer than usual, tilting her head to one side as if she was watching Toby. Helen leaned on the garage wall and gazed up at the fell. 'That was the best walk I've had in a while,' she said.

'You looked like you needed it,' Toby said softly. Helen turned and realised he was staring at her. For a moment, she thought he would reach out and pull her towards him. She could feel her heart beating faster. Then she blinked and the moment passed. Toby pulled down the garage door with a bang, making both dogs jump. Helen gave herself a mental shake. *Stop falling for the famous Toby Gordon charm*, she told herself. *You're with Seb, remember?*

'Well, you were right,' she said brightly. 'I feel as if I've cleared all the cobwebs away.' She called to Lucy and led Isla to her car. Toby climbed into his and waved at her as he drove off. Helen loaded the dogs and opened the windows. By the time she'd finished, both dogs were lying down in the back seat, their eyes closed. She glanced back at them and smiled. 'Thank you, Toby,' she said into the air. Tired, peaceful dogs, happy to sleep side by side. 'That's worth an entire trip to India.'

Chapter Twelve

The heat wave still hadn't broken by the middle of the week. Helen grabbed some cutlery from the drawer, took it outside and laid the little table in the garden. She had almost forgotten what it was like to eat indoors. She hummed under her breath as she went into the kitchen to chop tomatoes. It had been a good day at work, with more signs of progress from Tango. Though he was still on his drip, she and Mandy had removed the feeding tube and he had nibbled some biscuits from Helen's hand. He had even let out a croaky meow when he finished, as if he was asking for more. It was great to see his personality coming back, even though his face was still rather alarming to look at.

Seb had called half an hour ago to say he was on his way. Helen slid the cheese and bacon quiche out of the oven and put it on a plate. Lucy and Isla were lying on the stone flags, cooling their bellies. The two dogs had slept better both nights since their run on the moors, though Isla was still on her own in Helen's bedroom, with Lucy banished downstairs.

Seb's car pulled up and Helen smiled as she went to meet him at the gate. 'How are you?' she asked.

'Tired,' Seb replied, though he managed a smile. 'I brought you this.' He held out his hand to reveal a single tea light. Helen couldn't help but wonder what he'd done with the rest of the pack.

'Thanks very much,' she said lightly. 'Just what I've always wanted.' She walked over and put it in the middle of the table. To her surprise, Seb sat down in one of the chairs and pulled out his phone. Normally he went inside to say hello to the dogs and help Helen bring out the food. She fetched the quiche and bowl of salad and put them on the table. Seb was still studying his phone.

'Is everything okay?' she asked.

Seb looked up. 'Yes, fine. Why?'

Helen shook her head. 'No reason,' she said. 'How was your day?' She helped herself to a piece of quiche and nudged the plate towards Seb.

'So-so,' he said. 'Two stable inspections, a stray dog and a homing pigeon that got lost. How about yours?'

Helen spooned tomatoes onto her plate. 'Pretty good,' she said. 'Tango is starting to eat on his own. Toby's really pleased with his progress. The surgery he did really was something else.' She expected him to show some enthusiasm, but he was busy slicing a piece of lettuce.

'That's good,' he said eventually, seeming to realise she was waiting for a response. He smiled, but it seemed half-hearted. 'Sorry,' he said. 'Lot on my mind.'

'Anything I can help with?'

Seb shook his head. 'Not really,' he said. He speared a tomato and dabbed it in mayonnaise.

'Isla's so much happier,' Helen said when it seemed Seb was going to eat in silence. 'She loved being up on the moor.'

Seb looked up. His face was serious. 'Is she sleeping through the night yet? What about Lucy? Is she back in your bedroom?'

Helen felt a flash of defensiveness. 'Lucy's still downstairs, but Isla hardly wakes at all now.'

They finished their dinner in near-silence. Seb stood up to help Helen clear away and, for a few minutes as they carried in the plates and glasses, things felt almost normal. It was getting cooler as the sun began to set. Lucy, who had been lying inside, stood up and wandered out. Helen put the kettle on. 'Would you like some tea?' she asked Seb.

'I'll make it,' he replied. 'You sit down. I'll be out in a minute.'

Helen went outside and turned her chair round so that her back was to the sun-baked wall. The scent of strawberries reached her and, in the distance, she could hear the murmur of voices. The Mellors must have begun to open the pick-your-own fields in the evenings.

Lucy trotted over when Seb came back outside. 'I heard another rumour about Toby today,' he said, putting the mugs on the table and bending down to ruffle Lucy's ears.

Helen felt her shoulders stiffen. Why did everyone seem to feel the need to gossip about Toby?

Seb arranged his chair next to Helen's and sat down. 'Last thing I heard was that he was with Imogen Parker-Smythe. Then he left her for Chloe Benn, Sergeant Benn's daughter. Did you know about that?'

Helen had to fight not to roll her eyes at him. 'It's hardly the kind of thing we'd discuss over a cat spay,' she pointed out. 'What's it to you anyway? He's a free agent, isn't he?' Seb had never come home with rumours about Mandy or anyone else for that matter. Why did Toby fascinate him so much?

Seb seemed to think she wanted to hear more. 'Chloe took him home to a barbecue where he met her sister Megan and within two days he'd dumped Chloe for Megan.' He took a sip of tea. 'Megan's only twenty,' he added.

Helen could feel his eyes on her face. There was no way Toby would be looking at a twenty-year-old, she thought. She made herself breathe in and out before she replied. 'You know what Welford's like. You can't cough in the post office without half the population thinking you've got flu.' Isla pottered out of the kitchen and Helen got up to steer her gently towards the chairs. 'I can't imagine Toby has time for dating all these women when he's working full time and helping me with Isla.'

'Oh yes, your bike ride on the fells. That sounds like something I would have enjoyed, you know.'

Helen glanced at Seb. Was he *jealous*? 'Well, Toby had

the dog harness in his car, so . . .' She broke off, angry that she was justifying spending time with a friend and colleague. 'It didn't cross my mind you'd be bothered,' she went on. She pulled her shoulders back, forcing herself to relax. 'Tell you what, why don't we go out together and do something nice tomorrow afternoon? You're off until Monday, aren't you?'

Thursday was Helen's half day, and the Hopes had said she could have Friday off in lieu of the night she'd worked with Tango. She recalled Seb telling her that he had booked a long weekend as well.

To her surprise, Seb reddened. 'I'm afraid I can't,' he said. 'I couldn't get tomorrow off after all. We can do something on Friday if you like.'

'Sure,' said Helen, feeling unexpectedly annoyed. Seb couldn't blame her for going cycling with Toby if he was always at work! She was even more shocked when Seb stood up and put his chair back under the table. 'I'm off home,' he said. 'I could do with a good night's sleep.'

Was it another dig about Isla? Helen wondered. Seb kissed her briefly. 'See you Friday,' he said. 'I'll come over in the morning.' He paused as if there was something he wanted to say, but the moment passed. 'Bye, then,' he said.

'Bye,' Helen echoed. She listened to the sound of his car as it disappeared up the lane. It was finally getting dark. She looked at the tea light. No point in lighting it now. Isla came over and whimpered. Helen lifted the dog onto her knee and put her arms around the thin little body. Was Seb having a problem with Isla? Or her friendship with Toby? Or was he still angry that Helen hadn't jumped at his offer of renting a place together?

She felt a stab of melancholy. She didn't want to break up with Seb. But then hadn't she been wanting the freedom to go away? Toby had whetted her appetite to go beyond her horizons, see something more of the world. Would it really be so awful to be single again?

Friday dawned bright and clear, and when Helen turned on the radio the presenters were talking ominously about record temperatures and hosepipe bans. Helen knew that Steve and Anneka were relying heavily on their irrigation system, but they always needed it for their polytunnels. Personally, she was enjoying every minute of the glorious weather.

By the time Seb's car drove into the lane, she had taken Isla and Lucy out for a short walk and was drinking freshly brewed coffee in the kitchen. In contrast, Seb looked tired when he walked in, but at least he was smiling. Helen felt herself relax; she hadn't wanted to admit it, but she'd been half-dreading seeing him today after their uncomfortable evening on Wednesday. He held out a small gift. He'd even wrapped it up this time. Helen tore off the paper to find two packets of dog treats. 'Look at the name,' he urged.

'Helen's Meaty Nibbles,' Helen read. She grinned at him. 'Mmmm, they sound tempting!'

'I also brought these.' Seb held out his swimming trunks. 'I thought we could take a leaf out of Lucy's book and take a swim in the river.'

'That's an excellent idea,' said Helen, meaning it. 'I'll go put my swimsuit on.' She ran upstairs to her bedroom. Seb seemed much more like himself today, she thought. Maybe it wasn't all ending. Maybe she didn't want it to. She looked at herself in the mirror and pulled a face. Make your mind up, she told herself.

The water in the deepest part of the stream was icy cold, but just about bearable once you were under. Lucy seemed fascinated that Helen was in the water and kept pushing sticks at her. Even Isla came in for a paddle, though she seemed panicky whenever she went out of her depth. 'No wonder,' said Seb. 'It's okay, girl, you stay on the stones.' He seemed quite solicitous over the little dog, making sure she didn't feel left out while they were swimming.

When she realised she couldn't feel her feet or hands, Helen waded out of the water and sat on her towel in the sun. Isla came out with her, lay down beside Helen and closed her eyes. Helen rested one hand on her damp, tightly curled fur.

'Did you know dogs can shake seventy per cent of the water from their coats in four seconds?' Seb waded out and dropped down onto the towel beside Helen.

'They create so much force that they have to close their eyes to stop them getting damaged.'

'Really?' Helen said.

'Lots of different animals do it,' he added. 'Even horses.'

For a moment, it felt as if everything was back to normal. Helen lay back and waited for Seb to regale her with more fascinating facts. Then his phone rang. He lunged for his backpack.

'I have to take this,' he said. 'Back in a minute.'

Helen watched in surprise as he jumped up and jogged along the path until he reached the trees. Why did he need to be out of earshot? He'd never hidden anything from her.

It was very quiet beside the stream. In the distance she could just hear the drone of a chainsaw. Lucy was sniffing the air beside her, and Isla was nibbling the base of her tail. Then she heard the tramp of footsteps coming closer. Seb appeared from behind a bush. He was smiling, though his face looked a little strained.

'Who was that?' Helen asked.

'No one important.'

Helen felt a jolt of unease. The spell that had been woven by the sunny day had cracked and the chasm between them yawned even wider. 'I don't understand,' she said. 'How can it be no one important? You couldn't answer your phone fast enough.'

Seb concentrated on drying his feet. 'Like I said,' he told her, 'it was nothing important.'

Helen stared at him. Her legs felt shaky, as if she'd been running.

Seb didn't seem to notice. He stood up and began stuffing his towel into his rucksack. Helen packed her own towel, then clipped Isla's lead onto her collar. Seb seemed distracted to the point of rudeness. Helen found herself glancing at him, willing him to say something, but he didn't even look at her. It was almost as if she wasn't there.

They arrived back at the granary in near-silence. Helen's mind was whirling. She had filled the fridge with food, in case he decided to stay for lunch, but Seb didn't even come inside. *Why can't you tell me about that phone call? Whatever it is, how can it be worse than this?*

'I'll see you on Sunday,' he told her as he pecked her on the cheek. 'I take it you're still coming to my parents?'

Helen didn't know what to say. She gazed at him and nodded. The thought of him having to explain her absence to them seemed worse than playing along.

If I don't go, it will mean we're over. It can't be over. Not yet. I'm not ready . . .

Chapter Thirteen

Helen shifted the lamp until its beam was shining directly into the rabbit's mouth. 'Better?' she checked. Mandy nodded. It was Saturday morning and Mandy was doing an emergency dental on the rabbit. It was a French Lop: very sweet and impressively chunky. In fact, before Helen had met Lettuce, she would have said Nonna was enormous for a rabbit. Her owner, Mrs Chan, was a petite lady who adored her pet and was clearly very strong for her size.

'Will you be able to sort her out?' Helen asked. Nonna's front teeth were overgrown and, because she couldn't chew properly, her back teeth had needed some attention too.

'Almost there,' Mandy replied. She had already burred both incisors and trimmed the teeth farther back. She glanced up at Helen. 'What did you do on your time off?'

Helen grimaced. 'Seb came over yesterday. We went swimming in the river.'

Mandy nodded and picked up another instrument.

'Everything was fine until he got a phone call,' Helen

went on. 'He leapt up and hared off as if he didn't want me to hear what he was saying.'

Mandy looked up and frowned. 'How odd. Was he okay afterwards?'

Helen shrugged. 'Not really. I asked him what it was about and he wouldn't tell me. Hardly spoke all the way home, then left.' She straightened up and stretched her back, which was starting to ache from bending over Nonna. 'I don't know what's going on with him,' she admitted. 'It's as if he's keeping something from me. He's had all these extra shifts at work, and now this.'

Mandy put down her instruments and leaned her hands on the table. 'Well, there's one thing I'm sure of,' she said. 'Seb's not the type to have an affair. Are you sure it isn't something good? Maybe he's planning a surprise proposal?'

Helen didn't know whether to laugh at Mandy's optimism or sigh. She was absolutely certain Seb wasn't about to ask her to marry him. 'Are you sure you're not mistaking Seb for yourself?' she teased. 'I take it you haven't found an engagement ring that would fit Jimmy yet?'

To her surprise, Mandy flushed. 'Not yet,' she said, 'but I am looking.'

'You're definitely going through with it?' Helen said, picking up the used instruments to put in the steriliser. 'Maybe you and Jimmy can have a double wedding with James and Raj.'

Mandy's eyes widened. 'Oh gosh, that was quite the

bombshell at your lunch, wasn't it?' she said. 'I haven't had a chance to talk to James yet.' She ran her hand over the sleeping rabbit's ears. 'I know Raj's timing was off, but James will be a brilliant father.' Helen thought she could detect a note of wistfulness in Mandy's voice.

A movement at the edge of her vision caught her attention. Nonna had started to twitch and a moment later she started to kick with both back legs. Helen wrapped the blanket that was covering the rabbit more tightly around her. Rabbits could kick out so hard they broke their own spines. She had to keep Nonna still until she was properly awake. 'I'll take her to the recovery room,' she said to Mandy.

Heaving the furry body into her arms, she carried Nonna out and put her into a cage, then hung up the drip that was still attached to one large floppy ear. Rabbits needed to eat as soon as possible after any anaesthetic so as soon as Nonna was awake enough to swallow, Helen would give her some liquid food with a syringe.

Even under the blanket, Nonna looked enormous. Helen couldn't help thinking of Lettuce. Would Mrs Chan be interested in taking on another rabbit? she wondered. Nonna had been a rescue too, and Mrs Chan was obviously familiar with caring for giants. I'll suggest it to Mandy, Helen thought as she adjusted the drip rate.

★ ★ ★

'Hi, Toby. How'd it go?' Helen looked up from updating Nonna's invoice on the computer as the door opened and Toby walked in. He'd been at a calving at Upper Welford Hall.

Toby rubbed one hand over his face. He looked sombre and exhausted. 'The calf was breech,' he said, 'and I couldn't get the legs up. The uterus had clamped down and there was no room. I did a Caesar in the end, but it was too late. Good little heifer calf, too. Graham didn't say much, but I could see he was gutted.'

Graham was the dairyman at Upper Welford. Helen knew he was devoted to his herd. She also knew that Toby would be blaming himself for the bad outcome. 'I'm sorry,' she said.

Toby pulled out a chair and sat down. 'The calf was alive when I got there. If I'd done the operation straight away . . .'

'Sometimes things go wrong,' Helen said gently. 'Even when you do everything right.'

Toby managed a wry smile. 'True,' he admitted. 'The first ever cat I anaesthetised dropped dead half an hour after the operation had ended. The lecturer who was overseeing me couldn't explain it. He said the same as you.'

Helen thought for a minute. 'We could go out this afternoon,' she offered. 'Late lunch at the Fox and Goose? You're off, aren't you?'

'Yes, Adam's taking over at two.' He frowned. 'You are still with Seb, aren't you?' he checked.

Helen felt a brief prickle of conscience but pushed it aside. 'I am with Seb,' she said, 'but we're not tied at the hip. He's playing cricket this afternoon.'

Toby raised his eyebrows. 'And you'd rather have lunch with me than cheer on Walton?'

'Oh, for goodness' sake,' Helen said. 'I'm not asking you to marry me. It's pie and mash at the Fox and Goose, not *Gone with the Wind.*'

For the first time, Toby grinned properly.

'What?' Helen demanded.

'I'm just trying to imagine you as Scarlett O'Hara!'

At that moment the door opened and Mandy walked in. 'Did he just compare you to Scarlett O'Hara?' she said to Helen. She grinned at Toby. 'Tell me, is it the flouncy dress or the annoying Southern drawl?'

Toby laughed. 'Neither,' he said. 'We were arranging a tryst at the Fox and Goose.'

Mandy's eyebrows shot up.

'It's true,' Helen told her. 'It's ages since we've been out. Would you and Jimmy like to come?'

Mandy nodded. 'Sounds great. I'll let Jimmy know. Abi and Max are with their mum, so he'll be free once this morning's group is finished.' She glanced at the clock. 'Which should be very soon, actually.'

'Tell him to come here first,' Helen said. 'We can walk to the pub.'

★ ★ ★

By the time Jimmy arrived, they had changed out of their work clothes and Toby had showered. Adam appeared at two for the changeover. 'Have fun,' he told them.

Helen had assumed that by inviting Mandy and Jimmy, it would feel more like an afternoon out with colleagues, but after a few minutes she and Toby were walking so far ahead of Mandy and Jimmy that it felt as if they were alone. When Helen glanced round to see where they'd got to, they were strolling arm in arm, deep in conversation. She turned back to see Toby smiling at her.

'So,' he said. 'Tell me about yourself.'

Helen wanted to laugh. They'd been working together for months, and even if they hadn't it was such a corny question. Was this the best that the famous womaniser Toby Gordon could do? 'Hello, I'm Helen Steer,' she began. 'I'm twenty-seven years old and I'm a veterinary nurse.'

Toby rolled his eyes. 'Okay, fair enough,' he said. 'It was a silly question. I should have asked you about your star sign or something I don't already know.'

'My star sign? You claim to be a vet, but you believe in star signs? You'll be telling me next that the Earth is flat.'

'How did you guess?' he gasped. He picked a leaf from the hedge and rolled it between his fingers. 'Did you know there's a whole community online who call themselves Flat Earthers?'

Helen frowned. 'Do you think they really believe it? I mean, people have gone into space and taken photographs of the world, and it's clearly round.'

They reached the end of the lane and turned left towards the centre of Welford. The church tower rose ahead of them, a soft grey against the blue sky.

'Do you think,' Helen went on, 'that someone thought it up as a joke? That they never thought anyone would take it seriously?'

Toby grinned. 'You could be right. A few blokes having a quiet drink. What's the most outrageous thing we can come up with? Let's start a discussion on the internet.'

Helen punched him lightly on his arm. 'Are you absolutely sure they were blokes? Isn't that rather sexist?'

Toby shook his head. 'Definitely blokes,' he said. 'Women would never come up with anything so daft.'

Helen laughed, feeling lighter and more relaxed than she had since Seb's mysterious phone call. She felt a sudden urge to reach out and grab Toby's hand. The intensity of the impulse made her uneasy. She and Toby probably shouldn't be alone together. She glanced over her shoulder to see where Mandy and Jimmy had got to, but they were still a long way back.

The Fox and Goose wasn't far away now. 'We're almost there,' she said. 'We should wait for Jimmy and Mandy.' To her relief, Toby stopped and they stepped onto the verge to let a car go past. By the time Mandy and Jimmy caught up, Helen felt more in control. Toby flirted with everyone, she reminded herself.

'Sorry for keeping you waiting,' Mandy called out.

'It's quite all right,' Toby assured her.

They walked into the Fox and Goose and, with only a moment's hesitation, Helen sat beside Mandy and Jimmy and Toby sat down opposite.

The Fox and Goose always provided hearty local fare and today was no exception. Helen even found space for a passion fruit sorbet after her enormous ploughman's platter.

Mandy sat back with a satisfied sigh. 'That was lovely,' she said. 'I should probably go for a brisk walk on the moor to work it off, but I actually can't be bothered.'

Helen laughed. 'I share your idle inclinations. Shall we get another round of drinks?' She wasn't having alcohol because she had to drive home later, but she felt very mellow.

Toby pushed his chair out and stood up. 'In that case,' he said, 'may I suggest we adjourn to the beer garden?' Despite having had the best part of a bottle of wine, he seemed perfectly steady. 'Helen,' he looked across the table, 'could you give me a hand? And you two,' he looked from Mandy to Jimmy, 'perhaps you could go outside and see if there's a table?'

Jimmy threw him a salute. 'Yes, sir!'

He and Mandy began to make their way to the back door. It seemed unlikely to Helen that there would be a free table on such a warm day. She pushed herself upright and followed Toby to the bar.

'What would you like?' Toby was standing very close

to her, she realised. It was pleasantly cool in the bar, but she was suddenly aware of the heat from his body, and of his elbow touching hers. She could smell his cologne, too. A shiver ran down her spine.

Toby was grinning at her. 'Go on, live a little,' he urged.

'I'm living just fine, thanks,' Helen said. She had to put a stop to this. She and Seb were still a couple, even if things were rocky. She shifted away from Toby, planting her feet firmly on the worn wooden floor. 'I'll have a virgin mojito,' she said to Bev Parsons, the Fox and Goose's landlady.

Bev nodded. 'Coming right up,'

'And a jug of non-virgin mojito for the rest of us.' Toby leaned on the bar, still far too close for comfort.

'You go and sit down,' Bev told them. 'I'll bring the drinks out in a minute.'

'Ooh!' There was a squeal from the other end of the bar. 'Look who it is!' Helen turned to see Imogen Parker-Smythe shimmying towards them. 'What are you up to today?'

Helen felt the heat rising in her face. Was she wearing a cloak of invisibility? Imogen sidled up to Toby, bumped her hip against his suggestively, and then beamed in his face.

'Hello, Imogen,' Toby said calmly. 'It's good to see you, but as you can see,' he indicated Helen, 'I'm out with friends today.'

Imogen looked Helen up and down as if she was

itemising her wardrobe, calculating the value, and finding it sorely lacking.

'I see.' Imogen's voice was dry as she turned back to Toby. 'Well, anyway,' she reached out a hand and ran a predatory finger down his cheek, 'it's good to see you. Don't be a stranger,' she added, making a phone gesture with her hand. 'Call me,' she mouthed. With a last narrow-eyed look at Helen, she sashayed back to her table.

Helen fiddled with her hair, straightening out her grown-out fringe. It suddenly felt as if every woman in the pub was sizing her up. Did they think Toby could do better? She shook her head. It wasn't as if she and Toby were together. Why did it matter what they thought?

'Well, well, well.' Helen turned to see Jimmy had come in. 'Look at you, Mr Irresistible. Can't even stand in the Fox and Goose without women throwing themselves at you.'

Toby grinned. 'I bet you were the same before Mandy snagged you,' he said.

Jimmy shook his head. 'Whatever,' he said, his voice light. 'I just came in to say we've got a table outside, so whenever you and Helen feel like joining us . . .'

'Shall we?' Toby said to Helen. His hand touched the small of her back as he ushered her through the door and Helen tried not to shiver. Pull yourself together, she ordered.

Mandy and Jimmy were sitting side by side at the table. Helen had no option but to slide into place beside

Toby. He was sitting quite close to the centre of the bench seat and their thighs brushed.

Helen looked up to see Mandy's eyes on her. Could Mandy see what was going on? Not that anything was going on, she reminded herself. She was relieved when Bev arrived with the drinks.

'Here you go.' Bev unloaded the jug and glasses, then put Helen's drink in front of her. She winked. 'You want to watch that one,' she said, nodding at Toby.

Helen felt herself turning red. 'No need, we're just friends,' she said.

Bev patted Helen on the shoulder. 'That's what they all say,' she whispered.

Helen looked round to see whether Toby was feeling as uncomfortable as she was, but he was grinning broadly. 'Here's to us,' he teased, raising his glass.

Helen ignored him and pretended to be removing a fly from her drink.

'I had the most amazing couple in this morning.' Jimmy put down his drink and sat forward, leaning his elbows on the wooden table. 'They were both eighty years old and celebrating their sixtieth wedding anniversary. Can you imagine being married that long?'

Toby laughed. 'I can barely imagine being alive that long,' he drawled. He looked at Helen. 'How about you?'

'Well, I hope I make it to sixty,' Helen said. 'But it's pretty incredible to be married for that many years. Did you ask them their secret, Jimmy?'

'Of course.' Jimmy squinted a little as he looked at

her in the bright sunshine. 'He was an osteopath. They said keeping supple was key. Keep moving and keep doing things together.'

Mandy leaned into Jimmy's body with an affectionate nudge. 'You and I shouldn't have any problems at all, in that case,' she said.

'How right you are.' Jimmy smiled into Mandy's eyes.

'Stop it, you two.' Toby knocked on the table with his knuckles, then lifted his glass and drained his drink. 'Personally, I think another mojito is the answer,' he said. He lifted the jug and refilled his glass, topping up Mandy's and Jimmy's at the same time. 'Jug's empty,' he announced. 'I'll get another one in. Helen, do you want the same again, or will you join us?'

Helen glanced at her watch and felt her heart sink. 'I'm afraid I'll have to get home,' she said. It was well past Isla and Lucy's feeding time and she'd promised Anneka she'd do the irrigation again this evening. She stood up and edged out from the seat.

Toby stood up too. Instead of heading inside with the jug, he put it down and followed her to the side gate. 'Thanks for inviting me out,' he said. 'You were right. It was just what I needed.' His eyes met hers and, for a moment, Helen felt as if she was frozen to the ground. Her heart was thudding. Toby leaned towards her and she thought he was going to kiss her mouth, but it landed on her cheek. She could feel her knees shaking as he stepped away. 'See you Monday,' he said, and patted her on the arm.

'See you,' she replied automatically. She walked through the gate, then pulled it shut and leaned on the wall. What on earth was happening to her? She was far too old to be getting palpitations over a man. And she was seeing Seb tomorrow. Even though they hadn't talked properly, they were visiting his parents. Somehow or other, she had to mend things between them. This couldn't go on.

Chapter Fourteen

'Morning!' Seb called as he walked into Helen's kitchen. Lucy rushed towards him but Isla hung back, her ears twitching.

Helen bent down and stroked the little dog to calm her. 'Hi, Seb,' she said. She was so weary that even if she had been pleased to see him, it would have been hard to raise much enthusiasm. She had decided it was time to try again with Lucy and Isla in the bedroom together, and although they had made it through till dawn, Helen had been up and down so many times resettling them that she felt as if she hadn't slept at all.

Even without the dogs to disturb her, she lay awake in the long hours of the early morning worrying about the sudden lack of communication from Seb. On top of that were confusing thoughts of Toby. Guilt flooded her as she recalled the way he'd looked at her, the way she'd reacted. She had reminded herself again and again that she had done nothing wrong. And then found herself justifying her feelings. After all, Seb was lying to her. Then she was back at the mysterious phone call. Her mind had gone round and round until it was almost a relief to get up and sort out her fretful dogs.

Seb looked at her. 'Are you okay?'

'I'm tired, that's all,' Helen lied.

Seb held out his hand. 'For you,' he said. He dropped a pebble into her hand.

Helen ran her fingers over the smooth white stone. She wondered whether it was from the river where they'd gone swimming.

'I found it on Walton cricket field yesterday,' Seb said. 'Right in the middle of the pitch. Shockingly bad groundsmanship. It should never have been there.'

Helen managed a weak laugh. 'Just what I always wanted,' she said.

Seb glanced round the kitchen and spotted that Lucy's bed was no longer downstairs. 'Did they sleep together last night?' he asked. 'How'd it go?'

'Not bad at all,' Helen said. It was the second lie she'd told him in a matter of minutes.

'That's brilliant,' Seb said. He smiled a little anxiously. 'I was wondering whether it might be possible to leave them at home today? I know Mum and Dad love Lucy, but with the two of them it gets a bit . . .' His sentence was cut off as Lucy whirled round and snapped at Isla, who had bumped into her. Helen stared at the dogs in shock. What had happened to her beautiful gentle dog? The tears she had been fighting welled in her eyes. After all her efforts last night, Lucy and Isla were no more comfortable together than they had ever been. She blinked away the tears. 'I don't think we can leave them,' she said. 'What if Isla ends up getting hurt?'

Seb frowned. 'Can't Isla go into Hope Meadows for a day? I'm sure Mandy wouldn't mind.'

Helen cut him off. 'No,' she said. 'Isla's there already when I'm at work. I won't shut her away at the weekend as well. Anyway, Mandy is out with Adam and Emily today. Can't we just take them along? I'll make sure to keep an eye on them.'

Seb sighed. 'I guess we don't have a choice.' He pulled his car keys out of his pocket. 'Can you get their leads on? I need to clear a few things from the back of my car.'

They drove to Walton without talking. Lucy lay down and tried to sleep, but Isla cried noisily all the way. Every time Helen glanced back, she could see Lucy's tired eyes glaring at Isla. It was difficult for them both, she reminded herself. Isla couldn't see Lucy's body language and Lucy didn't understand why Isla seemed so unresponsive to her cues.

They arrived outside the bungalow and Seb pulled on the handbrake. They sat there for a moment, then Seb pushed open his door, climbed out and went to the rear of the car. 'Shall I take Isla in?' he suggested. 'Lucy can go with you.'

Helen looked at him. Had he been able to tell she was dreading having to control both dogs as they went into the house? It was the kind of thing the old Seb would have thought about. Lucy was bound to want to rush around re-exploring everything. It would have been diffi-cult to restrain her and comfort Isla at the same time. 'That would be great,' she admitted.

Seb's parents appeared on the front doorstep and both made a fuss of Isla and Lucy. Seb's mum Shirley was the first to straighten up. She opened her arms and hugged Seb first, then reached out to Helen. 'It's lovely to see you both,' she said.

Frank Conway hugged Seb, then put out a hand and patted Helen's arm. 'It is that,' he agreed.

They were a handsome couple. Frank had the same deep-set eyes as Seb and the gentle, open face. Shirley worked in the optician's in Walton and was forever sporting new glasses, but she too had a warm expression, with cropped grey hair and deep smile lines around her eyes.

'Come on in, lass,' Shirley said to Helen, pulling the door wider.

As soon as Helen stepped inside, she smelled a wonderful savoury aroma. 'I made your favourite,' Shirley told Helen. 'Rib of beef. You can let Lucy run around if you like,' she added. 'I've put Jess in the bedroom.'

Jess was the Conways' much loved black and white cat. Frank Conway had been a postman for almost thirty years and, as Shirley often joked, with him being a postie in the Dales, when Jess had appeared one day on the doorstep, it had seemed like fate. The Conways and Seb had spent weeks trying to trace Jess's owner but had finally accepted that they had been thoroughly adopted.

Shirley bustled about, making sure everyone was comfortable. She had bought Bonios for each dog. 'I just need to do the gravy,' she announced when Lucy and Isla were crunching happily.

'And I'll go and finish off the roasties,' Frank said. 'Don't worry,' he added in a loud stage whisper. 'I'll make sure my lovely wife doesn't put any lumps in the gravy.'

Shirley glared at him. 'I'll lumpy-gravy you in a minute,' she said, pretending to thwack him with the tea towel she was holding.

They disappeared and for a moment the silence was broken only by the sound of Lucy sniffing her way round the room. Isla was sitting as close to Helen as possible without actually climbing on her knee. A burst of laughter sounded from the kitchen. 'I wonder what they're up to,' Helen said. She couldn't help feeling wistful. Frank and Shirley Conway always seemed so comfortable in each other's company. The contrast with Helen's own family was stark. Her dad was out today on another date, after the previous lady turned out to be less keen on steam engines than he thought. And Helen's mum would have been wholly disapproving of roast beef on a hot summer's day.

She glanced around. The cluttered sitting room was filled with signs of happy family life. Pictures of Seb and his older sister Bridget had pride of place on the mantelpiece. Bridget's wedding photo stood beside Frank and Shirley's black and white one on the sideboard. Bridget's children, girls of five and two, smiled down from the wall opposite the window. There was just one gap, Helen thought with a sinking feeling. There was space on the sideboard for a third picture.

'Grub's up!' Helen's thoughts were interrupted by Frank's cheery shout. She stood up and Seb followed her through to the dining room.

The table looked full enough for several families. A vast tureen of roast potatoes jostled with carrots in butter and fresh green peas. There were crisp individual Yorkshire puddings and a bowl of horseradish sauce. As she helped herself to vegetables, Helen started to relax. This wasn't about her and Seb and whatever lay ahead in their future. This was about enjoying time with lovely people, and having someone else cook dinner. She was listening to Seb and his dad discussing Walton's latest cricket match when she spotted a movement out of the corner of her eye. Lucy had slunk into the room and was crouching down under the table.

'No, Lucy!' she said in horror. Before Helen could stop her, the dog started to pee.

'Stop!' Helen cried. Shoving her chair back, she grabbed Lucy's collar and pulled her towards the back door. 'Why on earth did you do that?' she exclaimed, then felt a wave of shame. It was the closest she'd ever got to shouting at her beloved dog. Lucy gave her a sideways look, then slunk out into the garden to finish.

By the time Helen got back, Shirley Conway was already on her knees with an antibacterial spray and a cloth. 'Not to worry, dear,' she said as she grabbed the back of one of the chairs and pulled herself upright. 'No harm done.'

Helen sat back down and picked up her knife and fork. Her dinner was almost cold. She took a few mouthfuls, then put her cutlery down. There was a sick feeling in her stomach. Was Lucy ill? She'd never, ever peed inside before.

'Had enough, dear?' Frank reached out to take Helen's plate. He and Shirley stood up and began to clear the table. Helen pushed her chair out, but Frank stopped her. 'You stay there,' he said. He bent down and put his head close to her ear. 'You look like you need a rest, love,' he said, patting her on the shoulder.

The room seemed very quiet as Helen sat alone with Seb. She could hear the clatter of pots through the kitchen door. Shirley would appear with something wonderful for dessert in a few moments, but Helen wasn't sure she could manage another mouthful. She risked a glance at Seb. He was staring straight ahead. Was he angry with her? Lucy had spoiled their meal after he'd asked her to leave the dogs at home, but usually Seb would take something like this in his stride.

'Do you think there's something wrong with Lucy?' she asked in a low voice.

Seb turned to look at her. 'Something wrong?' he echoed. 'Of course there's something wrong. She's stressed out the whole time about Isla. Probably not getting any sleep, just like you.'

Helen couldn't have felt any worse if he'd reached out and slapped her. She shook her head, feeling the lump in her throat growing. 'I know it's not been easy with Isla,' she said, 'but Lucy isn't stressed.' She looked over at Lucy, who had crept back into the dining room and was curled up in the corner. 'She isn't,' she insisted.

Seb sighed and glanced upwards, as if seeking strength from the swirls on the ceiling. 'You can't see it,' he said, 'but Isla's demanding all your attention. Lucy hardly gets a look-in.'

'That's not true,' Helen objected. Isla wasn't any more demanding than you'd expect any dog to be that was struggling with something new. 'She's getting much better,' she said. 'And I haven't stopped loving Lucy. She knows that.'

'Does she?' Seb sounded bitter, and for a second Helen wondered whether he was going to say something about their own relationship.

Shirley pushed open the dining-room door. 'Apple pie, anyone?'

'And cream!' Frank followed her into the room and set a huge jug of cream on the table.

Helen forced herself to smile. 'It looks delicious,' she said. 'You're totally spoiling us!'

★ ★ ★

The journey home was even more uncomfortable than the drive out. They had limped their way through the rest of the meal, but Seb's words lingered in Helen's head. She twisted around in the passenger seat and looked at Lucy, who was sitting up and looking out of the half-open window. Her ears were flapping and she was obviously enjoying the sensation of the air blowing in. She looked at Helen, then turned back to the breeze. She had clearly forgotten all about her mishap under the table, but Helen wanted to cry more than ever.

Her mobile buzzed as Seb drove past the huge old oak tree that marked the Welford boundary. She pulled it out of her pocket and looked at the screen. Gemma's beaming face grinned back at her. 'Everything fabulous!' the message read. 'Moondance and I wish you were here!'

Clicking on the button to clear the screen, Helen shoved the phone back into her pocket. She turned her face to the window and a tear ran down her face, then another.

How lovely it would be if they could rewind time, she thought. Back to Gemma's party. Back to the time when Seb wasn't angry with her. Before everything had gone so horribly wrong.

Chapter Fifteen

Seb dropped Helen off and left immediately. At bedtime, with a pang of guilt, Helen put Lucy's bed back in the kitchen and took Isla upstairs. She tried to make the effort to make a fuss of Lucy, taking her out into the garden without Isla, but Isla looked so unhappy when Helen came back in that her heart went out to the little dog.

At least with Isla and Lucy separated, Helen managed to get a decent night's sleep. She arrived at the clinic in good time on Monday morning and popped into the cottage. Emily was sitting in a comfortable chair beside the window. She was knitting with bright yellow wool. 'Look,' she said to Helen as she held up the tiny square. 'What do you think?'

'Very nice,' Helen ventured. 'What is it?'

'It's a cat blanket. I'm hoping to do one for every kitten and puppy that Mandy rehomes. They can take it with them so they can have something that smells like their mum.'

Helen couldn't help smiling. 'That's a gorgeous idea.' Emily was so kind, and so determined to keep going despite the devastating MS diagnosis.

Lucy finished sniffing her way around the kitchen floor and flopped down at Emily's feet. It was another little jab to Helen's heart. Lucy seemed more at home here than she did in the granary.

'Hello, girl,' Emily said, reaching down to pat her. 'Do I have the pleasure of your company again today? Lucky me.'

'She's lucky to have you,' Helen said. The lump that kept appearing in her throat had returned. 'See you later.' She bent to stroke Lucy's silky head and the dog's tail thumped lazily on the floor.

She walked back to the car, unclipped Isla and took her round to Hope Meadows. Mandy was in the cat room, tending to Lettuce, who was far too big to fit with the guinea pigs in the small-furries room. Mandy looked up as Helen walked in. 'Morning,' she said. She smiled at Isla. 'And good morning to you, sweet girl.'

'Do you think I'm neglecting Lucy?' The words burst from Helen's mouth before she could stop them.

Mandy looked so taken aback that Helen almost laughed. 'You'd never neglect Lucy,' Mandy said. 'Nobody would even suggest it. Would they?'

Helen shrugged.

Mandy closed Lettuce's cage and stood up. She peered closely at Helen. 'What's up? It's not like you to worry about how well you're taking care of your dog.'

Helen took a deep breath. 'I'm still having problems with Lucy and Isla,' she admitted. 'Sometimes they get on like a house on fire and it's lovely, but sometimes

Lucy gets so cross with Isla that she snaps.' She felt her face grow red. It felt disloyal to Lucy to suggest she was behaving badly. She was reacting to the change in her environment, that was all.

Mandy looked down at Isla. 'It must be difficult for both of them,' she said. 'Obviously dogs rely a lot on smell, but they need to see each other too.' She pinched her bottom lip thoughtfully. 'Is Lucy with Mum as usual?' she asked.

Helen nodded.

'Well, how about you leave Isla with me today?' Mandy said. 'I can do a few exercises with her and then I'll have a look at my behaviour notes and see what I can come up with. How does that sound?'

'It sounds great.' Helen smiled at Mandy. The relief at someone offering to help without judging her was enormous.

'Anyway,' Mandy bent down and began to brush the rabbit hairs from her trousers, 'I've got some excellent news for you. Thanks to your brilliant idea, Mrs Chan's agreed to take Lettuce. I was out there yesterday to do the home visit and she's all ready.' She straightened up. 'I was wondering if you'd like to take him over? Mrs Chan lives near York, so it's a bit of a drive, but it's not looking too busy today.'

'I'd love to go,' Helen said. Much as she enjoyed helping Mandy care for rescued animals, there was nothing more satisfying than seeing them off into their new homes.

'While I remember,' Mandy said, reaching into her pocket and pulling out a packet, 'James asked me for some worming tablets. Is there any chance you could drop them in while you're over that way?'

Helen grinned. 'This is feeling more and more like a day off,' she said. 'Are you sure?'

'Yes, I'm sure,' Mandy replied. 'Get some lunch while you're there. James has some wonderful fruit salad concoctions at the moment. Raj keeps bringing him all kinds of exotic stuff to try.' Mandy put her hands into the back pockets of her jeans. 'Here is Mrs Chan's address.' She pulled out a slip of paper and handed it to Helen. 'Hope it goes well.'

'I'm sure it will.'

Mandy left Helen alone with Lettuce. The magnificent bunny stood up in his cage with his front paws on the bars and regarded her, whiskers twitching. 'Come on, you,' Helen said. She opened his kennel and heaved him into one of the big carrying crates that Mandy used for cats with young litters. Lifting it, she staggered out to her car.

The drive to York was a treat in itself. The weather was scorching and Helen was glad of the car's air conditioning. She found herself humming as she steered her car between green fields and rustling, leaf-heavy trees.

The satnav led her directly to Mrs Chan's door. It was a gorgeous chalet bungalow, overlooking fields. A light breeze sent ripples through the ripening barley and, in the hazy distance, the moors rose up to meet the cloudless sky.

'Hello!' Mrs Chan greeted Helen as she hauled the heavy carrier out of the car. She was really quite tiny, dark eyed and smiling. 'And hello to you too!' She beamed at Lettuce through the bars of the cage. 'Let's show him his new home.' Mrs Chan ushered Helen round the side of the house. Her back garden was filled with tidy rows of hutches and runs. Healthy-looking rabbits with bright eyes and shiny coats lolloped gently around, nibbling at the grass.

'What a lot of rabbits,' Helen commented.

'I love bunnies,' Mrs Chan said unnecessarily. 'I grew up in Hong Kong in a high-rise apartment and my parents wouldn't even consider letting me have one. When I moved here with my husband fifteen years ago, the first thing I did was get a rabbit. Then someone gave me one that their children had grown out of, then another, and before I knew it, I had a whole garden full of bunnies. It's wonderful, don't you think?'

She looked down at Lettuce, who was sniffing the air. 'I've got just the place for you,' she told him. She led Helen over to a run on the edge of the lawn. Like all the other runs, its grass was smooth and green and it contained a shelter to provide shade from the sun or protection when it was raining. There was a fresh bowl of water and a large plate of chopped vegetables. 'You see, I'm all ready for you,' she reassured Lettuce.

Helen handed Lettuce over and Mrs Chan stroked

him, then set him down gently on the grass. He stayed beside her for a moment, snuffling at her feet, then wandered away and began nibbling at the grass.

'Would you like to see Nonna?' Mrs Chan suggested. 'She's doing so well. Eating everything I give her.'

'Yes, please.' Helen smiled. Mostly she didn't get to see patients until they were ill again.

Nonna looked splendid. Her coat was shiny and she had gained weight. Helen didn't need to look in her mouth to tell that her teeth were much better. Mrs Chan lifted her out of the run and held her in her arms while Helen stroked her soft coat. Lots of rabbits weren't keen on being handled, but Mrs Chan was so gentle and loving that it was hard to imagine she couldn't tame even the wildest bunny. Lettuce was going to be very happy here.

'Thanks for showing me Nonna,' Helen said as they walked back round to the car, 'and thanks for taking Lettuce. I get the feeling he's landed on his paws!'

'I hope so,' Mrs Chan replied. 'And if I have any problems with his health, I know where to come.' She stood beside the car as Helen got in. Helen could see her waving in the rear-view mirror as she drove off.

James's assistant manager Sherrie was standing behind the counter of the café when Helen walked in. Her white-blond hair was tied back and she was wearing a pair of cut-off dungarees with a tiny vest underneath. Judging by all the gaps behind the glass counter, they had been doing a roaring trade in rolls and sandwiches.

Sherrie looked up and smiled warmly when she saw Helen. 'Lovely to see you, Helen. James is through the back.'

James was standing in gloves and a hairnet beside what seemed to be a mountain of fruit. As well as melons and strawberries, Helen could see persimmons and passion fruit, and some red hairy-looking objects that she couldn't identify. James was dissecting an orange. He had cut the skin off and was slicing out each segment so that only the most succulent flesh remained. He had rings under his eyes as if he was tired, but he smiled when he spotted Helen. 'Hi,' he said. 'Welcome to the Hunter House of Fruit.'

Helen held out the packet of worming tablets. 'Mandy asked me to bring you these,' she said.

James went to the sink, removed his gloves and rinsed his hands before taking them. 'Brilliant,' he said. 'It's so mad here that I haven't had a chance to get over to collect them.' He slid them into his pocket. 'That'll be a nice treat later for Lily and Seamus,' he said with a grin. He reached over and plucked a new pair of gloves from a box on the table.

'Are you on your own back here?' Helen asked.

James picked up his knife again. 'Maria's on holiday,' he said, 'so I'm on cooking duty. I do love cooking, but it's not so much fun when it's on an industrial scale. We're selling so much fruit salad I can hardly keep up.'

'What are those?' Helen asked, pointing at the spiky red balls.

James rolled one in his hand. 'They're rambutan,' he said. He peeled off the skin and held out the white centre. 'Try it,' he said. 'They're like lychees.'

Helen took the rambutan and bit into it. It was unusual, but sweet and refreshing. 'Lovely,' she said. 'Can I give you a hand?' Mandy had told her she could have lunch here, but it would be better to help James out. She also wanted to ask how things were going with Raj. Despite his smiles, James had an air of sadness about him.

'I won't say no,' James said. 'Gloves are here.' He handed her a knife. 'Start with the passion fruit if you like,' he said. 'They're nice and easy.' He picked one up, sliced it in half, then scooped the seedy centre into an enormous metal bowl.

'I think I can manage that,' Helen said. 'It was good of you to come over to my barbecue,' she went on as she dissected her first fruit. 'Raj too. He must have been tired after his trip.'

'It was a good day,' James replied. He frowned, staring down at yet another orange. 'I hope we didn't wreck it too much. Raj certainly knows how to crash a conversation.' He was trying to keep his voice light, but Helen could hear the tension beneath the words.

She scooped some passion-fruit seeds into the bowl and looked at him. 'I'm not sure it's my place to ask,' she said, 'but are you okay? With what Raj said, I mean?'

'You mean, am I ready to become a father?' He was trying to joke, but Helen could tell his heart wasn't in it. His head fell forward as if he was exhausted with thinking about it, but he lifted his eyes to meet Helen's. 'Honest answer? I have no idea.' He finished dissecting his orange, cutting meticulously, then put the knife down. 'I think the main problem is that he didn't say anything before. Adopting a child is such a huge thing. Why wouldn't he have told me about it?'

Helen offered a tentative smile. 'It doesn't sound like he'd deliberately kept it secret,' she said. 'He seemed to think it wasn't happening. As soon as everything was confirmed, he looked for a chance to tell you. He just didn't pick his timing very well.'

'In front of all our friends.' James sounded despondent. 'Do you think he did it then to make sure I didn't react badly?'

'Goodness, no!' Helen said. 'I didn't get that impression at all.' She rolled a passion fruit on the counter. 'I don't see Raj being manipulative like that. He's impulsive, but not mean.'

James sighed and picked up his knife again. 'You're right,' he said. 'It's just . . .' He paused. 'It's just that I thought I was really getting to know him. And now I'm not sure that I do at all.'

The door swung open and Sherrie's head appeared. 'We're out of tuna salad rolls,' she said, 'and someone's just ordered three.'

'Okay, Sherrie.' James went to a different area of the kitchen to begin prepping the sandwiches.

Helen sliced open another passion fruit. 'I think you're

worrying about nothing,' she said. 'I don't have any doubt you know him very well.'

James put a handful of red onion into a bowl with tuna and mayonnaise and began to stir.

'You know that Raj will make an amazing dad, right?' Helen prompted.

James nodded without looking up from the bowl.

'And you would, too,' Helen continued. James's breathing sounded a little uneven. Was she wrong to push this hard? She was surprisingly desperate for James to forgive Raj. 'After all, you did say that you'd always wanted children one day,' she said.

James stopped mixing and pushed his glasses up his nose with the back of his glove. He turned and leaned against the counter and Helen saw real grief in his eyes. 'It was something Paul and I talked about, long ago. Before he got the cancer diagnosis,' he explained. 'Once he was ill, it was all forgotten. Nothing seemed more important than keeping him alive.' He fiddled with the spoon in his hands. 'And now . . . I don't know. I can't see a future without Raj in it, but that doesn't mean I'm ready to settle down the same way I did with Paul.'

Helen felt a little ashamed that she had told Seb they were too young to settle. For James and Paul, it had been a brief moment of happiness before Paul's death. No wonder he was afraid of making that kind of commitment again. She reached out and touched James's arm. 'It wouldn't be the same,' she said. 'Raj isn't Paul. He's never tried to be, has he?'

The muscles in James's jaw were clenched. 'I know he hasn't,' he said. 'It's just . . . we were happy the way we were. At least, I was.' He sighed. 'I thought he was too. Why does he have to change everything?' His voice had become ragged and Helen could see the glint of tears in his brown eyes. He turned round and began to slice the bread rolls.

'Perhaps Raj doesn't see this as changing everything,' Helen said carefully. She paused, her mind racing as she searched for the right words. 'Perhaps he sees this as sharing a great adventure with the man he loves.'

'But I don't think I'm ready,' James whispered.

The rolls were finished. To Helen's relief, Sherrie appeared, took them from James, then went back out without seeming to notice anything was wrong.

'You do have some time to get your head around it,' she pointed out. 'The adoption won't go through for several months if you're going to add your name to the paperwork, will it?'

James nodded.

'Well, think of that as your gestation period. Lots of couples have fewer than nine months to get ready for a baby. You and Raj are no different!'

James looked at her. His eyes were still troubled. When he spoke, it was so quietly that Helen had to lean towards him to hear. 'I feel as if he's forcing me into it,' he confessed. He swallowed hard.

Helen took hold of his hands. They felt cool and thin beneath the latex gloves. 'It's probably very normal to feel like that,' she pointed out. 'If it was an unexpected pregnancy, you wouldn't run away, would you? This isn't so different, is it?' She squeezed his fingers. 'If you look into your future, is Raj in it?'

James nodded.

'And children?'

'Yes, I think so.'

'Then the future is now!' Helen said. 'It's arrived before you wanted it, but it is what it is. What would Paul want, do you think? Wouldn't he tell you to live life while you can? We've no idea what lies around the corner. I think he'd be happy for you, James. Don't you?'

A tear rolled down James's cheek. 'I don't want Paul to think I've forgotten about him,' he croaked. He pulled off his glove and wiped away the tears with the back of his hand.

'He'd never think that,' Helen insisted. 'And I tell you something else. Your little boy will have an awesome godfather watching over him!'

James laughed shakily, then let out a long breath. 'You're right,' he said. 'Thanks, Helen.' He gave her a watery smile. 'I'm sorry to dump all this on you. I guess I've been bottling everything up.'

'Oh, now. Never ever do that,' Helen told him. She patted his arm, then grinned. 'Negative thoughts are like pus in an abscess,' she said. 'Better out than in!'

James laughed. 'Yuck,' he said, screwing up his nose. 'You vet nurses have the grossest analogies!'

'Anything to help!' Helen reached over and hugged

him, then stepped back. She checked her watch. Lunchtime was definitely past. 'I'm sorry, but I really must be going,' she told him.

James smiled. 'I'm glad you came,' he said. 'Sorry I didn't have time to eat with you. You can choose something on the way out. Eat it on your way home.'

'Thanks,' Helen said. 'That'd be lovely. I'm starving. And say hi to Raj from me. He really didn't spoil anything at the barbecue, I promise.'

Chapter Sixteen

Helen stopped in a layby halfway home and unwrapped her sandwich. She pushed open the door to let in some fresh air. Though it was hot outside, there was a breeze flowing down from the moors. She hoped she had helped James in some small way. He must feel as if the future was hurtling towards him like a train.

She ate the brie and cranberry baguette she'd chosen, then started the engine. It wasn't only James that was facing an uncertain future, she thought. Her own life seemed to be running away from her, and she had no idea where she wanted to go. She remembered what she'd asked James. If she looked into her future, was Seb in it? She didn't know. Not for sure. But the future without him looked equally bleak. Seb was a good person. He'd anchored her these past couple of years, and given her so much happiness. What would life look like if they chose separate paths?

* * *

Seb rang her mobile as she was pulling up outside Animal Ark. 'Hello.' He sounded so unsure of his welcome that Helen felt a spasm of pain. Had they really arrived at a place where they couldn't call one another without worrying?

'Hi, Seb.' She tried to make her voice warm.

'I was wondering whether you'd come out with me tonight?' he said. 'We could try the new Lebanese place in Walton.'

Helen felt her spirits lift a little. Maybe this was what they needed? They hadn't been out together for ages. 'I'd like that,' she said.

When work was over, she headed home. She pulled out her favourite shorts from the wardrobe and pulled on a crisp cotton shirt that she knew Seb liked. She dug in her bedside drawer for the gold necklace Seb had bought her when they started going out. You'll do, she told her reflection in the mirror. She put Isla in her bed, then closed the door. Lucy settled quickly in the kitchen without any of the whining she'd been prone to lately. It felt like a good omen. Maybe she and Seb could hit the reset button.

Seb was waiting outside the restaurant when she arrived and Helen felt a flutter of pleasure. He was wearing a light-coloured blazer over a stripy crew-necked T-shirt and beige chinos, and his spiky hair was still damp from the shower.

'Hello,' he said. He kissed her lightly, then glanced at his watch. 'We should go in. I booked for half seven.'

Helen followed him inside. The waiter took them to a table by the window and brought them menus. The restaurant was decorated in warm shades of terracotta and brown. Seb hadn't needed to book a table, she thought. Square wooden tables stood empty all around them, though the rich aromas emanating from the kitchen smelled delicious. It was probably just Monday-evening quiet.

Across the table, Seb seemed to be studying his menu very closely. Helen glanced down at her own. Every item on the first page seemed to involve aubergines and courgettes. She flipped it over to look at the other side. Mandy would like it here. There were loads of vegetarian dishes.

'What are you going to have?' she asked Seb.

He looked up. 'I'm not all that hungry,' he admitted. 'I might stick with the hot mezze. We could share, if you like.'

Helen looked down the list of dishes. Only one aubergine dish, and the rest sounded very tasty. 'That's fine with me.'

Seb called the waiter over and gave him their order. Another couple came into the restaurant and sat down. Their drinks arrived and then their food. Seb seemed quiet as he pulled apart a vine leaf stuffed with minced lamb and rice.

'I saw James today,' Helen said.

Seb looked across at her, eyebrows raised. 'How was he?'

'Not too bad,' Helen said. 'He was talking about Raj and the little boy, Taresh.'

'That's good,' Seb replied. He fiddled with his empty vine leaf. 'I've got some news,' he announced.

Helen felt uneasy as she looked at him. Was he going to tell her what the phone call had been about?

'I had an interview last week,' he began. A flush was creeping up his face. 'Well, two actually. I've been offered a job. Still in animal welfare, but more senior.'

Helen felt a rush of relief. Was that the big secret? 'Congratulations!'

But Seb was still staring down at his plate. When he looked up, his eyes were sad. 'It's in Aberdeen,' he said.

'*Aberdeen?*' Helen's voice came out as a squeak.

'Aberdeen,' Seb confirmed. 'It's a newly created post with special funding. They called me up about it and asked me to apply. I had to make a quick decision. I have to start training the week after next.'

Helen felt as if all the breath had been punched out of her. 'Why didn't you tell me?'

Seb let out a heavy sigh. 'I did try,' he said. 'The night after they'd phoned I came round. I asked if you'd consider moving in with me.' He swallowed and Helen could see the muscles of his jaw standing out. 'I thought you'd say yes,' he said. 'I was going to ask you to come to Scotland with me, but you seemed so angry. Then after that we always seemed to be arguing about one thing or another.'

Helen stared at him. There was a numb feeling in her chest. Even if he'd told her what was going on, would she have wanted to leave Welford and start all over again somewhere new? She wasn't sure. Hadn't she been craving adventure? *Why didn't he tell me?*

Seb crumbled a piece of flatbread onto his plate. 'I really thought you'd come with me,' he said. 'But things haven't been right between us recently, have they?'

Helen could barely move. Her whole body felt heavy. He was right. Their relationship had been so comfortable that it had hit her like a ton of bricks when it had begun to go downhill, but it was getting impossible to imagine they had a future together.

Seb reached across the table. His fingers felt warm when he held her hand. 'If you wanted to be with me,' he said, 'you'd have jumped at the chance to move in together. I hadn't realised we were drifting apart.'

Helen felt a lump forming in her throat. Her hand was shaking, while Seb's seemed completely steady. There was a part of her that wanted to tell him it wasn't true, that she loved him and would travel to the ends of the earth with him, but the words wouldn't come. They had reached a fork in the road that had been looming for a while. Time to choose one way or the other.

'I'm really sorry,' she whispered.

'I know you are,' he replied. His eyes were telling her he understood. 'So am I. I love you, Helen, but it isn't going to work, is it?'

Helen swallowed. Tears welled up, threatening to overflow. She put her hands on the table and pushed herself upright.

Seb looked up at her. 'You don't have to go now,' he said.

Helen took a deep breath. 'I do,' she said. 'Otherwise I'll just embarrass both of us in public.' She felt the urge to reach out to him, but she kept her arms by her sides. 'Take care, Seb,' she said. 'Good luck in Aberdeen. I hope it goes well.'

She stumbled outside, climbed into her car and put the key in the ignition. If she looked round, she would be able to see Seb in the window. She turned the key. The car burst into life and, without looking back, she drove off.

Helen clawed her way out of a deep, troubled sleep when the alarm went off the next morning. Isla was lying in the bed beside her. Lucy had been barking in the night. Helen had brought Isla upstairs to get some peace.

Seb. Thinking of him brought a stab of pain. She and Seb had split up. He was going to Scotland and she was staying here in Welford. She pulled the duvet up under her chin, blinking away tears, but she wasn't the only one who was awake. Isla whined, then scrambled up the bed and put her wet nose in Helen's ear. Helen sighed. Life was marching on, whether she wanted it to or not.

'Okay, okay, no lie-in for me,' she said.

Isla wagged her tail as Helen sat up. She dragged herself out of bed. Lucy was waiting downstairs and Helen crouched to fuss her. For a moment, Lucy's tail wagged, but when she saw Isla, her tail went down and her ears flattened. Helen let the dogs out, fed them and went for a shower. She couldn't face eating anything. Seb, Seb, Seb. He was on her mind with every step she took. There as she put the dogs in the car. There as she took them out again.

'Good morning!' Mandy called as Helen walked in to Hope Meadows.

'Hi,' Helen said, and stopped when she felt her voice wobbling. The sight of Mandy, the temptation to pour everything out, was bringing her close to tears yet again.

'Isn't it a glorious morning?' Mandy was standing in the reception area, cuddling Ziggy, the sweetest of all her cat rescues. The fluffy little tabby had tucked himself under Mandy's chin and was purring loudly.

Helen managed to drag a smile onto her face. 'Lovely,' she agreed. She gazed at her friend. Mandy had an air of excitement about her that couldn't be explained by Ziggy or the sunshine. 'Is something going on?' she asked.

Mandy turned to face Helen. Her blue eyes were sparkling and she was grinning so broadly that she would have outsmiled the Cheshire Cat. 'I've got something to show you,' she said. 'I'll just put Ziggy away.' She disappeared and returned in a moment, still buzzing. She crouched down behind the desk. Helen could see she was fishing inside her rucksack. With a flourish, Mandy pulled out a small green leather box. Prising it open, she held it out. Inside was a simple silver-coloured signet ring.

'Oh!' Helen felt a wave of self-pity. *Pull yourself together.* 'Oh, Mandy,' she cried. 'I thought you'd never ask.'

'You're hilarious,' Mandy announced, pretending to cuff Helen. 'It's for Jimmy. As you well know. I'm going to ask him to marry me.'

Helen took a deep breath. *Just be happy for her.*

Mandy's face had turned adorably pink. 'I know it's not usual for men to wear engagement rings, but I wanted to get him something,' she went on. 'Look.' She held out the ring to show Helen an engraving on the bezel: a bird of prey.

'Is that an eagle?'

'It's a red kite,' Mandy explained. 'I followed a red kite to its nest the very first day I met Jimmy.' She sounded so happy, Helen thought she was going to float away like a balloon.

To her dismay, there was a huge lump in Helen's throat. Mandy looked up from the ring. 'What's wrong?' Helen felt herself crumpling. A tear slid down her cheek. 'What is it?' Mandy asked again, her voice urgent.

Helen swallowed hard. 'I'm sorry,' she whispered. 'I'm really happy for you, honestly. It's a great idea. You two are made for each other.' She stopped and pressed her hand to her mouth, but the tears were coming faster now.

Mandy's face was stricken. She set the ring down, put

her arm around Helen and led her to a chair. 'Please tell me what's wrong.'

'Seb broke up with me.' It came out close to a wail. Helen gathered herself and tried again. 'He's got a new job in Scotland and he doesn't want me to go with him.' It wasn't the whole story, but it summed up her feelings right now.

'He's going to Scotland?' Mandy looked astonished. 'Without you? Seriously?' She paused and now Helen could see anger in her face. 'Why would he do that? Didn't he tell you what he was planning?'

She sounded so outraged that Helen held up a hand to stop her. 'He didn't tell me till last night,' she said, 'but it's not his fault. Not in the way you're thinking. We haven't been getting on for a while.' She ran her hands through her hair, which was still damp from her shower. 'We want different things,' she said finally. 'It wasn't just him. I've been thinking about ending it myself. It's just . . . it's a shock, that's all.' She tried to smile. 'Sorry,' she said. 'I didn't want to come and weep all over you. Especially when you have such lovely news with the ring and everything.'

Mandy rubbed Helen's shoulder. 'Don't worry about that.'

Helen pulled a tissue from her pocket. She blew her nose, then reached up to tighten her ponytail. Brushing away a final tear, she squared her shoulders. 'I need to keep busy,' she said. 'What would you like me to do first?'

'I've done almost everything. There's only Fluffybonce

left,' Mandy said. 'She needs food and water, but there's no rush.' She squeezed Helen's arm. 'I'm really, really sorry about you and Seb. You two always seemed like the perfect match.'

Helen sighed. 'We were,' she said. 'At least, it felt like it. But people change, I guess.'

Mandy nodded. 'Maybe it'll be easier if he's in Scotland. At least you won't have to see him every day.'

'I suppose so,' Helen agreed. She forced herself to smile. 'Honestly, men!' she exclaimed. 'Why do we waste so much emotion on them?'

'Well, some of them are worth it,' Mandy pointed out. 'But if Seb and you weren't right, then it's probably better to end it now than spend months fighting for a lost cause.'

Helen nodded. 'At least one of us has chosen well!' She was determined not to spoil Mandy's excitement completely.

'Let's hope so,' Mandy replied. 'Remember, I haven't asked Jimmy yet.' But Helen could tell that Mandy knew Jimmy would say yes. How wonderful it must be to feel so confident about the future, and the person you wanted to share it with. Mandy was very lucky – but Helen couldn't think of anyone more deserving of a happy ever after.

Chapter Seventeen

After Helen had seen to Fluffybonce, she walked round to the surgery. Adam was preparing his consulting room, Rachel was waiting for the computer to start and Toby was already out on a call.

'I've asked Dad if he can spare you for the morning,' Mandy said as Helen came in. 'Would you like to come out and give me a hand at Six Oaks?'

Helen's heart rose. Moondance wouldn't be at the stables, but she always felt better being around horses. 'I'd love to,' she said.

There was a welcome breeze when they pulled up in the cobbled yard. Molly appeared from the tack room as they climbed out of Mandy's RAV4. She was wearing a yellow tank top and blue shorts, but she had sturdy jodhpur boots on her feet. Helen could remember being told off one day when she'd arrived in sandals. Proper footwear was the rule around horses, whatever the weather.

Most of the horses were inside, waiting for their teeth to be checked and treated. Helen walked over to Coco's stable. He was a stocky bay gelding. He and Moondance often stood head to tail together when they were turned out. He greeted Helen by stretching out his velvety muzzle and snuffling in her ear. Helen put her hand up and held on to his neck, closing her eyes for a moment, breathing in the sweet scent of horse. 'Are you missing Moondance?' she whispered. Coco stamped his foot and Helen opened her eyes again. 'Me too,' she told him.

Mandy joined them with the dental gag in her hand. It had always looked truly fearsome to Helen: a great metal thing attached to a bridle headpiece, with two plates to fit round the teeth and a ratchet to prise the jaws open.

Molly ran through the list of horses, telling them what work was needed for each. As well as general rasping, one of the mares had a large hook on one of her upper molars, and there was a two-year-old gelding with a wolf tooth to be removed. Bill's teeth were due for a check, and Molly mentioned that he had been coughing a bit recently, too. Helen was very fond of the ancient draught horse that Mandy had rescued two years ago. He'd been in an awful state then, but thanks to Six Oaks and Molly, he had enjoyed two wonderful years of contented retirement.

'Can you hold this?' Mandy asked Helen, holding out the gag. 'I need to sort out my tools.' Helen took the heavy gag. Coco looked at it with suspicion, then snorted. Helen gave his nose a rub, then hid the gag behind her, leaning on the wall so Coco couldn't see it. There was no point getting him upset before they even started.

Mandy returned with both the normal rasp and an electric one with a power pack that was tied to a belt round her waist. In spite of the rather industrial nature of the equipment, horse dentistry was a delicate and painstaking process. Coco stood patiently with Helen steadying his head while Mandy operated the noisy rasp to smooth the sharpened growth on his molars. In a few minutes, it was over.

'One down,' Molly said with a grin. She had been watching from the doorway.

'What next?' Mandy lifted a hand to push back a strand of hair that had stuck to her forehead.

'Can we check Bill?' Molly asked. They walked over to the stable where the ancient horse was standing with his head over the half-door. His eyes were partly closed, as if he was enjoying the sun. 'He hasn't coughed for a while,' Molly said, running her hand down Bill's huge head, 'but he started again about half an hour after I'd brought him in this morning. He had quite a cough before we turned him out in the spring, but he seemed to get better.'

Helen watched as Mandy started to examine the gentle horse. She seemed to spend a lot of time listening to his lungs. Finally she put the stethoscope back in her pocket and turned to face Molly. 'So he's really only been coughing when he's inside?' she checked.

'Pretty much,' Molly agreed.

Mandy glanced at Bill again and he turned to lean his muzzle on her shoulder. 'I'm afraid it sounds like

COPD,' she said. 'That means he's become highly sensitive to the dust you get in hay and bedding.' She put up a hand and stroked Bill's whiskery nose. 'See how he goes,' she said. 'If he's fine when you turn him back out, we don't need to do anything at the moment, but if he struggles when he comes inside, we might need to do some tests.'

Molly nodded, though she looked sad. 'I thought it might be that,' she admitted.

'There are lots of things we can do to help him,' Mandy said. 'Different bedding, haylage instead of hay. And of course, he's a Hope Meadows rescue, so we can help with the costs.' She walked out of the stable. 'One good thing is,' she said, 'I checked his teeth and he doesn't need anything doing. We can turn him out straight away if you like.'

Molly clipped a rope to Bill's head collar and led him to the gate that opened into the nearest paddock. Bill followed her through. He was so placid, it was like a mountain being led by a leprechaun. Molly removed the head collar, then slapped Bill's rump, and he broke into a ponderous trot as he realised he was free again.

'Let's tackle Munro next,' said Molly. 'He hates the gag, remember?'

'I'll get the sedative ready,' Mandy said.

Munro was a Clydesdale cross. He was usually as docile as he was huge, but Helen knew he despised having his teeth looked at. Mandy returned with a syringe and popped the injection into his muscular neck.

'We'll give him a few minutes,' she said, rubbing his skin.

They strolled over and sat on the low wall that flanked the cobbled yard. A pair of white ducks waddled over and Helen watched them dabble their feet in a rather slimy puddle.

'Hello!' There was a shout from the lane and Susan Collins appeared. Her dark hair was neatly tied back and she was wearing a white T-shirt over beige jodhs. She flopped on the wall beside them, fanning herself with her hand. 'Goodness, it's hot,' she exclaimed.

'It'll be cooler up on the fell,' Molly said.

'Where's Jack?' Mandy asked.

'Douglas has taken him fishing for the day. Not that they'll catch anything. Jack would hate it if they did.'

Mandy laughed.

'I'm very lucky,' Susan admitted. 'Mum's away and with the summer holidays, Jack's bouncing off the walls.' She looked very pleased to have escaped.

'Handy man to have around, your Douglas,' Molly commented.

'He certainly is.'

Mandy moved her hand and gave Helen's fingers a squeeze. Helen felt tears prickling behind her eyes, but she felt a little comforted.

'You found Douglas on LoveSpark, didn't you?' Molly said to Susan. 'Maybe I should join. I've been single way too long.'

'You can try,' said Susan, 'but there were a whole load

of frogs on there. I met far too many of them before I found a prince. Maybe you should look closer to home. What about your new vet, Mandy? He's quite something, isn't he?'

'He is quite something,' Mandy conceded.

'Not that you're looking, of course.' Molly nudged her. 'Lucky Jimmy,' she added.

Jimmy and Molly had dated for a while, Helen remembered. But neither of them seemed to regret the split and Molly certainly didn't resent Mandy.

'Mind you,' said Susan, 'I'm not sure that Toby is a safe bet. There seems to be a new rumour every day about some woman he's picked up.'

A look of irritation passed over Molly's face. Did she have a thing for Toby? Susan wondered. 'I bet most of them aren't true,' Molly said. 'Imogen Parker-Smythe was all over him at one point. She's probably started a whole load of tall tales about him since he rejected her.'

Helen raised her eyebrows. Molly seemed rather protective of Toby's reputation for someone completely uninvolved.

Mandy shook her head. 'You should know better than to listen to the Welford Whispers,' she told Susan. 'I don't believe them, and I work with Toby. He's far more private than you might think.'

Molly leaned over and nudged Helen. 'You're very quiet. Has the delicious Toby confided any of his deep dark secrets to you?'

Helen felt as if her cheeks had caught fire, but before

she could speak, Molly laughed. 'Just kidding,' she said. 'But seriously, do you think he has something to hide? Surely nobody can be that gorgeous and charming and clever without a skeleton in the closet?' She grinned. 'What's he doing in a backwater like Animal Ark when he could be on TV?'

'I wouldn't call Animal Ark a backwater!' Helen objected, though she felt a touch of amusement that Molly had said that right in front of Mandy.

Molly waved a hand dismissively. 'Oh, you know what I mean,' she said. 'There are TV shows about vets on every channel. Toby'd be perfect. He'd make a fortune!'

'Maybe he's not interested in money,' Helen said. She felt suddenly like standing up for Toby. Maybe he didn't give away much, but no wonder with all this speculation.

'Maybe his secret is that he's fabulously wealthy and only works for the love of animals,' Susan suggested.

Mandy laughed. 'You'd really have to love animals to spend as much time trimming cows' feet as Toby does.'

Helen was relieved when Mandy looked at her watch. 'Munro's sedative should be working by now,' she announced.

Susan headed to the tack room to fetch a saddle and bridle for her ride. Helen followed Mandy over to Munro's stable.

The big horse's head was hanging very low. Without having to be asked, Helen fetched the tall padded head-stand from Mandy's car. It was like a tiny stool on one long metal leg. She propped it under Munro's feathered chin to hold his head up. It was much easier than trying to support him with her shoulder. She held Munro's head steady as Mandy placed the rasp in his mouth and began to work.

'Are either of you going to the cricket match on Saturday?' Molly almost had to shout to make herself heard over the rasp. 'There's a lovely tea at half-time and then Pimm's and a barbecue at the Fox and Goose after.'

Molly was a big cricket fan, Helen remembered. Seb had told her Molly was often there to cheer on the local teams. She felt a sudden stab of regret. Maybe she should have been there too, supporting Seb.

'Should be a good match,' Molly went on, still yelling. 'I hope Seb's on form.'

The noise of the rasp came to a stop. Helen gulped. 'I'm afraid Seb won't be there,' she said. 'He's moving to Scotland for a new job.'

Molly frowned. 'What about you? Aren't you going with him?'

Helen winced. Molly was lovely, but she could be painfully direct. 'I . . . I'm staying here,' she admitted. By sheer effort of will, she kept her voice calm. She wasn't going to break down. Not here, not now. 'We've broken up.'

Molly was gazing at her, though Helen couldn't tell whether the intent look in her eyes was fascination or sympathy. 'I'm sorry,' she said finally. She patted Helen's shoulder. 'God, men are awful, aren't they? Sometimes

I think we're better off single!' She grinned at Helen. 'We can be each other's wingwoman, if you like,' she said. 'Mind you, it does mean the Walton team has lost one of its best players.' Molly had the grace to look embarrassed. 'Not that that's the important thing right now!' she admitted. 'Me and my big mouth.'

Helen smiled, relieved that Molly had lightened the mood. 'It's fine,' she said. 'I know how it is with you cricket groupies. Nothing matters more than who's the last man in . . . or the number of runs . . . or whatever it is that's important on a cricket field.'

Molly raised her eyebrows. 'I'm sure those things are all very nice,' she said, 'but mostly I go to see all those good Yorkshire men in tight white trousers. And the Pimm's,' she added. 'The Pimm's is definitely important.'

Munro tossed his head as Helen and Mandy dissolved into giggles.

They arrived back at Animal Ark just before lunchtime. Mandy looked at Helen as she pulled up in the car park. 'I'm going to head home for a few minutes,' she said. 'I need to let the dogs out. Would you like to come?'

Helen shook her head. 'It'd be lovely, but not today, okay?'

Mandy patted her shoulder. 'Of course.'

Helen slid out of the car and walked inside. Rachel had just pulled a lunchbox out of the fridge. Her face lit up. 'You're back,' she said. She looked at Helen hope-fully. 'Would it be okay if I popped out? Brandon said he'd meet me for a picnic on the green if I had time.'

'That's fine,' Helen said.

Rachel nipped out of the door and walked briskly down the drive. Helen let out a sigh of relief. She was very grateful to Mandy for getting her out this morning, but it would be good to have some time alone. She booted up her account on the computer, checked the afternoon's patient list, prepared the consent forms for tomorrow's patients and then pulled out an insurance form to complete. She finalised two bills and after that went to each of the consulting rooms, checking all the syringes and needles were topped up. Short of pulling out a bucket and starting a spring clean, there was nothing left to do. She decided to go and see Tango.

She opened the door of the residential unit and slipped inside. Tango gazed at her through the bars and let out a rasping meow. Helen opened the door to his cage and carefully picked him up. He pressed the undamaged side of his face into her chest and began to purr.

Helen thought back to the night of his accident. She and Seb had been in the middle of an argument, but as soon as Seb heard Tango was hurt, he'd reassured Helen he would look after the dogs and sent her to help. A wave of sadness rushed over her. She felt a tear slide down her cheek, and then another. Burying her face in Tango's fur, she let out a sob.

She was startled by the sound of the door clicking

open. Frantically wiping her tears away, she turned round. Toby was standing behind her.

'What's wrong? It's not Tango, is it?'

Helen gulped, shaking her head. 'It's Seb. We've broken up.'

'Oh.' Toby looked surprised, and for a moment Helen wondered what he was thinking. Then he reached out and put his hand on her shoulder. 'It's always hard when that happens,' he said. 'I'm so sorry.'

He waited quietly, his hand warm and heavy. He reached out with his other hand and stroked Tango until Helen had gathered herself.

'Better now?' he asked.

Helen nodded. 'Thanks,' she said.

Toby smiled. 'Maybe you need a spell in the residential unit,' he suggested. He tickled Tango under his chin and the big cat began to purr. 'It seems to have done this old chap the power of good!'

Helen made a sound, half sob, half laughter. How lovely it would be to have someone to look after her until she didn't feel so broken.

'I'm really sorry,' Toby said, 'but I've got to go out on a call. I only popped in to get some penicillin. Will you be okay?'

'I'll be fine,' Helen told him. 'Thank you.' With a last pat on her shoulder, Toby turned and walked out.

Helen put Tango back in his cage and watched him flop down on the blanket. She suddenly felt very alone. Normally she would have gone to Gemma for hugs and wine, but Gemma was away. Moondance, too. She still had Lucy, she thought. She felt a stab of pain. And Isla. How come she could love them both so much, yet they couldn't get on?

She pulled her shoulders back. Mandy was going to help her with Isla. Gemma and Moondance wouldn't be away for ever. Seb had gone, but the world wasn't coming to an end. She took a deep breath and marched back out into the clinic.

Chapter Eighteen

Helen was driving to work the following Tuesday when she realised that a whole week had passed since her devastating evening with Seb. Almost every day, Helen had reached for her phone to text him, but each time she had put the phone away. Sooner or later she would make contact, but for now it seemed better to let him get on with his move. She knew the split had been inevitable. And surely it was better to be single than in a relationship where arguments and ill-temper were the norm?

It hadn't been a bad week, all in all. Helen had spent an evening with Anneka Mellor, baking fruit pies, and Susan had popped over to Sunrise Farm with Jack. Helen had turned down Molly's invitation to a night of speed dating in York. That wasn't exactly how she wanted to get over Seb.

The evening with Jack and Susan had been very sweet. She and Susan had shared some wine while Jack played with the dogs. He had listened carefully to Helen's explanation that Isla couldn't see.

'We have a cat that can't hear,' he had told her, his

face serious. 'But Mandy helped us lots with looking after him.'

Helen glanced over her shoulder. Isla was sitting in the back seat with her nose pressed to the partly open window. Lucy was curled up on the front passenger seat. The relationship between the two dogs had resolved into some kind of truce, but surely it must be possible to do better for both of them? Mandy had said she would help, but between the split from Seb and a busy week at work, Helen hadn't had a chance to follow it up. She would ask Mandy when she got in, she decided.

She pulled up outside the clinic. The weather had broken overnight with a dramatic storm, but the sky had already cleared again. Helen climbed out of the car, took Lucy into the cottage, popped Isla into a kennel in the rescue centre, then headed into the surgery.

Adam was behind the desk, tapping away at the computer. He looked up when Helen came in. 'Morning,' he said.

'Is Mandy here yet?' Helen asked. She should ask about help for Isla while she had it in her mind, but Adam shook his head.

'She's taking Abi and Max back to their mum's in Walton,' he told her. 'Jimmy had an early meeting at Running Wild.'

The door between the cottage and the clinic burst open and Emily rushed in. 'Bill Ward just rang on the house phone,' she said. 'Sable's been hit by a car. I told him to come straight in.'

'Is he badly hurt?' Helen asked. Bill Ward had worked alongside Frank Conway as a postman for years. He loved his cat Sable as much as the Conways loved Jess.

'He thinks he has a broken leg,' Emily said.

Adam pushed out his chair and stood up. 'Can you get the X-ray machine fired up?' he said to Helen. He leaned over to check the appointment list. 'Luckily it's quiet this morning,' he said, 'and Mandy should be here in a minute.'

'Where's Toby?' Emily asked.

'He's out at Riverside looking at a bull,' Adam told her.

Emily nodded. 'I'll sit here with the phones until you're done, Helen,' she said.

Helen ran into the X-ray room, flicked the power switch on the wall, then held down the button on the machine, watching until the numbers stopped flashing. She looked around the room. Everything was in place. She headed back out into reception.

A car pulled up outside. It was probably Mr Ward. Helen turned and set off to open the door, but stopped dead. Seb's dark green van had drawn up outside. Helen felt her heart hammering. Had he come to say goodbye? The van door swung open and a short, sturdy red-haired young woman stepped out. The heat suddenly left Helen's face. The woman was wearing a familiar uniform and carrying a clipboard.

'Goodness me!' Emily exclaimed. 'It's the new animal welfare officer. Mandy said she was coming, but it slipped my mind.'

The woman had closed the van door and was striding towards the entrance.

'I'm sorry, Helen,' Emily said. 'Would you mind showing her round Hope Meadows? I can manage here until Mandy arrives.'

Helen realised her legs were shaking. Seb had already gone. The clinic door opened and the young woman marched across the room, smiling. She shook Helen's hand and then Emily's. 'Hi,' she said, 'I'm Jo Rankin. I just started as Walton's new animal welfare officer. I feel so lucky! I've always wanted to work in this part of the world.'

Helen stared at her.

'Will you give Jo the guided tour?' Emily prompted.

Helen forced herself to smile. 'I'd love to,' she said.

She led Jo outside and across the parking area to the rescue centre. Jo followed her through the door and stopped.

'What an amazing place.'

Helen felt the usual sense of pride that she felt when showing newcomers round Hope Meadows. Like the surroundings, the building itself was stunning: made of stone and wood and soaring beams. Everything was clean and well maintained.

Jo seemed highly impressed when she saw the well-equipped rooms, the cat kennels, the wildlife room, the small-furries room and the dog kennels. She spent a few minutes in each and listened with interest while Helen explained about Mandy's interest in animal behaviour and dog training.

'It's all very professional,' Jo commented. 'Do you have an isolation ward for sick animals?' She looked round, as if expecting to see another door, then turned back to Helen, eyebrows raised.

'We certainly do.' Helen took her outside and led her round to the quarantine area. 'We have a separate door so they're not sharing airspace,' she told Jo.

Jo was clearly knowledgeable and very friendly, but Helen was glad when the visit was over. She watched the familiar van drive away with a fresh pang. Seb hadn't even said goodbye.

Emily was still behind the desk. 'How did it go?' she asked.

'Fine.' Helen kept her voice brisk.

The door to Adam's consulting room opened and Bill Ward appeared. 'Thanks very much, Adam,' he said.

Adam followed him out. 'No problem,' he said. 'As far as I could tell from the X-rays, there's nothing broken. He's a bit sore, but the painkillers will kick in soon. We'll keep him in today, just to be on the safe side, but I'm sure he'll be fine.'

Bill's green eyes crinkled with relief. 'I'm so glad,' he said. 'I felt such an idiot. He's never gone out the front before. Normally he goes out behind the house where there's only the sheep to worry about.'

Adam patted him on the shoulder. 'Our cat was hit by a car not long ago,' he said. 'Cats will be cats. You can't keep them shut in, not if they're used to going out.'

Bill nodded at Emily and Helen, sketched a wave and walked out.

Mandy's car drew up as Bill's van left. 'Sorry I'm late,' she gasped. 'I got held up behind a herd of cows.'

'You missed the new welfare officer,' Emily told her.

Mandy smacked her forehead with the heel of her hand. 'I'm sorry,' she said. 'It went clean out of my mind.'

'Helen showed her round,' Emily said.

Mandy glanced at Helen. 'Thanks,' she said. A look of concern passed over her face, as if she realised that Helen might have found the visit difficult. 'Did it go okay?'

Helen smiled. 'Fine. Jo was very impressed.'

She was glad when lunchtime came round and Mandy and Emily disappeared into the cottage for lunch. They had invited her, but she had made the excuse that she had some admin to catch up on. She found it easier if she could have a break from everyone in the middle of the day. She finished updating her notes while eating a sandwich, then swept the floor. It was amazing how much dirt came into the waiting room in the summer.

She opened the door to the cat ward quietly to check on Sable. Tango had moved back into the cottage, where Emily was looking after him, so Sable was in solitary splendour. He was sleeping when Helen went in, but as soon as he heard the door, he woke up and stared at her. Like all Persian cats, Sable had huge eyes, which often looked full of disdain for the humans who were bothering him. Despite his glare, Helen went over to the cage and stroked him until he was purring.

'You're an old fusspot really, aren't you?' she told him. She closed the cage door and went out just as Toby rushed in.

'Hi, Helen,' he said. 'I was hoping you'd be here. I'm really sorry to ask this, but could you do some washing for me again? It's too hot for waterproofs just now so I was wearing overalls, but I was at a farrowing and they stink of pig. I've got a spare set, but only one.'

Helen pulled a face. Not only did the overalls stink of pig, but there was blood and afterbirth staining both knees, not to mention a smear of poo right across his chest. 'You look like you've been rolling around the pig pen,' she said.

'I pretty much was,' he confessed.

'Did the farrowing go okay?'

'Mother and piglets all well.' Toby beamed. 'How's your day been?'

Helen shrugged. 'Not too bad.'

'That's good.' He looked as if he meant it. He patted his overall pockets. They were bulging and Helen could see the head of his stethoscope hanging out, as well as what looked like the plunger of a twenty-millilitre syringe. Goodness knows what else was in there.

'Don't forget to empty your pockets!' she called after him as he dived into the washroom.

He emerged ten minutes later, dressed in fresh overalls and looking disturbingly handsome with damp hair and glowing skin. 'Overalls are on the floor,' he said. 'I really am very grateful.'

Helen laughed. 'I'll send you the bill,' she said. She watched as he walked out of the door to his car, then headed into the shower room to collect his dirty overalls. She lifted them up, holding them at arm's length. An empty pill box rolled from the pocket. Helen bent down to pick it up and something caught her eye. There was an envelope lying on the floor under the wooden bench. She stared at the address.

The Rt Hon Tobias Auberon Wemyss Gordon
Craighenry Castle
Caithness
Scotland

Rt Hon? Helen frowned. That was short for Right Honourable, wasn't it? Was Toby some kind of lord? She looked down again. His address was a *castle*? Toby Gordon? Tobias? It was definitely his. Why did he say that his dad ran a business? She recalled that Toby hadn't told her what kind of business. Maybe lords did run businesses. She'd never met one.

Helen walked slowly through into reception. The envelope was empty. She took one last look at it, screwed it up and threw it in the bin. Toby had kept his identity a secret. It wasn't her place to tell anyone, not even Mandy. Toby had been a mystery already and now the mystery had deepened. Everyone was speculating about Toby

Gordon's background, but only Helen knew the truth. She hugged the secret to herself. It felt rather good.

Mandy returned after lunch and went straight to check on Sable. The cottage door opened again and Emily appeared. She looked paler than she had this morning.

'Are you okay?' Helen asked.

Emily smiled. 'I'm a bit tired, but I need to get the holiday rota sorted out, and Mandy wants to order a new brand of dog food.'

Mandy came back out from the residential unit. She frowned when she saw Emily. 'You're not doing my food order, are you? I told you I'd sort it out later.'

'It's no problem,' Emily insisted. 'Just that and the rota and then I'm going for a walk. It's much better for me now it's not quite so hot.'

'Just don't do too much,' Mandy urged.

'I won't,' Emily promised. She winked at Helen.

The door opened and the first client arrived for afternoon surgery.

'Hello, Mrs Burton,' Helen said. Mrs Burton's cat Sandy was here to have stitches removed.

'You can come through now,' Mandy called.

The door opened again and Helen beamed when she saw who it was. 'James!' she cried. James held the door to let Seamus and Lily trot in.

'Hello.' Emily looked up. 'How lovely to see you. How are things?'

'Pretty good,' James told her. Seamus and Lily dashed across the room and rushed behind the desk to greet Emily. Both their tails were wagging frantically. James grinned. 'Well, one thing's for certain,' he commented. 'Neither of those dogs is scared of the vet's.'

'What can we do for you today?' Helen asked. 'Is it just a social visit, or . . .'

'Kind of,' James said. 'I'm visiting my parents, but I wondered if you or Mandy could give me a hand clipping the dogs' claws.' He smiled ruefully as he glanced down at Lily, who had returned to his side and was sitting on his foot. 'I know I should be able to do it myself,' he admitted, 'but Lily's a terrible wriggler. I'm terrified of cutting them too short and going into the quick.'

'I'll gladly give you a hand,' Helen said. She stood up just as Mandy's door opened and Mrs Burton reappeared. Helen sat down again to print out Sandy's bill. Mandy greeted Seamus and Lily, who looked ecstatic to see her.

When Mrs Burton had left, Mandy looked at the computer screen. 'I've got a few minutes before my next client,' she said. 'I'll help you with the nail clipping, if you like.'

They took the dogs into Mandy's consulting room. James hoisted Lily onto the table. Mandy wrapped one arm around her neck and the other round her body to stop her pulling away. 'There are some treats over there.' Mandy pointed to a plastic box. 'Can you feed her them slowly, James? Hold them in your fingers and let her nibble on them.'

While Lily was focused on the treat, Helen gripped one of her front paws and wielded the clippers. 'At least she's got white nails,' she observed. 'Much easier to see the quick.'

'Is that it?' James asked when Helen lowered the fourth paw. He stroked Lily's head. 'You're making me look like a wuss for not doing the job myself.'

Mandy placed Lily gently on the floor. 'It's much easier with three of us,' she pointed out.

Seamus's claws were dark, but he sat so still that it was quite straightforward. James rubbed the dog's ears as he lifted him down. 'Thanks so much,' he said. He reached into his pocket and pulled out his mobile phone. 'I've got something to show you.'

He swiped the screen, then turned it to reveal a beaming brown-skinned baby. His cheeks were chubby and he had the most enormous dark eyes. 'This is Taresh,' James said.

'Raj's nephew?' Mandy said.

'Raj's son,' James corrected. 'Shortly to be my son too.'

Helen smiled. James looked so happy.

'You've decided to go through with the adoption?' Mandy sounded thrilled.

James nodded. His face had turned rather pink. 'It's still in the early stages but I've signed the initial paper-work,' he said. 'All I have to do now is get used to the idea of being called Dad!' He glanced down at the photograph again.

Mandy reached out and pulled him into a bear hug. 'That's amazing! You're amazing!' she said. 'Lucky Taresh. I'm so glad you decided to go ahead.'

James winked at Helen. 'It wasn't all down to me,' he admitted. 'I was being a bit of an idiot about it. Fortunately I had some rather excellent advice . . . as well as a nudge to remind me that I need to live the life I want now.'

Mandy turned to look at Helen. 'So we have you to thank, do we? You said you'd chatted when you were over in York, but you didn't tell me what about.' She grinned. 'Then again, you've always been one of the most sensible people I know.'

Helen shrugged. 'Much easier to give advice than take it,' she said. She took the phone from James's hand to study Taresh's picture again. 'Congratulations,' she said. 'He's a gorgeous little guy. It'll be wonderful to meet him.'

James fished in his shirt pocket and pulled out a leaflet. 'Raj and I have signed up for parenting classes with the local fostering agency. I've cleaned out a thousand animal cages but I've never changed a nappy!'

'Sounds great,' Mandy said.

'There's just one thing,' James said. 'Raj is going to provide Taresh with a legion of aunts and uncles, but I've no brothers or sisters. Would you two do me the honour of being honorary aunties?'

Mandy's eyes widened. 'That would be wonderful,' she said.

'As long as that means I can choose his first pet,' Helen added.

'And his second, and third,' Mandy joined in. 'I hope they'll all be from Hope Meadows.'

'Where else?' Helen replied.

James grinned. 'I think I should be off before you lumber me with half a dozen guinea pigs in a starter pack. Bye for now, Aunty Mandy and Aunty Helen!'

Chapter Nineteen

Though Helen's mood had been lifted by James's news, the afternoon was difficult. The contrast between Mandy and James's full lives and her own suddenly empty one was tough.

Evening surgery was busy, at least. There wasn't time to think as she saw the patients in and out, juggling clients for both Mandy and Adam. In a rare pause, she looked round the room. Mrs Jenkins was waiting with Sybil, her cat. He was having his claws clipped. Sybil had been named when he was a kitten. A routine visit to the surgery had revealed that Sybil should probably have been Cyril, but Mrs Jenkins had chosen to keep his name. Araminta Greenwood was in too. Her black cat, Pumpkin the Second, had been fighting again. Araminta was looking delightfully eccentric, as usual. She had to be more than eighty years old, but she still wore the trademark stripy tights and big black boots that had caused children to whisper she was a witch for as long as Helen could remember.

The door swung open and Susan Collins strolled in. Jack was holding her hand. 'Can I go see Sybil?' he asked when he spotted the tiger-striped tabby. Susan smiled as she let him go.

'What can I do for you today?' Helen asked.

'I need some worming tablets for Frostflake,' Susan said. 'And Jack wanted to ask if he could see Tango. He heard he'd been hit by a car and he was really worried.'

Poor Jack, Helen thought. Before Frostflake, Jack and Susan had had a cat called Marmalade. He'd died after a car had hit him. No wonder Jack was concerned. 'Tango's actually back home in the cottage,' she told Susan. 'I'll just check with Adam that it's okay to go in.' She stuck her head round Adam's door. 'Is it okay if I pop into the cottage with Susan and Jack?'

'Of course,' said Adam. 'Emily's just popped out for a few minutes, but the door's open.'

Helen took Jack's hand and led him and his mum through into the kitchen. Tango was lying on the window-sill in the sun. His face was almost fully healed and he stood up and stretched when they came in. Jack sat down on the floor and Helen put Tango on his knee. Jack bent down and studied Tango's scars.

'He was really hurt,' he said.

'He was,' Helen agreed. 'But Toby put him back together again like a jigsaw, and now he's good as new!'

Jack laughed. 'You're a jigsaw cat,' he told Tango, and the ginger cat purred.

Susan touched Helen's elbow to get her attention. 'Now we're somewhere private, there's something I want to tell you,' she murmured. 'I heard some rather alarming gossip and I know it's none of my business, but I thought you'd want to know. People are saying that Toby is the reason you and Seb broke up. That you and Toby have been seeing each other behind Seb's back.'

Helen felt her face turning red. She shook her head. 'That's rubbish,' she said. She felt a wave of anger. 'There's nothing going on between Toby and me! We're friends that's all. Seb and I . . . Seb and I . . .' She broke off and took a deep breath. 'Seb and I weren't getting on, that's all,' she said. 'There was no way I could go to Scotland with him. It really had nothing to do with Toby.'

Susan put a hand on Helen's shoulder. 'I know,' she said. 'I'm sorry. I didn't know when I saw you at Six Oaks that you and Seb had split up at all.' She blushed. 'We were all gossiping about Toby that day. I should have known better.' She gave Helen a squeeze. 'This'll be yesterday's news in no time, but I wanted to give you a heads-up. Better than hearing it from someone else, I hope.'

'Thanks,' Helen said. Her heart felt heavy as she took Jack and Susan back into the clinic and said goodbye. Gossip was nothing but a nuisance. She had felt sorry for Toby because there was so much speculation about him, and now she'd been dragged in too. Remembering the envelope with his home address, she felt doubly uncomfortable. If he wanted a bit of privacy, he deserved it. Not that being a member of the landed gentry was anything to be ashamed of, surely? Although knowing the people of Welford, they'd find something negative about it. Helen suddenly felt quite fierce. It would be a much better place if they all stopped gossiping and minded their own business!

The final half-hour of the day seemed to drag. There were so many things going round in her head that it was hard to concentrate, and she'd forgotten to ask Mandy whether she'd found anything out that would help Isla. She sighed as the last client came up to the desk.

'Long day?' Helen looked up. Araminta Greenwood was staring down her crooked nose at her.

'A bit,' Helen admitted. 'How did it go with Pumpkin?'

'Oh, not too bad.' Ms Greenwood waved a gnarled hand. 'He's a wild one, though.' She put her head on one side. 'You look sad,' she said. 'I expect you're pining after some young man or other, but really I recommend you get a cat.' For a moment, Helen wanted to laugh. Araminta Greenwood was the epitome of the crazy cat lady that nobody wanted to be, yet at eighty years old, she seemed much happier than Helen.

'Maybe I should,' she agreed. Would Lucy and Isla be united against a common enemy? Ms Greenwood walked out. She was remarkably nimble and Helen wondered what her secret was.

By the time Helen was able to go home, it suddenly seemed unbearable to go back to her empty house. Isla and Lucy should make it feel more like a home, but there were some nights when they turned it into a battleground. Helen thought for a moment. Even if she couldn't ask Mandy about the dogs right now, she could do some work with them herself. It was ages since she and Lucy had done a proper training session.

Leaving Isla in her kennel in the rescue centre, Helen went into the cottage to collect Lucy. They walked outside side by side, Lucy keeping to Helen's heel as if it was second nature. Once in the field behind Hope Meadows, they began to run through some familiar exercises. As well as the standard commands, Helen had taught Lucy some more difficult tasks, such as running to her and standing perfectly lined up by her side, then being sent out to do distance work.

For the first time in weeks, Helen felt uncomplicatedly happy. It was obvious, as Lucy cantered towards her at the end of the session, tongue lolling, that she felt the same. Yet even this caused a pang. Seb had said Lucy felt pushed out by Isla. Helen had been so caught up in working out how to bring the two dogs together that she hadn't been paying enough attention to them individually. She knelt down on the floor and rubbed Lucy's fluffy tummy, then grabbed a tug toy from her training belt and they spent a few minutes playing together.

As she took Lucy back into the rescue centre, Helen felt herself coming back down to earth. What was she going to do about Isla? Perhaps it was time to admit defeat. It wasn't fair to make Lucy unhappy.

Leaving Lucy in reception, she walked into the kennel room. Isla was sitting calmly in her cage, but when she heard Helen's voice, she stood up and came to the bars. Her skinny tail waved back and forth and her fuzzy ears were pricked.

'Hello.' Mandy came in behind Helen. 'That was a wonderful show with Lucy,' she said. 'I watched you through the consulting-room window after my last patient left. It was a masterclass in advanced training!'

Helen smiled. 'Thanks. I'd forgotten how good it was to work together. I feel like I've been neglecting her.'

'You clearly haven't,' Mandy said. 'Your connection is as strong as ever. I've been in touch with some friends about Isla and they've suggested a few things. If you like, we could go out and do a session together now.'

They left Lucy on a blanket with a chew. Isla trotted cheerfully into the paddock beside Helen. When she was in familiar surroundings and on her lead, it was obvious she was confident and relaxed. It was only when she was with Lucy that the problems seemed to start.

'I spoke quite a lot to Robin,' Mandy said. Helen had heard of Robin before. She was one of Mandy's vet friends in the US, and very keen on positive training in dogs. 'She suggested going right back to basics. Have you done any clicker training with Isla?'

Helen felt her face going red. It was so long since she'd used the clicker with Lucy that it hadn't even crossed her mind. It made perfect sense because the sound would let Isla know exactly when she was doing something correct.

Mandy pulled a clicker from her pocket and handed it to Helen. 'Worth a try,' she said.

They walked to the gently sloping ground at the edge of the field. Helen and Mandy sat down on the grass with Isla beside them. Helen pressed the clicker, then gave Isla a treat, then did it again several times. It only took a few tries before Isla started to look for the food after she'd heard the sound.

'She's picked that up very quickly,' Mandy commented. 'There were some other things Robin suggested,' she went on. 'Verbal cues for turning left and right. Telling her "Watch" when there's an obstacle in her way.'

They walked round the paddock with Isla on her lead. Helen gave the commands as they went. It was obvious Isla was a fast learner. As soon as Helen called 'Watch', she paused and checked around with her nose. Then she would proceed with far more confidence than before. They finished with another clicker session. Mandy pointed to the big glass window that looked into the reception area of the rescue centre. 'I think Lucy heard you,' she said with a laugh.

Lucy was sitting in the window. Her ears were pricked and there was interest in every line of her intelligent face. Helen felt a burst of love for her beautiful dog.

'Go and get her,' Mandy suggested. Helen went over and pulled open the door. 'Come, Lucy,' she called, and Lucy rushed towards her, dropping into a sit at her feet and looking up at her expectantly. Helen still had the clicker in her hand. She pressed the button, then reached for one of her very best treats.

They finished the session with some play. Mandy played tug with Isla, while Helen threw a ball for Lucy. They left the paddock and walked a little way up the track that led to the fell. They reached a bench and sat down. Both dogs flopped down on the ground, panting.

'That was brilliant,' Helen said. 'Now all we have to do is to get them both to sleep at night.'

Mandy nodded. 'Actually, Robin suggested crate-training Isla. I've never bothered with Sky because she gets on so well with Jimmy's dogs. They all lie in a pile wherever they are, so I've never felt the need to give her a safe space. But if you trained Isla to love her crate and use it as somewhere she could feel secure, maybe she wouldn't feel the need to be in your bed all the time. And Lucy's space would be protected, too.' She pulled out her mobile. 'Robin sent me a crate games video,' she said. 'I'll send it to you and you can have a look.' She clicked on the screen and the mobile in Helen's pocket buzzed.

'Thanks,' Helen said.

Mandy stood up. 'This has been a great start,' she said. 'We can do some more in a day or two, if you like. Now, I must go before Jimmy thinks I've fallen down a hole. I'll see you all tomorrow.' She patted each of the dogs and set off down the track.

Helen pulled her mobile out of her pocket and brought up the video. The young dog seemed to enjoy the different games, rushing in and out of the crate in return for clicks and treats. Lucy and Isla both sat up and looked at her. Helen laughed and turned the sound down. 'I must remember not to watch clicker videos while you're here,' she said. She gave them both a treat and they lay back down.

'Ahem.' She was startled by the sound of someone clearing their throat from farther up the track. Toby was striding down the hill towards her.

'What're you doing, creeping up on me?' Helen demanded.

'I wasn't creeping,' he objected. 'You were lost in your phone. And what kind of guard dogs do you call those? Just lying there all calm as strange men come up to you?'

'Well, there's one thing you're right about,' Helen said. 'You *are* very strange.'

Toby laughed. 'Mind if I sit down? I've walked over from Silver Dale and my legs are about to give way.' Helen shifted sideways to make room. As soon as Toby lowered himself onto the bench, Lucy sat up and put her head on his lap. He fondled her silky ears.

'Maybe I should get a dog,' he said. 'We always had dogs at home.'

Helen pictured the envelope she had found. Should she ask him whether the home he'd mentioned so casually was actually a castle? She shook the thought away, though she was smiling inside. 'Mandy's always got plenty of dogs coming in and out,' she reminded him. 'I'm sure she'd be happy to help.'

Toby was still stroking Lucy. Both of them seemed to be enjoying it. 'What are you doing at the weekend?' Toby asked suddenly, looking at Helen. His eyes looked very bright. 'I'd love to go for another bike ride with the dogs. Isla didn't seem to mind being on my back and Lucy loved it.'

Helen felt a burst of happiness. It would be lovely to have some weekend plans. Then a cloud scudded across her thoughts. What would the Welford hive mind say if she was seen out with Toby again?

'I'd love to go,' she said, 'but Susan Collins told me something today that might change your mind.' She reached down and put her hand on Isla's warm fuzzy head. 'People are gossiping about you and me,' she said. 'Apparently they're saying I broke up with Seb because you and I were seeing each other.'

Toby's eyebrows shot upwards. 'That's a new one!' A grin spread across his face. 'People will make up any old thing, won't they?'

Helen's face was burning. 'Don't you mind?'

Toby shrugged. 'I don't like it, but I can't help what people say when I'm not around. It's their problem if they choose to believe something that isn't true.'

He sounded genuinely calm. Was it part of being raised as part of a noble family? Helen wondered. Was he used to being gossiped about? Or was he so sure of his own place in the world that he didn't care?

'Anyway,' Toby went on, 'I've heard way worse things about myself. It wouldn't be so awful for you and me to have fallen for one another, would it? Even if you were with someone. These things happen all the time.'

Not to me.

'So how about it?' Toby didn't seem to notice that his latest comment had left Helen speechless. 'Saturday on the moors, mountain bikes and dogs in harness to pull us up the hill are non-negotiable.'

Helen blinked. Toby really was . . . what? Incorrigible? Irrepressible? Irresistible? 'I'd love to,' she said.

Toby stood up. 'That's settled,' he said. 'And I, for one, am looking forward to it.'

Helen let out a long breath. 'So am I,' she said.

Chapter Twenty

It was Thursday morning. Helen smiled as Mrs Bell walked into the waiting room. 'I've brought Croissant in for his check-up,' she announced.

'How is he?' Helen asked. She walked round the end of the reception desk and glanced into the basket Mrs Bell was holding. The enormous yellow eyes glared at her, then Croissant let out a furious hiss.

Mrs Bell looked pained. 'I'm sorry,' she said. 'He's really good at home, even with his injections.'

Helen patted Mrs Bell on the shoulder. 'It's quite normal,' she said. 'Lots of animals hate me. It's nothing personal. And if he's good for you at home, that's the main thing. If he didn't let you inject him, it'd be impossible to keep his diabetes under control.'

'He likes the new food,' Mrs Bell said. 'And he's got used to having his meals at exactly the same time every day. He comes looking for me if he thinks I'm late.' She held out the cage. 'Would you mind awfully if I waited out here?' she said. 'I know you have to get a sample, but I don't like seeing how much he hates it.'

'Of course,' Helen replied. In fact it was a relief that Mrs Bell didn't want to be there. Having an owner's eyes on you made almost any task more difficult.

She called Mandy to give her a hand. Mandy watched Helen hold the blanket over Croissant's carrier, then swoop in to gather up the cat, wrapping the fabric round the flailing paws. 'I see you've mastered number eighty-nine from my tutorial,' she commented.

'One hundred and one ways to wrap a cat?' Helen laughed.

Mandy fished under the blanket and gently extracted Croissant's hind leg. A moment later, she held up the filled test tube. 'Brilliant,' she said. 'I'll put it in the machine. Can you get him back in his box?'

'Probably.' Helen held on to the blanket until Mandy had left the room, closing the door behind her. If she lost hold of Croissant and he started doing the wall of death around the room, it would take ages to catch him again. She lifted him into the carrier, still wrapped in the blanket, and closed the lid to give herself a breather. Tussling with unwilling cats was always more energetic than you'd expect. Now all she had to do was extract the blanket. She lifted the lid an inch and began to pull the edge of the soft material.

A paw shot out through the narrow gap and, before Helen could move, Croissant's claws were embedded in her arm. Holding down the lid with her elbow to stop any more of him escaping, she picked out the claws from her arm one by one. Croissant pulled his paw back.

Grabbing the blanket, Helen tugged it out quickly and slammed the cage lid shut.

She inspected her arm. Two tiny holes and two deeper ones. Blood began to well from all four. She felt a little sick. She knew from experience that it wouldn't last long, but somehow being bitten or scratched always made her feel queasy.

There was a knock on the door. 'Is it safe to come in?'

'Fine,' Helen called.

The door opened and Mandy walked in. 'I checked the blood glucose,' she said. 'It's absolutely fine.' She stopped, her eyes on Helen's arm. 'He got you,' she said.

Helen managed a smile. 'It's only fair,' she pointed out. 'We've drawn his blood enough times.'

'I'll take him back to Mrs Bell while you go and wash,' she said.

'Thanks,' Helen said. She knew as well as Mandy that cats could have horrible bacteria under their claws. She picked up a gauze pad and put it over her arm, then walked into the prep room.

'Are you okay?' Toby looked up. He had been peering into a microscope, but when he saw Helen's arm, he stood up. 'Want a hand?'

'Yes please,' Helen said. It would be easy enough to wash it, but bandaging your own arm was always tricky. She washed her arm under the tap while Toby assembled swabs and bandages.

He pulled out a chair and offered it to her. 'Sit down,'

he ordered with a smile. She obeyed and held out her arm. Despite the wounds being flushed with water, blood was still seeping out. Toby grasped Helen's wrist, turning her hand from side to side to look at her injuries more clearly. His fingers were warm, his grip steady. 'Not too deep,' he pronounced. Helen felt her heart begin to beat a little faster. He was so gentle as he swabbed and cleaned. His movements were efficient and when he glanced up to see how she was doing, she felt heat rising in her face.

Once he was finished, Helen stood up quickly. She felt a little shaky. 'Thank you,' she said. Her voice sounded much higher than usual.

'No problem. My invoice will be in the post!'

Helen leaned on the table. Part of her wanted to scamper away, but it seemed rude to rush off when he'd been so kind. He regarded her quietly.

'Are you doing anything this evening?' he asked. 'If you don't have any plans, do you fancy a picnic by the river?'

Helen brushed a strand of hair out of her eyes. 'I'm not doing anything,' she mumbled.

Toby's blue eyes crinkled at the corners. 'Great,' he said. 'I'll pick up a few things after work and then I'll come over and we can walk from yours, if that's okay? Bring your swimming costume if you like.'

★ ★ ★

Helen felt surprisingly jittery as she drove home. Once inside, she rushed upstairs and pulled open her wardrobe. What should she wear? She pulled out a couple of dressy blouses. Lucy and Isla had followed her upstairs. Isla barked. Helen looked down and laughed.

'I'd almost forgotten you two were invited as well,' she told them. She was being daft, she thought. We're going for a walk by the river with the dogs. 'It's not some big date,' she informed Lucy, who was watching her with her ears pricked. 'You're going to go in the water, aren't you?' she said. And if Lucy was in the water, everyone in the vicinity was bound to get wet. Despite telling herself it was just a walk, she pulled on a smart pair of hotpants and a freshly ironed white V-necked T-shirt. Toby always looked as if he'd stepped into a brand-new outfit. Helen looked at herself in the mirror, then stripped everything off again and put on her swimming costume underneath. If Toby fancied a swim, she wanted to be prepared. She pulled on the T-shirt again, then took it back off. Her yellow swimming costume was showing through. She picked out a slightly looser white shirt and put it on, buttoned quite low. As an afterthought, she put a waterproof plaster in her backpack. She could hardly swim with a bandage on her arm.

She was still inspecting herself when the doorbell rang. The dogs rushed to the door. Helen made her way downstairs, holding on to the banister. She didn't want to look as if she'd rushed. Toby was leaning against the door jamb, looking effortlessly cool. He was wearing pale chino shorts, an open-necked blue shirt and a pair of Ray-Bans.

Helen felt herself going red and cursed her ability to blush for no reason. 'You look great,' she said. She suddenly felt self-conscious and tugged her blouse together to cover her swimsuit, which seemed to have turned her into a buxom medieval wench.

Toby looked her up and down with clear appreciation in his eyes. 'You look great too,' he said. 'Come on. We should get going if we want to make the most of the daylight.'

Isla showed off her new training on the lead. Helen gave her instructions for left and right, up and down, and she trotted confidently along the riverbank. Lucy ran ahead, her tail in the air. Now and then she ran back to check on them, then rushed off again.

'Isla looks like a different dog,' Toby commented.

Helen was thrilled that he could see a difference already. 'It's mostly thanks to Mandy,' she admitted.

'I'm sure you've been putting in some hard work too,' he said. He pulled a squashy ball out of his pocket. 'I brought this for Lucy,' he said. 'I thought she'd like something to chew on while we're eating.'

Helen felt another frisson of pleasure. He really had thought of everything.

'May I throw it in the river for her?' Toby asked.

'Of course,' Helen said, 'though you should probably let her see it first so she knows what she's looking for.'

Toby called Lucy and showed her the ball, then, with a graceful swing of his arm, he threw the ball into the deepest part of the river.

Lucy let out a single, joyous woof and launched herself into the water. Isla pricked her ears, then started to pull towards the sound. Helen bent down and touched the little dog gently. 'You stay here with us for now,' she said. 'We'll take you in soon.'

Lucy scrambled up the bank, rushed over to Toby, sat down and dropped the ball at his feet. 'Good girl,' he said. He picked up the ball and offered it to her.

'Carry,' Helen commanded Lucy. Lucy took the ball from his hand very carefully.

'She really is brilliant,' Toby said. 'I can't remember any of the dogs at home being this well behaved!'

Helen glanced at him. Was this a chance to ask him about his childhood? 'Did your family have lots of animals?'

Toby shrugged. 'Well, we had a farm,' he said non-committally.

'Is that the business your dad wanted you to take over?'

Toby sped up to walk ahead of her as the path narrowed. 'Kind of,' he said. 'Shall we stop here? I'm starving.'

'Sure,' Helen said. She couldn't help noticing that he had dodged away from talking about his past yet again. She couldn't push him any more without giving away the fact that she'd seen the envelope.

'How about a dip before we eat?' Toby suggested. He pulled his shirt over his head and undid his shorts to reveal smooth black trunks.

Helen could feel her cheeks starting to warm. We're not doing anything wrong, she reminded herself. Just two friends going for a swim. She peeled off her outer layers and stood on the edge of the river. There was no pebbly beach here and she gasped as she slipped off the edge of the bank up to her knees. 'It's freezing!' she squeaked.

Toby laughed. He had already waded in up to his waist. 'Must be all the rainwater from last night's storm.'

Helen tiptoed in until the water reached her thighs.

'Come on,' Toby called from the middle of the pool. 'It's fine once you're in.' He dived under the water like an otter and reappeared at the far side. His hair was slicked back and his brown shoulders bobbed in the water. Helen gritted her teeth. There was no way she was going to wimp out in front of him. Taking a deep breath, she pushed off and sank into the water.

When she surfaced, Toby was swimming towards her. 'You were absolutely right,' he yelled.

Helen blinked at him, shaking water from her eyes. Her teeth were already beginning to chatter. 'What about?'

'It's bloody cold!'

'Why did you tell me it was fine when you were in?' Helen glared at him.

'I couldn't have you thinking I was a wimp!' His eyes sparkled. 'Race you back!'

Even though it was only a few strokes to the bank, Helen was panting and shivering by the time she arrived. Toby pulled himself out of the water, then held out a hand to help her onto the grass. The sun felt blissfully warm on her wet skin. Toby was still holding her hand. Helen felt a shiver run down her spine. He reached out with his other hand and pulled her towards him. Then he lowered his head and brushed his lips against hers. Helen froze.

Toby took a tiny step backwards. His face looked flushed, though there were still droplets of water on his face. 'Did I do the wrong thing?'

Helen shook her head. 'Actually, no. You really didn't.' She reached up to his face and pulled him towards her. He kissed her again and this time she let his lips explore hers, breathing her in. He lifted his head and they broke apart. Both of them were shivering. They dried themselves off and pulled their clothes on. Helen realised she had forgotten to bring a bra. She felt rather exposed as she sat there with only her blouse covering her but Toby seemed oblivious – or was too gentlemanly to comment.

The sun was sliding down the sky now and Helen was starting to feel cold. When Toby edged towards her and put his arm around her, she didn't move away. Instead, she leaned against him until his chin was resting on top of her head. 'Are you sure you're okay with this?' he murmured into her hair.

'Very okay,' she replied, twining her fingers around his other hand.

'I was worried when you told me what Susan had said,' Toby admitted. 'I thought you'd run a mile from the gossipmongers of Welford.'

Helen felt her heart beating faster. He had been worried? Did that mean he'd been interested in her for a while? Toby Gordon. The Right Honourable Tobias Gordon. He could have had any girl in Yorkshire . . . maybe anyone in the whole of the country. And here he was, holding her hand.

'I've wanted to ask you out for ages,' he admitted. 'I never thought there'd be a chance. Not while you were with someone else, but now . . .'

Helen looked up at him. 'You can stop worrying,' she said. 'You're single. I'm single. We're free to do whatever we like.' She reached up and found his mouth again. This time it didn't feel so strange. A moment later, he had pulled her down onto the ground and was kissing her hard.

Chapter Twenty-One

It was the first time in ages that Helen was late for work. She rushed in at two minutes past eight, dropped Lucy off with Emily, put Isla in the rescue centre, and raced back to reception. There were no clients in and she took a moment to gather herself. She flicked the switch on her computer and waited for it to boot up. Then she went into the first consulting room and started pulling open drawers and cupboards to check what was running short. There were no two-millilitre syringes in the drawer beside the sink, only a couple of green needles. One of the antibiotics was running low. Stethoscope was in place, thermometer, ophthalmascope. She walked through to the stock room and almost bumped into Toby.

'Morning,' he said with a grin.

Helen could feel the heat rising in her face. He grinned at her and she found herself grinning back. 'Did you get home okay?' she asked.

He nodded. 'Finally,' he said. 'Not that I slept very well,' he added, with a smile so wicked that Helen felt an urge to kiss him.

'Morning, you two.' Helen jumped when she heard Adam's voice behind her. 'Toby, could you just hand me over a bottle of penicillin, please?' She didn't dare turn round. She was sure Adam would be able to tell what was going on from her face.

Toby picked up the bottle and handed it to Adam with a polite nod. He carefully avoided meeting Helen's eyes. She felt a giggle rising in her throat.

'Thanks,' Adam said. 'I'm heading out to Kimbleton to see a horse. Mandy's already out but she'll be back shortly.'

Helen heard his footsteps retreating, then the sound of the clinic door opening and closing. She let out a long breath. 'I felt like I was back at school and Mr Jamieson had caught me in a cupboard with one of the third years.'

Toby laughed. 'I might have to give you a detention,' he threatened.

As they returned to reception, Mandy came in. She nodded to them but before she could say anything, the phone rang and she picked it up. 'Hello, Animal Ark, Mandy Hope speaking.'

Toby touched Helen's arm. 'Dinner at the Fox and Goose tonight?' he whispered.

Helen nodded.

'Must get on,' Toby said. He glanced round to check Mandy was still on the phone. 'See you later.' He reached out, squeezed Helen's fingers for a moment and then scooted off.

A client walked in as he left, and then another and another. For the next hour Helen didn't have a chance to think about anything but work. She was relieved when ten o'clock came round and Rachel arrived.

Mandy checked the call list when the last client had closed the door behind them. 'No one else seems to need me right now,' she remarked. She looked at Helen. 'Shall we do a bit more training with Isla? Rachel, can you hold the fort? Just shout if you need us.'

'No problem,' said Rachel. 'I need to update the client database so I'll make a start on that.'

'Before I forget,' Mandy said to Helen as they crossed the waiting room, 'did you get a chance to look at the crate games? I actually brought a crate in today if you'd like to give it a try.'

'That would be great,' said Helen.

Mandy fetched the flat-pack crate from her car and carried it into the rescue centre. She unfolded it and fixed the sides into place with metal clips. Helen led Isla out from the kennel room. The little dog sniffed the crate curiously. Mandy put a dog treat inside the crate and Helen steered Isla's head towards the open door. To her delight, Isla stepped in, following the scent of the treat, and sat down to crunch it up.

'Good girl,' said Mandy. She took a clicker out of her pocket, clicked it, and gave Isla another treat. Next they tried closing the door with Helen holding Isla on her lead at the front of the cage so that she could feel she was being shut in. After ten minutes of clicks and treats,

Isla got the hang of walking in and out of the crate, and sitting quietly while they shut the door.

'She seems really comfortable,' Helen commented.

Mandy nodded. 'I really think she's going to enjoy having her own safe space.'

Before Isla had a chance to get bored with the crate training, they took her into the orchard to work on her on-lead commands. Mandy was impressed with Isla's progress, and Helen admitted they had been practising.

They stopped by the paddock fence to feed Fluffy-bonce some handfuls of grass. 'Is there anything you want to tell me, Helen?' Mandy asked lightly.

Helen felt her face growing very red. 'I don't think so,' she said.

Mandy raised her eyebrows. 'I may have been imagining it,' she said, 'but you and Toby were looking very shifty when you came out of the stock room this morning.'

Helen stopped stroking Fluffybonce and turned to face her friend. 'What is this, the Spanish Inquisition?' she demanded. 'Animal Ark has turned into a hotbed of gossip!'

'Hmmm, an evasion with no denial. Don't tell me you've fallen for that Gordon charm?'

Helen shook her head. 'Not a chance!' She felt a twinge of guilt. Why did she feel so uncomfortable admitting it? *It's just too soon after Seb. Everyone would think so.*

Mandy looked at her for a long moment, then

shrugged. 'Okay, then,' she said. 'Shall we pop Isla back and bring Lucy out for a quick training session?'

They set off across the orchard towards the gate. Helen realised that with everything going on with Seb and Toby, she'd forgotten about the ring Mandy had bought. 'Oh, gosh,' she said. 'I meant to ask about you and Jimmy. Have you popped the question yet?'

Mandy shook her head. 'I'm waiting for the right moment,' she said. Her eyes were shining. 'The twins are going away with their mum next weekend so Jimmy and I'll have the place to ourselves. I thought I'd do the full works – flowers, candles, music.'

Helen grinned. 'I'd love to be a fly on the wall!'

Mandy pretended to frown. 'I'll have you know there are no flies in my house!'

As Helen unlatched the gate, a figure appeared around the side of the rescue centre. It was Anneka Mellor from Sunrise Farm. 'Hi, Anneka!' Helen called. What was she doing at Animal Ark? she wondered. She felt a stab of worry when Anneka got closer. Her face was pale and her eyes looked red.

'Is something wrong?' Helen handed Isla's lead to Mandy and slipped through the gate. 'Is it Birdie?'

Anneka stopped and shook her head. 'Birdie's fine . . . we're all fine,' she said. Her voice was so hoarse it was hard to hear her. 'It's the farm.' She sniffed. 'Starlings has pulled out of this year's harvest. Steve and I . . . we don't know what we're going to do.'

Helen stared at Anneka in dismay. Mandy was looking

mystified so Helen quickly explained. 'Starlings is the wholesaler that takes the majority of the Sunrise Farm fruit.' She turned back to Anneka, who was shaking. 'You've been their client for years! They can't pull out now!'

Anneka swallowed. 'They can,' she said. 'There's been a takeover.' A tear ran down her cheek and she brushed it away. 'The new owners don't want to deal with the smaller suppliers.'

Helen reached into the pocket of her tunic and pulled out a tissue. She handed it over and put her arm around Anneka. 'Don't give up hope,' she said. 'Can't you find another buyer?'

Anneka blew her nose. 'Steve and I have been ringing around all day,' she said. 'The market's flooded. Lots of us have lost our contracts. We're too small and too far from most of the distributors to be able to offer a competitive rate. It's hopeless.' Her shoulders slumped. 'We're going to lose everything we've grown this year.' Her face crumpled.

'Can you sell some of it locally?' Mandy asked. 'I'm sure lots of us would be happy to buy direct from you. I can post a notice on the Hope Meadows website and we can send out an e-mail to Animal Ark's clients. James might take some for the café and I'm sure Jimmy can take a supply of fruit for Running Wild.'

Anneka managed a faint smile. 'That's very kind,' she said. 'And please don't think I'm not grateful. But there's so much fruit that we'd still make a massive loss. We can't even afford to pay our seasonal workers. I've left Steve ringing the agency to cancel this year's contract.'

'Don't you have some kind of insurance?' said Helen.

'Not for this kind of thing,' Anneka admitted. 'Look, I'm sorry to burden you with all this. I just wanted you to know what's going on.' She took a deep breath. 'I'm afraid it's going to have an effect on you too. It's not just this year, you see. We've barely covered our costs for the last three years. Starlings closing down is the last nail in the coffin.' She blinked and lifted a hand to wipe away a tear. 'I'm really sorry, Helen. Sunrise Farm will have to be sold.'

Helen gulped. The gnarled trees of the orchard seemed to swim in the bright summer sunshine. First Seb and now this. Was she going to lose everything?

'I know it's your home,' Anneka went on. 'We'll try to sell the farm with your rent agreement in place, but there's no way we can guarantee it.' She paused, squeezing Helen's fingers. 'We'll give you as much time to find somewhere else as we can. We'll be here for at least a couple of months, but after that . . .'

The trees had stopped spinning. Helen forced herself to smile. 'I'm the least of your problems! Don't worry about me. Deal with the harvest first.'

'Thank you, Helen,' Anneka said, reaching out and squeezing her hand. 'We've loved having you in the family, we really have! Right, I need to get back. I still have a few wholesalers to try.' She turned and headed back to her car.

Helen stared at Mandy. 'I'm going to be homeless!' She was filled with a strange feeling of grief.

'Steady on,' Mandy said. 'There's plenty of time to find somewhere else. We can help.'

Isla had been sitting beside them while they spoke, but as they began to walk back towards the rescue centre, she hung back and started to whine. Then Lucy let out of a chorus of deafening barks as they came into sight through the big glass window. 'You can help all you like,' Helen said. 'What landlord would want the hounds of hell as tenants?'

'They're not that bad,' Mandy said. 'Lucy wants to come out and Isla's just picking up on how you feel.'

Helen bent down and lifted Isla into her arms. 'Poor little girl,' she said. Isla reached up and licked her face.

'Do you want to bring Lucy out?' Mandy asked. 'Or do you want to leave it for another day?'

'Leave it,' Helen replied. She sighed. 'I'll take them out for a walk later, but I don't think I'm in the right mood for training at the moment.'

Helen felt as if she was working on autopilot for the rest of the day. Anneka Mellor's tragic face haunted her. She knew it was awful for them, losing their business as well as their home. But then she would remember that the granary was also being taken away, and that made her feel a hundred times worse.

She had changed out of her uniform and was hanging

it up in her locker when Toby rushed in. He was carrying a bundle of letters, which he shoved into his pocket when he saw her. 'I was hoping I'd catch you,' he said. 'What time do you want to eat? Shall we give the dogs a run before dinner?'

Helen shrugged. 'Up to you.'

Toby frowned. 'What's wrong?'

Helen could feel tears pricking her eyes. 'Anneka Mellor came over earlier,' she explained. 'You know, the Mellors that own Sunrise Farm?'

Toby nodded.

'They're selling up,' she said. 'Usually a company called Starlings buys their fruit, but they've just been told the contract isn't being renewed.'

Toby's blue eyes were troubled. 'So you're going to be turfed out?' He sounded angry and Helen couldn't help feeling touched. He reached out and wrapped his arms around her, then dropped a kiss on the top of her head. Helen leaned against him. The clean scent of his cologne was mingled with warmth from a hard day's work, and his arms felt strong and safe. 'Poor you,' he said. 'Let's talk about it over dinner. You still need to eat!'

They set off on foot towards the Fox and Goose, stopping beside the village green to let Lucy off her lead. She ran for a minute or two, then came back, wagging her tail. Helen clipped her lead back on and crossed the road.

'Shall we sit outside?' Toby suggested.

'If you like,' said Helen. She was struggling to care about anything.

Toby reached out and squeezed her hand. 'Hang in there,' he said. They walked into the beer garden and found a table. Toby fetched a menu. 'Is there anything you fancy?'

Helen scanned the list of dishes but nothing tempted her. It all sounded very hearty for a hot summer day, even if she had been feeling hungry. She handed the menu back to Toby. 'I'll have whatever you're having,' she said.

Toby looked closely at her for a moment, then nodded and headed into the pub. Coming in with Toby had felt fine, but now Helen was on her own, she suddenly felt very exposed. There was a loud burst of female laughter from a table on the other side of the garden. Helen felt her heart sink. Isobel Parker-Smythe and several equally glossy friends were sitting together, shooting glances at her that landed like tiny arrows. It was obvious that Toby was still the hottest topic in Welford.

Toby reappeared with a pint in each hand and slid onto the bench beside Helen. He reached his arm around her waist, pulling her close, then lifted his glass to take a sip. Helen stiffened as she heard more laughter. She shuffled slightly away from Toby. He looked confused for a moment, then glanced at Isobel's table.

'Ignore them,' he murmured. 'If we're the most interesting thing they have to talk about, they must have very tedious lives.'

Helen took a gulp of her beer. Another loud peal of giggling rang out and then the most ridiculous snort. Helen tugged at the neck of her T-shirt. Her face felt bright red. She turned and spoke quietly. 'I'm sorry, Toby,' she said. 'I can't ignore them. I know they're idiots, but I hate being gossiped about.'

Toby grinned. 'You should be more like me,' he said, giving her a squeeze. 'You need to get a thicker skin.'

Helen felt her irritation rising. It was one thing to have a meal together. It was quite another to be under the gaze of half of Toby's exes. 'How do you suggest I do that?' she snapped. 'I'm not like you. I haven't lived my life looking down on the peasants.'

Toby pulled his arm away. 'What do you mean by that?'

Helen gulped. Why had she said that? She could hardly tell Toby she'd been snooping through his mail. 'I just mean you're always so self-assured,' she stammered. 'Everyone else must seem very humble to you.'

Toby looked puzzled. 'Is that what you think?' He put down his beer, then ran his finger down the side of the glass, drawing a line through the condensation. Then he smiled at Helen. 'Tell me about the farm,' he said. 'Do you know what the Mellors are going to do?'

Helen shook her head. 'I don't think they know either,' she said. 'They needed Starlings to buy their harvest. They can't even afford to pay the people who normally come and pick the fruit for them.'

'So you don't know how soon the farm will go on the market?'

Helen shrugged. 'Anneka said they'd be there for a couple of months at least, but beyond that, I don't know.' To her dismay, Chloe Benn had just come into the garden. Hadn't Seb told her Chloe and Toby had been out together too?

'Will the granary be put up for sale separately?' Toby persisted.

Helen closed her eyes. Why did he have to ask all these questions now? She opened her eyes again. 'I don't know about the granary. All I know is that in a few months' time, me and the dogs are going to be homeless.'

Toby regarded her quietly for a moment. 'You don't want to be here, do you,' he said. It wasn't a question.

Helen shook her head. She didn't trust herself to speak.

'Come on.' He took her hand and helped her up. 'I'll take you home. Wait for me outside.' He disappeared into the pub and emerged a few minutes later with a Tupperware box. 'Chicken salad to go,' he said, waving it at her.

Helen let Toby steer her back to the surgery. She was too tired to do more than put one foot in front of the other. 'We'll take my car,' he said. He helped Helen into the passenger seat and lifted first Lucy and then Isla into the back.

'Mandy brought me a crate for Isla,' Helen said as he slid into the driver's seat. 'I'm really sorry, would you be able to fit it in the boot? It's all folded up.'

'Of course I could.' Toby climbed back out of the car and returned a few minutes later.

It felt strange for someone else to be driving her home. Instead of watching the road, Helen's eyes followed the lines of the hillside as they drove up onto the moor. They topped the ridge and began to drop down into the valley where Sunrise Farm lay. The red brick buildings were bathed in golden sunset and Helen felt a lump form in her throat. Her home had never looked more beautiful.

Toby pulled up on the gravel drive and came round to open her door. She was greeted by the sweet scent of strawberries and raspberries. In the quiet evening air, she could hear the whisper of the stream beyond the garden.

'I can see why you love it here,' Toby commented.

Helen led him through the garden, unlocked the back door and led him into the kitchen. She opened a cupboard. 'Can you take these?' she asked, handing him some glasses. She pulled out plates and cutlery and they carried their dinner into the garden.

As they ate, Lucy and Isla snuffled around the flower beds and the orchard trees threw long shadows across the grass. 'Isla seems to be getting more confident every time I see her,' said Toby.

Helen watched as Isla pottered slowly from bush to bush. She had learned to follow the winding stone pathway that split the lawn into two. Helen's breath caught in her throat as she remembered again. Sunrise

Farm was going to be sold. Isla would to have to start finding her way around all over again. Helen felt tears welling up.

Toby reached across the table and took her hand. 'Try not to despair, Helen.' His voice was gentle. 'You'll be okay.'

'I don't know if I will,' Helen admitted in a small voice. Toby stood up and walked round the table. He grasped her hand and pulled her into his arms. Lifting his hand, he wiped away her tears with his thumb, then bent down to kiss her.

It seemed to last a long time. They broke apart and Helen rested her head on his chest. She had the sudden fierce feeling that this was exactly what she needed. This was the only place she wanted to be.

'Better?' Toby whispered. Helen nodded. He squeezed her fingers, rubbing his thumb across the back of her hand. 'Come on,' he said. Without letting go of his hand, Helen followed him inside.

Chapter Twenty-Two

Helen blinked herself awake. Sunlight was streaming through a gap in the curtains. Behind her, she could feel Seb shifting in the bed. Her mouth felt dry. Still half asleep, she reached out her arm for her morning cup of tea, then stopped. The bedside table was empty.

Helen jolted awake. Seb was gone. The man in her bed was Toby. He stirred again, breathing in and letting out a heavy sigh. Helen felt an arm reaching around her waist. She stiffened slightly, then reminded herself to relax. Seb was gone. She and Toby were together now.

He shifted again and she rolled over to face him. He looked very young when he was asleep. As she watched, he opened his brilliant blue eyes and smiled at her.

'Morning, gorgeous,' he said. Pushing himself up on his elbow, he leaned over to kiss her.

There was a bark from the side of the bed where they had set up Isla's crate. Helen realised that Isla had slept through the night. Lucy was in her bed in her favourite corner, just waking up. 'I'll let them out,' Helen said.

She pushed back the duvet, very aware that she was naked. Toby propped himself up on his pillows and put his arms above his head. He was watching her with obvious enjoyment. Helen grabbed her dressing gown from the back of the door. 'Don't cover up on my account,' he told her with a grin.

Helen pretended to glare at him as she hauled the dressing gown on. 'Come on, Lucy,' she called. She opened the door of Isla's crate and the little dog walked out and stretched. The two dogs followed her downstairs and trotted outside. Helen watched them relieve themselves on the grass and trot back in, leaving faint paw prints in the dew.

The kettle had boiled by the time she had given them both their breakfast. She glanced at the clock. It was still only 6.30. She poured the water into two mugs to make tea, aware that she was smiling. Last night had been an unexpectedly good end to a really bad day.

Toby was in the bathroom when she carried the tea upstairs. Helen placed his mug on the table at his side of the bed and climbed back under the duvet, still wearing her dressing gown. She heard the sound of the bathroom door opening, and a moment later Toby appeared in the bedroom. He didn't seem to have any shyness about being naked in front of her. He threw himself back down on the bed and took a sip of his tea.

Helen turned away, lifting up her own tea and taking a sip to give herself a moment. It was her room, her bed, yet Toby seemed to feel completely at home. *Have you been in so many women's bedrooms that this seems normal?* She pushed the thought away.

Putting his mug down, Toby reached out and rested his hand on her thigh. 'Are you feeling better this morning?'

Another memory from yesterday thudded into place. She was going to lose Sunrise Farm. 'I slept well,' she said. 'Thanks to you.'

'As did I,' Toby said. 'Eventually.' He was smiling again. He trailed a strand of Helen's hair through his fingers. 'Thank you for letting me stay.'

'My pleasure.' The words came out automatically and Helen told herself to stop acting like an idiot. But this was starting to feel rather peculiar. Toby was her colleague. She was used to him in scrubs or work clothes, cheerful and efficient.

'You're looking very serious,' Toby said. 'What are you thinking about?'

Helen shook her head. 'Very little,' she said. She finished her last mouthful of tea. 'I must get in the shower or we'll be late for work.' She threw the duvet back and stepped out of bed.

To her surprise, Toby stood up as well, wearing nothing but a broad grin. 'I have a great idea to save time and water,' he said. 'Do you think there's room for me?'

★ ★ ★

They pulled up outside Animal Ark with minutes to spare. Helen felt a surge of embarrassment when she saw her car in the parking area. Mandy's RAV4 stood on the other side. All the Hopes must have guessed what had happened. She was doing nothing wrong, Helen reminded herself. She and Toby were both adults. He reached out and squeezed her hand. 'Have a good day, lovely,' he said. She couldn't help feeling glad he hadn't kissed her.

She climbed out and let Isla and Lucy out of the back. 'See you inside!' Toby called. Helen was bending down attaching the clip to Isla's lead when she heard the sound of a car door opening. She looked round to see Mandy climbing out of her SUV. Helen felt a sinking feeling in the pit of her stomach. Mandy must have been there the whole time.

Mandy was looking at her, eyebrows raised. 'That escalated quickly.'

Helen's face was burning. 'I'm not going to say it's not what it looks like.'

'Good,' Mandy said. She had a bland expression on her face that Helen couldn't read.

'Shall I come and give you a hand in the centre?' Helen asked.

'If you like,' Mandy replied. They walked side by side across the drive, Lucy, Isla and Sky at their heels.

An awkward silence hung between them and Helen found herself feeling more and more uncomfortable. She stopped when they reached the door. She could feel her fingers shaking on Isla's lead. 'Say something,' she begged. 'You're making me feel like I need to explain myself.'

Mandy pulled out her keys. She turned to look at Helen with her hand on the door handle. 'I'm not *making* you feel anything,' she pointed out.

Helen took a deep breath. 'Perhaps I feel like I need to explain things to myself, then.'

Mandy shrugged. 'That's up to you.' She pushed open the door and walked inside. Helen paused. She could just put Isla in a cage and walk away, she thought. There was plenty she could be doing in the clinic. Mandy was holding the door open, waiting. Helen stepped inside. She was going to have to face up to this sooner or later. Whatever Mandy thought, they had to work together.

The silence stretched out again as they began the morning's tasks. Finally Helen couldn't stand it any more. She went over to Mandy, who was standing at the sink, filling up one of the dog's bowls. 'What are you thinking?' she prompted. 'Do you think it's too soon after Seb?'

Mandy reached out and turned off the tap. 'Do you?'

Helen blinked. 'I guess I do, sort of,' she admitted. 'But it's not like I'm going to marry Toby tomorrow. We're having fun, that's all.'

'Are you trying to convince yourself or me?' Mandy said. She turned and squeezed Helen's arm. 'If you're genuinely having fun,' she said, 'then I'm pleased. I'm worried about you, that's all. The news about Sunrise Farm was a real shock. And when I saw you and Toby together . . .'

'I didn't just invite Toby back because of the farm.'

Mandy smiled. 'I never thought you did,' she said. 'It just seemed very sudden.'

Helen glanced down at the floor. 'It felt sudden to me, too.'

Mandy lifted the bowl out of the sink. 'It really doesn't matter,' she said. 'As long as you're happy. Though that's not easy at the moment. Not with the whole house thing hanging over you.' She walked through to the kennel room and placed the water inside a cage.

Helen wiped some water drops off the counter. 'I can hardly feel sorry for myself when the Mellors are going to lose everything,' she pointed out.

Mandy grabbed a lead and handed one to Helen. 'Bring Bobby, will you?' she said.

Helen clipped on Bobby's lead and watched Mandy wait outside Flit's kennel. She knew Mandy wouldn't go in until Flit was sitting down.

'Bloody Starlings!' Helen cursed. The lingering anger she had been feeling on and off had returned with full force. 'It's crazy that a company doesn't care about its suppliers!'

Flit was sitting quietly at last. Mandy opened the door of the kennel. She glanced up as she clipped on Flit's leash. 'It sucks,' she agreed. 'I know how hard Steve and Anneka have worked, and their fruit is amazing. Poor kids, too. Sunrise Farm is a brilliant place to grow up. I wish there was something we could do to help.'

'Do you think we could open a massive jam factory?' Helen said. 'How many jars do you think Dorothy could churn out?'

Mandy laughed. 'I'm sure Gran would accept the challenge!' They took the dogs outside and watched them race around in the sunshine. 'I've definitely found homes for these two,' Mandy said.

'Where?' Helen asked. It was always good to hear when Mandy's furry tenants found new homes.

'Bobby's going to a young family,' Mandy told her. 'I went out and had a look yesterday evening. And all being well, Flit's going to a sheep farm up near Richmond. They seem to think they'll be able to train her as a working dog.'

Helen sighed. 'Lucky dogs,' she said.

'Not just them,' Mandy said. 'I got a message last night on the website from a farm that might be interested in Fluffybonce.'

'Really?' Helen had thought the sweet Jersey cow would be with them for a while. 'Where's the farm?'

'It's in Nidderdale,' Mandy told her. 'I think you've been there.' She rolled up the lead in her hands. 'It was actually Seb who recommended they get in touch.'

Helen realised her friend was looking at her with concern. 'It's okay,' she said. 'I can cope with Seb existing in the same universe. I'm glad he helped out with Fluffybonce. She deserves a good home, bless her.'

'And a new name?' Mandy said.

Helen laughed. 'We can only hope.'

They put the dogs away. It was time to head over to the clinic for morning surgery. Helen touched Mandy's elbow as they walked across the drive. 'Are you going to say anything to your mum and dad about me and Toby?'

Mandy shook her head. 'It's none of their business,' she said. 'Unless you think it should be?'

'No, not at all,' Helen said. She glanced at the waiting-room window, half expecting to see Toby or Adam looking out. 'If it all goes south,' she said quickly, 'I promise it won't affect my work.'

Mandy smiled. Her eyes were twinkling. 'I think we can trust you both to be professional.' Her gaze became serious. 'You will be careful, though, won't you? There's a lot going on at the moment. Don't rush into anything.'

'I won't,' Helen promised.

Toby was out on a call all morning. He reappeared just before lunch. Helen was sitting at the reception desk when she saw his car pull up outside. He smiled as he walked in and glanced around. Apart from Helen herself, the waiting room was empty. 'Fancy sharing some sand-wiches?' he suggested. He held up a paper bag. 'I didn't think you'd want to go to the Fox and Goose again, so I got something from that new bakery in Walton.'

Helen nodded. 'I'll get Lucy and Isla,' she said.

She felt her spirits lift as she followed Toby to the orchard. Once they were through the gate and out of sight of the surgery, he reached for her hand. They sat down in a sheltered, sun-soaked patch beside the wall of the rescue centre. For the first time that day, Helen felt a sense of peace as she watched Lucy trotting in and out of the trees in pursuit of rabbity smells. Not to be outdone, Isla sniffed her way bravely towards the fence to say hello to Fluffybonce.

Helen leaned her head on Toby's shoulder. 'Thanks for getting the sandwiches.'

'Don't thank me before you've tried them,' he warned. 'They had some truly weird concoctions in that place. I got you avocado and blue cheese.'

Helen nibbled at the corner of the sandwich. 'It's . . . interesting,' she admitted. 'They could have eased off on the chilli sauce, I think.'

'Chilli sauce?' Toby made a face.

'What have you got?' Helen asked.

Toby waved his baguette at her. 'Cheese and ham,' he said. 'I'm a man of plain tastes.'

Helen sent him a mock glare. 'Well, that's not very nice,' she said.

Toby looked at her. His eyes were puzzled, then he seemed to get the joke. He bent his head to give her a kiss. 'Plain tastes: present company excepted,' he amended. He balanced his baguette on his knee and wiped his fingers. 'How are things at Sunrise Farm? Any news?'

Helen put her own sandwich down, suddenly feeling

less hungry. 'Well, they've lost their buyer for the entire harvest,' she said. 'That's the main problem I know about, though Anneka said things hadn't been great for a year or two.'

'Wow.' Toby whistled. 'That sounds pretty grim.'

Helen nodded. 'But it's so frustrating! You wouldn't think it would be that difficult to find another buyer for the fruit, would you? It's not like they have to shift the European Strawberry Mountain, just a few fields' worth.' She tore up some grass beside her and sprinkled it from her fingers.

'When you put it like that, it does feel like a problem that could be solved,' Toby remarked.

Helen rolled the last blades of grass between her fingers. 'Well, I guess it's not just about finding a buyer for the harvest. They need an entire staff to pick it. From what Anneka said, there's no money to pay them. Not without a guaranteed payment from Starlings.' She forced herself to smile up at Toby. 'Free, instantly available labour, and a destination for a whole farm's worth of fruit. Not quite so solvable, is it, really?'

Toby put his hand on her thigh. 'Don't lose hope,' he said. He lifted up his baguette and took a bite. Isla pottered over, her nose in the air. 'I think she can smell my sandwich,' he said, fondling her curly ear.

'She loves ham,' Helen said. She leaned back against the wall. The stone felt warm through her polo shirt. She felt her eyes drifting shut. She shook her head, blinking. Toby was talking again.

'One thing I really like about Welford is the feeling of community,' he said. 'Sometimes it feels like we've travelled back in time to when people looked out for each other. It's a bit like it was in Caithness. The whole village acts together like a swarm of bees.'

'And knows everyone else's business,' Helen muttered.

'Well, there's a downside to everything,' Toby acknowledged. 'But there's a great sense of public spirit. Look at how they support the rescue centre. I've seen tiny kids coming in with their pocket money to give to Mandy!'

'That's true,' said Helen, nodding without lifting her head from the wall.

'And I can't believe there's a single home that doesn't have a rescue pet of some kind or another.'

Helen opened one eye to look at him. 'Mandy doesn't hand out the animals willy-nilly.'

'I know that,' Toby said. He took the last bite of his sandwich, wiped his fingers and reached out to touch her hand. 'I'm just trying to show how great the people around here are. So welcoming and helpful, even to a newcomer like me.'

For a moment, Helen wanted to roll her eyes. Some of them had been a bit too welcoming for her liking.

'I was wondering if we should appeal to the local folk to help Steve and Anneka?' Toby went on.

Helen opened her eyes and sat up. 'With donations?' she asked. 'I'm pretty sure they won't want charity. Not even from the people of Welford.' She blinked. 'Wait a minute. Do you mean, ask everyone to help pick the harvest?' She could feel her heart starting to beat faster.

Toby nodded. 'You said they needed free, instantly available labour, right? If we asked everyone to give up one day, do you think we could get it done?'

'It's a brilliant idea! I know all our clients would help, and Steve and Anneka have loads of friends in the farming community.' For a moment, Helen felt like jumping up and racing into the rescue centre to start phoning round. Then her heart sank. 'And what do you propose we do with all the fruit? People will pay for some of the stuff they pick, but they're not going to take industrial quantities, are they?' She fiddled with the wrapping on her baguette. 'We need the world's busiest tea-room to decide they're going to use ten times as many strawberries in their cream teas this year. Or a jam-maker to quadruple production.' She sighed. 'Even the Welford WI wouldn't be able to use up all the Sunrise Farm fruit.'

Toby didn't respond, and Helen looked up at him. His expression was thoughtful. 'Are you thinking of opening a jam factory to help out?' she asked. 'Just how fond are you of raspberries? Do you have a never-ending supply of champagne to dip them in?'

'Not exactly.' He rubbed his hand across his chin. 'Give me a bit of time, that's all. If I come up with something, will you come with me to see Steve and Anneka? Tell them about our idea for getting the locals to help with the harvest?'

Helen shrugged. 'Okay,' she said. She reached over and shook Toby's hand. 'It's good to meet you . . .' she said, '. . . Toby Gordon, Esquire, hero of small animals and soft fruit! Once you've finished organising the whole village, do you think you can spare a kiss?'

'I thought you'd never ask,' he said.

Chapter Twenty-Three

Adam opened the consulting-room door to let Helen back into the waiting room. Emily was sitting at the reception desk. She looked up and smiled. 'Mandy's had to go out on a call,' she said, 'and Toby's having the afternoon off. Would you be okay to see a couple of clients? Reverend Hadcroft's bringing Tallulah in. He wants help giving her a worming tablet.' She glanced at the screen. 'And Mike and Jo Hapwell have just got a puppy and they'd like someone to check him over.'

Helen frowned. Toby was having the afternoon off? Half an hour ago, they'd had lunch together and he hadn't said anything. 'Sure,' she said, though her mind was racing. Where had Toby gone? Was he trying to find a buyer for the Sunrise fruit? Where on earth could he try that the Mellors hadn't?

'The Hapwells are here,' Emily said as a silver car pulled up outside.

The puppy was an adorable Bernese Mountain Dog. Jo Hapwell looked very proud as she lifted him from the car. Mike Hapwell, who had recently returned from an overseas stint in the army, pulled the door open and ushered Jo and their five-year-old daughter Sophia inside.

'This is Busby,' he announced as they walked up to the desk.

'He's gorgeous,' Emily said. 'Helen's going to take a look at him for you today.'

'We'll weigh him first,' Helen said.

The little dog was the perfect weight for his breed and age. Helen carried him into a consulting room and put him on the table. Busby was full of energy and his coat looked very clean and shiny. Helen checked his eyes, ears and teeth. 'Watch out,' Mike warned her. 'They're sharp.'

Helen reached for the stethoscope. 'What made you choose a Bernese?' she asked.

'I'm sorry we didn't get a dog from Hope Meadows,' Jo said, 'but I've wanted a Bernese for ages. We had pugs when I was growing up, but I wanted a properly big dog.'

'They don't come much bigger,' Helen replied with a grin.

'We got him from a reputable breeder in Leeds,' Jo assured her. 'Liz Butler recommended them.'

Helen nodded. 'It's absolutely fine to buy a pedigree puppy if that's what you want,' she said. 'With a good breeder, you get a chance to see them with their mother and have access to their parents' medical history. It's a great way to preserve pedigree lines.'

'We got a book from the library about looking after

a puppy,' Sophia told her, standing on tiptoe to stroke Busby.

'That's a very good idea,' Helen said. 'This is a really important time in Busby's life.' She looked at Mike and Jo. 'The more positive experiences you can cram into the next few weeks, the better. While he's here, we should give him something tasty to eat, make him think that coming to the vet is a nice thing to do.' She grabbed the tub of treats that was sitting on the side table, selected a puppy-sized morsel, and fed it to Busby. In return, he planted his front paws on her chest and licked her chin. She laughed as she fended him off.

'I think he's got the message,' Mike said.

'Bring him in a few more times before his next vaccination is due,' Helen suggested. 'You're welcome to come in and weigh him and let him sniff around.'

She watched them leave, already looking forward to the sweet pup's next visit. She had a weakness for big dogs herself, especially the mountain breeds.

Reverend Hadcroft's cat was not so much fun. Tallulah had always been something of a nightmare with tablets, but as she'd got older, she'd become even worse. Reverend Hadcroft was apologetic as he bundled the big black and white cat back into her cage. 'I'm so sorry. She won't take the sachets in her food and if I try to mix the tablets in, she won't touch it at all.'

'Not to worry,' Helen reassured him. She looked down at the scratches on the back of her hands. Tallulah hadn't been quite as difficult as Croissant. But next time she came in, they needed to make sure there were two staff to hold her.

Her phone buzzed and she pulled it out. There was a message from Toby. 'Can I come over tonight? Speak to the Mellors?'

Helen replied with 'OK'. Her mind was whirling. Surely he couldn't have come up with a solution that quickly? Not when Steve and Anneka were already trying everything.

Mandy came into the surgery as Helen was putting her phone away. 'Anything else happening?' she asked.

Emily checked the computer screen. 'Nothing,' she said. 'And your dad's on his last patient.'

'That's good.' Mandy grinned. 'Because I just passed Gran and Grandad in the lane. And Grandad was carrying a cake tin.'

Dorothy and Tom Hope were Adam's parents. Though they were both almost ninety, they were still remarkably active. Helen gave the reception floor a quick sweep and joined the family in the kitchen. Tom Hope had put the cake tin on the table and Dorothy had prised off the lid. Inside was a huge sponge cake stuffed with fresh strawberries and cream.

'My own strawberry shortcake,' Dorothy announced. 'It's an old recipe, but it still works.'

'Thank you,' Helen said as Adam handed her a slice. 'And thank you,' she added, grinning at Dorothy. Thick cream oozed out from between the light golden sponge. 'It's absolutely delicious,' she said.

For a moment, she wondered where Dorothy had got the strawberries. Perhaps they were from the Mellors' pick-your-own. She found herself thinking about Sunrise Farm again. If by some miracle they did find a buyer for the harvest, could they really get people from the village to help? Toby hadn't been in Welford long, but Helen knew he was right about the people who lived there. They did pull together when things went wrong. And wouldn't it be lovely to have some kind of festival, if they could arrange it? A kind of summer fruit solstice?

Mandy finished her cake and pushed her chair back. 'I'd better get on,' she said.

Adam stood up too. A moment later, Helen and Emily were alone at the table with Tom and Dorothy.

'How are the animals in the rescue centre?' Tom asked. He had been an enthusiastic helper when the centre first opened, although he'd slowed up recently after a nasty virus.

'They're great,' Helen replied. 'Even Fluffybonce might be getting a new home soon.'

Tom shook his head. 'That's still the most crazy name I've heard for any cow,' he said. 'And I hear you've taken on a new dog?' he went on. 'Isla, is that right?'

Helen nodded. 'She's lovely,' she said. 'I couldn't resist her.'

'Mandy told me she was blind. You're very good to take her on. It must be a lot of work.'

Helen pulled her half-empty mug towards her. 'It

hasn't been easy,' she admitted. 'But things are going much better now that Mandy's helping.'

Tom's eyes crinkled as he beamed. 'That's our Mandy,' he said. 'Best granddaughter in the world, that girl!'

Helen felt a rising sense of excitement as she drove home that evening. Whatever Toby was going to tell the Mellors – and she really couldn't see how he'd come up with a way to save the farm in a single afternoon – she was looking forward to seeing him. When she had unloaded the dogs and followed them into the kitchen, she took a bottle of white wine from her larder and put it into the fridge. Hopefully Toby would stay for dinner after talking to Steve and Anneka.

The dogs began to bark and a moment later Toby appeared in the doorway. He looked handsome and polished as usual, and Helen realised she hadn't had a chance to get changed. She reminded herself he had already seen her in her work clothes that day and hadn't shied away in horror, so she went over and greeted him with a kiss.

'That's a welcome welcome,' he said.

Helen stepped back, studying him. 'So?' she demanded. 'Have you found a direct line to the Soft Fruit Enthusiasts' Association?'

Toby laughed. 'Not quite, but I do have a suggestion for the Mellors. Shall we head over to the farmhouse?'

Helen felt a stab of frustration. Why did he have to

be so mysterious all the time? 'I'd like to know what it is first,' she said stubbornly.

Toby looked surprised. 'Okay.'

They sat down at the kitchen table. Toby had brought a folder with him. He opened it up, pulled out a glossy green brochure and handed it to Helen.

'*Craighenry Estate Produce,*' Helen read, admiring the shiny gold lettering. She frowned. Where had she heard Craighenry before? It sounded familiar. She glanced up at Toby and remembered the address on the envelope: Craighenry Castle.

She suddenly felt breathless. Toby was looking at her with a smile that she couldn't read. She opened the brochure. Half of the first page was taken up with a photo of a rather austere-looking grey-haired man wearing a Harris tweed suit and matching tie. '*The Laird of Craighenry welcomes you to his estate, and invites you to share some of the food that his family has been producing for hundreds of years.*'

She flipped through a few more pages. The brochure offered a wide range of game, dense-looking fruit cakes, jams and preserves, and multiple flavours of ice cream. At the end there was a section on visiting the estate with gorgeous photos of places to stay, from a bothy for two people to a fully restored gamekeeper's cottage that slept ten.

'*Ideal for Hogmanay in the Highlands!*'

Helen looked up at Toby. 'This is your home, isn't it?' She flipped back through the brochure until she found the photograph of the Laird of Craighenry. 'And that's your father.' She lifted the photo into the light. Lord Craighenry's piercing blue eyes and straight nose stared up at her. He was the spitting image of Toby.

Toby held up his hands. 'It is, and he is.' He tilted his head. 'You don't seem too surprised.'

Helen swallowed. 'I recognised the name,' she said.

Toby looked puzzled.

'I . . . I saw it on some redirected post,' she confessed. Toby's eyebrows lifted until they disappeared under his fringe.

'So the comment about peasants wasn't completely off the cuff, then?'

Helen felt her face growing hot. 'No,' she admitted. 'I knew you had a title.'

Toby rolled his eyes. 'Oh God yes, we mustn't forget the title,' he drawled. 'Though technically just now, I'm only an honourable.'

Helen giggled. 'Only,' she said. 'Why don't you use it?'

'Can you imagine if I insisted on being called the Right Honourable Tobias by every client?' he said. 'They'd die of boredom before I'd finished introducing myself.'

'It's kind of cool, though, isn't it?' Helen traced her finger along the edge of the brochure. 'I don't think I could resist using it if I had one!'

Toby laughed dryly. 'Trust me,' he said. 'The novelty soon wears off. Still,' he went on, 'thank you for not telling anyone. I guess they'll all find out after this. But hopefully it'll be worth it.'

Helen flipped through the brochure again. 'Is this where the fruit is going to go?'

Toby nodded. 'I spoke to my father's factor this afternoon.'

Helen looked at him with a frown.

'The factor is the general manager,' he explained. 'Lairds of the Highlands like their hierarchy. What can I say?'

Helen felt a laugh bubbling up. You can say lots and lots more, she thought. She swallowed her laughter. There would be plenty of time for questions later.

'It was you who gave me the idea, actually,' Toby went on. 'You asked me if I was going to open a jam factory, or the world's biggest tea-room. Not exactly, but as you can see, Craighenry has a busy restaurant, and we also make our own preserves. Both of which use up pretty impressive amounts of soft fruit, especially at this time of year.'

Helen stared at him. Was she dreaming? Or was Toby actually coming up with the very solution she had wished for?

'Noel – the factor – spoke to Peter, the executive chef. Noel thinks they can commit to a large proportion of the fruit, especially the blackcurrants. They do grow those here, don't they?'

Helen nodded, unable to speak.

'We usually pride ourselves on using local fruit,' Toby

said, 'but it just so happens that Scotland had a bad summer last year, and yields were much lower than usual. I know Peter has been having problems getting enough supplies, so it would be doing him a huge favour if Sunrise Farm could step in. And I told Noel we'd get a great deal because of the situation.'

For the first time, Helen felt uneasy. It had seemed up till now that Toby was some kind of knight in shining armour, riding up with the perfect solution. But the Mellors hadn't agreed to any deal. She looked across the table at Toby. Was he going to take advantage of her friends?

'It sounds amazing,' she said slowly. 'Let's go and speak to Steve and Anneka, hear what they think.' She wanted to make it clear that her friends still had a choice about accepting Toby's offer. She gave his hand a squeeze. 'Thanks for doing all this. Even if they don't go for it, it's really kind of you.'

Toby shrugged. 'Family connections have got to come in useful some time,' he said. Though he was trying to sound light hearted, Helen could feel the undertone. Toby had kept his secret for months and now he was going to reveal himself. Why would he do that? *Is he doing all this for me?*

It was stiflingly warm in the Mellors' kitchen. Anneka smiled as they came in. 'Would you like a slice of pizza?' It looked as if the children had just finished their supper and several pieces of leftover pizza lay in the middle of the table. Steve was collecting the used plates.

Helen felt her cheeks going red. 'We're not really here for a casual visit,' she said. 'We're kind of here on business. Toby wanted to talk to you.'

Steve raised his eyebrows. 'Come on through to the office.'

He showed them into a small, white-painted room at the back of the house. A long shelf was filled with books about fruit and there was a large, rather cluttered desk. Steve pulled out a couple of chairs from the wall so that there were enough for them all to sit around the desk.

Toby reached into his folder and took out two of the Craighenry brochures. He handed one to Anneka and one to Steve. 'This is my father's company,' he said.

Steve looked at him in surprise. Anneka flicked through the brochure.

'I've spoken to Dad's manager and he's willing to take a commercial quantity of fruit from you,' Toby went on.

Steve glanced down at the booklet in his hands. 'A commercial quantity?' he echoed. 'How much is that, exactly? How do you even know what we grow here?' To Helen's dismay, he sounded almost angry.

'I don't know exactly what you have,' Toby admitted, 'but I did see round a bit one day when I was visiting Helen.'

'This would be for your food production, would it?' Anneka asked, the brochure resting open on her lap.

Toby nodded. 'And to use in the restaurant on the

estate. We get through a vast amount of fruit at this time of year.'

Steve frowned. 'What about your usual suppliers? Aren't you committed to them?'

'We are, but we've been having trouble with local farms because of last year's bad harvest. And it's always a competitive market. If you can offer us the right deal, we'll switch suppliers to make up our stock.' Helen stared at Toby in astonishment. The efficient, single-minded vet had vanished, and it seemed like a stranger was sitting here. He wasn't as detached from his family business as he had made out.

'We're not going to sell our fruit dirt cheap just to get shot of it,' Steve grunted.

Toby seemed unruffled. 'Of course not,' he said. 'We always pay a fair price. It'll be based on the market value of your crop.'

Anneka was gazing at Toby with a mixture of hope and worry. 'There's something else you need to know,' she said. She reached out and took Steve's hand. 'We have a major problem with the harvest. We don't have any staff, you see. Even if you were willing to buy it, we can't commit to delivering the fruit at its peak.'

Toby smiled. 'I know that too,' he said. 'I'm sorry if it seems like we're overstepping the mark, but Helen here was worried enough about what was happening to tell me everything. I'm really, really sorry for the situation you're in. But Helen had a bit of a brainwave about the staffing issue. How would you feel about asking the local people to help?' He smoothed his hair back with one hand. 'If there's one thing I've learned in the short time I've been here, it's that Welford rises to the occasion when it's needed.'

Helen's neck had become hot as she listened to him. Would the Mellors think that she had betrayed their confidence? Or worse, that she had been plotting with Toby behind their backs?

But Steve seemed to be thinking about practicalities. He shook his head. 'I'm afraid even if we sell to you, and even if they did it cut price, we can't pay anyone from the village to do our harvest,' he said. For the first time in their conversation, there was regret in his face.

Helen took a deep breath. 'That's not what Toby meant,' she said. 'We thought we could turn it into an event. Not for people to be paid, but to volunteer. People should have a chance to take home some produce as well, paying for it, of course . . .'

Anneka held up her hand. 'No! If people are helping us, we won't charge them.'

Helen felt a prickle of optimism. Anneka sounded genuinely enthusiastic. 'Like I said,' Helen went on, 'we could make a special day of it. We can organise some children's games like biggest strawberry or smallest apple. Maybe have a harvest supper to follow. Bring and share, something like that. And Mandy's gran has always been a staunch member of the WI. Maybe the WI ladies would agree to produce some summer fruit recipes.'

She felt Toby's eyes on her. She was pleased to see

him looking surprised and impressed with her rush of ideas. He leaned towards her. 'True Welford spirit,' he murmured. He put out a hand and squeezed her knee under the table.

To Helen's delight, Anneka was nodding. She had pulled out a pen and was making notes.

But Steve was still frowning. 'Look, I appreciate you offering to help,' he said. 'But I'm not sure it's going to work. The harvest is ready now. We can't organise something like this in such a short space of time, and it doesn't seem fair to ask so much from our neighbours.'

'I think you're wrong,' Anneka argued. 'We've helped some of them out before. It's what friends do. Anyway,' she added, her voice filled with spirit, 'what have we got to lose? I think we should give it a try.' She put her hand on her husband's arm. 'At least let's talk to the people at Craighenry and see what kind of quantities they need.'

Steve sighed. 'All right, love, we'll give it a go.' He looked at Helen. 'Don't go rousing the locals just yet, will you? We'll have to work some things out.'

'I won't,' Helen promised, 'but as you say, we need to move fast. When do you think you'll be able to speak to Craighenry?'

Steve looked at Toby. Toby's face showed no sign of triumph as he held out a card. 'Here's Noel's private number,' he said. The card had the same distinctive gold and green lettering as the brochure. 'He won't mind if you call him tonight. He understands the pressures of farming well enough.'

'I'll do that,' Steve said. He smiled tightly. 'Thank you,' he said. There was emotion in his voice. 'I don't know if this will save the whole farm, but Anneka's right. It sounds like it's worth a punt.'

They stood up and Steve shook Toby's hand, then turned and offered his to Helen, but she reached out her arms and hugged him. 'You're not on your own,' she said. 'I know you and Anneka love Sunrise Farm. I love it too. Let us help, please.'

Anneka took Helen's hands. 'Thank you,' she said. There were tears in her eyes. 'I'm sorry. I don't want to cry all over you again, Helen. It's just that Sunrise Farm means so much to us.'

Helen nodded. 'I know it does. And we're not going to give it up without a fight.'

Chapter Twenty-Four

'Shall we take the dogs out?' Helen asked Toby as they walked back across the garden. A million ideas were fizzing in her head. It seemed impossible to go and sit quietly in the granary. They collected Lucy and Isla from the kitchen and took them through the orchard, over the bridge and up the shoulder of the fell.

After several minutes of brisk striding, Helen stopped to catch her breath. She sat down on a pile of flattened, sun-warmed stones and gazed at the polytunnels and fruit fields below. Had Toby really found a way to save the farm?

'Thanks again,' she said. 'Today's been amazing.'

'No problem,' Toby replied. To her surprise, his voice sounded flat.

She glanced at him, but he was watching Lucy sniffing around the base of the stones and she couldn't read anything from his face. 'Are you okay?'

'I'm fine,' he said. 'It's been a busy day, that's all.'

'Hasn't it?' Helen agreed. 'I don't know where Toby the vet went,' she continued, 'but I quite liked the international businessman that took his place.'

She grinned at him, but Toby was fiddling with a piece of dry grass. 'Don't worry,' he said, 'I'm back to being Toby the vet now.'

Helen reached out and turned his face towards her. 'Would you be willing to talk to me?' she pressed gently. She felt Isla lie down at her feet with a small sigh. Lucy had flopped down on the other side of Toby and seemed to be enjoying the view, her ears lifting in the breeze.

'You told me before that your father wanted you to join the family business,' Helen said, 'but you wanted to be a vet, yes?'

Toby twisted the stalk in his fingers, watching the seed head spin. 'Family business,' he echoed. 'It sounds so gentle when you put it like that.'

'Couldn't you have combined the two things?' Helen asked. 'Be a vet somewhere nearer to home? Noel runs the estate, doesn't he?'

Toby turned to look at her. He was smiling, but there was an edge to his voice when he spoke. 'Family business sounds like something cosy,' he said, 'like Animal Ark. For me, it's something different. To an extent, yes, I could have done what you said. It might have worked while my father's alive.' He stretched out his legs, careful not to disturb Lucy. 'But the lairdship is a proper hereditary peerage. It carries a place in the House of Lords. Of course, not all hereditary peers go there on a regular basis, but my father always has. He has this sense of duty, of tradition and honour and all that goes with hundreds of years of history.'

He made it sound like a bad thing, but Helen wondered whether he realised he had inherited the same work ethic and sense of loyalty to his clients. 'How often is he in London?' she asked.

'Outside the recess, he tries to be there four days a week. Then, of course, there's all the travelling. He has a house in London, but he likes to get home every weekend. "The estate doesn't run itself." He's forever telling me that.' He gazed out over the valley. 'Craighenry is beautiful,' he said, 'but it's freezing cold and it eats money. And then there's pressure to marry the right woman to produce yet another son and heir.' He gave a short laugh. 'Of course, it has to be a son,' he said. 'The irony is, my sister would love to take over. But that would never do.'

'You have a sister?' Helen felt a small rush of surprise. How did she still know so little about the man sitting beside her? For some reason, she'd never imagined that he had any siblings.

'Maggie,' said Toby. 'Margaret really, but that's never suited her. She lives in a cottage on the estate with her partner Cara.' He glanced at Helen, and for the first time there was humour in his eyes. 'You can imagine how that went down with my parents. Actually, my mother was fine but it nearly gave my father a stroke at first.' He flicked the blade of grass onto the ground. 'Cara's fab. She's a music teacher specialising in traditional instruments. I think part of my father's problem is that she's far better at the bagpipes than he'll ever be!'

'What does Maggie do?'

'She's a ceramic artist,' Toby replied. 'She has a studio in the old stableyard. She's really good, sells her pots all over the world. Loads of Americans come especially to see her.'

Helen found herself smiling. 'Well,' she said, 'aren't you a dark horse! Not only a lord in waiting, but you also have a famous potting sister!' She tipped her head to one side. 'Why do you keep it all a secret?' She couldn't help feeling genuinely baffled. Why did it matter so much?

Toby shook his head. There was resignation in his face. 'All that's my family, not me! It was awful growing up, being constantly reminded of all the things my future held. All that weight of expectation.' He gently lifted Isla onto his knee and ran his hand across her back. 'One of the nannies gave me a box set of James Herriot videos one Christmas. She could see how much I loved animals. After that, I only ever wanted to be a vet but that wasn't what my father had in mind.'

He scratched Isla's ear and the little dog leaned her head into his fingers. 'Father was bloody furious when I got into Glasgow to study veterinary medicine. He told me it was a waste of time. He said I should do estate management and marry some blue-blood as quickly as possible to get on with producing an heir and a spare. He wasn't bothered that I'd been awarded a full scholarship, or that I had ambitions of my own. It's all about the family to him, nothing else.'

Helen stared at Toby. Different emotions were coming from him in waves: pain, bitterness, frustration. No wonder he tried not to talk about it. What would it be like to grow up with so much pressure? All that weight of history looming on top of you from the moment you were born.

Her own childhood might not have been perfect. She had often longed for a traditional family: Mum and Dad living together, a brother or a sister for company. Yet they'd both encouraged her to do whatever her heart wanted. They'd helped her through her years of study and supported her when she first started work.

'What about now?' she asked him gently. 'Your parents must be proud of you now, surely? When you've done so well?'

Toby concentrated on untangling a tiny knot in Isla's fur. 'In their own way, yes, they are. Mum is, anyway. I think my father is too, but everything has strings attached. When I told him I wanted to leave Glasgow to set up my own practice, he offered to finance the whole thing. But it was on condition that I was based on the estate. He wanted me there so I could take on a share of his responsibilities.' He sighed. 'I told him I'd rather raise the funds on my own and be independent. It didn't go down too well.' Isla wriggled off his knee and began pottering around on top of the rock. Toby's mouth twisted into a rueful smile. 'Is that the definition of cutting off your nose to spite your face?'

Helen shook her head. 'Not to me it isn't. I'd feel

the same, I think. How else would you know that your clinic was really yours?' Toby nodded. 'Not only that,' Helen went on, 'if I was building my own practice, I'd want to be there all the time. If you had to keep stopping to do your father's work, you'd be pulled in two directions.'

Toby wrapped his fingers around hers. 'I'm glad you understand. Lots of people don't.'

'So what made you come here?' Helen asked. She couldn't imagine that working at Animal Ark was much better paid than his post at the university, so it wasn't an obvious step towards setting up his own practice.

'I wanted to increase my large-animal and rural experience,' Toby explained. 'I thought I'd be here for a year or two, and then move on, but I'm more content than I expected. Animal Ark's a great place to work.' He sent Helen a look that was hard to read. 'I'm not so far from being my father's son that I don't want to live in the country,' he said. 'And I'm quite traditional in my own way. I want a family, and children, maybe even sons that have the family name, but I want to do that in my own time, with the person that I choose.'

Helen started to feel uneasy. Was he suggesting she was that person? They'd been having a fling for a few days. A bit of fun. Had Toby read something more into it?

But he smiled rather sadly as he went on. 'All that's probably a long way off, though. I think my father is coming round to the idea of who I am, rather than who he wants me to be. I know my mother is on my side, at least. And Maggie helps. She's dead proud of me.'

'Maggie sounds great,' she said. 'I'd love to meet her.'

'You would?'

Helen felt her uneasiness return. She had wanted to compliment Maggie, not request a meeting.

Toby put his hand down and pushed himself off the rock. 'Well, there you go,' he declared. 'That's my sordid backstory.'

'Hardly sordid,' Helen said. She told herself to relax and stop seeing proposals of marriage everywhere. Toby was just Toby, as he'd always been. 'It seemed interesting to me.' Toby stiffened. 'But if you don't want me to say anything, I won't,' she added.

Toby nodded. 'I guess some things are going to come out if Sunrise Farm starts supplying Craighenry, but we don't need to talk about it to anyone else, do we?'

Helen squeezed his fingers. 'Absolutely not. Nobody needs to know your deepest, darkest secrets.'

To her surprise, Toby bent down. 'I'm quite willing for *you* to know everything,' he teased.

Helen laughed. Here he was again. Funny and flirtatious. 'Down, boy!' she told him. 'We need to get these dogs home before they think they're being starved. Race you back!'

They fed the dogs and Helen cooked a bowl of pasta while Toby sorted out the wine. 'Very nice,' he said, lifting up the bottle and studying it. Helen found herself wondering about the pedigree of the wine. Not that she bought very cheap wine, but it was hardly the Bollinger that he seemed to take for granted.

It felt almost like an evening with Seb. Toby washed the dishes and Helen dried them. 'Shall we watch *Supervet*?' she suggested.

'If you like,' Toby said.

Isla sat on Helen's feet and Lucy stretched out in front of Toby. An hour drifted past and then another. Helen had wondered whether Toby would head home, but he seemed to have settled in for the night.

There was a tap on the kitchen door. Lucy jumped up and barked and Toby, who had been half asleep, jerked awake. Helen stood up and walked over to open the door.

Anneka was on the doorstep. Her eyes were still tired, but she was smiling. 'Sorry to disturb you so late,' she said. 'I just wanted you to know that Steve spoke to Noel, and to Peter the chef, and it looks like we have a deal! They'll take twenty pallets of mixed soft fruit, as long as we can deliver by the end of next week.' She sounded so excited that Helen wanted to hug her.

Anneka looked at Helen, wide eyed. 'Do you think we'll be able to organise the harvest by then?'

'Of course we will,' Helen said with determination. There was a lot to sort out, but organising was one of her strengths.

Toby joined them at the door. Anneka grasped his

hand in both of hers. 'Steve and I can't thank you enough,' she said. 'Even if Craighenry only uses us this season, it'll give us a chance to find another wholesale client before next year. I can hardly believe it. It feels like a dream come true!'

'Happy to help,' Toby said.

'We need to get the fruit picked first,' Helen warned. For the first time, she felt a tremor of doubt at the size of the task. 'I'll get straight on to that tomorrow.' A million thoughts were already rushing round her brain. She should write them down or she would never sleep.

'Well, obviously Steve and I'll help with sorting out the pickers,' Anneka told her.

'You should probably get on with some harvesting,' Helen said. 'Or at least making sure everything's ready for the onslaught.'

'We'll work it out between us.' Anneka's enthusiasm lifted Helen again. She didn't have to do everything on her own. It would be a team effort. 'I'll leave you in peace now,' Anneka said. 'And thank you, both of you. It feels like you're our guardian angels, it really does.'

She turned and rushed off, leaving the door open. Helen pushed it closed. Toby was standing in the kitchen, leaning against the counter with his arms folded. He had a look of relief on his face. He was a mass of contradictions, Helen thought: super-confident and filled with uncertainty. Fiercely independent but very aware of his roots and his good fortune. He seemed far more vulnerable than she could ever have suspected.

She waltzed over, and put her arms around his neck. 'You . . .' she said, looking up at him, '. . . future Laird of Craighenry, are the hero of the hour!'

Toby smiled down at her. 'Oh yes,' he said. 'Well, you know what they say about us Scottish lairds?'

Helen shook her head. 'I really have no idea. What do they say?'

He swept Helen into his arms. Helen felt a wave of shock to find herself lifted clean off the floor. 'We're always hiding our best assets,' he told her. 'Would you like to see what I keep under my kilt?'

They were both laughing so hard that Helen was afraid he was going to drop her as he carried her upstairs.

Chapter Twenty-Five

'You're early!' Mandy glanced at her watch as Helen pulled up in front of Animal Ark. 'Isn't it your late start today?'

Helen reached into the back seat of her car, grabbed a folder and waved it at Mandy. 'I need to use the printer,' she said. She grinned, as she had been doing on and off since she woke up beside Toby. It was a long time since she had felt so full of energy, and ideas had been swirling around her head half the night.

At five o'clock, when the sun had risen high enough to shine in at the edge of the curtain, she had left Toby snoring and crept downstairs. Lucy and Isla had followed her. They had spent an hour cuddled together on the sofa, Lucy on one side and Isla on the other, as Helen made frantic notes.

'What's going on?' Mandy opened the door to the clinic and waved Helen through.

'We've found a way to save Sunrise Farm!' Helen declared.

Mandy stared at her. 'Really?'

'You know Toby took yesterday afternoon off?'
Mandy nodded.

'Well, he was chasing up some family connections. He managed to find a buyer for the entire harvest.'

Mandy began spooning coffee powder into mugs. 'Goodness,' she said. 'You can't fault Toby's dedication to the Helen Steer cause. What did you do to him?'

Helen felt her face grow warm. She looked down at the folder, pretending to ruffle through the pages. Her mind had been so intent on her Fruit Festival plans that she had barely thought at all about Toby since Anneka's announcement last night. Yet all this was his doing. What would he think when he woke up and found she'd left?

She shoved aside her guilt and held out the folder. 'What do you think?' Mandy had often rallied the people in Welford before, but mostly it had been done by word of mouth. This time the scale of the task meant they needed a coordinated plan.

Mandy gazed down at the pages of lists. 'You seem to have thought of all kinds of things,' she said.

'We need to recruit as many volunteers as we can. The harvest has to be delivered to Craighenry next week,' Helen explained.

'Next week?' Mandy's eyebrows shot up. 'Blimey, you don't ask for much! I guess the main thing you need is publicity,' she decided. She thought for a moment. 'How about we put a notice on the Animal Ark Facebook page? There isn't time to change the clinic website, but

I can put something up on the Hope Meadows page, if that would help?'

'That would be brilliant,' Helen said. She added tentatively, 'What about your rescue centre sponsors? Do you think any of them might help?'

'I'm sure James would love to get involved,' Mandy said. 'As for the others, I'm not sure, but I can e-mail them for you.'

'Thanks ever so.' Helen looked down at page two of her list. 'How about some flyers? If we get going, we could print them off and deliver them today.' She ran her finger down her notes. 'As well as posters for the pub, church and post office.'

Mandy's eyebrows had disappeared under her fringe. 'All good ideas,' she said. 'But you're talking about a lot of work.' She glanced at the clock on the wall. 'Morning surgery begins in half an hour.'

The door to the clinic clicked open. Helen felt a stab of annoyance. Animal Ark wasn't open yet. This wasn't an emergency, was it? To her relief, Nicole Woodall was standing in the doorway. Tall, blonde, and with a smile that was completely infectious, Nicole was Mandy's student helper in the rescue centre.

'Hi, Mandy,' she said. 'Any special chores for me today?'

Mandy glanced at Helen. A triumphant gleam had appeared in her eye. 'Actually, yes,' she said to Nicole. 'How do you feel about rescuing some soft fruit for a change?'

Helen had rarely seen anyone look so confused. She

pulled out the chair in front of the computer. 'Come on, whizz kid,' she said. 'I bet you can whip up a page for the website faster than either of us. We need to save Sunrise Farm and we only have a week to do it!'

By the time they had finished their mugs of coffee, their work was well under way.

'How does that look?' Nicole asked, turning the screen to show Helen. She had created a whole new page for the Fruit Festival on the Hope Meadows website. It was bright and strawberry-coloured, decorated with pictures of animals holding fruit. There was also a cosy picture of Sunrise Farm that Helen had downloaded from her phone and the caption 'Help Us Save Sunrise Fruit Farm!' in green lettering. Underneath was a clear explanation of how people could help.

Between them, they had also come up with some flyers. The printer was churning them out as fast as it could. *Pick Your Own And Save The Farm! This Sunday! Support your local fruit farm by joining in with harvest! Generous harvest supper and baskets of soft fruit to take away!*

Helen picked up one of the flyers as it slid out from the printer. She frowned as she read the blurb. 'Erm . . .' she said. Mandy had come up with the text and she hadn't checked it. 'Where are we going to conjure a harvest supper from?'

Mandy grinned. 'That's easy. I'll get Grandma to rally the WI! Ham, cheese, bread and some salad should be okay, shouldn't they?'

Helen felt a wave of relief. That was one less thing she would have to organise. 'Perfect,' she said. 'I'm hoping we can persuade Upper Welford Hall to provide some cream to have with fruit for afters. And I might have offered a WI cake sale to Anneka and Steve to raise more funds . . .'

'I'll ring Gran right now and ask her to come over!' Mandy said.

Emily appeared just as Mandy was heading out to use the cottage phone. She looked around at the office, taking in the growing pile of flyers, and Nicole at the computer. 'Is this a veterinary clinic or a printing office?' she asked.

Helen felt her cheeks reddening. 'Oh gosh,' she said. 'I'll pay for a new toner! And for the paper. It's for a good cause, honestly.' She handed Emily one of the flyers. Emily read it with interest, then looked up with a smile. 'I should have known you wouldn't take the sale of Sunrise Farm lying down. And I agree it's a very good cause. We're lucky in Welford to have so many fine local producers.'

The door opened and Mandy rushed back in. 'Hi, Mum,' she said, then turned to Helen. 'Gran is up for the challenge!'

'What challenge?' Emily asked.

'She's going to rally the WI,' Mandy explained. 'Ham sandwiches, teas and lots of cakes.'

'That's right up Gran's street,' Emily agreed.

Helen felt as if she was standing in a pool of bright

sunlight. Amazing as it was, somehow everything was coming together.

'Finished!' Nicole sat back in her chair. Mandy and Helen walked over to look at the screen. 'Shall I upload it?' Nicole asked.

Mandy patted her on the shoulder. 'Please do,' she said. 'And would you mind e-mailing a link to the supporters, please? I'll type a quick note to go with it.'

'This does sound like fun,' Emily said. 'Adam and I will come along to help, if that's okay?'

'Definitely okay,' Helen told her.

Emily took the flyer through the door that led to the cottage. 'I'll go and warn Adam what I've let him in for!' she called over her shoulder.

'Jimmy and I will be there too,' Mandy said, 'though we won't have the twins with us.'

Helen suddenly remembered that it was this weekend that Mandy had been planning to propose. 'You don't have to come,' she said. 'I know you've got important things lined up.' She kept her voice low. Fortunately Nicole was engrossed in the computer.

Mandy grinned. 'It's okay,' she said. 'Not to undermine your day, but maybe it'll be a chance for us to share the good news!' She stood up and wandered over to the window, then turned to look at Helen. She looked so happy that Helen smiled. 'We can only be romantic for twenty-four hours, anyway. I know Jimmy. We'll both want to get back to normal life.'

'We'll toast you with strawberries,' Helen promised.

'That's the e-mails done,' Nicole announced. 'If there isn't too much to do in the centre, I could go out and deliver some of those flyers, if you like?'

Helen beamed at her. 'That would be brilliant.'

'No problem,' Mandy confirmed.

Helen picked up a pile of the leaflets and helped Nicole put them in a cardboard folder so she could carry them on her bike.

'Can you do the houses along the Walton Road and the new estates?' Helen suggested. 'I'll do the village centre, if that's okay?'

'Fine by me!' Nicole cycled off with the folder slung in a bag over her shoulder.

Helen placed the rest of the flyers in another folder, put the dogs' leads on, and headed outside. Toby's car drew up as the door closed behind her. For a moment, she felt nervous. What would he say about her deserting him in the middle of the night? But Toby grinned and kissed her, then looked down at the folder.

'Flyers,' Helen explained. She took one out to show him.

'You've been busy,' he commented.

'It's all thanks to you,' she told him. 'Honestly, I can't thank you enough for helping Steve and Anneka.'

Toby bent forward in a small bow. 'My pleasure,' he said. His eyes were glittering, but then he looked more closely at her face. 'This really matters to you, doesn't it?' he said. 'Saving the farm?'

Helen nodded. 'Of course it does.' She felt a little surprised that he would have to ask. 'It's my home!'

For a moment, Toby paused as if there was something else he wanted to say. Then he shook his head. 'Hope it goes well with your delivery,' he said. 'I'll see you later.'

As she strode up the lane to the village with the dogs beside her, Helen was glad that the weather had turned slightly cooler. There were even a few grey clouds dotted across the sky. As long as it didn't turn in the next few days, she thought. She pulled out her mobile, checked the forecast and let out a sigh of relief. Dawn-till-dusk sunshine for the next few days.

'Helen!' She looked up as she heard the hearty yell.

'Hello, Douglas,' she said.

Douglas MacLeod was marching towards her. His big red beard and chaotic hair made him look like a Viking. He was walking a small terrier, which looked quite ridiculous beside his sturdy frame.

'Hello, Bounce!' Helen said. 'You're looking well.' Bounce had been in the rescue centre just before Christmas. He had been rehomed to Susan's elderly neighbour, who had recently lost his much-loved dog. Douglas must have offered to take him out. Lucy wagged her tail as the little dog came towards them. Even Isla seemed calm. 'You're such a good girl,' Helen told her, running her fingers through the little dog's curly hair.

'You're very cheerful today,' Douglas commented.

Helen reached into her bag and pulled out a flyer. 'Cheerful – and hopeful,' she said as she handed it to him. 'What are you doing this Sunday?'

Douglas was studying the flyer. 'Saving Sunrise Farm,' he said. 'Sounds fantastic. And lots of fun. Susan and Jack would probably love to come as well. Jack and I could bring some shortbread, if you like? Our baking is getting rather good, if I say so myself.' He took a couple of the flyers, promising to give them to friends outside the village, then he saluted Helen and carried on, turning left to cross the road to the village green.

Helen turned right into Honeysuckle Lane. She stopped in the shade of one of the tall trees beside the Old Vicarage. She should give Anneka a quick call, she thought. Let her know what they were doing.

'That all sounds wonderful,' Anneka said when Helen told her about the flyers and the e-mails and about Dorothy Hope and the WI and the cakes. 'We're getting things ready here too. We've made up plenty of collecting baskets and we've made a start on some of the fruit that's already ripe. We don't want any of it to go to waste.'

Helen ended the call, then marched up one side of Honeysuckle Lane, turned round and walked back down the other side, dropping leaflets into all the letterboxes. 'Don't Stop Me Now,' she sang as she turned right onto the High Street and started along the row of houses near the church.

She was still humming when she reached the Fox and

Goose. Bev Parsons looked with interest at the leaflet. 'Leave a few with me,' she told Helen. 'We can put them on the bar. What day is it again?'

'Sunday.'

'I'll send Gary up with a keg of beer and some soft drinks for the harvest supper, if you like,' she said. 'I can't stay to help with the picking, but can you reserve us a few punnets of fruit, please? We can use some for desserts on the summer specials.' She shook her head. 'It's daft really. Soft fruit is so popular this time of year, but we never thought to look for a local supplier. Maybe we can buy some more, if you manage to save the business.'

Helen and the dogs headed back out into the bright sunshine. Two middle-aged women were walking across the green and she handed them a flyer each.

'Sounds great,' said the taller woman. She was wearing bright green trousers and a white T-shirt. 'I've got three sons and it'll do them good to get off the Xbox for a day. What about you, Madeleine?'

'Definitely,' Madeleine agreed. She folded up the flyer and pushed it into the back pocket of her jeans. 'See you on Sunday,' she said to Helen. She bent down, gave Lucy's ear a tug, and walked on.

By the time Helen got back to Animal Ark, her legs were trembling from all the walking. Even Lucy and Isla were panting.

Mandy watched the dogs as they walked into the clinic. 'Are you carrying on with the training?' she asked

Helen. 'Those two look way more comfortable together now.'

Helen felt a swell of pride. It came almost naturally now to guide Isla with verbal commands while they walked. Isla loved retreating to her crate at home, which made Lucy happier. It wasn't perfect yet at night. Isla occasionally cried in her crate, but Helen was still working on that.

Adam stuck his head around the door. 'Anyone want a drink?' He led them into the cottage garden, where a jug of fresh lemonade was standing on the table. 'I hear you're planning a festival,' he said to Helen. 'Count me in, won't you? I love raspberries . . . and strawberries . . . and cream!' He patted his stomach and Helen laughed.

Emily joined them and sat down in a garden chair that Mandy pulled up for her. Adam drained his glass and glanced at his watch. 'Suppose we'd better get on,' he said to Mandy. 'That colt at Hare Hill Stables isn't going to castrate itself.'

'I need to be off too,' Emily announced. 'I've got a physio appointment.'

'Help yourself to more lemonade,' Adam told Helen. 'You look like you need it. There's nothing else in till after lunch.'

He put Emily's folding chair in the shed. A minute later, Helen saw Adam's car set off down the drive, then Emily's. Helen poured herself another glass. There was a wooden bench standing beside the wall, partially shaded by a trellis with climbing roses. Helen had a quick look over the wall to check no one had turned up, then flopped down onto the bench.

Though she was exhausted, she found it hard to switch her mind off. There were only four days until harvest day. Would they manage to find enough volunteers? Would they get all the fruit picked? Her eyes drifted shut. Biggest strawberry competition, she thought. What if one of the strawberries was huge? Massive enough to roll towards her. It would crush her in a heap of sticky red juice . . .

She woke with a start, feeling a hand on her arm. It was Toby and he was smiling. 'Hello, Sleeping Beauty,' he said. 'I'm afraid it's time to work. I need a hand in theatre.'

Helen blinked herself awake. She never, ever fell asleep in public. She surreptitiously lifted a hand to the side of her mouth. Had she been dribbling? She wished Toby would stop looking at her.

'You'll be pleased to know I left some of your flyers with every client I visited this morning,' Toby said. 'They've all promised to come and give us a hand, and they're going to tell others as well. Noel won't know what to do with the avalanche of fine Yorkshire fruit that's about to land on him.'

Helen stood up and tried to smooth out the creases in her polo shirt. As usual, Toby was making her feel scruffy and underdressed, even though she was in her everyday uniform. 'Thank you again for everything you've done,' she said. 'Maybe being the son of a laird isn't so bad?'

Toby shrugged. 'Only time will tell.'

The afternoon flew by with a tricky spay followed by a run of clients. Whenever they were working together, Toby was nothing but professional, for which Helen was heartily grateful.

'What are you doing this evening?' he asked as they walked into the warm air at the end of the afternoon. 'Shall I come over to Sunrise Farm? I can pick up some food on the way.'

Helen looked at him. What she really wanted was a quiet evening in front of the TV and then an early night. 'Thanks for the offer,' she said, 'but I told Susan and Rachel I'd go out with them in Walton tonight. I felt like a night with the girls, okay?'

A strange look passed over Toby's face. Helen couldn't quite tell whether he was angry or disappointed. Then he nodded. 'You missed out on a lot of sleep last night,' he said. The mischievous sparkle had returned to his eyes.

Helen lifted an eyebrow. 'Yes,' she said, 'because I was up making lists while you were snoring.' She laughed and was relieved when Toby joined in.

She fetched Isla from the rescue centre and loaded the dogs into her car. As she crested the ridge and began to drop down towards the farm, she pulled in to the side of the road. The farmhouse had never looked more beautiful. She could see the windows of the granary from here, kitchen and bedroom. The tall fir tree that stood in the back garden. And beyond that, rows and rows of fruit trees.

Could their crazy harvest plan work? she wondered.

She pulled herself up straighter in the driving seat and looked at the open fields where the strawberries and raspberries grew. She could see Anneka bending over the plants. Halfway across the field, Steve was carrying two buckets filled with bright red strawberries. Steve and Anneka were part of Sunrise Farm. They couldn't lose it. She had a sudden yearning to call Seb and tell him all about the plans. He knew how much Sunrise Farm meant to her, and how much she would want to help her friends. Then Helen reminded herself that it was none of Seb's business now. He was in Scotland, lost in his new job with new friends and a completely new home. He probably wasn't giving Helen or Sunrise Farm a second thought.

She felt a pang of sadness in her heart, and twisted around to look at the dogs sleeping peacefully side by side in the back seat. She reached out and gently stroked Lucy's silky ear, then Isla's curly one. Seb might be somewhere else, but she wasn't alone. Steve and Anneka, Barney, Connie, Harry and Birdie. They were part of Sunrise Farm and part of Helen's life. And so were Lucy and Isla.

We're not going to lose Sunrise Farm, she told herself. It's our home. Crazy or not, the plan had to work.

Chapter Twenty-Six

Helen put Isla's food bowl down on the floor. The little dog's ears were pricked forward, waiting for Helen's voice. 'You can have it,' Helen told her, and Isla began to wolf down her breakfast. Helen watched her proudly. Sometimes it was hard to believe Isla was blind at all. She put down Lucy's bowl, and went through the same command. She didn't need to feed them at separate times now.

Her mobile phone buzzed. She picked it up from the kitchen table. She had made coffee and the cafetière and a mug were standing on the table. There were croissants in the oven.

The text was from Toby. *'Hope your head isn't too sore! Cricket match today. Fancy coming to cheer me on?'*

Helen felt a wave of guilt. She had been out yesterday evening with Susan and Rachel. They had planned to stay out late, but all three of them had agreed at about 9.30 that they were ready to go home. She had been tucked up in her comfy bed by ten, with a book and a cup of tea. She had toyed with the idea of messaging Toby; she was sure he would have come over. But the thought of an early night with the dogs had been too tempting.

She picked up their bowls and put them in the sink. The croissants were ready and she took them out of the oven. They smelled wonderful. She set them on the table, sat down and poured the coffee.

She was going to have to answer the text. Was it the idea of cricket or Toby that brought a sigh to her lips? It would be lovely to stay at home and relax in the garden before the busy day tomorrow. She told herself to stop being so lazy. She hadn't seen Toby outside work all week. He would start to think she was avoiding him. And if the cricket was as dull as she feared, she could always have a nap in the sun. She picked up her mobile and started to type.

'Yes, I'll come. See you there. Are pom-poms appropriate for an English cricket match?'

A smile emoji came winging back. *'Only for Scottish cricket matches. Even then it has to be the correct tartan.'*

She set off at two o'clock. Steve and Anneka's eldest son Barney had been drafted in to let Lucy and Isla out at regular intervals. It had been a busy morning. She and Anneka had sorted out a table for people to pick up their baskets, while Steve had set up a separate area for the filled baskets to be weighed and packed onto pallets. They'd put several refreshment stands around the farm. Anneka had found a huge white tablecloth to cover the trestle table they had borrowed for the cake sale, and several more tables were waiting to be set up for the supper afterwards.

Helen pulled up outside Walton's cricket ground. It was very scenic, a flat field on the edge of the town surrounded by ancient oak and beech trees. At one end there was a low brick building. Round the edge of the grass, square white pillars separated the car park from the field. There were a few people on blankets and folding chairs scattered at one end. Helen knew that the closely mown rectangle in the centre of the pitch was where the action happened, but beyond that she was a complete ignoramus. She hoped it wouldn't be too obvious.

There had been excited chatter in Welford when Adam had persuaded Toby to join the cricket team. Toby had played cricket at school to county level. Even Helen, who didn't usually listen to cricketing gossip, had heard all about it. There had been an unexpected shortage of players last season, so they had dropped out of the local league. Now, with Toby in place and a couple of young farmers who had signed up, they were back in business.

Despite being Yorkshire born and bred, Helen had never developed an interest in cricket. Even when she met Seb, who played regularly for Walton, she had resisted getting involved. She felt rather strange as she climbed out of the car. Her first ever match, and it was Welford versus Walton. The rivalry between the two was the stuff of local legend.

Without needing to chase after dogs, she was wearing a strappy yellow sundress and a pair of sandals with wedge heels. She had stowed her book in her handbag. If the game was too dull, at least she'd be prepared. Rather rashly, because Toby had told her it looked nice, she had chosen to wear her hair loose. As she walked towards the edge of the field, the breeze started blowing it into her face. She grabbed her sunglasses and pushed them up onto the top of her head. For a moment, the sun was blindingly bright. She blinked a couple of times, and then stopped. Seb was standing in front of her, dressed in his cricket whites.

Helen felt as if her whole body was burning. 'I didn't expect to see you here,' she blurted out.

'Ditto,' he said dryly. 'I thought you'd rather watch paint dry than a cricket match.'

Helen tried to make a joke. 'I couldn't miss the grudge match of the century, could I?'

The crunch of wheels on gravel sounded behind her and she turned. To her horror, it was Toby. He grinned and waved at her as he climbed out of the car, tugging on his cricket sweater with one hand. He jogged towards her, grinning broadly. 'Best-looking cheerleader I've ever seen,' he declared. He pulled Helen to him and planted a kiss on her mouth. Helen winced. She wasn't a fan of public displays. Especially not with Seb as an audience of one.

Though she tried not to, Helen could see Seb staring at her over Toby's shoulder. If Helen had thought it was uncomfortable bumping into Seb, it was nothing compared to this. She lifted her hands and wormed her way out from Toby's grasp. Forcing herself to smile, though she knew it hadn't reached her eyes, she waved at Seb. 'Good luck!'

Seb also managed a smile, though his jaw was clenched. 'Make sure you cheer on the right side,' he said in a strangled voice. He gave her one last long glance before heading for the pavilion, his thick white pads slapping against his knees.

Toby rested his hand on Helen's shoulder. To his credit, there was embarrassment in his eyes. 'I'm sorry,' he said. 'I didn't see it was Seb when I pulled up. I wasn't expecting him to be here.'

'Me neither,' Helen said. She reached up and twitched the glasses higher on her head.

Toby made a face. 'I hope I haven't made things worse for you,' he said. 'Or him,' he added.

Helen shrugged. 'He'll be fine,' she said. She took Toby's hand and plastered a smile on her face. 'Now, explain to me again what a duck is.'

Toby rolled his eyes. 'If I were you, I'd just watch the numbers on the scoreboard,' he advised her.

They walked across the grass together and Toby followed Seb into the pavilion. Helen stood on her own, feeling a bit lost. Perhaps Molly would be here.

'Hello there!' To Helen's relief Roo Dhanjal was waving at her. Roo and her husband Josh ran Moor View campsite on the edge of Welford. As ever, Roo was wearing a colourful salwar kameez, this time pale blue that matched the sky. She and her children, Herbie and Kiran, were sitting on a blanket. Between them was an old ice-cream box stuffed with home-made samosas. Roo beckoned Helen over and patted her hand on the blanket. 'Sit with us,' she urged. Kiran grinned up at her, his eyes like enormous chocolate buttons.

Helen lowered herself onto the blanket. 'Are you here to see your daddy play?' she asked Herbie.

The little girl nodded. She put her hand into the tub and pulled out a samosa. 'Would you like one?' she offered.

Helen realised that she'd forgotten to have any lunch. 'Yes, please.'

Kiran had a samosa in each hand and was toddling round the mat, waving them in the air. Before Roo could stop him, he wobbled over to a Westie on a lead, whose owner was sitting beside them, and handed it a samosa. 'Good doggie,' he said as the Westie lay down and began to chew.

Roo rolled her eyes at Helen. 'Can you believe Josh wants another baby?' she whispered. 'I've told him I'll run the campsite and he can look after the children if that happens!' She jumped to her feet and walked over to pick Kiran up. 'Sorry about that,' she told the Westie's owner, but he was laughing.

'She looks like she enjoyed it,' he said as the little terrier licked her lips and gazed longingly up at Kiran.

The players had emerged from the pavilion. They

looked very dashing in their whites. Trying not to look at Seb, Helen waved at Toby and at Dean Warrington, who worked at Upper Welford Hall. Adam emerged with his bat over one shoulder and strode over to the wicket. 'He's going to bat first for Welford,' Roo explained.

Helen clapped her hands and whooped. 'Go on, Adam!' she called.

Apart from a subdued round of applause, nobody else made a sound. Several heads turned to stare at her. Helen felt her cheeks go red. 'Oops. Bit loud?' she whispered to Roo.

'Cricket audiences tend to be a little more . . . reserved,' Roo said with a grin. 'But don't let that stop you. It's lovely to see a bit of enthusiasm.'

The Walton fielders spread out around the field. To Helen's embarrassment, Seb ended up close to where she and Roo were sitting. She pulled her sunglasses down and dropped her head to look at the tartan rug. The last thing she wanted was to catch his eye. Roo sent her a sympathetic look. Like everyone else from Welford, she knew exactly what was going on.

Though Helen resisted getting out her book, it was hard to focus all her attention on the match. Everything happened at a snail's pace. The players seemed to spend at least half the time discussing the rules with Reverend Hadcroft, who was acting as the umpire. There were a number of clients in the crowd. Helen spotted Dawn Fenwick, who had rehomed two dogs from Hope Meadows. Dawn came over to ask Helen for some worming advice for Flame and Birch, and Helen was delighted to have a diversion. Dean Warrington's wife Alex also wandered over. She asked when it would be suitable to get their cat Soupy's claws clipped and told Helen all about Soupy's itchy left eye. Helen advised her to wash it with salty water and phone for an appointment on Monday.

Roo smiled at her when Alex had returned to her folding chair on the other side of the field. 'You're very patient,' she said. 'Don't you ever get a day off?'

Helen laughed. 'Not really. Luckily I love my job, and anyway, it's nice to be recognised without my uniform.'

'Quite the local celebrity,' Roo commented. She nudged Helen in the ribs. 'Look,' she said, pointing.

Toby was walking out to the wicket. Helen glanced at Seb. He looked very serious as he watched Toby.

Toby positioned his bat and fixed his eyes on the bowler. The bowler began his run, his arm swung up and the ball hurtled towards Toby. Almost casually, Toby flicked the ball away. It flew over the head of the nearest fielder, bounced twice then rolled over the rope that marked the boundary.

'Four!' Herbie said. She turned to Helen. 'It's a six if it gets to the boundary without touching the ground,' she explained, 'but that was a four because it bounced.'

Roo leaned towards Helen. 'Josh has indoctrinated her,' she confessed.

When Helen looked up, Toby raised his bat and winked at her. She grinned back, then found herself looking to see whether Seb had noticed. To her relief, he was talking to another fielder.

The bowler sent another scything ball towards Toby. This time, he swung the bat sideways. There was a loud thwack and the ball rose high into the air. Surely this time it would be a six. The ball arced towards them, a red dot in the sky. Closer and closer. Helen held her breath. As the ball fell towards the ground, Seb made an enormous leap, raised his hand and grabbed it. He tumbled onto the grass, cradling it, then held it up.

It was a brilliant catch, and a polite wave of clapping ran through the crowd. Toby was looking at the ball in Seb's hand as if he couldn't quite believe it. After a moment, he slung his bat over his shoulder and, without looking at anyone, set off towards the pavilion. He disappeared inside, and Helen looked at Seb. He was concentrating on throwing the ball back to the bowler.

'Has your gallant knight been defeated by his rival?' Roo teased.

Helen felt her cheeks turning pink. 'It's not like that,' she protested.

It was Josh's turn to bat. Roo, Herbie and Kiran joined in the applause as he strode out onto the pitch. Josh played carefully and ran up a respectable thirty-six runs before his wicket fell. Roo looked pleased as she studied the scoreboard. 'Best score so far,' she said to Helen.

The crowd had begun to shift, standing up and stretching their legs.

'Time for tea!' Roo announced. She ushered the children towards the pavilion and Helen followed.

It was much cooler inside. A large table was packed with several Tupperware containers and plates of cakes and buns. Roo started to remove the lids of the boxes and use them to stack up the sandwiches. There were egg sandwiches in one box and several more of cheese, ham and beef. Helen joined in, and Roo found a knife to slice up two large chocolate cakes. Another of the wives produced a tray of scones and was laying them out onto paper plates. Someone else had brought a dustbin-lid-sized quiche and a massive package of sausage rolls.

The cricketers came up and helped themselves, closely followed by their families and friends. Helen took a cheese sandwich, though having eaten two of Roo's delicious samosas, she wasn't especially hungry. It was slightly chilly thanks to the breeze blowing into the pavilion. She pulled a white linen scarf from her bag and draped it round her bare shoulders. She looked round for Roo, but couldn't see her. Spotting an empty chair at one of the corner tables, she sat down and took out her mobile.

A chair scraped at the table behind her, then another. Helen recognised one of the voices. It was Miranda Jones, Susan's mother and grandmother to Jack. Miranda had been in a soap opera many years ago when Helen was a child and her voice was very familiar. Helen felt sure she knew the other voice too. She turned, but the women had their backs to her.

Miranda was talking. 'I hope Jack will start riding very soon. I don't want to take him to Six Oaks, though. The young woman there seems a bit flighty. She had a fling with that Aira Kirkbryde last year. You know, the one from *Survival 101* on the Beeb.'

Helen blinked, but the second woman seemed matter-of-fact as she replied. 'I'm sure Molly Future is perfectly competent,' she said. 'I wouldn't have sold her Six Oaks if I'd thought otherwise.' Helen glanced round again, and this time she recognised the owner of the voice. It was Mrs Forsythe, who had owned Six Oaks Stables before Molly Future had taken over.

'There's a new stable opening over towards Richmond.' Miranda breezed on as if Mrs Forsythe hadn't spoken. 'I shall look into it. Jack needs a firm hand if he wants to learn.' She paused as if she was taking a sip of tea. 'Anyway,' she went on, 'what do you think of Toby Gordon? Quite an addition to the Welford team, isn't he?'

Helen pushed back her chair. The last thing she wanted was to listen to any gossip about Toby. There had been enough of that already. She headed for the door with her head down. Too late, she realised she had walked straight up to Seb. He smiled at her, and for a moment it was as if time had turned backwards, but then his smile slipped and the last few weeks fell back into place.

'Hello.' Toby's voice sounded behind Helen and he slid an arm around her waist. Helen stiffened, and pretended that she needed to put her teacup on a nearby table in order to extract herself. When she came back, Toby was smiling at Seb. 'I must congratulate you on your brilliant catch.'

Seb was the first to drop his eyes. 'I got lucky, that's all,' he muttered.

'It was a great catch,' Helen said without thinking.

Both Seb and Toby stared at her, eyebrows raised.

'Turning into a cricketing expert, are we?' Seb had found his smile again.

Helen pretended to frown at him. 'Catching's the easy part to understand. You're on your own with the scoring!'

'Remember how I tried to explain with Lego people at my sister's house?'

Helen rolled her eyes. 'You were rabbiting on about mid-sillies and legs before wickets and all kinds of nonsense,' she pointed out. 'It didn't work. I was more confused after than before. Toby told me to watch the scoreboard instead.'

Seb's face fell. He managed a tight smile, then nodded to Toby. He glanced around the room and gestured with his teacup. 'Excuse me, I must go and say hi to John.' He began to thread his way across the crowded room.

Toby gazed at Helen with approval in his eyes. 'Nice scarf.'

'Thanks,' Helen replied. She couldn't help but feel a little uneasy that he had his arm around her in public again. She had never been a fan of showing off her relationships.

'Are you enjoying the match?' Toby asked.

Helen nodded. On the surface, she was paying attention to Toby, but she kept catching sight of Seb as the people between them shifted. How was he getting on in Scotland? she wondered. It seemed odd that she had no idea. Did he like his new colleagues? Was he dealing with any interesting cases?

Toby had wrapped his arm more tightly round her. Helen glanced down at her watch and did a double-take. 'I have to go!' she gasped. 'I still have a million things to do before tomorrow.'

Toby leaned towards her. To her relief, he kissed her cheek and not her mouth. 'I'll call you later,' he said with a grin. 'I'm sure you'll be dying to know the result, though we're being trounced at the moment.' He didn't sound too concerned. He looked at her face, as if trying to read her thoughts. 'I'd suggest coming over later,' he said, 'but I'm guessing you'll need to reserve your energy for the big day, am I right?'

Helen nodded, with a rush of gratitude to him for being so understanding.

'I'll be there bright and early tomorrow morning,' he promised.

'You'd better be!'

It was a relief to climb back into her car. Helen sat for a moment with her hands resting on the warm steering wheel. She had never imagined that she would see Seb today. It would have been nice if she could have talked to him some more. It crossed her mind that she should have told him before that she was seeing Toby but there hadn't been a chance. Not without contacting him specially. She tried to imagine sending that message. What could she have said? The last thing she wanted was to hurt him, but sometimes life just moved fast.

That didn't stop her feeling strangely guilty, though. Somehow she didn't want Seb to think she had forgotten him the moment he left. And she still couldn't believe that he didn't know about Sunrise Farm, and everything Helen was doing to save her home. *Old habits die hard*, she told herself firmly. Once upon a time, she would have told Seb everything. But that time had passed, right?

She started the car, put it in gear and pulled out onto the road.

Chapter Twenty-Seven

Helen woke with a jolt and glanced at her clock, panic rising in her chest. The room was flooded with light, but it was only 5.30. She lay her head back on the pillow, looking up at the beamed ceiling. She loved this little room. To her right, Lucy was still asleep in her bed, and when Helen turned her head, she could see Isla in her crate, also curled up peacefully. For a moment, she toyed with the idea of just lying here. There was an hour until she needed to get up. But the sunshine was calling to her. It was Harvest Day. There was so much to do. She threw back the covers, opened Isla's crate, called Lucy and headed downstairs.

When she opened the kitchen door to let the dogs out, she saw a mist hanging over the valley. For the first time, Helen could feel the faintest breath of a chill in the air. A few more weeks and autumn would be on its way. She took a deep breath, trying to push down the nerves. Lots of people had said they'd come, but would they really? Would they get the fruit harvested in time? The kettle boiled, but she sat down at the kitchen table, suddenly feeling dizzy.

A wet nose probed her hand and she looked down. Isla's little face gazed up at her. Helen bent down and buried her face in the curly fur. Lucy trotted in, her claws rattling on the stone floor. Isla skittered away and Helen gave Lucy a hug too, then stood up. Come on, she told herself. There's no point in wasting time worrying.

She was sitting at the table half an hour later, showered and dressed, when Lucy and Isla pricked up their ears. Isla stood up and started to bark and Lucy rushed outside. Mandy appeared in the doorway with Sky beside her.

'Hello,' Helen said. 'You're nice and early.' She stood up and reached into the cupboard for a mug. 'Would you like a coffee?'

She turned to Mandy, then stopped in her tracks. Mandy's eyes were red and swollen and her face was deathly pale. 'What's wrong?' Helen gasped.

Mandy's face crumpled and her shoulders started to shake. Helen pulled out a chair and gently sat her down. Sky hovered at Mandy's knee, her small furry face filled with worry. Helen took Mandy's hot hand and waited until the worst spasm had passed. 'Can you tell me what's wrong?' she pressed gently.

Mandy swallowed, then took a tissue from her jeans pocket and blew her nose. 'Sorry,' she said. Her eyes were brimming with tears again.

'Just tell me what's happened,' Helen urged.

'Jimmy said no,' Mandy sobbed.

The proposal. Surely not. Helen felt sick.

Mandy sat up a little straighter. She picked up her coffee, took a sip, then leaned back in her chair. 'I had everything set up,' she said. Her mouth twisted. 'There were candles on the table. We'd had a wonderful mushroom stroganoff that James had made for me. Raj had matched the wine. I had the ring in my pocket.' She dropped her head, then raised it again. 'I opened the box and got down on one knee . . .' She gulped. 'What was I thinking?' she wailed.

Helen touched her shoulder. 'That you're a bold and brilliant feminist who knows how to take the initiative?'

Mandy closed her eyes for a moment, then opened them again. 'He looked . . . *horrified*,' she whispered. 'He took the box away from me and made me sit down. He was saying all the right things: how much he loves me, that everything's great, the twins love me, blah blah. But . . .' Another tear escaped from Mandy's eye and ran down her face. 'He doesn't want to change anything. That's what he told me. His life is exactly how he hoped it would be, you know, after the divorce and everything.' She ran her hand along the top of the table. 'He doesn't see how it can be improved. God, I'm such an idiot!'

'You are not an idiot,' Helen said hotly. 'That's the last thing you are.' *He's the idiot. He should have been falling at your feet in gratitude . . .*

She pulled herself onto her chair and sat on the edge, leaning towards Mandy. 'Maybe this isn't the right time for him,' she suggested gently. 'If he says everything's perfect, that's good, isn't it? Does he know you've been thinking about having a baby? A child of your own?'

Mandy shook her head.

'I think you need to tell him,' Helen said. 'Let him know that you would like to move your relationship on for a very specific reason. It's great that he's happy now, because that makes two of you, but you need to share your plans for what happens next.' *If you want a baby and he doesn't, then perhaps he's not the right man for you.*

Mandy looked away for a moment. A tear ran down her nose, and then she turned back to face Helen. 'He's going to the Arctic.'

'He's going *where?*'

Mandy sniffed. 'The Arctic. Aira Kirkbryde has asked him to join an expedition to track polar bears north of Hudson Bay. They leave in two weeks. He'll be back just before Christmas.'

Helen's mouth had fallen open. She closed it.

Mandy shot her a grim smile. 'Do you think he needs some space?' There was a kind of desperate humour in her eyes. 'The whole of Canada should do the trick, shouldn't it?'

Helen squeezed Mandy's shoulder. 'That's not the reason he's going,' she said. *Arsehole!*

Mandy shrugged. 'So why didn't he mention it sooner?'

Helen paused. Hadn't Seb done exactly the same thing? 'Because men are crap at sharing stuff like that,' she said. There was a bitter taste in her mouth. 'Seb didn't tell me about his amazing new job, did he?' Her voice rose. 'It doesn't seem to occur to them that we might like to know what's happening beyond the middle of next week. They're so bloody stupid.'

Mandy was staring at her. Helen calmed down and tugged the end of her ponytail. 'Sorry,' she said. 'Just venting. I know there probably isn't, but is there anything I can do to help? I mean, there's not much room but you're welcome to stay here . . .'

'I'm not leaving Wildacre,' Mandy said. 'It's mine, not his. And it's not like we've broken up. At least, I don't think we have. I don't know. Anyway, he'll be gone in two weeks . . .' She started to crumple again.

'Hang in there,' Helen told her. 'If he's going away, at least it'll give you some time . . .' She looked at the clock on the kitchen wall. It was nearly eight o'clock.

Mandy followed her gaze. 'Oh!' she cried. 'I'm holding you up! Sunrise Farm needs you!' She jumped up from her seat. Sky got up too.

'You don't have to rush off,' Helen said. 'There's still plenty of time.'

Mandy shook her head. She seemed more like her normal self now. 'There really isn't,' she said. 'I know you've got a lot to do.' She walked towards the door, shadowed by Sky. 'I'm really sorry, but I can't face joining in today. I'm going to take Sky for a walk on the fells, clear my head, you know?' She looked at Helen with a small smile.

'That sounds like an excellent idea,' Helen said. She gave Mandy another hug, then held on to her elbows as she spoke. 'Give the dust a chance to settle with Jimmy, okay? If he has any sense at all, being in the Arctic will make him realise how much he misses you and how amazing you are. And when he comes back, he'd better damn well put a ring on that finger!'

Mandy gave a weak laugh. Helen felt her heart go out to her friend. It was such a sad sound. 'That's the best-case scenario, I guess,' Mandy said. 'Anyway, you've got enough to think about today. I hope it goes well.'

Helen followed her outside. Mandy opened the car door to let Sky in, then climbed in herself. She waved as she reversed, then the car sped off up the lane.

'Poor Mandy,' Helen said, looking down at Lucy and Isla. 'Let's hope Jimmy comes to his senses and doesn't lose her while he's romping in search of polar bears.' She straightened up. 'Right. It's harvest time!'

Anneka was standing in the farmhouse kitchen looking flustered. Hi-vis vests lay in a bundle at one end of the table. There was a stack of clipboards and a scatter of pens at the other end. An entire army of plastic bottles was lined up against the wall.

Barney and Connie were at the sink. Barney was carefully adding orange squash to the bottles and Connie was topping them up from the tap. 'We're in charge of drinks,' Connie explained. Four-year-old Harry was sitting at a corner of the table, colouring in a large sign with the word 'Toilets'.

The door opened and Steve Mellor swept in. 'Finished, Harry?' he said. He ruffled his son's head, then grabbed the sign and marched out again.

Anneka laughed at Harry's surprised face. 'It's mayhem,' she said. 'We must be mad!'

Helen found herself wanting to giggle too. Anneka's laughter had a nervous energy to it that Helen couldn't help sharing. 'I'll go and start getting the welcome tables organised,' she said.

Two trestle tables stood on the gravel drive outside the farmhouse. Each one had a stack of cardboard trugs beside them. Helen had brought one of the clipboards outside and she glanced down at the list of people she'd asked to help run the day. It was almost time for them to arrive.

Right on cue, Rachel and Brandon Gill walked into the farmyard. Helen smiled at them and Rachel smiled back. Brandon looked away, then looked back again and nodded slightly. Even after all these years, he still suffered from crippling shyness.

'Thanks for coming,' Helen said.

'Just tell us what we should do,' Rachel replied.

'I'd like you to be the welcome committee, please.' She pointed to the trugs. 'Hand those out and allocate people to the different fields.' She gestured to the clipboard. 'At least twenty people are needed for the strawberry tunnels and field,' she explained, 'ten for the raspberries, ten for the currants, and four for the gooseberries.'

Rachel took the list, picked up a pen and began to create tick boxes for each category.

'Anneka said you need to check that gooseberry pickers are wearing sturdy gloves,' Helen added. 'There are gloves behind the table, but they're strictly only for the gooseberries. We don't have enough for everyone.'

A bright green Morris Minor with wooden trim pulled into the yard. The driver's door was flung open and Douglas unfolded himself from behind the wheel. Susan appeared on the far side and tilted the front seat forward to let Jack out. Douglas strode round, pulled open the rear doors and lifted out a large plastic box. His watermelon smile was already in place. 'Where do you want us?' he asked, beaming.

'You're in the garden,' Helen said. Douglas tramped off through the stone archway that led into the garden. Jack glanced at Susan for permission and then scampered off after Douglas.

'Thanks for organising the games,' Helen said, walking over to stand beside Susan. 'I know you spend all week child-wrangling. Sorry to ask you to do it again at the weekend.'

Susan laughed. She was looking very pretty with a gingham handkerchief holding back her hair, and pale denim dungaree shorts over a pink short-sleeved shirt. 'Don't be daft,' she said. 'I'm thrilled to help.'

Jack reappeared and rushed up to stand in front of Helen. 'So am I,' he told her. He looked up at Susan. 'Shall I get the fruits now?' he asked. Susan nodded and he rushed over to the car. Helen frowned. Why would anyone be bringing fruit with them? Jack came back staggering under the weight of a crate filled with brightly coloured plastic fruit.

'For the Hunt the Fruit game,' Susan explained. 'Come on, Jack,' she said, 'let's go and hide them.'

Helen followed them into the garden. They found Douglas unfolding an easel. 'Pin the Strawberry on the Vine,' he explained. He unrolled a beautiful picture of a strawberry plant, complete with shiny green leaves and several tendrils. Lifting it up, he attached it to the easel. 'Prizes if you get your strawberry at the end of a tendril,' he said.

'It looks fabulous,' Helen said. She would have to come back later and have a go herself. She glanced at her clipboard. 'You're also doing apple bobbing, is that right?'

Douglas nodded. He strode back to the car and returned holding up a bag of apples and a bucket. 'Just add water,' he said cheerfully.

Helen checked her list again. 'Martha Walsh from Welford Primary is coming to do face-painting,' she said. 'She should be here any moment.'

Douglas patted her on the shoulder. 'Everything's going swimmingly. It'll all be fine, you'll see.'

Helen walked out through the archway and headed to the barn. She found Steve sitting on his mini-tractor.

He was loading large white plastic crates onto a small trailer, but he stopped the engine and came over to speak to her. 'Anneka'll be down in a minute or two,' he said. He pointed to the crates. 'That's how we'll carry the fruit,' he explained. 'Then the crates will be loaded onto pallets in the barn. That's Anneka's job.' He looked at Helen and gave her a sudden, rather shy smile. 'Thanks for doing all this,' he said, waving a hand.

Helen gave a nervous laugh. 'Thank me later,' she said, 'when we see if it works.'

'Even if it doesn't, at least we're doing something,' Steve said.

Helen jogged back to the garden. Better make sure Martha had arrived and that Douglas and Susan had everything they needed. She stopped in surprise when she rounded the corner. The Welford WI had come up trumps yet again. Dorothy Hope and Amelia Ponsonby were setting out a vast cake stall at the top end of the lawn. Despite the heat, Mrs Ponsonby was wearing one of her more amazing hats. It looked like someone had scattered several flowering strawberry plants onto an upturned doily. The sturdy woman was breathing heavily as she unpacked sponge after sponge onto paper plates. 'Keep the pavlova for later, Dorothy, dear,' she ordered. 'We should be able to get some strawberries to decorate it.'

Helen spotted plastic bananas and peaches poking out from bushes around the garden. Now Susan, Douglas and Jack were setting up an obstacle course across the lawn. Brandon Gill was putting up signs directing people to the various fruit-picking areas. Helen felt a surge of excitement. It was all starting to take off.

A pair of warm hands landed heavily on her shoulders and she jumped. She whirled round. It was Toby. 'Hi, beautiful,' he said.

Helen felt her face going red. With everything that was going on she'd almost forgotten he'd be coming. She was dressed in practical clothes, old shorts and a faded Rolling Stones T-shirt. As usual Toby looked immaculate. Helen pulled herself together. If it wasn't for Toby and his father's estate, there would have been no chance of saving Sunrise Farm. What she wore was really not important.

He kissed her and she kissed him back briefly, then pulled away to see whether anyone was watching. Mrs Ponsonby was arranging a pile of chocolate brownies and Susan and Douglas were fixing some bunting to Brandon's signs.

'What's in the box?' she asked Toby. There was a large cardboard package at his feet.

He bent down and pulled it open. Inside, boxes of Scottish tablet and shortbread jostled with jars of heather honey, all in the distinctive dark green Craighenry packaging. 'I asked Dad to send down a few goodies,' he told her, lifting out a pack of tablet. 'I thought we could offer them as prizes.'

'That's a great idea. Thanks so much.' She glanced around the garden again, then reached up and hugged him. She didn't want Toby to think she wasn't grateful. 'As if you hadn't done enough already!'

Toby kissed her forehead. 'I just hope everyone turns up,' he said. 'Is there anything I can do to help?'

'Could you help Brandon with the signs?' He nodded and set off towards Brandon, leaving the box beside Helen. She heaved it into her arms and carried into the kitchen. She could unpack it later, when the prizes were required. She checked her watch. It was almost nine. In a few minutes, the first people would start to arrive. She went out to the front of the farmhouse.

Tom Hope was coming up the drive. 'Morning,' he said, then glanced at the sky. 'Lovely day for it.'

'It really is,' Helen agreed.

'I'm looking forward to a proper harvest supper,' Tom continued. 'There were lots of 'em when I was a boy. I used to help out on the farms at harvest time, you know. Someone would always bring a fiddle and we'd all dance. I liked a bit of dancing back then.'

'I'm sorry,' Helen said. 'There isn't any dancing. I didn't think of that.'

Tom patted her arm. 'Don't worry, dear. Times have changed. I don't think fiddles have the same appeal they once did. Besides . . .' He waved an arm towards the garden and the fields beyond, dotted with people setting up for the harvest. 'It looks like you've thought of everything else.'

'Good, I've found you.' Dorothy Hope appeared from behind the house. 'Did you remember the cashbox?'

Tom Hope lifted his hand. The cashbox was dangling from his fingers.

'We've had lots of cakes donated for the stall,' she said.

'Mandy will be pleased,' Helen said. She had originally thought they could sell cakes to help Sunrise Farm, but Anneka and Steve had said they couldn't possibly accept donations. They had agreed with the WI that the cake stall money should go to Hope Meadows.

Dorothy looked around. 'Is Mandy here yet?'

Helen felt a stab of sadness. 'Something came up,' she said. 'She's not going to make it, I'm afraid.'

Dorothy smiled. 'That's our Mandy,' she said. 'She's always working.'

A car appeared on the lane and then another. Helen went for a quick walk around. Everything seemed to be in place. By the time she walked back into the yard, a queue had formed in front of Rachel and Brandon's table.

'Hello, Roo!' Helen called, and Roo waved. Josh was beside her, holding on to Herbie and Kiran. Helen smiled at the children. Kiran was looking adorable in a huge sunhat and Herbie had a brand-new pair of sunglasses.

'Don't forget,' Rachel told them, 'there's a prize for the biggest strawberry and one for the reddest apple. Games in the garden for the children. And you can sample some of the fruit, but please don't eat it all!'

Brandon was handing out gloves for a family who would be picking the gooseberries.

'It's this way.' Helen showed them to the gooseberry polytunnel, then returned to collect the next group. The air was filled with excited chatter.

'Lovely ripe fruit,' someone called.

'These strawberries are delicious.' One of the farmer's wives winked at Helen.

'Don't eat too many,' Helen warned her with a friendly smile.

'I'll start at this end, if you do that side . . .'

Steve walked past with a mallet over his shoulder. 'All the signs are finished,' he called. Helen gave him a thumbs-up.

There was a squeaking sound and Helen turned to see Barney and Connie wheeling their little wheelbarrow towards her. It was filled with bottles of squash.

'Mummy says we need to make sure everyone gets one,' Barney said.

''Cause it's so hot,' Connie added.

In the garden, children were racing around, hunting plastic fruit. Jack rushed up to Helen. His face was painted orange with black and white stripes. 'Look,' he told her excitedly. 'I'm a tiger.' He roared and Helen covered her ears.

There was a burst of laughter from Douglas's straw-berry picture. Helen walked over to see Toby in an eye mask, waving a picture of a strawberry in the air. Half a dozen children were watching him in rapturous giggles. Douglas grasped Toby's shirt and guided him back to the picture on the easel. 'Pin it here,' he said, placing

Toby's hand on the edge of the easel. 'Mrs Ponsonby's hat is out of bounds.'

Helen had just reached the yard when Anneka emerged from the farm office. She waved a sheet of paper at Helen. 'I've been moved on to keeping track of the produce,' she explained. 'Brandon offered to supervise the pallet-stacking.'

Emily Hope had joined Rachel at the welcome tables. Adam appeared a moment later with a large sunshade. He nodded at Helen, then began to set up the shade to protect Emily and Rachel.

Helen walked over. Emily looked tired. 'I'll get you a chair,' Helen told her.

'You don't need to,' Emily insisted.

'Is Mandy around?' Adam asked.

'Not at the moment,' Helen said. 'I'll get your chair,' she told Emily, and walked away before they could ask where Mandy was.

She returned five minutes later, carrying one of her own kitchen chairs. 'Here you go,' she said to Emily.

James and Raj were next in the queue. Helen smiled. James was looking very dapper in a striped shirt, green knee-length shorts and deck shoes. 'I wasn't expecting you,' Helen said. 'This is hardly just round the corner!'

'I know I live in York now,' James said, 'but I'll always be part of Welford.' He glanced at Raj. 'Besides,' he said, 'we have to start networking with other parents. We need to line up a few Welford-style play-dates for Taresh.

Can't have him growing up without seeing what village life is really like.'

Helen handed James and Raj a trug apiece. 'You're on currants,' she told them.

Raj frowned as he studied the signs that Brandon and Toby had put up. 'Biggest strawberry and reddest apple,' he said. He shook his head at Helen with a stern look. 'I think someone's forgotten to add the smallest currant competition.' He grabbed James's hand. 'Come on, Dad,' he said.

Helen stepped back as Steve drove into the yard. The little trailer was piled high with the first crates of strawberries. This is it, Helen thought. The harvest was in full swing. Her wonderful, wonderful neighbours had joined together to save her home.

Chapter Twenty-Eight

It was very quiet in the farmhouse kitchen after the hustle and bustle outside. Helen had left Lucy and Isla there with Birdie for the day. It was cooler than the granary, and with the kitchen being at the back of the house, they would be disturbed less. Helen had brought Isla's crate round, thrilled to have portable security for the little dog. Isla was sitting calmly in it now, her ears pricked towards the sound of Helen's footsteps.

She put Isla's lead on and took them all outside. They all had a pee, then seemed happy to leave the noise and go back into the kitchen. Helen gave them a biscuit each. She would take them out for a proper walk later. She closed the door and walked back out into the yard.

The queue had finally vanished at the welcome table. Rachel had disappeared, but Emily Hope was sitting under the umbrella. 'It seems to be a huge success,' she said.

'Hello!' Helen heard a familiar voice behind her. 'Are we too late?' Helen turned to see Frank and Shirley Conway walking down the drive.

'Y-you came,' she stammered. 'That's so kind.'

Shirley held out her arms. Helen hugged her, then

kissed Frank on the cheek. 'It's lovely to see you both,' she said, meaning it.

'Ah, here's Seb.' Shirley waved as Seb appeared at the bottom of the drive, jogging briskly. 'He was just parking the car,' she explained to Helen.

'Oh,' said Helen faintly. So Seb did know about Sunrise Farm, and the trouble they were in. What's more, he'd come to help. *Of course he has*, Helen found herself thinking. Without any fuss, without holding any grudges, he'd shown up in her corner. *As always*.

Seb came up, kissed Helen lightly on the cheek (no big displays of affection, she thought with relief), then went over to the table. 'Do we take one of these baskets?'

'Yes,' said Emily. 'I think there's room for a couple more pickers in the strawberry field.'

Helen felt a rush of gratitude to Seb and his parents. 'You didn't have to come,' she said.

Seb raised his eyebrows. 'And miss the chance to snaffle a few raspberries? You know they're my favourite!'

Helen laughed. 'I'll show you the way. But be warned, we'll be watching you like hawks!'

She led them through the gate and across the lawn. She realised that Toby was watching her over his bottle of squash, his eyes narrowed. Helen tensed, then told herself that she had known the Conways a long time. It felt natural to be friendly towards them. And Seb would always want to help her out. That was something Toby would just have to get used to.

* * *

Summer Days at Sunrise Farm

Helen was standing in the field by the lane, helping to load crates of strawberries onto Steve's trailer, when an old-fashioned bell sounded from the farmhouse. She looked at her watch. It was four o'clock.

'That's it,' she said. 'Harvesting is over!'

Steve nodded to the plants, which were almost bare of fruit. 'I'd say that's perfect timing,' he declared.

All around the field, people were straightening up and stretching. One by one, they handed their half-filled trugs to Steve and Helen before making their way back to the farmhouse. Helen carefully emptied the trugs into the plastic crates. The smell of fruit was almost overwhelming.

Seb was one of the strawberry pickers. 'You've done a great job,' he said as he handed over his basket.

Helen could feel her face reddening. 'It wasn't really down to me,' she said. 'It was the whole village.'

Seb smiled at her, the corners of his eyes crinkling in a way that was so familiar. 'I heard it was your idea,' he said. 'Even up in Scotland, the Welford drums beat loudly, you know!'

Helen laughed. Seb walked away and Helen started to stack the crates on the trailer.

'Are you almost done?' Toby was striding along the edge of the field. 'I'll give you a hand.' He hoisted the last crate onto the stack and they sat on the back of the trailer as Steve drove slowly to the barn.

Helen jumped off in the garden, where Douglas and Adam were setting up trestle tables. Seb was helping

Susan pack away the toys. Anneka had produced several large white tablecloths and was shaking them out. All the WI ladies were poised with platters of sandwiches and cake, ready to set the tables. Dorothy Hope was firing up the tea urn and Emily was unloading cups and saucers from a cardboard box.

James and Raj had brought an array of breads with cheese and cold meats which had been stowed in the farmhouse fridge all day. The Dhanjals had brought delicious-smelling Indian bread and two large bowls of rice salad, as well as more of their tasty samosas. On a separate table, the bowls of fruit that Anneka and Steve had picked the day before were complemented by several pots of cream sent from Upper Welford Hall.

The hungry villagers queued up to load their plates. The garden was soon filled with people sitting on blankets and chairs, perched on the walls, anywhere a space could be found. Helen had found a quiet seat in the corner. She was glad of a chance to sit down as she tucked into a slice of James's focaccia. Toby had been commandeered by Gary and Bev Parsons to help with the drinks that they had brought from the pub. Helen watched him for a while. If he hadn't been a vet, he would have made a good barman, she mused.

There was a ringing noise as Anneka tapped a teaspoon on a glass and everyone stopped talking. Steve stood up. 'I just wanted to thank everyone who's come along today to help,' he said. 'We've never done an entire harvest in a single day before. Quite an achievement, and something we couldn't have done without all of you.' There was a ripple of quiet clapping. Steve waited until it finished before he went on. 'We also want to thank Toby Gordon. We're incredibly grateful to both him and the Craighenry Estate. We know our fruit will be in excellent hands.' Steve looked at his wife and smiled. 'If there's one thing Anneka and I have learned,' he said, 'it's how lucky we are to live in such a wonderful place. Here in this beautiful dale,' he waved an arm, 'there's a whole community ready to help out. Sunrise Farm means the world to us. We hope that all of you here today will feel able to come along in the future as friends.'

Anneka stood beside Steve and together they raised their glasses. 'To you,' they said.

The crowd raised their glasses in return. 'To us,' they chorused.

'And now,' Anneka said before the chatter could start up again, 'I think you know that there were some very serious competitions taking place today. On top of everything else, Toby has provided some wonderful prizes. First of all,' she lifted up a small hamper which contained a packet of tablet, four Ecclefechan tarts and a packet of shortbread, 'we have the prize for the biggest strawberry. It goes to . . .' she checked her list '. . . Roo Dhanjal.'

Roo looked very pleased as she walked up to collect her prize.

'Next up is the prize for the reddest apple,' said Anneka, 'which goes to Tom Hope.'

Tom went over to collect a jar of heather honey. 'I shall enjoy that on my porridge,' he announced.

'And last and most definitely least, by popular demand . . . or at least demanded by James and Raj, we have the competition for the smallest currant. This was a hotly contested event,' Anneka said, 'and the currant in question was, in fact, so small that there's some doubt that it's even a currant at all. Steve and I were quite suspicious that perhaps it was actually a speck of dirt. But in the end, we decided we had to give the prize to Raj himself. So here you go, Raj.'

With a flourish, she held out a plastic chilli, taken from the fruit that Susan had used for the children's games. Raj walked up and accepted it with a huge grin, then held it up over his head like a trophy.

'Finally,' Anneka said, 'I want to remind everyone that you're welcome to collect a punnet of fruit from the table in front of the farmhouse before you leave. Thanks again, everyone, for coming. We really are very, very grateful.'

Toby threaded his way through the crowd to join Helen. His face was glowing from a day in the sun but he still looked polished and tidy. Helen found herself wishing she'd taken a moment to nip into the granary and change her shirt, and maybe drag a brush through her hair. Toby looked down at her, smiling. 'Mission accomplished!' he declared.

'Yes indeed,' Helen said, feeling a wave of tiredness overtake her.

'There's been a suggestion that we relocate to the pub to carry on celebrating,' Toby said. 'And wash down all those strawberries, of course!' He held out a hand to Helen. 'Coming?'

She looked at his hand, then up at him. 'Actually, would you mind if I didn't? I'd like to stay here, have an early night.' More than that, she wanted to be on her own with Lucy and Isla. This was their home, and she had saved it for the three of them. She winced. Was it really obvious that she was excluding Toby? She knew Sunrise Farm owed everything to him and his family business, but somehow this victory felt very personal right now.

There was a flash of surprise in Toby's eyes, then he nodded. 'Of course. I'll see you tomorrow.'

'Bright and early!' Helen managed a grin. She waved as Toby turned and headed off to the front of the house, then went to help the Mellors with the clearing up.

It was almost dark by the time she had a chance to take Lucy and Isla down to the stream. The sweet scent of fruit hung heavily in the air. The first of the trucks had already arrived to collect the pallets. The rest would be dispatched to Scotland tomorrow. Helen walked through the strawberry field, surrounded by empty vines. Their harvest was stripped, their fruit was safely stored. Helen felt a bubble of joy welling inside her. Sunrise Farm was safe.

Chapter Twenty-Nine

When Helen arrived at Hope Meadows on Monday morning, she found Mandy in the room set aside for nursing cats. She was kneeling down, watching a litter of newborn kittens feed from their mum. Helen crouched down beside her. The kittens were so tiny, you could easily fit two of them in the palm of your hand. Their eyes and ears were still shut tightly as they lay in a row, kneading their mother's flank.

Mandy didn't look up, even when Helen placed a hand on her shoulder. 'Are you okay?' Helen whispered.

Mandy nodded. 'Hanging in there,' she said. 'I'm sorry about baling out on you. Mum and Dad said it was a great day.'

'It was,' Helen agreed, 'though I think I'd be happy if I never had to see another strawberry in my life. But everything got picked and Steve and Anneka are so pleased with everyone's help. How are things at home?' she asked gently.

Mandy sighed. 'Properly weird,' she said. 'Jimmy's still at Wildacre but I didn't see him all day yesterday because he was briefing his replacement at Running Wild. He's off to meet Aira in Manchester today, and then he's got an expedition to the Cairngorms to test some equipment at the end of the week.' She looked pale and exhausted, and Helen's heart went out to her. 'It feels as if he's gone already, to be honest,' Mandy said.

'How would you like to take the dogs for a walk tonight?' Helen suggested. 'Isla and Lucy could do with a decent leg-stretch after being shut up yesterday. You've got Jimmy's three as well as Sky, haven't you?'

'I'd like that. Thanks.'

Helen was doing her morning check of the consulting rooms when Toby arrived.

'Morning,' he said, pushing open the door and sticking his head round. 'I just want to say congratulations again for yesterday. It was all brilliant.'

He came into the room and closed the door. For a moment, Helen thought he was going to kiss her, but Rachel pushed open the door again. 'Sorry, you two,' she said. 'Mr Hawthorne is here with his terrier.'

Toby pulled a face. 'Can you give me a hand with this one?' he said to Helen. 'Coriander took an instant dislike to me last time he was here. He must have heard about my terrible reputation.'

Mr Hawthorne was a meek-looking man with short sandy hair and anxious eyes behind enormous glasses. Despite Toby's comments, Coriander trotted in wagging his plumy tail. He was a Jack Russell with rather long legs and a sweet face. He tried to lick Helen's hand as she lifted him up onto the table.

'I don't know what's wrong with him exactly,' Mr Hawthorne began. 'We noticed on Friday night that he seemed to be pawing his face a lot, and this morning there was an awful smell about his mouth.' He looked down at Coriander, who was crouched on the table. 'All right, lad,' he told the little dog. 'Dr Gordon will put you right.' Helen felt the feathery tail twitching against her arm.

It took Toby only a few moments to find the cause of the problem. 'Look,' he said, holding Coriander's jaws apart. 'He has part of a stick stuck across the top of his mouth.' It was an easy manoeuvre to grasp the stick and twist it out. 'There's very little damage,' he said, looking up at Mr Hawthorne. 'I think it'll probably heal itself.' He gave Mr Hawthorne a warning about letting Coriander play with sticks – a rubber toy was always better – and Helen showed the dog and his owner back to reception.

She left Mr Hawthorne settling his bill with Rachel and headed into the prep room. Adam had a dog castration coming in later. Toby followed her in. 'Are you doing anything this evening?' he asked as she pulled on her scrub cap and tucked in her hair. 'We could go out for dinner if you like?' He grinned. 'Nowhere with soft fruit on the menu, of course.'

'Sorry. I've already arranged to go out with Mandy and the dogs.' She felt a twinge of guilt.

Toby nodded. 'No problem,' he said.

Though Helen was watching him closely, she couldn't read him at all. Would he suggest tomorrow instead? But he smiled at her and opened the door. 'I'd better get on,' he said. 'Got to be at Burnside in half an hour.' He smiled again and walked out. Picking up the surgical kit, Helen pushed open the double swing doors and pressed the switch that turned on the bright theatre lights.

Mandy opened the gate of the paddock to let the dogs through and then held it open for Helen and Isla. They set off up the track at a brisk pace, their rucksacks bouncing gently on their shoulders. Mandy's contained sandwiches and some of Dorothy Hope's wonderful carrot cake, and Helen was carrying bottles of water and mats to sit on.

They stopped to catch their breath at the top of the slope. The moor stretched ahead of them, all purple and gold. When they turned, they could see all the way back along the valley, past the church spire and the roofs of the houses to the winding river and the Pennine hills in the distance. Over in the west, the sun's golden rays were tinged with red.

'I love Yorkshire,' Helen declared.

'It's sacrilege to say anything else round here,' Mandy pointed out. 'But you're right. God's own country, for sure.'

They carried on, the dogs bounding around them in a zealous swirl. Other than the sound of their own feet and the panting of the dogs, there was perfect silence. They reached a drystone wall with a stile built into it. Helen helped Isla through the gap, but the other dogs scrambled over themselves.

Mandy glanced at Isla, who was walking confidently at Helen's heel. 'She's doing so well. What do you think about trying her off the lead?'

Helen frowned. 'Won't the other dogs bump into her? What if she walks into a rock or a hole?' She had been very naïve at the beginning, she thought, with her fond hope that Lucy would be Isla's constant guide. Now the idea of letting her off the lead seemed impossible.

'There's only one way to find out,' Mandy prompted gently. 'Give the other dogs a chance. I think they understand much more than most people give them credit for.'

Helen's fingers were trembling as she unclipped the lead. 'Off you go!' she told Isla, using the same command she would give to Lucy.

Isla held her head high, sniffing at the air. At the corner of her vision, Helen could see the other dogs chasing around after rabbit scents. If Isla got caught up in their paws, she could be really hurt.

Isla took a step forward and then another. Her ears were pricked and she was tilting her head from one side to another. She seemed to sense the movement in the air as Lucy trotted towards her. The big retriever came up to Isla's flank and sniffed her. Sky joined them, and

Zoe and Simba and Emma. Each dog brushed against Isla, letting her breathe their scent. Then, as a pack, they started to trot slowly along the path. Hesitantly at first, steadily gaining in confidence, Isla followed.

Helen felt a lump in her throat. Her blind dog, her brave, good girl, was running free. 'You dear sweet girl,' she whispered under her breath.

Lucy broke into a run, followed by Mandy's dogs, and then Isla was bounding along with them, her ears lifting in the breeze. She stumbled occasionally but kept going, letting her nose brush against Lucy's flank to check she was still with the pack.

Helen looked at Mandy. 'I never thought this would happen.'

Mandy smiled. 'There's always room for hope,' she said.

They sat down on a flat stone to eat their sandwiches. Isla flopped down among the other dogs, almost lost against the large hairy bodies.

Mandy watched them. 'Animals have an amazing instinct for helping others,' she said. 'Not just dogs. I've seen it in cats and horses too. Some of them really seem to understand if one of their friends can't see or needs help.' She took a sip of water. 'Lucy and Isla have had time to get used to living with each other. They've figured out their own rhythm. Animals can work a lot of things out for themselves, if they're given time and a safe environment.' She sighed. 'Unlike humans, who just make everything ridiculously complicated.'

Helen patted her shoulder. 'You've done nothing wrong with Jimmy,' she said. 'Let him go and chase polar bears for a while. If he has an ounce of sense, he'll realise exactly what he's missing.'

Mandy looked down into the valley, where shadows were starting to pool. 'Time to go,' she said.

At that moment, Helen's phone chirruped. She looked at the screen and felt herself beaming. Gemma had sent another picture of Moondance, this time knee-deep in a meadow of wildflowers. 'Hi, Mum!' read the caption, as if Moondance was writing. 'I'm having a great time as you can see, but I wish you were here too! Maybe next year? Aunty Gemma says we'll be home in two weeks. Can't wait to see you!'

To her surprise, Helen realised her eyes were filling with tears. Her dear, sweet mare was coming home. All three of her animals would be exactly where they should be, in her care, lifting her heart and reminding her where she belonged. She texted back quickly: 'My darling girls, I can't wait to see both of you too!'

Helen's heart was singing as she drove over the ridge and down towards Sunrise Farm. She kept picturing Lucy and Isla, running across the moor in a joyful, confident pack. She drove into the yard and felt her heart sink. Toby's car was parked on the gravel. As Helen unloaded the dogs, she could hear voices coming from the garden.

'Hello.' Anneka popped her head over the wall. 'Come and join us. We're celebrating with Toby. Steve's found some very dodgy swede wine that he made for a bet.'

'It's a tempting offer,' Helen replied, 'but I need to go and feed the dogs.'

'Okay,' Anneka said. 'But you're welcome to come out afterwards if you're not too tired.'

'Thanks,' Helen said. She led the dogs towards her back door.

Toby stood up. 'Thanks for the drink,' he told the Mellors. 'I'll be in touch if there's anything else we need to sort out.' He jogged across the grass to Helen. 'Mind if I come in?'

Helen bit back a sigh. She was so tired, she just wanted to change into her pyjamas and watch mindless TV with crisps for dinner, but she could hardly turn Toby away. 'Of course. I need to go and have a shower,' she warned him. 'Help yourself to whatever's in the fridge.'

'Can you just give me a minute?' Toby said. 'There's something I want to say.' He walked over and took hold of both her hands. 'Come over here and sit down,' he said gently. He pulled out a chair and they sat down at the kitchen table. Helen felt a sinking feeling in the pit of her stomach. Was Toby going to propose? *Please God, no!* She forced herself to look at him.

'This is a difficult thing to say,' he said, tracing the grain on the wooden table with one finger. 'But I've been around a bit.' He stopped and pushed his hand through his hair. 'There's no easy way to say this, but . . .' *Don't propose, don't propose.* '. . . I can tell you're not that into me.' He sent her a rueful smile, trying to take any sting out of the words. 'It's a great shame,' he told her, 'because I'm actually rather smitten with you. Maybe it's true what they say. We all want what we can't have.'

Helen stared at him, unable to speak.

'I guess the Welford Whisperers would say it was about time I had my heart broken,' he added.

Helen placed her hand over his. 'That's not true. You haven't done anything wrong. You don't deserve to have your heart broken. Anyway,' she went on, 'it's early days between us. Isn't it too early to tell how we're going to feel?'

Toby shook his head without taking his eyes off her. He looked so kind that Helen wanted to cry. 'I know that if the feelings aren't there now, they aren't going to turn up later,' he said. 'And I can tell they aren't. Can you look me in the eye and tell me you were glad when you saw I was here tonight?'

Helen blinked. It was on the tip of her tongue to tell him that of course she was glad. She opened her mouth, but nothing came out.

Toby sighed. 'I have my answer, then,' he said. 'I guess it's been a crazy summer for you. I probably moved too fast. I should have given you more time.'

Helen wrapped her fingers more tightly around his hand. She knew he was right. She didn't feel the way about him that he deserved. He had moved heaven and earth to save Sunrise Farm – and she had just wished she could have had Seb beside her to fight the battle. Toby had been proud and unabashed about showing his affection in public – and Helen had only missed Seb's reserve and quiet affection. Toby was lovely, but it would be unfair to him to pretend they were a perfect match. It wouldn't have mattered how much time he'd given her.

There was a lump in Helen's throat that made it impossible to speak. She stared at him, hoping he could see the gratitude and affection in her eyes. *You are a dear, dear friend. Thank you for making this easy for me.*

Toby stood up. 'I'm going to go now,' he said, bending down to kiss her cheek. She caught a hint of his scent and for a moment she wanted to reach up and cling to him, beg him to carry her up to bed once more. She kept very still. That would just make this conversation even worse, the next time it came around.

'Thanks for the time we did have,' Toby said, straightening up. 'This seems like a real crossroads in your life,' he said. 'Lots of opportunities, as well as a chance to figure out what really matters. Don't rush into anything, take your time to see where you want to go. And if you're worried about work, don't be. We'll be fine. Grand, even. See, I've been spending too much time with the locals!' He smiled, but the sadness in his eyes left a crack in Helen's heart. 'I'll see you in the morning. Okay?' He gave her hand one last squeeze, then turned and walked out.

It was almost dark in the kitchen but Helen stayed at

the table, unable to move. Should she feel more upset? she wondered. She ached for Toby, yet she felt relieved. She thought back over the past couple of weeks. They had shared a huge amount of fun and some pretty extraordinary moments, with the Harvest Day and saving Sunrise Farm. Everything had happened in a rush, larger than life, lit up by the scorching sun. Toby was right. She needed to work out what she really wanted.

Lucy pattered over and sat down on her foot and a moment later Isla followed and slumped against her other leg. Helen leaned down and put her arms around both dogs. She smiled at the two precious faces, just visible in the dusky light from the window. 'No regrets,' she said aloud. Isla reached up to lick Helen's hand and, to her delight, Lucy stretched over and licked Isla's ear.

No regrets at all.

Chapter Thirty

Emily Hope was sitting in the reception area of Animal Ark. It was early Saturday morning. She looked up when Helen walked in. 'Hello,' she said. 'You're not due in this weekend.'

'I know, but I'm running out of Isla's food. I thought I'd pop in and get some.' She fetched a bag from the storeroom and brought it back to settle up. Emily was watering one of the bamboo pots. 'I'll put it through,' Helen said. She sat down and pulled the computer keyboard towards her. It knocked a packet of worming tablets that was lying on the desk, sending them spinning onto the floor.

'Drat!' Emily exclaimed as Helen bent to pick them up. 'Are those still here?'

'Who are they for?'

'Jess Conway. I meant to put them in the post yesterday.'

'I could drop them in,' Helen said. 'I was going to take Lucy and Isla to Duskham Reservoir this afternoon. It's only a tiny bit out of my way.'

Emily raised an eyebrow as she looked at Helen. 'No plans with Toby this weekend?'

Helen shook her head. 'No,' she said. 'Actually, we're not together any more.'

Emily blinked at her. 'Are you okay with that?'

'Oh yes. He's a lovely man, but this isn't what I want right now.'

'Well, I'm sure you're still feeling a bit sad,' Emily said. 'But I'm glad he hasn't chased you away!'

Mandy pulled up as Helen was walking out. To her surprise, Abi and Max were in the back of the car. They scrambled out, followed by the three dogs.

Helen looked at Mandy. 'I thought Jimmy was in the Cairngorms?'

'He is,' Abi said in a clear voice. 'But we wanted to come and stay with Mandy.'

Mandy grinned down at Abi. 'Couldn't resist my cooking, could you?' she joked.

'You said we could have pizza tonight!' Max protested.

Mandy laughed. 'Don't worry.' She reached out a hand to ruffle his hair. 'Takeaway it is! And if you're lucky, I might even manage to open a tub of ice cream for pudding!'

Abi was jumping from foot to foot. 'Can we go and see the kittens?'

Mandy nodded and the twins raced off.

'They're so happy with you,' Helen commented.

'They're great.' Mandy sounded wistful.

'You'll see them while Jimmy's in the Arctic, won't you?'

'Of course.' Mandy folded her arms across her chest. 'We haven't told them anything beyond the fact that their dad will be away for a while.' Her face clouded.

Helen squeezed her arm. 'Never lose hope, remember?'

'I do try, but then reality gets in the way,' she said. 'Are you going to the reservoir? Have a great time.' She bent down to pat Lucy and Isla, then set off to rescue the kittens from the twins.

Helen couldn't help feeling sad as she climbed into her car. It was obvious that Mandy adored being with Abi and Max. They really seemed like a family, but without a baby of her own, was that enough for Mandy? Jimmy was forcing her to make an impossible choice. And what would it be like when James and Raj came home with Taresh? Happy families all around. It would be hard to watch.

Helen relaxed as she drove to Walton. She lowered the car windows and the warm air brought the sweet scent of freshly cut grass into the car. She still couldn't quite believe that Sunrise Farm had been saved. The Craighenry factor had been delighted with the quality, Toby had told her. He had joked that their customers might even forgive the fact that it was Yorkshire fruit and not Scottish. They seemed to have slipped back to being friends in a way that made Helen realise just how fortunate she was. Animal Ark had always been a happy place to work. It would have been truly sad if their relationship had spoiled that.

She pulled up outside the Conways' bungalow and picked up the packet of worming tablets from the front seat. Frank was already opening the front door and waving to her.

'Hello!' He called over his shoulder. 'Come and see who's here, Shirl!'

Shirley appeared behind him. 'Hello, Helen. I've just put the kettle on. Would you like a cup of tea?'

'That would be lovely,' Helen said. 'The dogs will be fine for a little while.' She had left the windows open and the car was parked under the shade of a leylandii hedge. She followed Frank and Shirley through the house to their patio. The garden backed on to a steep bank, with a row of poplar trees along the top. Helen handed over the worming tablets and sat down.

Shirley inspected the box. 'Thanks for bringing these,' she said. 'I'm sure Jess will be very grateful!'

Frank appeared carrying a tray with three mugs of tea and put them down on the low glass and wickerwork table. 'We had a lovely afternoon at Sunrise Farm,' he said. 'Did the fruit go off all right?'

Helen nodded. 'It's already in Scotland.'

Shirley looked at Frank, and for a moment Helen

thought she was going to say something, but then she looked up at the poplar trees. 'We've had a lovely spell of weather,' she commented.

'I'm taking the dogs to Duskham Reservoir this afternoon,' Helen said.

'That sounds nice,' Frank said.

There was another silence. Frank sipped at his tea, while Shirley brushed an invisible piece of fluff from her skirt. Then, with a final glance at Frank, Shirley sat forward in her chair as if she had reached a decision. 'Has Seb been in touch?' she asked.

Helen blinked in surprise. Why would Shirley think Seb would have been in contact? 'No. Is he okay?'

Shirley added another spoon of sugar to her tea and stirred it. She seemed reluctant to meet Helen's eye. 'That new job of his,' she said, 'the one in Scotland . . . Well, it hasn't worked out exactly. He called us a couple of days ago to tell us he's coming home.'

'I'm sorry,' Helen said, meaning it. 'I know he was really excited about the new position.'

'Seems it wasn't the opportunity he thought it was going to be,' Frank said gruffly.

'Walton Council has offered him his old job back,' Shirley said. 'And a pay rise!'

'Good,' Helen said, suddenly feeling light headed. Seb was coming home? Well, it would be nice to see him again. She and Toby were friends. Perhaps she and Seb could be, too.

Helen finished her tea and stood up. She didn't want

to leave the dogs in the car any longer. 'Thanks very much for the tea.'

Shirley hugged her at the front door. 'You're welcome to call in any time,' she said.

Frank followed her to the car. 'I'd like to see the dogs,' he said. Once there, he patted her on the shoulder slightly awkwardly. 'You mustn't worry about Seb coming home,' he assured her. 'We know things won't go back to . . . to how they were before.' He paused, rubbing the stubble on his chin. 'I think Shirley just wanted to share the news, that's all.'

Helen smiled at him. 'You and Shirley will be very happy to have him back, won't you?'

'That we will,' Frank said. Helen climbed into the car and started the engine. She could see Frank gazing after her in the rear-view mirror as she drove away.

It wasn't far to Duskham Reservoir. She pulled into the car park that lay close to the dam and sat there for a moment, staring at the huge concrete wall. Then she twisted round and looked at the dogs. 'Well,' she said. 'Seb's coming home. How do we feel about that?'

Lucy stood up in her harness and wagged her tail. Isla's tail thumped against the seat. She let out a single bark.

'Are the wagging tails for Seb coming back, or the prospect of a walk?' Helen asked.

Isla barked again. Lucy turned round in a tight circle and stopped, her bright eyes fixed on Helen.

'I'll take that as yes to both!' Helen said, laughing. 'Okay, buddies. Let's go.'

The weather broke dramatically the night after their walk at the reservoir and it poured with rain for two days. Helen had spent a happy Sunday pottering around the granary, listening to the rain hurling itself at the windows, only venturing out to walk the dogs. Isla had been fascinated by all the puddles. To Helen's amazement, she seemed to love splashing into them, pawing at the water with her front legs until she was soaking.

'It's just as well I have lots of towels,' Helen had told her.

The rain continued on Monday, but by Wednesday the weather had settled, though the sky remained grey. There was a chill in the air which hinted that autumn was only just round the corner.

Helen stretched her back as she drove over the ridge and Sunrise Farm hove into sight. It had been a long day at work. Fluffybonce had been dispatched to the farm in Nidderdale and Helen and Mandy had spent several hours cleaning out the orchard field shelter. There was a batch of rescue sheep on the way. Helen realised as she climbed into the car that Lucy had rolled in something that smelled almost as bad as Toby after the abscess incident, but she bundled both dogs in and opened the windows. They could all have baths once they were home.

There was a dark green van parked outside the farm-house. It looked familiar. Helen's heart started to beat faster when she spotted the registration number. It was the van that Seb used to drive. She felt slightly breath-less as she pulled to a halt. Was it Seb's van again now? Or had Jo Rankin come to see Steve and Anneka?

She climbed out of the car with the dogs. On the other side of the barn, someone was talking. It was Steve's voice. 'I'm pretty sure they're all occupied,' he said. 'We often see the bats coming and going in the evening.'

'That's great.' Helen felt the tension in her shoulders rise a notch. It was definitely Seb. 'I won't need to come and check the boxes again this year, but do let me know if there are any problems.'

Helen found herself straining to hear what was being said. Seb must be checking the bat boxes he'd put up in the autumn. She glanced down at her trousers. They were covered in hair and unnamed muck from the field shelter. Whatever Lucy had rolled in, Helen had it on her arm. She wouldn't have been surprised to find a cloud of flies was hovering about her head. For a moment, she wondered whether she had time to rush inside before anyone saw her, but then Seb and Steve appeared round the corner of the barn.

Steve shook Seb's hand. 'Right, then, I'd better get on,' he said. He turned and strode away.

'Hello Helen,' said Seb. His face was slightly red. He might have been checking the bats, but he must have known she was due home, Helen thought. It was unlikely he was here by accident. Lucy cantered towards him and Seb bent down to greet her.

'I wouldn't get too close to her,' Helen warned. 'Or me, for that matter. I've been mucking out the field shelter and I think Lucy has treated herself to some fox cologne.'

Seb wrinkled his nose as he patted Lucy at arm's length. 'She does smell quite piquant,' he said.

Helen took a deep breath. 'I heard from your mum and dad that you were coming back,' she said. 'I'm really sorry it didn't work out in Scotland.'

Seb made a wry face. 'So am I. It wasn't at all what I expected. They wanted me to work in the abattoir, overseeing the welfare of the animals that were brought in. I don't have anything against that. It's important work, but it's not what I want to be doing, day in and day out.' He gave a taut smile. 'I'm lucky Walton were willing to have me back. I'm going to stay here a while and see if a promotion comes up in York or Richmond. At least then I'll know what I'm getting into.'

They stood looking at one another for a long moment.

'Are you finished for the day?' Helen said impulsively. 'It's just . . . I was going to take the dogs down to the river for a quick swim. Would you like to come?'

'Won't Toby mind?'

Helen flinched. She felt heat rising in her face. 'I doubt it. Toby and I . . . we're not together any more.'

Seb raised his eyebrows and Helen braced herself for

a caustic comment but he just said, 'I'd love to come for a walk with you.'

'Would you mind if I quickly get changed?'

''Course not. I'll wait in the garden with the dogs.'

Helen ran upstairs, rushed into the bathroom, had the world's quickest shower, then dried herself. She dug out some clean clothes and put them on. It was a relief to be able to pull on a pair of old jeans and a sweater without feeling she was letting herself down. No need for dressing up or fancy clothes. She stopped to look at herself in the mirror. Her reflection stared back. This is me, she thought. *Good enough, just as I am.*

She walked more sedately down the stairs, clipped on the dogs' leads and led them across the garden. Seb was waiting for her beside the gate to the orchard. 'A vast improvement,' he said.

'Thanks,' Helen replied. They filed through the gate and she unclipped Lucy's lead. 'Would you like to see what Isla can do?'

'Sure.' His smile was so gentle and familiar that Helen felt a twist in the pit of her stomach. *I've missed him.*

Helen pulled the clicker from her pocket and took Isla through her exercises. She felt herself going red with pride as Isla sat and lay down, stood up again and followed at her heel.

'That's incredible!' Seb said.

Helen's heart expanded a little more. 'She's even happy off the lead,' she said, unclipping the lead from Isla's harness. 'Off you go!' She felt very proud as Lucy rushed over and the two dogs trotted off side by side.

'You'd hardly know she was blind,' Seb observed. 'How about at night? Do she and Lucy manage in the same room?'

'Isla sleeps in a crate now,' Helen explained. 'It gives her and Lucy their own space, and Isla seems really comfortable.'

'That's great.'

They headed downstream, following the dogs. For a while, neither of them said anything. Helen tucked her hands into the sleeves of her sweater, conscious that the evening was turning chilly.

'There was something I wanted to talk about,' Seb said finally.

Helen looked at him. 'What?'

Seb stopped and held her gaze. 'I wanted to apologise,' he said. 'For something I did . . . or rather something I didn't do.' He reached out and took her her hand. His fingers felt warm against Helen's palm. 'There was a day I came round a couple of months ago,' he went on. 'I asked you about saving up for a mortgage. It wasn't long after Gemma had left. I brought you round a sachet of tomato sauce, I don't know if you remember?'

'I remember,' Helen said. The sachet of sauce was still in her fridge.

Seb's jaw was working. 'Well, that was the day I heard about the job in Scotland. I meant to come home and tell you about it.' He swallowed. 'I was going to ask you to marry me . . . but I bottled it.'

Helen stared at him.

Seb took a deep breath in through his nose. 'I didn't know how you'd take it, if I came out and told you about Scotland straight away,' he admitted. 'I knew you were happy here. It seemed such a big thing to ask you to come away with me . . . So I asked you about moving in together.' He paused and tightened his grip on her hand. 'You had no idea what I was asking. You were talking about going on holiday. But my mind was caught in this crazy spiral of Scotland and you and my job and how to work it all out. And then I lost my temper.' He looked at the ground. 'I should have been honest with you. I thought we'd talk about it the next time I was round, but . . .'

'But Isla was there,' Helen said. His fingers were trembling slightly, she noticed.

'Yes. And I was so tired. I'd driven up to Edinburgh for the interview and came straight back again. I was desperate to talk to you, but it wasn't the right time. There was never a right time, and I suppose I ended up thinking you'd be happier if I just went. You never knew what was going on. I'm really sorry.'

Helen put her free hand on his arm. 'I'm sorry too. When you started talking about mortgages, I freaked out. Your mum and dad obviously have this wonderful relationship, but my mum and dad . . .' She pulled a face. 'Well, they were barely together. They married fast, had me, and that was it. I'd always promised myself I wouldn't make the same mistake.'

'You're right about my parents,' Seb agreed. 'Ironically, I think I was as nervous as you about settling down, but for a different reason. They've always had such a strong relationship. I've constantly been scared I won't be able to live up to it.'

He glanced at Isla and Lucy. They had paddled right across the stream and were standing on the far bank. There were a series of holes in the ground. Both dogs were looking at them with fierce concentration.

'They're waiting to see if a rabbit comes out,' Seb said. He looked at Helen, his eyes warm. 'I was wrong about Isla, too. She belongs here as much as Lucy. I should have known you could help her.'

The breeze picked up, carrying a hint of dampness. By unspoken agreement, they started walking again, their backs to the wind. When they reached a stand of oak trees, Seb stopped again. His face was serious. 'What's the deal with Toby? Is it really all over?'

Helen felt her cheeks turn to flame. 'It was almost over before it began,' she said. 'I think we got caught up in all the drama about the farm being sold, and Toby's dad being able to save it. When that was over, I knew things weren't going to carry on.'

'When did you start to like him?' Seb asked. Helen winced, but Seb persisted. 'No, I could tell you did. I was so jealous, but it was just something else we couldn't talk about.'

Helen chose her words carefully. 'I don't know exactly,' she confessed. 'He was mostly just there in the practice. But he flirted with everyone. I didn't think there was anything in it.' She took a breath. 'And then you and I started to row and he was being so nice to me. It felt like an easy option, being around him. I had no idea he was interested at first, but it was fun and I was flattered. When you left – honestly, not before – he asked me out and, well, that was that.'

'Oh.' Seb looked downcast. 'You're saying I pushed you to him.'

'No! No, you really didn't. It was my fault. I was feeling trapped and confused and I just wanted a bit of light relief, I think.' Helen desperately wanted him to believe her. 'I was glad when he . . .' She stopped. Should she gloss over the fact that Toby had left her? Would it be better to let Seb think it had been mutual? She looked into his honest blue eyes and knew that nothing mattered but the truth. 'I was glad when he told me it was over,' she said. 'I think I'd known it from the first time he kissed me. I should have stopped it there and then. That kind of thing, jumping into another person's arms . . . Well, it's not me. It's not like I'm afraid to be on my own.'

Seb put his head on one side. 'Really? Are you happy on your own?'

Helen looked at the dogs. 'I'm never completely on my own,' she pointed out. 'Not with the dogs. But yes. If you're asking if I could be happy with just them, the answer is yes.'

354

It was true. The realisation had hit her suddenly, but she had known it for a while in her heart. As long as she was here on Sunrise Farm. She had always been happy here. It was her home. Her home, and Lucy's and Isla's.

She looked at Seb and grinned. 'But just because I could be happy on my own,' she told him, 'that doesn't mean I couldn't be even happier with someone else. So long as it was the right person. And they loved Sunrise Farm as much as I do, of course.'

Seb blinked. There was something new in his eyes, and it was a moment before Helen realised what it was. Hope. It was hope.

'What about India?' he said. 'I know you were desperate to visit.'

'I'd still love to go there one day,' Helen said. 'But I'd need the right person with me, like I said.'

'I started to read up a bit about India,' Seb confessed. 'Very big on cricket there. Did you know?'

Helen raised one eyebrow. 'It's lucky that I'm a cricketing expert now. It might be quite nice to go to a match.'

'Really?' Seb said. He was standing very close, Helen noticed. He took her hand again. 'I know you don't want to plan too much for the future,' he said. 'But . . .' He smiled that achingly familiar smile, the one that warmed Helen to the tips of her toes. '. . . if you ever did find yourself booking a ticket to Asia, I'd love to be the one to go with you.'

Helen's heart was pounding. She put her hands on

Seb's hips and pulled him gently towards her. It felt like putting an old, well-loved puzzle back together. 'I've heard Goa is a lovely place to go on honeymoon,' she whispered. Seb wrapped his arms around her, holding her body close against him. He smelled wonderful and she breathed him in. *This is what coming home feels like.* He bent down, finding her lips, and Helen closed her eyes and kissed him back.

They were interrupted by a soft bark. Lucy and Isla were sitting at their feet, looking up at them with matching quizzical expressions. 'Are you feeling left out, lovely girls?' Seb murmured, reaching down to stroke their heads.

Helen waited for him to stand up again. He raised his eyebrows at her. 'What?'

'You didn't give me an answer,' she pointed out. 'To what I said about Goa.'

Seb looked down again at the dogs, then back up at Helen. 'Goa, eh?' He rubbed his cheek, his eyes fixed on hers. Helen could see he was close to laughter. 'Suits me,' he said, and he pulled her towards him for another, longer kiss that was filled to bursting with hope and joy for the future.

Summer at Hope Meadows

Lucy Daniels

Newly qualified vet Mandy Hope is leaving Leeds – and her boyfriend Simon – to return to the Yorkshire village she grew up in, where she'll help out with animals of all shapes and sizes in her parents' surgery.

But it's not all plain sailing: Mandy clashes with gruff local Jimmy Marsh, and some of the villagers won't accept a new vet. Meanwhile, Simon is determined that Mandy will rejoin him back in the city.

When tragedy strikes for her best friend James Hunter, and some neglected animals are discovered on a nearby farm, Mandy must prove herself. When it comes to being there for her friends – and protecting animals in need – she's prepared to do whatever it takes . . .

HODDER

Christmas at Mistletoe Cottage

Lucy Daniels

Christmas has arrived in the little village of Welford. The scent of hot roasted chestnuts is in the air, and a layer of frost sparkles on the ground.

This year, vet Mandy Hope is looking forward to the holidays. Her animal rescue centre, Hope Meadows, is up and running – and she's finally going on a date with Jimmy Marsh, owner of the local outward bound centre.

The advent of winter sees all sorts of animals cross Mandy's path, from goats named Rudolph to baby donkeys – and even a pair of reindeer! But when a mysterious local starts causing trouble, Mandy's plans for the centre come under threat. She must call on Jimmy and her fellow villagers to put a stop to the stranger's antics and ensure that Hope Meadows' first Christmas is one to remember.

HODDER

Springtime at Wildacre

Lucy Daniels

In the little village of Welford flowers are blooming, the lambing season is underway . . . and love is in the air.

Mandy Hope is on cloud nine. Hope Meadows, the animal rescue and rehabilitation centre she founded, is going really well. And she's growing ever closer to handsome villager Jimmy Marsh. What's more, James Hunter, her best friend, is slowly learning to re-embrace life after facing tragedy.

But when an unexpected crisis causes Mandy to lose confidence in her veterinary skills, it's a huge blow. If she can't learn to forgive herself, then her relationship with Jimmy, and the future of Hope Meadows, may be in danger. It'll take friendship, love, community spirit – and one elephant with very bad teeth – to remind Mandy and her fellow villagers that springtime in Yorkshire really is the most glorious time of the year.

HODDER

Snowflakes over Moon Cottage

Lucy Daniels

As far as Susan Collins is concerned, this Christmas is all about quality time with her family, especially her son Jack. After a string of terrible dates she's given up on love, and Susan's certainly got plenty to keep her busy.

That is, until she meets handsome children's author Douglas Macleod. Dishevelled in appearance with bright red hair he is the opposite of Susan's usual type, but an undeniable spark soon lights up between them. But then Michael Chalk, Jack's father, turns up on the scene wanting to be a family again – and Susan finds herself torn.

With snow settling on the ground and the big day fast approaching, who will Susan and Jack be choosing to spend Christmas at Moon Cottage with this year?

HODDER

Christmas at Silver Dale

Lucy Daniels

Although Christmas should be the happiest time of year, Mandy Hope is struggling. Her relationship with Jimmy Marsh is on the rocks, possibly beyond repair, while her best friend James has a gorgeous new son which only confirms how much Mandy wants children of her own.

Desperately in need of a friend, Mandy strikes up a close relationship with new Welford resident Geraldine Craven. Geraldine looks to be a lifeline for Mandy in these troubled times, until she reveals a devastating secret about Mandy's past.

Will the magic of the season be enough to save Christmas?

HODDER